Love Is Never Painless

Love Is Never Painless

Three Novellas

ZANE and
EILEEN M. JOHNSON
V. ANTHONY RIVERS

ATRIA BOOKS

New York   London   Toronto   Sydney

ATRIA BOOKS
1230 Avenue of the Americas
New York, NY 10020

ISBN-13: 978-0-7434-9862-3
ISBN-10:   0-7434-9862-3

First Atria Books hardcover edition November 2006

10   9   8   7   6   5   4   3   2   1

ATRIA BOOKS is a trademark of Simon & Schuster, Inc.

Manufactured in the United States of America

For information about special discounts for bulk purchases,
please contact Simon & Schuster Special Sales at
1-800-456-6798 or business@simonandschuster.com.

CONTENTS

*I*ntroduction   vii

*H*ow the Other Half Lives

EILEEN M. JOHNSON   1

*L*ove Is 2 Blame

V. ANTHONY RIVERS   103

*S*taring Evil in the Face

ZANE   203

*A*cknowledgments   275

A Word from Zane   277

INTRODUCTION

*H*ave you ever felt like you have done everything conceivable to make a relationship work and there is nothing but drama anyway? Have you ever loved someone more than life itself, but they disvalue that love? Have you ever sacrificed something for another, only to have them not appreciate your generosity? All of us, as we all have feelings, have experienced something like this.

Life is strange. So many people cross our paths during our predetermined amount of years on earth. Many of them will be in our life from day one to the final hour. Many will come into our lives later and hang in there until the very end. Then there are the "other ones." People who are only in our lives for a minute, a day, a week, a month, a year, or a few years. We cannot understand how the relationships with them can start out seemingly perfect and end in total madness.

Whenever I think of a love lost, I hear the words to "Isn't It a Shame?" by LaBelle in my head. The questions asked throughout that song have always hit home with me. How can two people love each other, create children together, cohabitate, build a life together, and then end up hating each other in the end? No one enters into a relationship or marriage expecting it to fail. No one gives of their heart and soul in exchange for being mistreated, either mentally or physically. Yet, anger happens. Abuse happens. Cheating happens. Death happens.

While all of the above can be devastating, the truth of the matter is that old adage: "It is better to love and have lost than to never have loved at all." No matter what the circumstances, no matter what the outcome, love is what makes life worth living. Love is the center of the universe. Love can move mountains. Love can also tear down walls. Love can also kill. Love is never painless.

I know that from personal experience. I have been hurt by those who claimed to love me. It was disappointing, but it does not mean that I will ever give up on finding the right one. There is a man out there who complements me on every level, who can appreciate what I have to offer more than he craves his next high, who can mirror my ambitions with his own, who can uplift me instead of trying to hold me back. Meanwhile and between while, I have children to raise, challenges to meet, and history to make.

Thanks to V. Anthony Rivers and Eileen M. Johnson for participating in this anthology. If you walk away from this book thinking that you should reevaluate your outlook on love, then we have accomplished our goals. I wish you success, I wish you happiness, but most of all, I wish you love.

Blessings,
Zane

How the Other Half Lives

EILEEN M. JOHNSON

I would like to dedicate my novella to my husband, Demond,
and kids, Saadiq, Nasir, and Sanaa.
They have truly taught me the meaning of real love.

*J*amellah pulled the heavy Persian rug toward the hallway and off the wall-to-wall carpeting. Grabbing the vacuum cleaner and wrapping the thin cord around her slim brown hand, she turned the power on and began the task of cleaning the carpet. Humming an old Commodores tune, she pushed and pulled the vacuum until beads of perspiration formed above her nut-brown upper lip. Not only was today Friday, her usual cleaning day, but she was expecting company. Not just any company, but that of the sexy black male persuasion. Kenny was thirty-three years old, the owner of a small but profitable construction company, and very married.

The fact that Kenny was married did not disappoint Jamellah. All of her boyfriends were married. As she always told her best friend, Fernecia, the more happily married they were, the better. Married men were low maintenance and that was right up Jamellah's alley. Married men required no commitment, you didn't have to deal with them 24/7, and they were usually extra passionate and extra generous. That's the way she liked her men. She had actually started dating married men at a very young age after quickly growing weary of young, inexperienced boys who were in her face constantly. So at nineteen, she had gone out and met Clarence at an after-work happy hour. Clarence was a twenty-eight-year-old dreamboat who already had his own small investment banking firm, the fabled house on the hill, and his own Benz. He also had a very somber and sexually unresponsive wife. This was a disappointment for Clarence but a blessing for Jamellah. She and Clarence participated in a hot and heavy fling that lasted until she turned twenty-one. In those two years, he managed to give her a used but still fashionable Audi, a pair of stunning two-carat diamond solitaire earrings, and a nearly permanent headache from his complaining about how unhappy his home life was. So after getting him to secure the financing on a snazzy little town house and helping her to set up a small but lucrative stock portfolio, she gave him a well put together story. With well-rehearsed but very persuasive tears rolling down her cheeks, Jamellah told Clarence about how she could no longer sleep at night without him and how she wanted him to leave his wife. As much as Clarence wanted to be with the cute and sexually uninhibited Jamellah, he realized that the state they lived in was a community property state, and under no circumstances was he ready or willing to give his tight-lipped wife half in a divorce. After an Oscar-worthy performance, Jamellah told him that she might be willing to get over him in exchange for a few parting gifts. Relieved that Jamellah withdrew her staunch ultimatum and waved the white flag, he presented her with a nice diamond tennis bracelet, tuition for her last semester of college, a discreet and heavy deposit in her money-market account, and grateful thanks for the two years of her life that she'd devoted to him. Amazingly, they parted as friends, and would occasionally meet for a drink and a quickie.

Three months later, feeling pleasantly boosted with her car, town house, stock portfolio, and degree, Jamellah was once again on the prowl. Love could definitely wait a few more years. Right now, she craved more security. After landing a job as an entry-level adjuster for a large insurance agency, she soon began to use her huge office building as a hunting ground.

She paired crisp linen business suits with soft, lacy peekaboo camisoles and tall heels for a look that was professional yet sexy. Each morning, she painstakingly applied her makeup and arranged her extension-enhanced tresses to look like she had just stepped out of a magazine. Her good looks immediately drew the attention of several of her colleagues. Pretty soon, both her looks and her strong work ethic drew the attention of one of the company's VPs. In the first six months that Jamellah worked for Southwestern Life and Casualty, not only did she do desk work but she also did her homework. She knew which of her suitors had the most pull within the company, who earned the most, who drove what, who was married to whom, and who could get her where she wanted to be.

After chatting with Hugh McDonough, vice president of operations, at the Christmas party, Jamellah soon made him her prey. From that point on, she always made it a point to look extra sexy at the Thursday afternoon staff meetings that he presided over. It also helped that she was always full of provocative conversation at all social functions.

Within three months of the Christmas party, Jamellah was taking all of the gifts that Hugh presented her with, and he, in turn, accepted all her free time and talent. From her prior research, she knew that his wife, Meredith McDonough, cared only about the *Times-Picayune* society page and the city's black bourgeoisie.

Although Hugh was a lusty and insatiable lover and much older than she generally liked them, he was definitely the route that Jamellah needed to take.

By the time Christmas rolled around again, Jamellah had been promoted to a competitive yet promising position as an underwriter. She received this promotion partly because of her hard work but more so because of Hugh's iron influence on the powers that be. With her cushy new job came a cushy new gift from Hugh. Jamellah gladly got rid of her old car for Hugh's gift, a brand-new, shiny black Audi A8 that she drove to her office with pleasure and pride.

No matter how discreet the two attempted to keep their involvement, it was unmistakable. One minute Jamellah was trudging around the city assessing claims and the next she was three floors up in the building, her mind far from flood, fire, and accident damage. Of course, this did not sit well with the other sisters in the office. They had spent years at Dillard, Xavier, Southern, Alcorn, and Grambling, studying and preparing for corporate America. Some graduated magna and even summa cum laude and were shocked to find out that no matter how much education you got, you often wound up in a surplus pool of black college graduates fighting for entry-level jobs not even near your field. The shock went even further when they realized that a simple blow job or two could catapult a 2.5 GPA graduate like Jamellah into a job it would take them years to move up to. This of course led to their extreme dislike of her.

AT FORTY-FIVE, HUGH WAS handsome, wealthy, and wise beyond his years. However, for a brief time, he felt something for the twenty-three-year-old Jamellah that could have been mistaken for love. She returned the favor of his expensive gifts and favors with practiced sexual skills and unlimited affection, which he never got at home. Of course it would bother Jamellah when she would see Hugh and Meredith at social gatherings and on the society page, but she understood her place in his life and his place in her career. Hugh, in turn, would often get angry when the water-cooler talk by the agency's black male employees was about Jamellah and her fabled sexual escapades. But since no one in the office building knew about his relationship with her, he had to keep his anger to a minimum in public, but when he was alone with her, he lashed out at her with contempt and disgust.

Contempt and disgust soon turned to jealousy and abuse, and that was when Jamellah decided that it was time to end their allegiance. Knowing that he would not agree with her decision, she came up with a surefire plan to keep her newfound prestige and at the same time end the troublesome relationship. With the urine of a hugely pregnant Fernecia and a Fact Plus pregnancy test, Jamellah managed to convince Hugh that she was carrying his baby. Afraid of the scandal the pregnancy would cause in the uppity black community and the jeopardy it would put his job and marriage in, Hugh quickly ended the relationship, but not without pacifying a threatening Jamellah. Not only did he give her three thousand dollars for a false late-term abortion, but Hugh also gave her five times that amount in hush-hush money. Jamellah could not believe her good fortune, while Hugh could not believe his stupidity. He made it a policy long before he'd met Jamellah not to get involved with anyone who was connected with his job. Now he was sharing an office building with a walking time bomb who could easily destroy his life. But for some reason, he had actually fallen in love with the young girl who had given him relieving icy rubdowns when he was in physical pain and soothing hot-oil massages when he wanted to feel pleasure.

Sometimes when his heart and his dick overpowered his reasoning, he contacted her and attempted to renew their ties, but his requests were met with firm refusals and idle yet convincing threats. After one of these threats, which sounded more lethal than usual, Hugh decided to wean and save himself from Jamellah. At the same time, he decided to show her that his love for her had not been in vain.

Jamellah was just coming out of the adjustment period in her new position when a corporate headhunter, who happened to be Hugh's fraternity brother, contacted her about a better-paying and more secure position with an old and stable company in the northeastern part of the city. Overjoyed and aware that this was of Hugh's doing, Jamellah promptly turned in her immediate resignation to Southwestern Life and Casualty.

THAT WAS A YEAR and a half ago, and now Jamellah's salary was 25 percent larger and her conscience 100 percent smaller. Since then, she had been through three other married men who she'd become involved with for material reasons, and a single black attorney who she'd been involved with purely for pleasure.

At twenty-four, Jamellah felt that she was on top of the world. She had a great job, an expensive automobile, and a professionally decorated town house that was on its way to being paid for. She was childless, free, and beautiful, which to her were the most important things in the world. Her family marveled at her success and her friends were mystified by how quickly she'd climbed the corporate ladder and gained material wealth. They always knew that she'd get out of the New Orleans ghetto that she'd grown up in, but they never guessed that she'd come this far. Unbeknownst to her friends, Jamellah was whoring just as they were, only at a much higher price.

SATISFIED WITH THE CLEANLINESS of the carpet, Jamellah placed the Persian rug back over it. The beautiful pattern of the rug matched nicely with the solid royal blue carpet. A matching tapestry hung on the wall, and a simple yet tasteful replication of a Synthia Saint James painting was framed and hanging on the opposite wall. Passing an appraising and appreciative eye over her living room, Jamellah decided that Kenny would be impressed.

Rolling the vacuum cleaner into her hallway closet, Jamellah headed upstairs to prepare herself for Kenny's arrival. Now, what does one wear to sweep such a fine man off his feet? Contemplating this, she hurried into her bedroom to see what she could do.

FERNECIA FRANKLIN SWIRLED THE last chitterling around her fork and popped it in her mouth with great relish. It had been so long since she'd eaten them. Too long, in fact, but her husband, Fernando, would never allow the smell of cooking chitterlings to permeate their museum-like home. Not only that, but Fernando did not even know how much his wife of two years loved chitterlings, pig's feet, and the other soul food that she often sneaked back to BeeBee's Soul Kitchen in her old neighborhood to eat.

Extracting five dollars from her Coach billfold, Fernecia left the money on the table as a tip for her doting young waitress, who was the proud owner of a mouthful of gold teeth. Shuddering at the thought of dental gold, she picked up her heavy, matching Coach purse and walked out of the dilapidated restaurant. Quickly walking across the parking lot toward her car, Fernecia glanced over both her shoulders. She was acutely afraid of getting mugged, and she was afraid of being seen by her girlhood friends, who she avoided at all costs. She had been born and raised here in the Third Ward. In fact, the run-down project she'd grown up in, where her mother and older, younger, and twin sisters still lived, was only two streets away. Earlier, she'd had a notion to go and visit, but that was quickly dismissed because she knew that Fernando would be furious if he found out. She also decided against it because she knew that her mother and sisters would not hesitate to ask her for huge loans that they had no intention of paying back.

She had the urge to enjoy a bit of the Indian summer that New Orleans was famous for, so she decided to take the long way home.

She drove down Lakeshore Drive, easily navigating the curves. Coming to a deserted spot on the lake, she pulled into a space. Rolling down her windows and sliding back her sunroof, she inhaled deeply while glancing out at the serene Lake Pontchartrain. September was always her favorite month, and no matter how many foreign and beautiful places she traveled to, the lakefront was always her favorite refuge. The squeal of her cell phone broke her reverie, and she answered it after seeing her home number on her caller ID.

"Hey, Big Daddy," she answered playfully.

"Where are you?" Fernando asked sharply, ignoring her coyness.

"I just finished showing a house near the lakefront and am on the way home," she lied smoothly.

"You should've called. Try to hurry, I hate when we have dinner after six," Fernando said before disconnecting the call.

Fern held the dead phone in her hand and let out a sigh. Sometimes, the man she loved could be so callous!

Making a left turn out of the parking lot in her steel-gray car, she headed south to I-10 East and her Pontchartrain Park home. Popping an Anita Baker CD into the drive, she hummed along with the songstress and navigated the freeway. When she neared the exit to her house, she put her window down and sprayed perfume on herself and the interior of the car, which smelled like the food she'd eaten only minutes ago. Exiting off the freeway and pulling over into the parking lot of a day-care center, she shifted the Acura into park and pulled out her makeup bag. After repairing her Claret lipstick, which she'd eaten off, and powdering the shine from her skin, she sprayed more Jessica McClintock perfume on her body and in her hair to mask the pungent and clinging smells of soul food until she could take a shower. Satisfied, she pulled out of the lot and continued on her way.

After about ten minutes, she turned onto a tree-lined street and drove past the houses of New Orleans' black elite. Slowing down as she approached a large, split-level, hacienda-style home, she turned into the driveway. Seeing Fernando's Range Rover parked, she smiled at her earlier decision to pull over and primp up. Parking in the carport, she pressed lock on her car-alarm activator and went into the house.

The aroma of spicy Mexican food met her as she stepped into her kitchen. Esperanza, the middle-aged Latina who was their part-time housekeeper and nanny, always cooked something delicious in the large, restaurant-style kitchen before taking the Metro bus back to her own seedy apartment building in the city. After opening the oven and savoring the smell, Fernecia closed it and went to look for her husband and thirteen-month-old son, also named Fernando but affectionately called Hugs.

Before proceeding down the hall, Fern stopped and took a deep breath. Slowly counting backward from twenty, she cleared her mind, felt her true person slip away and be replaced by another familiar being. She was now Fernecia Franklin, wife of Fernando Franklin. Everything in her life was near perfect and she wanted for nothing. She loved her husband and pleasing him made her happy. When her counting was down to one, she lifted the corners of her mouth and assumed her "game face." Deep down, she hated having to assume another personality simply to please her husband and didn't know how much longer she could do it. As she'd been doing this since the day she met Fernando and became a part of his world, the personality switch was now a force of habit. Fern felt so blessed to have someone like him. He'd basically rescued her from what could've been a ghetto disaster. She owed him, didn't she?

Throwing her shoulders back, Fern shook out her weave and sucked in her stomach. Hearing the infectious sound of Hugs's high giggle and Fernando's deep laugh, she followed the noise to the sunken den. Her husband was crawling around on all fours while her son rode his back and laughingly struggled to stay on.

"Hey, you guys!" Fernecia called as she stepped down into the den. Walking toward them, she lifted Hugs up and gave him a huge kiss on his chubby cheek. Standing to his full height of six feet six inches, Fernando drew her into a close and comforting embrace. He smelled strongly of the splendid cologne that he'd worn since they'd met.

"How was your day, Fern?" his deep and articulate voice asked her.

Looking up into his dark cocoa face and deep brown eyes, she excitedly told him about her newly listed property in Gretna, on which a contract had already been drawn. He congratulated her over his shoulder as he walked down the hall. Balancing Hugs on her thick hip, she followed him toward the wood-paneled dining room.

Taking a seat at the heavy oak table, she put Hugs down and called to Fernando as he went into the kitchen to get the food.

"Can't we eat in the kitchen? It's just us and I really don't mind." Night after night, the three of them ate dinner in the large and museum-like room. No matter how simple their meals were, they ate off the best china, and only the finest silverware touched their lips. She felt that this was the silliest thing in the world. Although she wasn't born with it, Fern always had a silver spoon in her mouth. Esperanza was a great help and a stellar cook, but Fern was a black woman, for God's sake! Like so many others, the girl could burn. What sister felt comfortable with a Mexican woman cooking for her every night? Just for once, she wanted to come home, bake some chicken or something that she defrosted that morning, mix up some rice, chop up some vegetables, and throw it all on some plates. She wanted to sit at the jazzy little bistro-style table that they'd paid so much for when they were decorating the kitchen. She wanted to talk, and laugh, and joke with her husband. She wanted dinner to be a joy, for once, instead of an event. It seemed her whole life was onstage and there was an audience.

COMING BACK INTO THE dining room, Fernando was carrying the enchiladas, which he had placed on a beautiful glass serving plate.

"Did you hear me, baby? I asked if we could eat in the kitchen for a change," Fern said.

"I heard you, and I was hoping that my lack of response would be your answer, but I guess it was not good enough. How many times do I have to tell you, only common people eat in the kitchen, baby. If I wanted to eat in kitchens, I would have rented us an apartment in your old stomping ground after we got married," he replied firmly. He was actually wagging his finger at her, kind of like he was the adult and she was the disobedient child. "I grew up having dinner in a dining room and I don't plan on having it any other way, so quit asking."

Biting her tongue, Fern held back a flip reply. He always managed to hurt her feelings by making references to her upbringing. Fernando always took every opportunity to make her feel small, so much like the letter after Z.

Sighing, Fernecia looked down at Hugs, who was nodding off to sleep. She excused herself and got up from her seat at the table. She brought Hugs down the corridor to his room, which was decked out in Winnie the Pooh decor. Setting him down on his bed, she placed his stuffed Piglet in the crook of his arm, switched on his Eeyore lamp, and turned off his light.

Returning to the dining room, she sat in front of the full plate that her husband had served her. She was still full from her earlier meal, but she managed to take a few bites as she listened to her husband recount the day's events from the all-black private high school where he was principal. Looking into his handsome face as he talked, she recollected how this same handsome face had rescued her from a dead-end life in the Third Ward.

Fernecia was seventeen and she and her best friend, Jamellah, worked their asses off and were rewarded with scholarships to Texas A&M University. They had both been planning to get out of the ghetto since they had been in the eighth grade. Successfully avoiding the pitfalls of sex, drugs, and early pregnancy that many of their friends fell into, they made it to their last year of high school. The week after they graduated, they boarded a Greyhound bus bound for College Station, Texas, and their bright futures. They both joined the small minority of girls from the New Orleans ghettos who had gotten out without becoming statistics. When the long bus pulled out of the station, they both stopped looking back and started looking toward the summer semester and their new lives.

The girls took to life at the large college campus with gusto. In their sophomore year they both pledged the same sorority and were listed in *Who's Who Among College Students*. They concentrated on losing their ghetto ways and habits and on adopting the practices of their peers and well-bred sorority sisters. Soon, they were indistinguishable from the well-mannered and cultured girls that they shared classes and dorms with. Careful to hide their ghetto background, the girls told anyone who asked that they were from Metairie. Anyone who knew anything about New Orleans knew that Metairie was a wealthy and affluent part of the metro area.

At the beginning of their senior year, Jamellah was dating a lean but muscular football player whose roommate was a transfer student-athlete from Prairie View A&M University. Tired of seeing Fernecia date loser after loser, she decided to introduce her to her current boyfriend's roommate. The four planned to go out on a double date on a Saturday night after a football game. As the girls waited outside the locker room for their dates, Fernecia almost changed her mind. For a while, she had the notion to dash back to her dorm, because she was sure that her blind date would take a look at her overweight body and crooked teeth and run. Just as she was about to put her plan into motion, the locker room door opened and Jalyle, Jamellah's date, walked out with the most attractive man that Fernecia had ever seen. To Jamellah, he was much too big, but she knew he was right up Fernecia's alley. Fernecia took one look at Fernando's towering height, extra-beefy body, and dark skin and instantly knew that she would never look anywhere else. After six months of heavy dating, Fernando told Fernecia that he was ready to make a lifelong commitment. Fernecia felt ready to do the same, but she knew that Fernando, with his wealthy upbringing, would never accept her true background. So rather than tell him the truth, she started ignoring his phone calls and avoiding his visits.

By this time, Jamellah had moved back to New Orleans and was dating a man who set her up in a terrific-looking town house. She was in love and had transferred to Dillard University, where she would complete her last semester. With Jamellah gone, Fernecia was able to hide out without anyone growing suspicious.

Fernando finally caught up with her as she left the student union, where she had gone to pick up her graduation cap and gown. Cornering her, he demanded an explanation for her disappearing act. Tearfully and reluctantly, she broke down and told him that her mother was not a doctor, but cleaned a doctor's house for a living. She also confessed that she didn't do occasional charity work in the low-income areas of the city, and that she was actually from the Third Ward.

Slowly digesting the fact that almost everything the woman he loved had told him was a lie, Fernando decided that he still loved and wanted to marry Fern, as he lovingly called her, but he also knew that he had his work cut out for him.

When he introduced his parents to Fernecia at their college graduation, they immediately turned their already skyward noses up at her. Even with her careful updo and real strand of cultured pearls, they sensed that she was nothing but trash. Determined not to let his parents put a damper on their graduation day and on his love for Fernecia, he went ahead with his plans and proposed to her. Immediately accepting his proposal, she tried extra hard not to let the looks of horror on the faces of his parents make a permanent brand in her mind.

Fernando and Fernecia had a breathtakingly beautiful wedding at Saint Benedict the Moor Cathedral and a lavish reception at the prestigious ballroom of Fernando's Masonic Lodge. To Fernecia's chagrin, her mother and sisters had spread the word about the location, time, and date of the wedding to half of the Third Ward. Fernecia and Jamellah, who made a beautiful maid of honor, watched in disturbed horror as a large number of old acquaintances and neighbors marched into the reception and took over as if it were a house party. Fernecia's mother made a scene as she demonstrated her skills in doing the Electric Slide. She was wearing her special mother-of-the-bride outfit that she had purchased down the street from her house at Chong Lee's Beauty Supplies and Fashions. The bright pink dress overlaid with white lace contrasted starkly with the baby pink pearl-studded stockings and hot pink vinyl pumps. If anyone had told her that she didn't look good, they would have had a major fight on their hands.

As if her mother weren't causing a big enough scene among Fernando's subdued parents and their expensively and tastefully dressed guests, Jamellah's mother and her current boyfriend, who were both suited up in head to toe fire-engine red, were on the dance floor grinding away to all the songs from "Electric Slide" to "Ribbon in the Sky." While this strange tableau was taking place, all the rest of the uninvited guests who had ridden uptown to the wedding on the Metro bus were causing a great commotion by drinking the expensive champagne like it was Boone's Farm wine, and wrapping up large and numerous plates of wedding food in aluminum foil before all the guests could eat. Jamellah and Fernecia's sisters, who were dressed like *Soul Train* dancers, flirted with all the male guests and groomsmen, married and unmarried alike. Despite the embarrassment of Fernecia's guests, everyone ended up having a good time. Fernando's parents and their friends had secretly enjoyed the free show that the ghetto guests had put on. Jamellah and Fernecia were overjoyed that they had both gotten degrees and that one of them had already landed a good husband. Fernando had a smile on his face because he had married the woman he loved and because he had received a wonderful serenade from his Masonic and fraternity brothers. Fernecia's mother was happy because, in her mind, she had wowed all the guests with her gorgeous outfit and her skillful dancing. She was also overjoyed because she felt that Fernecia's marrying into money would mean that she, as her mother, would benefit.

BRINGING HER FOCUS BACK to her plate of half-eaten enchiladas and her husband's animated conversation, Fernecia was once again reminded of how far she had come. A few years ago, she would have been at her mother's cheap dinette set eating smothered turkey necks and drinking cherry Kool-Aid with a sickening amount of sugar. Now she was sitting at her very own cherrywood dining room table with her husband and eating a meal that was prepared by her very own maid. As she absently laughed at one of her husband's anecdotes about his day, she thought, Yes, Lord. . . . I have come a long way.

JAMELLAH WAS AWAKENED BY the sharp buzz of the alarm clock and the movement of her soft mattress. Momentarily forgetting that she was not alone, she jumped in instant surprise. Then, catching her breath, she turned just in time to see Kenny's big and healthy body slide into her bathroom. Turning back over and looking at the clock, she noticed that it read two thirty, which meant that it was actually five thirty.

Jamellah had a system that was part of a much larger system. When she planned on bringing a man that she wanted to get rid of quickly into her bedroom, she set the alarm and the time on the clock ahead about four hours when he finally dozed off. Then, she would awaken him, and seeing how late it was, he would quickly get up and go home to his wife, which allowed Jamellah to be alone but bask in the memories of their earlier sexual activity and count the money or admire the gift that he left on her bedside table. But when she had someone with whom she wanted to spend more time, such as Kenny, she set her clock back a few hours so that he would think that it was still early and he had more time to get back home to his wife than he really did.

"I can't believe that the time went by so slow," Kenny called from the bathroom. Stepping out, he fastened the buttons on his now wrinkled shirt. "It's still so early yet it feels like I've been asleep for hours."

Suddenly glancing at the clock and then his Tag Heuer watch, he let out a loud groan.

"Awww, shit!" he exclaimed. "Your clock is a piece of shit. It's damn near six o'clock. My wife must be having a shit hemorrhage."

"Oh my God," Jamellah improvised. "It must have stopped during the night. I'm so sorry, baby." Smiling inwardly at her lie, she let fake tears of sorrow slide down her cheeks. Hearing her sniffling, Kenny came and sat down on the edge of the bed.

"It's all right, Jamellah. It was just a mistake. Don't cry, boo. I'm sorry for yelling." Kenny could not stand to see a woman cry and at this moment he would have given Jamellah anything. Anything besides more of his time, that is, because now he had to go home and face his angry wife. "I had a great time, baby. You threw some hellified pussy on me!"

Chuckling at the face of the now smiling Jamellah, he stood and grabbed his blazer and headed toward the bedroom door.

"I'll show myself out. I'll call you and we can have lunch Monday, okay? See you."

"Good-bye, Kenny," Jamellah called in her best little-girl voice. She smiled as she recalled the night before.

They had eaten a delicious eggplant parmigiana that she'd prepared, and after polishing off a whole bottle of Martel, they headed upstairs for some serious lovemaking. After the two-hour sweat session, Kenny had fallen immediately asleep and stayed asleep until the alarm clock woke him up. Hearing the front door close, Jamellah jumped out of her bed and looked in the top drawer of her dresser. Right after Kenny had fallen asleep, she had carefully and quietly gotten up and dragged his pants to her bathroom, where she'd copied down his Social Security, driver's license, and bank account numbers. She also helped herself to a crisp hundred-dollar bill that she knew he wouldn't miss. First thing Monday morning, she would call TRW and request a copy of his credit report to see who and how much he owed. Then, she would call the banks' automated systems and see just how much money he had in his accounts. After doing this, Jamellah would be able to determine whether or not he was a keeper. Getting back in her warm, king-size bed, Jamellah pulled the silk sheets and the warm down comforter over her head and went back to sleep with a large and satisfied smile on her face.

JAMELLAH STOOD BY THE bay window in her entranceway and waited for Fernecia to pull up. Just as she was about to go to the phone to call and see what was delaying her, she saw Fern's gray Legend pull into her driveway. Grabbing her chocolate-colored Liz Claiborne bag, she stepped out and locked her door.

"Hey, Fern," Jamellah said as she got in the car and gave Fern a kiss on the cheek.

"Girl, I'm sorry I'm late but Fernando decided at the last minute that he was going to his school to organize the new football equipment because the season starts next week. So I had to bring Hugs to the babysitter's house," Fernecia breathlessly explained.

Smiling at her best friend's apology, Jamellah noticed for the thousandth time how cute Fernecia was. Although many people would consider Fernecia fat, Jamellah felt that she was merely superfine. She was about five feet eight and weighed well over two hundred pounds, but she carried her weight like she was less than a hundred. Her warm brown face was smooth, with a very tiny mouth, high cheekbones, and slanted hazel eyes. Braces that her mother could not afford to give her when she was a young girl now adorned her teeth and only added to her cuteness.

Along with social status, Fernecia had also gained a terrific sense of style.

Essence, *Mode*, and *Belle* were her fashion bibles and everything she wore complemented her large chest and heavy hips. She had blossomed from a dumpy fat girl into a well-dressed plus-size woman.

"Girl, I hope that Precious didn't take anyone else because I really don't feel like waiting," Fernecia said. Precious was the only person besides Jamellah who knew that Fern's shoulder-length auburn hair was actually a weave. She'd worn weaves since she started at A&M and was careful to conceal that fact. When she and Fernando became intimate, there had been some very close calls, but she had always steered his hands to another part of her bountiful body. When she could finally afford it, she switched from the near perfect bonded weaves that she did herself to the more sophisticated and undetectable fusion weave that she was currently sporting. She had no qualms about letting Fernando run his thick hands through her hair now that the tracks had been replaced by invisible drops of acrylic glue.

"I know that's right," Jamellah answered. "LaJoyce said that I was her only client this morning and there is no way I'm going to let anyone see me look this tore down!"

Laughing at Jamellah's statement, Fernecia reached over and clicked on the radio.

"Oh, girl, remember this one?" Fernecia exclaimed as Jeffrey Osborne's smooth voice flooded the car. LTD's "Love Ballad" was one of their favorite girlhood songs and they were always overwhelmed with memories when they heard it. Singing along with Jeffrey's affirmations of how he'd never been so much in love before, they continued down I-10. The song always reminded Jamellah of her mother, who used to always play the record when her old boyfriend Melroy would come over. Most of all, it reminded Jamellah of how hurt her mother had been when Melroy had told her that he couldn't leave his wife and walked out of her life on that rainy August night so many years ago. It had taken her mother months to get over it, but she eventually got back in the saddle.

Feeling the big car come to a stop, Jamellah looked up out of her reverie and noticed that they had arrived at Lady Ebony Beauty Salon. Getting out of the car, she was determined to enjoy her day of beauty.

Stepping into the cool interior of the beauty shop behind Fernecia, she was immediately comforted by the sizzle of Marcel irons and the smell of Dudley's Oil Sheen. After checking in with LaTagnia, the bubbly receptionist, the two women sat down in the comfortable chairs of the lobby until they were called.

Lady Ebony was one of the only full-service beauty shops in New Orleans that was not in the ghetto and that didn't specialize in the ridiculously gaudy hairdos that black women in New Orleans were famous for. Plus, you could get a tasteful weave, braided style, nail services, color, cut, relaxer, or shampoo without having to deal with the sight of the B-girl hoochies who populated the city. You could sit back and enjoy complimentary Evian or soft drinks while you listened to the latest gossip, the gossip being the only thing that Lady Ebony had in common with any of the other New Orleans salons.

The interior was decorated in shades of gray, black, and white and the comfortable chairs were all gray steel and soft black cushions. A large television was set in the lobby and tasteful soul music was piped through the work area. All in all, it was a place where a black woman could go to get beautiful, regroup her thoughts, and forget about life for a while. "Precious and LaJoyce are ready for y'all now," LaTagnia came up and said to Fernecia and Jamellah in her melodic Louisiana accent. Getting up, they followed her rhythmic hip-sway to Precious and LaJoyce's designated areas.

As Precious attached the last few strands of weftless hair to Fernecia's own thin hair, Malaika applied a clear top coat to her Parisian pink toe- and fingernails. She had come to enjoy being pampered in these last few years. As Malaika gathered her tools, Jamellah strolled in from LaJoyce's cubicle with a headful of fresh shoulder-length auburn microbraids. The braids were virtually invisible and the total effect resembled bouncy and full curls. "Jamellah in the house!" she said as she swung her head from side to side and laughed. Her springy braids flew back, then forth, then right back into perfect order.

"Those look so good, Melly! Did you go a shade lighter?" Fernecia asked.

"You know it. So how are you gonna have her style yours?"

"Well," Fernecia sighed. "It took so long to put this hair in, I don't have the courage to wait to get anything complicated done. But I do want something different. What do you guys think?"

"I think you should let me pull it up into a simple ponytail and I'll leave a few sexy tendrils here and there," LaJoyce answered.

"I don't know . . ." Fernecia hesitated. "What do you think, Melly?"

"Girl, go for it. But when Fernando sees it, he'll be as horny as a goat because he'll think about the old days."

Laughing at her friend's fresh sense of humor, Fernecia spun around in her chair to face the mirror and let LaJoyce work her magic.

• • •

"REALLY, HOW DOES IT look?" Fernecia badgered Jamellah as they sped back down the I-10.

"Girl, I told you already. It looks tight. It reminds me of the A&M days! It also makes those chubby cheeks sleek," Jamellah told her as she appraised Fernecia's sophisticated yet playful ponytail.

"So what's up with this new one? Is he a keeper?" Fern asked.

"Yeah. A keeper for his goddamned wife!" Jamellah laughed.

"Girl! You're still at it?" Fernecia chuckled. "There are single men in New Orleans."

"But not for me. Ever think about cheating on Fernando? One of them may be for you!"

"Biiitch! Now, you know better! I wouldn't give a single man this pussy, he may want me for himself! Then you would have a free shot at Fernando," Fernecia screamed as she tried to hold on the steering wheel through all her laughter. "So where you wanna eat?"

"Now, do you even have to ask? Take that next exit puhleeze!" Jamellah said as she whipped her lipstick out of its case. "I can already taste those wings!"

"Say that, girl! I want me some pig feet!"

Forgetting the proper English that they had become accustomed to using, they laughed and talked in their old Third Ward dialogue about what they were going to do and eat once they got to BeeBee's. Within minutes, they were pulling up in front of their old childhood haunt. Fernecia pulled down the visor mirror in her car and inspected her new hairstyle once more. Satisfied, she repaired her Fashion Fair Chocolate Strawberry lipstick and looked over at Jamellah.

"You ready, girl?"

"Greedy, can you *please* wait until I finish powdering my nose?" Jamellah replied.

"Damn, girl! You already have enough powder on that damn nose to bake biscuits. What more do you need?" Fernecia laughed.

"Fuck you, fatty!"

Laughing, the women got out of the car and practically ran up to the front door of BeeBee's. As soon as they opened the greasy but welcoming door, the aroma of greens, hocks, and crackling bread hit them like a brick wall. Without noticing each other, the girls both stopped and let nostalgia overtake them. To them this place was so full of memories, it was not even funny. For a moment, Fernecia was that skinny twelve-year-old, and her mother's boyfriend of the moment, who just like all the rest was married, had given her two dollars to get rid of her so he could use her mother. Instantly, the grown-up Fernecia began feeling sorry for herself. Shaking off the sorrow before she sunk too deep into it, she glanced around, hoping not to see any familiar faces.

"Wanna sit over there in that corner?" Jamellah asked her.

Following Jamellah over to the right front corner, Fernecia felt several pairs of eyes on them. Although she knew that they no longer blended in with the rest of the Third Ward residents, it was still hard for her to believe that she and Jamellah had changed that much. Wiping off the red plastic seat of the chair, she plopped down and picked up the dirty, grease-coated menu.

After a few minutes had passed, Fernecia noticed that instead of looking at the menu, Jamellah was staring into space with a worried, clenched look on her face.

"What's wrong?" Fernecia inquired.

"I was just sort of reminiscing. Thinking about how far we've come. You know, Fern, deep down inside, I still get scared of falling on my ass and having to go back to square one. Everything is still so fresh. I can remember all of the times I used to dream that I'd get out of the Third and never look back. Now I have to look back and face everything that I left there in order to carry on with my future, and looking back scares the hell out of me. Do you feel me?"

Feeling Jamellah's words all too much but not wanting her to know that she also feared looking back, Fernecia plopped down the plastic menu, pasted on a happy and unconcerned smile, and said, "I think I want the stuffed turkey wings. What about you?"

THE CLEAR OPAL BUBBLES hissed and made soft swishing sounds as they burst around Fernecia's thick thighs. The once steaming hot water had turned tepid and a chill was beginning to take over her body. Reaching over, she pulled the tub plug and let out some of the water. Turning on the hot-water tap, she refilled the tub with hot water. Squeezing more foam into the water, she settled back and closed her eyes.

Hearing Hugs's screams and Fernando's coaxing, she wasn't ready to get out of the tub and face the life that she now called her own. Everything that she had always wanted was now hers, but she still couldn't decide whether or not she was satisfied with it. She had a husband who pleased her mentally and physically, a son who she adored, and all of the material things she could want. But, at times, she still felt a certain emptiness that she could not explain. Maybe it was because she hadn't experienced life and different men as much as she should have. Or maybe it was because she had such a distant relationship with her family. Maybe it was because of something she hadn't discovered yet. Whatever it was, it crept up on her every so often and made her feel like the proverbial motherless child.

Fernecia felt the warm and salty tears slide down her face but could not explain their presence. The two initial tears soon turned into a rainstorm of weeping that she could not control. Feeling that she was no longer in control of herself, she began bawling as she hadn't for years.

"Fern!"

The banging on the bathroom door, which she always locked, was accompanied by Fernando's shouting.

"Fern! Open the door. What's wrong?"

Fernecia stopped her crying and looked at the bathroom door as if it were a Sunday crossword puzzle with no possible solution. Dismissing the knocks and shouts, she abruptly went back to her bawling.

Hearing the pause and then the louder continued crying, Fernando grew angry on the other side of the door. Ever since they met, Fern had a habit of shutting him out of what was going on with her and inside her head. When they got married, he was sure he'd cured her by allowing her to be honest about her past. From then on, he'd expected openness, but for the past few months, she'd had the habit of shutting herself in the bathroom or the baby's room for hours on end. When he complained about this, she began to go on long drives at all hours of the night whenever she seemed troubled. To him, it would have been much easier for her to talk to him and let him know what was bothering her.

"Fine. Don't answer me. Just stay in there and feel sorry for yourself. If you don't care, I don't either." Lying and instantly feeling bad about the lie he told, he turned away from the door and went to tuck Hugs into bed. Sometimes, he felt as though his wife were a world away.

COMING OUT OF THE bathroom wrapped in a terry robe, Fernecia sat on the edge of the bed. Releasing the robe from her ample body, she began to smear on Palmer's Cocoa Butter, a staple from her girl-hood. Enjoying the smell and smooth feeling of the lotion, her spirits were instantly lifted.

"As much of that shit as you use, we should buy stock in the company," Fernando said from his post in the doorway.

Looking up, Fernecia wondered how long he had been standing there. Dismissing his joke, she squeezed more lotion into her hands and rubbed it into the skin on her smooth arms. Satisfied with the results, she snapped the bottle closed. Kneeling at the edge of the bed, she said a quick prayer and then slid under the starched cotton sheets of their bed. While most people preferred satin or silk sheets, Fern was a stickler for freshly washed and starched cotton sheets sprinkled with cornstarch baby powder. At first this aggravated Fernando, but soon, he too couldn't sleep on anything but starched cotton sheets sprinkled with powder. When they went to his parents' for the weekend, his mother thought the practice to be extremely odd and ghetto, but whatever her son wanted, she soon adapted to and accepted. Now, whenever they slept at his mother's, the bed felt like their own.

Watching his wife with a smile on his face, Fernando felt relieved to see her seemingly happy. When they had first become intimate he was tickled to learn that Fernecia was in the 10 percent.

She'd explained to him that 10 percent of the world's population slept naked and generally felt more comfortable wearing no clothes. From then on, whenever he heard the words "ten percent" in any type of conversation, he could not stop the grin that crept onto his face. He could recall only a few times that Fernecia actually wore clothes to bed, not counting the times when she had her period and the last few months of her pregnancy. Those times, she explained, were times that she felt gross and needed to wear clothes. Other than that, she was quite comfortable being ass-naked.

Crossing the room, Fernando stripped down to his boxers and got between the sheets. Telling his wife good night, he rolled over with his back to her. Before Fernecia could count to twenty (which was the longest it ever took), Fernando had turned back around to face and embrace her. Too tempted by her warm and fragrant nakedness, he caressed his wife's large and gracious body. Placing her face in his hands, he leaned in for a warm and sensuous kiss.

Soon taking the lead, Fernecia slid down and planted hot kisses on her husband's navel. Going further downtown, she took him into her mouth and gave him the pleasure she knew no other woman was willing or able to do. When his groans of delight turned into yelps of mercy and pleasure, she moved back up his body and placed her mouth on his. Laying her flat on her back, Fernando slid down Fernecia's body and with his mouth brought her to the climax he never failed to give her. Exhausted but not spent, Fernecia let out heavy, rushed breaths as Fernando took her breasts in his rough yet gentle hands and sucked, licked, and kissed them as if his life depended on it. Entering her, he gently and then roughly brought her to the point of no return. After what seemed like hours of his moans and her screams of pleasure, he collapsed on top of his wife. Totally satisfied, they both let out constant heavy breaths until they could once again achieve normal breathing.

"I love you," Fernando whispered.

"And I love you too," Fernecia quietly reciprocated.

For Fernando, the evening had turned out perfect. Starting out not so good but ending with their always passionate and perfect lovemaking. However, his ideal evening was soon ruined by the silent tears that he knew were now running down his wife's face. When he reached out to touch her, his feelings were hurt by the unexplainable way she shook him off. Disappointed, he rolled over and soon indulged in some tears of his own.

SLAMMING THE PHONE DOWN when she heard Kenny's wife murmur hello, Jamellah felt like an elevator that had dropped several floors to the basement. She'd been waiting all night for him in her sheerest lingerie and her coldest bottle of Merlot. Seconds of anticipation grew into minutes, which soon grew into hours. Polishing off the bottle of Merlot, she threw a Chinese silk robe over her body and grabbed her car keys. Speeding over to Kenny's house, she passed it and parked two houses down. Slipping on the shoes that she had hastily thrown in the car, she tiptoed back down the street to his house. Standing under a tree and staring at the house, Jamellah felt both her courage and anger grow. Walking under the garage, she circled both Kenny's and his wife's cars, contemplating doing damage to both. Instead, she walked around the side of the house, peering into the first window she came to. A small part in the curtains revealed what seemed like a complete and warm home. Walking to the rear of the house, Jamellah hit the jackpot. On a large four-poster bed lay Kenny and his wife. Trying her best to turn away, Jamellah could not tear her eyes away from the tableau. As Kenny's wife reclined on the seemingly comfortable bed, he lovingly ran a brush through her long silken locks. Bending over her, he planted a kiss on her eyes, then her nose, then her mouth. Spinning away from the window before she started to scream, Jamellah ran to her car as if the dead were chasing behind her. Sticking her key in the ignition, minutes went by before she could calm and comfort herself enough to turn the key and start the engine. Taking off, almost blinded by a veil of tears, hurt, and anger, she drove around in lost circles until she saw the sun rise above the New Orleans skyline. Only then could she find it in herself to go home to her empty bed.

• • •

WALKING UP THE SEEDY sidewalk, Fernecia felt like she was walking to her own execution. Looking over her shoulder to make sure her Legend was still there, she turned back around and knocked on the torn screen door. Through the greasy glass, she could see the unkempt living room where she had learned to walk, talk, and think. She could feel that familiar feeling in the pit of her stomach.

Okay, Fern. Just remember, you're only here to visit. You'll be leaving here in a few minutes. You don't live here anymore. Looking up, she saw her twin sister wiggling to the door.

Bernecia no longer looked like Fern's twin. She now looked like a fat and run-down version of the stunning and statuesque woman at the door. Childbirth and constant partying had taken their toll on her once good looks. Now, looking at Fern was no longer like looking in the mirror. It was more like peering in one of the catalogs that had served as wish-books for them when they were young girls.

"Girlyouknowyoudon'thavetoknockwhenyoucomehere!" Bernie exclaimed loudly. "Wherethebagsat? Whatyouboughtme?"

Hating to disappoint her sister, Fern made hasty promises to clean out her closet and bring Bernecia all of the things that no longer fit.

Walking into the door that Bernie held open for her, she was greeted by damp darkness and the smell of day-old chicken grease.

Half listening to Bernie's story about a dope pusher who had taken her to get her hair done two weeks earlier, Fern was once again reminded of why she hated to visit. Her mother, all gold teeth and gold hair, soon came into the dank living room to greet her "rich daughter," as she often referred to Fern. Proud of her daughter's new status, she still dreamed and had faith that the rest of her daughters would somehow meet Fernandos of their own and be swept away from the ghetto, taking her with them.

For an hour, Fern sat listening to her mother and sister complain, prod, and beg. When she knew she could take no more, she opened her purse and wrote out two checks, one for her mother and one for Bernecia. Handing the checks to them, she was instantly disgusted when their complaints were replaced by fake inquiries about Fernando and Hugs. Growing more disgusted by the minute, she gathered up her purse and made a hasty excuse to leave, taking her full heart with her.

Jumping in her car and driving to the freeway ramp, she let the tears flow. Why couldn't she have a family who was happy with her success instead of in love with it?

As the tears collected under her chin, she knew what she needed. Reaching for her purse, she dug out her cell phone and dialed Jamellah's number.

Jamellah answered after the third ring.

"Talk to me!" Jamellah answered.

"Hey, it's me."

"Fern, what's wrong, honey?"

"I . . . I just needed to hear the voice of someone who's on my side." After completing the sentence, Fernecia broke down in a myriad of fresh tears.

"Aww, Fernie . . . Look, gimme a few minutes. Let's meet up and we can talk about this. I'm here for you."

Instantly feeling better, Fern made plans to meet Jamellah in the mall. When all else felt caved in, she knew Melly would be there like a stone shelter.

FLORA AND FAUNA PRINTS competed with loud plaids and stripes for Fernecia's undivided attention. There were chartreuses and watermelons alongside centurions and ochers. Throwing her arms up in disgust, she stomped over to a full-length mirror placed on a dressing room door.

She stared at the mirror, and a large but very attractive young woman stared back. She had warm, light brown eyes, lustrous hair, and a killer smile, complemented by silver braces. Instead of seeing this woman, Fern saw a fat, ugly girl with a hidden ghetto accent, trying to impress her in-laws for the first time. The fat girl inwardly cringed at her reflection and instantly hated herself.

"Whatcha looking for?"

Jumping at the voice that shocked her out of her thoughts, Fernecia turned around to see Jamellah beaming at her.

"I've been up and down this store three times and I didn't find your big ass!" Jamellah joked.

"I was hidden over there, in those prints. I swear, these buyers must want big, beautiful women to look like big, beautiful tents. Look at some of this shit!" Fern exclaimed, motioning to the clothes around her.

Flipping through a rack of clothes, Jamellah's face soon adopted a mask of heavy disgust. The prints and colors would do nothing for any figure, not even a stick figure.

"Ewwweee! Why are you even looking in this store? There have to be at least a million other places to shop besides this one. Unless you want to look like Ma Rainey, I suggest we go somewhere else immediately."

"Okay. I usually find some cute things in here. Maybe they changed buyers. Then again, maybe I am even fatter than I was last time. Either way, let's go, these clothes are depressing me." Slinging her purse over her shoulder, Fernecia led the way out of Plus Size Paradise.

"Look at this dress!" Jamellah exclaimed. "Better yet, look at the price!"

"Dang . . . How much is it?" Fernecia asked, examining the nicely cut linen dress.

"Forty percent off the ticket price. Here, go try it on."

Walking toward the dressing room, Fernecia held the khaki dress close as if it were a new friend. Closing the door and removing her denim jumper, she slid the dress over her ripe figure. It slid down her curves and came to a rest seven inches above her knees. The crisply pleated linen did wonders for her large bustline, while the high empire waist took inches off her thick midsection. Twirling around, she felt and looked like the confident woman she knew she should be. She already knew that Fernando would have a conniption when he saw how short the dress was, but she also knew that this was the newest addition to her feel good–look good wardrobe.

The door to the dressing room swung open and out walked a woman who looked, in Jamellah's opinion, just like Fern. Except this woman was a sexier, more confident Fern. Spinning around once again, she gave Jamellah a good view of the great dress and all it did for her figure. Overcome with emotion, Jamellah ran up to her friend and gave her a big, near suffocating hug. The salesgirls looked on in a state of confusion while Fern and Jamellah held each other and let the happy tears flow. Looking at each other's face, heart, and soul, the friends knew that no words or explanations were needed for the show of emotions.

"Now, while you're in such a good mood, let me tell you why I need a dress. Also, lemme tell you why you need one also," Fernecia said.

Jamellah laughed. "Why, why, why did I know there were strings attached."

Linking her arms with Jamellah's and walking toward the cash wrap area to pay for her dress, Fernecia filled Jamellah in on the happenings for the following weekend.

FLOPPING DOWN ON HER bed, Jamellah reached out and pushed the stop button on her bedside answering machine. Every time she listened to Kenny lie about why he had been unavailable for the past week and a half, she grew sick to her stomach. Tired of his lies but too weak to move on, she felt like she was in limbo. Turning over onto her back, she started at her mosaic ceiling and weighed the pros and cons of Kenny.

She was young, single, intelligent, and beautiful. In her and everyone else's opinion, she had the world at her feet. She wasn't weighed down by children or other obligations. She was more than halfway to owning her house, and had a great car and a wonderful job. The only person that depended on her was Jamellah. She was totally self-sufficient and able to stand on her own two feet.

What she also knew was that she was also very addicted to some

Kenny. She drove past his house at all hours, popped in at his job, and even went as far as calling him at work.

Although she knew this aggravated him, she continued to do it. In fact, she could not stop herself. In reality, she knew he was a married man who probably would never leave his wife. Knowing this, she still could not stop herself from yearning for him. He was what she wanted and very rarely did Jamellah not get what she wanted. She considered it a challenge when she hooked up with a man that "couldn't be had." The more inaccessible he made himself, the more she wanted him. The fact that Kenny was an obsession was staring her in the face, yet she continued to hope that it would turn into love.

When they got together, she rewarded him for his time by giving him great dinners, even better conversation, and an unlimited amount of herself. In return, he paid her with fake smiles, false intentions, and empty promises. The woman in Jamellah recognized this but the girl in her wanted it to be love. Either way, she knew that the situation was damned near impossible.

IN MANY WAYS, JAMELLAH wanted her own man. A man who could park his car in front of her house without being paranoid. A man who could spend the whole night without worrying about the time. A man who did not reek of another woman. But Jamellah was sometimes scared. Scared that she could not hold a man's attention without another woman to take over when she grew tired, disgusted, or disenchanted. She was scared of being deserted, loved, cherished, and abused. Jamellah was just scared.

Seeing Kenny and his wife through the open window, Jamellah felt as if the last stone had been thrown. She decided then and there that it was time to go on with her life and make a change while she was at it. She was sick and tired of being sick and tired.

She spent the morning of each and every holiday in bed, mad as hell, with only her TV to keep her company. With every man came the same tired excuses and cancellations. She wallowed in her anger and cursed herself for being stupid over and over. Fern usually

called around noon and harassed her until she reluctantly agreed to
end her melancholy solitude and join whatever celebration was going on. Men had a funny way of having emergencies happen on the
few days of the year that she really needed someone to be around,
and Fern always had to rescue her during these times. Although she
loved spending time with her best friend, she sometimes felt like the
third arm. Sex always played a large part in her relationships, but
she was tired of putting unnecessary mileage on her ass. Years of doing this had earned her some security, but she needed to stop before
she became a used car, sitting alone and collecting dust, because no
one wanted something that everyone else had already ridden in.

She'd done her share of trickery and deception, but it wasn't all
about game. She'd really invested a lot of time in these men and in
the process developed feelings that always went unrequited. Jamellah decided that with the next man, she wanted to get what she
gave.

Resolving to make things better, Jamellah packed away all the
anger and sadness. The past was just that, the past. Rising, she put
on a smile and walked toward her bathroom, humming a happy
tune. Stopping to glance at herself in the mirror, she noted a few
instant changes she wanted to make to her appearance. Tomorrow
was the first day of the rest of her life and she was going to start her
new life looking as fierce as possible!

"BABY, DOES THIS DRESS make me look extra fat?" Fernecia whined
from her dressing room. "I felt really good about buying it but now I
think I made a mistake."

Letting out a heavy sigh, Fernando spun around to inspect his
wife for the umpteenth time that night. What he saw was the pretty,
plump woman that he fell in love with and was still so in love with.
He just had to convince her of this.

"Fern, you look perfect. Your hair, your face, especially your
dress." Before she could object to his answer, the soft doorbell
chimed. Glancing at the clock, Fernecia was both surprised and delighted that Jamellah was on time. In fact, her usually tardy friend

was a few minutes early. Sliding into her new Kenneth Cole pumps, Fern lighted out of the room to greet her friend.

Opening the door, Fernecia was greeted by a girl who she thought looked like her best friend. It was Jamellah, just Jamellah without the dark eye circles and worried expression that she'd been wearing lately. She was decked out in soft dove gray and looked perfect in it. Her million curly microbraids framed her face and added to the beautiful total package. She was wearing the tallest pair of dove-gray platform heels that Fernecia had ever seen. The effect was wonderful.

The two friends stared, smiled, and admired until they were disturbed by the sound of Fernando clearing his throat. Turning toward him, they smiled at the sight of the handsome, gentle giant in his suave navy suit.

"Fernando, are you sure you don't want to leave us home and go to pick up some broads to pimp?" Jamellah joked.

"Don't know about that, Melly, but I do know that if you and my wife don't hustle outside and get in the car, you'll both be all dressed up with no goddamned place to go!" he smartly replied.

Laughing but heeding his words, they walked outside and got inside of his Range Rover. Hugs was with Fernando's parents for the weekend, so they went straight to the ballroom where the charity function for the school Fernando taught at was being held.

WALKING TO THE ENTRANCEWAY behind Fernecia and Fernando, Jamellah felt reluctant to go through with the evening. Had she been in her own car, she would have promptly turned around and headed home. A function like this, where the black elite congregated, was sure to be packed with a few has-beens from her all too recent past.

Turning around and seeing Jamellah slowly approaching the entranceway as if it were the gas chamber, Fern took her arm and led her through the doorway. The mellow, soft sounds of Frankie Beverly and Maze could be heard, and in the low, dim lights, the black important people of New Orleans danced, swayed, and name-dropped.

Walking up to Fernando as he was turning to them, the girls assumed the air of good breeding and quality that they had adopted in their college years.

"This is my wife, Fernecia. I don't think you've met her," Fernando was telling the swollen Barry White look-alike he was talking to.

"And who is the other fine female with her?" Barry bellowed, more to Jamellah than to Fernando.

"And that is her lifelong friend Jamellah. The two are inseparable . . . Think you could get her off my hands so that I could spend some time alone with my wife?" Fernando joked.

Cringing inwardly at the thought of being anywhere with the Jheri-curled and potbellied man, Jamellah made a mental note to punch Fernando when they were out of public view.

Before Barry could answer, the sound of someone tapping into a microphone could be heard. Turning her attention toward the stage, Jamellah was surprised but not shocked as she watched her old lover, Hugh, walk to the front of the decorated stage with a microphone in his hand.

"I want to start by thanking everyone for coming out for Harvest Acres' third annual Harvest Moon Charity Ball," Hugh began. "Every fall, we gather here and show our love for Harvest Acres. If it were not for alumni, and great benefactors like you and me, our prestigious school would go defunct. Thanks also go out to my lovely wife, Meredith, for the beautiful decorations and to all of you who bought and sold tickets to this ball on behalf of Harvest Acres. Harvest Acres started seventy-five years ago as a one-room school shack for Negroes. Today, it is a three-story, fifty-five-room high school for young black men who will soon take their places as movers, shakers, and world leaders." Gazing over the well-dressed crowd, Hugh's eyes momentarily locked with Jamellah's. Tearing his eyes away, he continued on. "Now, let us eat, dance, drink, and be merry as we all paid fifty dollars per ticket to do!"

The crowd roared with laughter at Hugh's joke as Jamellah's head roared inside. She had been spotted by Hugh and was unconsciously searching for the nearest escape route.

Fernecia laughed. "Well, girl, first chance, last offer. Barry's twin wasn't all that bad!"

"Ewwwe!" Jamellah said with a disgusted look on her face.

"You guys can laugh and 'ewwwwwe' all you want . . . 'Barry' laughs all the way to the bank," Fernando said. "I'll bet you all didn't know that he is the Wilson in Wilson, Carter, and Albrecht."

"Wilson, Carter, and Albrecht as in trial litigators?" Fernecia asked in disbelief.

"No other," Fernando answered.

Jamellah gave Fern an "Ican'tbelieveIletthatonego" look and returned to her thoughts of escaping. Just as she was about to open her mouth and plead a headache, the smell of his cologne permeated the air. Turning to follow the smell, she observed Fernando exchanging intricate handshakes and hugs with a man who was a slightly smaller and even darker version of himself. Fernecia looked on in amusement as Jamellah dropped her mouth open to let her tongue wag and then closed it to assume an air of nonchalance.

"So who are you here with?" Fernando was asking the pot of dark honey.

"I'm with Glen, but he bumped into Shelda a few minutes ago and I haven't seen the brother since," the dreamboat said. "Who are you here with?"

Spinning around, Fernando waved an arm to indicate Fernecia and Jamellah.

"Fern, baby, you remember O'Kelley Pounds, don't you?"

"I think so . . . You're his lodge and frat brother, plus you have a dog named Diamond?" Fern guessed.

"Good memory, except Diamond is now my mother's burden. Carpet was getting too expensive," the life-size Hershey's bar chuckled, showing perfect ivory teeth.

"And this is Jamellah, the third wheel for the evening," Fernando said dryly.

Turning toward O'Kelley slowly, almost as if he weren't there, Jamellah gave a weak hello and turned back toward Fernecia. She could feel his eyes burning holes in the sides of her face and on her body, but she pretended not to pick up the vibe.

The beginning chords to Luther Vandross's "The Night I Fell in Love" could be heard. A glance between the married couple was all it took. In no time, Fernecia and Fernando had walked to the dance floor and were swinging as if they had just stepped off of *Soul Train*. By doing this, they had left poor Jamellah all alone with the delicious O'Kelley.

Jamellah was about to make the mistake of excusing herself from O'Kelley to check out the food when she spied Hugh making a purposeful beeline toward her.

Turning to O'Kelley, she gave her most dazzling smile and said, "So, do you know how to swing out?"

Not waiting for an answer, she gracefully made her way to the dance floor, exhaling with relief as she and O'Kelley began to dance. Looking at the edge of the crowd, she could see that Hugh was staring at her with a pained and lustful look on his face. Quickly averting her eyes, she looked up charmingly into O'Kelley's face and said, "I hope you have enough energy in you for a few more—I love to dance."

Grinning like the cat who swallowed the canary plus a double bowl of cream, O'Kelley nodded, grinned, and swung Jamellah around in a perfect turn. Beaming at her, he knew it was his lucky night.

THE BIG, BLACK CHEVROLET Yukon was parked in the parking lot of the ballroom among the luxury cars and expensive SUVs. It stood out and looked just as good, if not better than the other cars. Deactivating the Viper alarm and hitting the keyless entry button, O'Kelley walked to the passenger side and opened the door for Jamellah. After taking her hand and helping her inside, he reached over and pulled her seat belt into its lock. Giving her a dazzling and satisfied grin, he walked over to the driver's side and started the engine. Opening a case, he grabbed a CD and pushed it into the CD changer. The funky and luscious sounds of Slave filled the air. Buckling his seat belt, O'Kelley pulled out of the parking lot.

"Oh no! You didn't!" Jamellah exclaimed.

"I didn't what?" O'Kelley asked with concern in his voice.

"Oh no, you didn't put this on! I can't believe someone else besides me has soul!"

"Well, meet Mr. Soul," O'Kelley joked, sticking out his hand for her to shake. "Slave is one of my favorite old-school groups. Many of these new groups need a lead singer like Steve Arrington to take them to the top . . . But they don't hear me, though!"

Sharing a long laugh, Jamellah savored learning the fact that they already had something in common.

"So what's your favorite track?"

"Well," O'Kelley answered while slowing at an intersection, "I like 'Weak at the Knees,' but 'Dancing in the Key of Life' is my jam."

"Okay . . . now I know that you've been eavesdropping on me before you met me because those are my songs!" Jamellah laughed.

Noticing that she was laughing by herself, she turned to O'Kelley to see why he had grown quiet.

"What's wrong?"

Turning to her with a sheepish grin on his face, he handed her a cell phone.

"You know, Jamellah, it would be nice if we called Fern and Fernando to let them know how and why you disappeared from the function."

Laughing and feeling guilty that she had completely forgot about her friend and her husband, she took the phone and punched in the numbers to Fernecia's Motorola pager, which she knew Fern always kept stuffed in her bosom. Fern was the kind of mother who always worried about Hugs but was still too cheap to keep her cell phone powered on all the time. When the call was connected, she punched in O'Kelley's cell phone number as he recited it. Pressing pound and hanging up, she handed the phone back to him.

"What's wrong now?" she asked, noticing that he wore a semi-worried expression.

"Ummmm, Jamellah . . . I know it's kinda late for me to be asking you this, but how do we get to your house?"

Laughing, Jamellah gave him directions and sat back to enjoy the ride across town.

Lost in her good thoughts, she jumped at the ringing of the phone.

"Hel—" O'Kelley answered, not getting a chance to finish the greeting.

"Girl, where is your rusty ass?" Fernecia screamed into the phone.

"Oh hi, Fern," O'Kelley chuckled before handing the phone to Jamellah.

"Hey girl, whatcha doing?" Jamellah said nonchalantly to Fernecia.

"Sitting here with Fernando in the parking lot, waiting for your ass to pop back up."

"Well, when O'Kelley and I left, you guys were too busy cutting the rug to Earth, Wind and Fire to notice us. We got tired of waiting and decided to leave," Jamellah said.

"Melly," Fern said in a low voice so O'Kelley could not hear. "How much do you know about this guy?"

"Well," Jamellah answered. "Any friend of Fernando's is a friend of mine. I introduced you two, remember?"

"You know I can't help playing the mother role sometimes. Anyway, call me tomorrow with all the details and in the meantime, I'll get the scoop on him from Fernando. Be safe."

"Toodles," Jamellah said before pressing the off button on the phone.

Turning toward O'Kelley, she gave him a delicious catlike smile and sweetly said, "So, tell me a little bit about yourself."

O'KELLEY MADE A RIGHT turn into Jamellah's driveway and parked in back of her Audi. The forty-five-minute drive across the city had given them a chance to learn some pretty interesting things about each other and discover a few of the many things they had in common. A mutual love of black automobiles and Asian food only scratched the surface of the interests they shared.

"So, O'Kelley, would you like to come in for some Kahlúa and coffee?" Jamellah asked.

"That really sounds tight, but I wouldn't want to make you uncomfortable," he answered.

"Oh, you wouldn't make me uncomfortable. I'll be up for the next few hours anyway. Weekends are my time for staying up late and sleeping in."

"Well, pretty lady, if you insist," O'Kelley replied.

FLIPPING ON THE LIGHT in her foyer, Jamellah led O'Kelley inside her lavishly decorated town house. She gave herself an imaginary pat on the back for cleaning up earlier out of sheer boredom. Her place was spotless and smelled delicious, like the dried citrus peels that she constantly kept simmering on her stove.

O'Kelley stepped into Jamellah's domain and instantly knew that it would be hard for him to ever leave. Not only did she have a great sense of style and a flair for decorating, she knew how to make a place feel like home.

Walking around her spacious living room, Jamellah turned on two touch-sensitive lamps and then crossed the room to dim the room's main lights. "I'll be right back with our cordials," Jamellah called as she walked into her kitchen. "Make yourself at home."

Walking around the room, O'Kelley stopped to look at some pictures on Jamellah's mantel. Casting his eyes over the beautifully framed snapshots, his eyes stopped on a picture that Jamellah had taken at Fernando and Fern's house the previous Christmas.

Jamellah was sprawled out on the floor with Hugs, surrounded by torn Christmas wrap and bows. She and Hugs embraced each other and gave the cameras huge smiles. While her smile was perfect and she seemed to have been so happy, he could sense emptiness in her eyes. Not so much emptiness as longing. The longing to be with her own family, in her own house, opening gifts with her own child. The longings that he also had.

In the three hours that O'Kelley had been acquainted with Jamellah, he already determined that he wanted her. He had grown up in an upper-middle-class black household with a genuine, June Cleaver–like mother and a philandering father. O'Kelley had grown to hate the women who called their house night and day, harassing his mother and searching for his father. His mother had been passive, but O'Kelley knew that deep down inside, these things had eaten away at her. Although he loved his father, who still lived with his mother in their same spacious Hammond home, he would never forgive him or his whores for hurting his mother. He despised women who made it a habit of trying to break up happy homes and families. His father had since apologized to his mother, whom he showered with expensive cars, clothes, and gifts to make up for the hurt and lost time. His mother, being the wonderful and big-hearted person that she was, accepted her husband's apologies and his newfound love for her. O'Kelley wanted all the things that his parents had, minus the hurt and extramarital affairs. And somehow, he knew, Jamellah was capable of giving him these things.

"Here you go," Jamellah said as she handed O'Kelley a steaming mug of coffee spiked with Kahlúa. She had returned with the two cups, wearing a soft black satin robe. It was pulled tight across her chest and hips and was enough to make the average mind wander.

"Thank you . . . this is quite a place," he said, meaning the room but taking a sweeping inventory of Jamellah's luscious body. "How long did it take you to collect all of this?"

"Well," she said with a secretive grin, "I started a few years ago, picking up pieces however and wherever I could. And when I looked again, voilà, I had a collection."

"Mind if I put on some music?" O'Kelley asked, standing.

"Go right ahead. I can usually tell a lot about a man and what he has on his mind by what he puts on."

Walking toward the entertainment center, O'Kelley began to look through the scores of CDs, cassettes, and records that were shelved tastefully in alphabetical order. Pulling out a Phyllis Hyman CD, he placed it into the disc changer.

Jamellah was not fully aware of his choice until she heard the first few melodic chords of a very familiar song . . . I'll be damned, she thought. He just put on "It's Our First Time Together." Looking up at him, she noticed that he was planted right in front of her.

"I feel that we didn't have enough dances at the party. What about you?"

As Jamellah nodded, O'Kelley reached out a hand to her and pulled her up off the couch. He took her into his scented arms and they began a slow, seductive rock while Phyllis's honey poured out of the speakers. Placing his left hand under her chin, he tilted her face up until they were gazing deep into each other's eyes.

"Jamellah, I don't know you but I want to know you . . . I don't know you but I know that I want you. Not just for now, not just for tonight. I want you for always."

"But," Jamellah whispered, "how can you know this already? How can you know this if you don't know me?"

"Because I know," he said confidently. "I know that I want you. Not just all of you and what you have to offer. I want your good, your bad . . . I want your all."

Jamellah giggled. "That's a lot to ask for. You're asking for trouble."

Moving her face so that she was looking back into his eyes, O'Kelley responded to her with the same serious expression that he had been wearing when he made the admission.

"I don't care. Just give me a chance to give you what you want. Give yourself the chance to give me what I want, Jamellah. If we just gave ourselves a chance, we could be two very happy people."

Softly, so softly that he almost didn't hear, Jamellah responded, "I will, O'Kelley. I will."

Wrapping her even tighter in his arms, he brought her face up to meet his.

Parting her lips with his own, he opened her mouth and tenderly began to explore it with his tongue. Feeling the slow burn, Jamellah responded by returning his passionate kiss. She was completely enthralled by his kiss. Pulling away, O'Kelley looked again into her eyes with his passion-filled ones. Drawing her to him, he continued the fire-starting kiss that they were both caught up in.

Jamellah reached out and began to rub the smooth skin of his cheek. Feeling his penis grow hard against her satin-covered pelvic area, she began to return his kisses in a needy frenzy. Sensing this need, O'Kelley knew that it was time to take the lead.

Laying her down on the soft Persian rug, he let his hands part the low neck of Jamellah's wrap. Untying the sash at her waist, he watched in amazement and admiration as her very large and firm breasts tumbled free.

"Tell me you want me," he whispered as Jamellah sank to her knees in front of him. Resisting the strong temptation of what she was about to do, he pulled her back up. "Tell me you'll give us a chance, Jamellah."

Becoming mildly frustrated, Jamellah let out an audible sigh. She had only known O'Kelley for a few hours and he was talking about a relationship. Sex in this situation was fine, but a relationship? Deciding that she really wanted to have sex with him, she willed herself to agree to anything for the time being.

"Yes, O'Kelley," she said breathlessly. "Yes, I want to give us a chance."

"Baby, I promise you that you will not regret it," he happily and lustily replied.

Sinking back to her knees, Jamellah reached out to undo O'Kelley's zipper.

"Baby, don't. You don't need to do that."

"But I want to," Jamellah whined.

"Only whores do that, baby. I want you to be my lady, not my whore."

Before she could protest any further, he had bent his head to her caramel breasts. Taking one into his mouth, he sucked gently and savored her taste and smell. Swirling his tongue around her nipple, he took his other hand and began to caress and fondle her other nipple.

Not being able to stand anymore, Jamellah gave O'Kelley a gentle push onto his back and pulled his pants down the remaining length of his body. Taking his solidly erect penis into her hand, she angled it straight up and gently eased it into her waiting vagina. Slowly lowering herself, she almost climaxed right away from the feel of his rock-hard member. Even slower than she had lowered herself, she rose back up the shaft so slowly that she could hear him gasp. When he called out for mercy from the slow torture, she slammed herself back down, swallowing his penis with her vagina. Clenching her PC muscles, she could hear him moaning louder and louder as he felt her muscles biting down on him. When his moans became shouts, she raised herself off him and got down on her hands and knees. Within seconds, he had entered her from behind and was slamming into her vagina as if his life depended on it. Feeling herself near climax, she tried to control herself but couldn't.

"I'm coming . . . Oh gosh, I'm coming!" she shouted.

She could hear O'Kelley loudly gasping and moaning behind her, and before she could pull away, she felt his orgasmic juices flooding her insides. Remembering that she had been too caught up to fit him with a condom, Jamellah pulled away from him and ran toward her bathroom.

"Where is my fucking douche bag when I need it?" Jamellah muttered to herself, slamming a bathroom cabinet closed and trying to catch her breath. Opening and slamming closed drawers and cabinets, she finally located it under the sink. Filling the bag with solution, she squatted over the toilet and frantically tried to rid herself of the traces of their lovemaking. Repeating the process, Jamellah rose from the toilet and stepped into the shower. While she was lathering her body and trying to calm down, she heard soft knocks at the door.

"Jamellah?" O'Kelley called out. Not getting any answer, he gently pushed the door open. "Is something wrong?" he asked, his voice full of concern.

Jumping at the sound of his voice so close, she stuck her head out of the shower. "I am fine . . . I guess I am kinda surprised about the way that things went down."

"I am sorry, Jamellah."

"No, no . . . you didn't force me to do anything. I wanted it as much as you did."

"Well, when you get out, would you like to go somewhere and get something to eat? This area of town has a few cool all-night cafés."

"I'd like to but I am so tired. Plus, I am supposed to meet Fern tomorrow morning at a ridiculous hour. Can I take a rain check?" she asked.

"Sure. I'll leave my numbers and you can give me a call. I'd like to hook up and spend some quality time."

"Sounds good," Jamellah said.

Approaching the shower, he brought his face to hers and gave her a kiss.

"I had a wonderful time," he whispered. "I can't wait to see you again."

"Me too," she answered.

"Call me," he said, turning away.

"Okay," she told him, starting to grow aggravated and wanting to return to the warm water.

After a soothing and refreshing shower, Jamellah stepped out and wrapped herself in a thirsty terry-cloth robe. Walking into her bedroom, she flopped down on her bed. As thoughts of "What did I do" invaded her head, she drifted off into a dreamless sleep.

"I KNOW THAT YOU aren't still asleep!" Fernecia screamed into the phone as Jamellah contemplated placing it back in its cradle.

"What time is it, Fern?"

"Really early. Only two p.m.," Fernecia replied sarcastically.

"Damn! I can't believe I have been sleeping that long."

"So, did the dick put you to sleep?" Fern chuckled.

"As a matter of fact, he did. It took so long for him to get his shit and get out of my house that he made me tired." Jamellah laughed. "Gotta give it to him, though, it was pretty good."

"So can he work it or what?"

"Girl, he can work, twerk, and anything else you can think of!"

Screaming into the phone, Fernecia laughed at Jamellah's tawdry humor.

"So, are you guys hooking up today?"

"He told me to call him but I am not so sure that I'll get around to doing that," Jamellah said frankly.

"Well, honey, if you knew what I knew, you would call. Fernando gave me the scoop. The brother is not married, has no kids, and has been saving his money ever since he landed a job. Already has a smooth ride, which you already know about, and owns his own house. Not renting an apartment, not renting a house. Not paying a mortgage but he owns a house."

"Well, girl, maybe I did right to throw this pussy on him," Jamellah said, feeling instantly brightened.

"Who haven't you thrown that pussy on?" Fernecia joked. "I am sure he was very grateful. Well, gotta go, but I'll give you a holler later on, that is, if you're not too busy throwing the pussy on him again."

Erupting in giggles, Jamellah agreed to catch up with Fern later and hung up the phone. Turning to her nightstand and seeing where O'Kelley had left his home, cell, pager, and work numbers, she rolled back over and reached for the phone. It was turning out to be a lovely day after all.

Hanging up the cordless phone, Fernecia placed it back on its base and turned toward her bedroom. Fernando was blocking her way into the hall. She had no idea how long he had been standing there and really didn't care. Ducking under his extended arm, she started off toward her bedroom.

The conversation that he'd walked in on really unnerved Fernando. With all the time and effort he put into making Fernecia his perfect woman, she refused to get rid of the last tiny bit of raunchiness that was embedded in her. He'd picked her up when she was nothing and made her into what she was today. When she first obtained her Realtor's license, she struggled. What she didn't realize was that he'd been the co-borrower and silent partner in the duo that purchased her first listing. The office building, which was located in Lafayette, was leased out to full capacity. The healthy lease checks were quietly deposited into one of his personal accounts that she had no knowledge of or access to. This same account was used for little luxuries like the new Acura she drove and the nice jewelry he always presented her with.

Because of that quick sale, her career skyrocketed. Her firm had been wary of allowing a rookie straight out of college to handle a property so large, but she'd done it in record time. Pretty soon, everything she listed turned to "Sold" and it was all because of him. Did she appreciate it? Obviously not. Her new life couldn't be that important to her, because she made it clear that she missed the world she came from. On several occasions, he noticed her sitting in her car, frowning in the direction of their house, like it was some type of chore to walk through the door to greet him. This pissed him off. The fact that Fernecia spent so much time with Jamellah also made him sick. Of course he realized that without Jamellah, he never would have met his wife, but let's face it, the girl was trifling. She reminded him of an eight-ounce medium-rare filet mignon, a side of fragrant creamed spinach, a luscious lobster tail, and a glass of the finest red wine—all served on the lid of a garbage can. She looked great on paper and even better in person but had the reputation of a common street hooker. In college, he instantly fell in love with Fern but was a bit reserved about committing to her because of her choice of friend. It was common knowledge that Jamellah slept with any- and everybody. Not much had changed since their days at A&M. Geographically, New Orleans was large, but people were separated by only three degrees. Someone always knew somebody who knew somebody and people talked.

Over the past three years, he'd been privy to much talk about Jamellah and her escapades with men all over the city. As a matter of fact, that very afternoon on the golf course, Hugh gave him a very detailed account about his dealings with Jamellah. He pretended to be amused but he was furious. When Hugh and his wife, Meredith, let it be known that they were searching for a new house,

Fernando immediately recommended his wife, who located their dream house. The deal was closed the very next week. They had so much respect for and gratitude toward his wife, but how long would that last? His friends envied his marriage. When they came around, Fernecia was perfect, like the tamed shrew. When they entertained, she always offered the right drinks, always gave intelligent input on all the right conversations, always wore the right clothes, and always put the right mix of people together. He had built the perfect beast. Gave her a life that was sweeter than her sweetest dreams, yet she missed her old life. He needed to give her a quick reality check. Remind her of who she was then, who she was now, and who made all that possible. He would also remind her of how quickly he could send her back to where she came from.

"How was golf?" Fernecia called from down the hall, rousing him from his diabolical thoughts.

"It was fine. In fact, my day was fine until I came home and caught my wife talking like a whore on the phone to a whore."

"You really need to watch what you call my friend," Fernecia hotly replied, stepping into the hallway. "It was that whore who introduced us and I didn't hear you complain then." Ducking back into the bedroom, she slammed the door. With Hugs away for the weekend, she planned on catching up on some much needed rest.

As soon as she had slammed the door shut, she heard it fly open. "Don't you ever, as long as you live, slam another fucking door on me!" Fernando screamed. "Before I came along, you didn't have any doors to slam, remember?"

"Ohhh . . . I'm scared," Fernecia said, giving a fake shiver.

Taking a deep breath, Fernando fought the urge to slap her.

"Fuck you," she said simply, staring him down with a cold gaze. Dismissing him, she turned her back and began to undress. After all her clothing had been removed, she continued to ignore him and slipped between the sheets, turning her back to him. A nap, not an argument, was what she needed.

"I told you, you need to watch your goddamned mouth."

Letting out a sleepy sigh, Fern plumped up her pillow and assumed a sleeping position.

Seeing that his wife was ignoring him, Fernando grew angrier. Lately she'd had a mind of her own. When she wasn't being flip, she was ignoring him and slipping into her own little world. He had put up with her moods for long enough and felt that something had to be done.

"Okay, Fern. I'm sorry. I just want to know why you allow Jamellah to drag you into the same habits I took you away from."

Furious, Fernecia sat up and faced him.

"What do you mean, 'same habits'? It is not like I fucked him. Jamellah did. Besides, she is my friend. I should be able to discuss what I want with her without having you eavesdrop."

"She did the fucking but you condone her whorish ways. Do you think I want my son around someone like her?"

"Excuse me," Fern retorted. "*My* son can be around his god-mother whenever she chooses to have him. You should quit judging people and concentrate on your own life. Now, if you don't mind, either close my fucking door or shut the fuck up. I am trying to take a nap." Grabbing another pillow, Fern turned back toward the wall and shut her eyes, trying to find sleep.

Quickly drifting into dreamland, she was disturbed by a weighing, stinging feeling across her cheek. Lifting her head up, she realized that she'd just been slapped. Focusing on Fernando, she realized that he had his hand drawn, as if to hit her again.

"This is *my* goddamned house and I close the door and shut up when I am ready!" he shouted. Before either of them knew it, he had slapped her hard across the face again.

"Fernan—" Before she could finish, he had straddled her body and was hitting her repeatedly. It seemed like a nightmare. Fernando, the gentle man that she had married, had never given any indication that he would ever hit her. Screaming and crying, she tried to get him to stop. Much to her horror, she realized that her fighting back was not the right thing to do. Her struggle was actually starting to arouse him.

Fernando had unzipped his shorts and was soon trying to force his way inside his wife. Becoming frantic, Fern began to thrash and scream and resorted to punching him in the mouth. Her doing this angered him, but he was determined to finish what he started. Placing his mouth hard over hers, he began to kiss her while he thrusted hard inside of her. The painful, degrading sex had gotten the best of Fern and pretty soon, she quit fighting back. She lay back, crying, and tried to separate her mind from her body.

"Tell me you love me," he muttered, unaware that he was hurting her.

Forgetting his request, he began moaning and thrusting even harder, signaling his orgasm.

When the thrusting came to an end, he lay weak, spent, and out of breath on top of her. Fernecia took the opportunity to push him off her and run into the bathroom. Locking the door behind her, she sank to the floor in an explosion of fresh tears. With all of the bad things that had happened in her life, she had never been raped. Women every day were raped by strangers. By desperate, dirty men. Now here she sat crying on the floor, ashamed, hurt, and shocked after being raped by her own husband.

After growing cold on the floor to the point where she began to shiver, Fernecia stepped into the shower and turned the tap until the water became scalding hot. Stepping out of the stall briefly, she yanked open a drawer and grabbed a rough cotton towel. Getting back under the spray of steaming hot water, she picked up a bar of soap and, along with the towel, proceeded to scrub her body until she thought her skin would fall off. She soaped and rinsed and rinsed and soaped. She filled her douche bag with scalding hot water and rinsed herself out. Feeling as though her insides were boiling after the douche, she went back to the scratching and scrubbing of her skin. She was unconscious of how hot the water really was. Feeling impossibly dirty after being handled so badly by her own husband, she was determined to cleanse herself of all traces of his abuse. After almost a half hour of nearly scrubbing her skin off, she turned off the water and stepped out. Grabbing a white cotton towel that was equally as rough as the washrag, she rubbed her skin dry. Pausing near the door, she could hear that Fernando was standing on the other side. Taking a seat on the toilet, she sat, her mind boggled and fresh tears running down her face. The silence was killing her and she wanted to open her mouth and scream, like the roaring in her head.

Before long, she heard Fernando's engine in the distance start up and rev for a few minutes. Then she heard his Range Rover back down the driveway. Feeling that the coast was clear, she ran out of the bathroom and ran naked around her bedroom, blindly throwing clothes and toiletries into a suitcase. Yanking a linen shift out of the closet, she pulled it on and slipped her feet into a pair of soft leather mules. Grabbing her car keys, she went outside, started her car, and hauled ass away from the place she called home. Speeding down the middle of her street, she drove aimlessly, not knowing where to go. I could check into a hotel, she thought. But then the silence would kill me. I could go to my mother's . . . Hell no. Her mother's was the last place that she wanted or needed to be. As she approached a stoplight, she noticed Fernando's vehicle coming down the block toward her. When he approached and crossed the intersection, he slowed and the driver's-side window began sliding down. Putting all of her weight into her right foot, Fernecia put the gas pedal down to the floor, speeding toward the freeway. The freeway would lead her to Jamellah's and, hopefully, to sanity.

"DAMN!" FERNECIA SWORE AS she slammed down the controller pad and watched Yoshi's cart spin out of control. She was stretched out on Jamellah's floor, where she had been for the past four hours playing Mario Kart on Nintendo. She really didn't know or care how long she had been there. The only thing she cared about was the fact that she wasn't in her house and she didn't have to constantly think about what had happened earlier.

"Damn what?" Jamellah asked, coming into the room wearing a short red robe. She perched on the couch, opened the robe, and started rubbing Palmer's Cocoa Butter from her face to her feet.

"Damn this Yoshi. I'm gonna switch players."

"Oh," Jamellah said blankly. It was great having her best friend over, but she wondered why Fernecia had come and how long she planned on staying. It wasn't that Fern was not welcome in her house for an extended period of time, she was simply trying to gauge the situation at home. Hmmm, she thought to herself. There must be trouble in paradise.

"Where ya going?" Fernecia asked while she comfortably lolled on the floor.

"I'm meeting O'Kelley at his house for dinner. Why? Wanna come?"

"Naw . . . I don't believe in being the third wheel. I figure I'll stay here, play some Mario, and chill out."

"Fern, that is exactly what you've been doing since yesterday. While I am gone, do something constructive. Organize my cabinets . . . clean out my closets . . . you know, something creative," Jamellah joked, barely able to control her laughter.

"That is why I have a maid, bitch. You think I'd actually do your housework?" Fernecia replied. "Now, if you don't mind parting with some cash, I can send her over here!"

"Sorry, but I doubt that she would be of any service to me after picking up behind you, Fernando, and Hugs all day long. Speaking of Hugs, when is he coming back from your in-laws'?"

"I don't know," Fernecia replied, seemingly unconcerned.

"Well, have you called to ask?" Jamellah questioned.

"No, let Fernando handle that for a change."

"Have you even spoken to him since yesterday?" Jamellah asked.

"Nope."

"Does he even know where you are?" Jamellah asked.

"Uh-uhn," Fern grunted.

"Well, do you even plan on calling him and letting him know where you are?" Jamellah asked, growing impatient with Fern's short answers.

"Not really. I don't give a fuck where he thinks I am. If he was concerned at all, he would have come looking for me by now."

"Did you two have a fight? Girl, why are you staying away from your house?" Jamellah asked.

"Oh, you are supposed to be my friend, right?" Fern said, growing defensive.

"I didn't mean it like that, girl. I was just concerned about you. You can talk to me about anything."

"Hey," Fern said, standing up and changing the subject. "Do you have any of that pasta salad left?"

Giving up on trying to get to the thick of Fern's situation, Jamellah sighed and replied, "There's plenty, girl. It's in the fridge."

FERNANDO STEPPED OUT OF the shower and dried himself off with a towel. Sniffing, he noticed that the towel smelled just like Fern. In fact, everything in the spacious house smelled like Fern. Pulling on some striped pajamas that Fern had ordered from L.L. Bean for him, he sat on the bed and pulled out his lesson planner. He had to work tomorrow but definitely didn't feel like it. He didn't know exactly where his wife was and he missed his son.

In his opinion, the fight he and Fern had gotten into had grown way out of hand. He really had not expected the argument to end like it did. Fernando had never had to force himself on any woman in his life. The fact that he had forced himself on his wife made him feel like a heel. He wanted to call her up, apologize, and make everything all right. It wasn't that easy. First of all, he didn't know where to call her. She had not answered her cell phone and the messages he left on her voice mail and pager had went unanswered. He had the feeling that she was at Jamellah's house but was afraid to call there. Maybe Fern told Jamellah the whole story. If she had, Jamellah would chew him out like an angry tiger or ignore him like he carried the plague. Either way, he didn't want to take any chances.

The quiet in the house was starting to drive Fernando crazy. He tried some CDs and the television, but they didn't help. Getting up, he threw on some shorts and a T-shirt and headed to his parents' house to pick up Hugs. He missed him and was sure that Hugs could shake up the quiet in the house.

• • •

"Hello?" Fern mumbled blindly into the phone. She was half asleep and was still dead tired. Jamellah had come in at two in the morning and woken her up to tell her about her date with O'Kelley.

"Hey," Fernando whispered simply.

"Yes?" Fern said, recognizing his voice and sitting up.

"What are you doing?" he asked softly, trying to break the ice.

"Whaddaya want?" Fern asked him.

"Well, I was wondering if you were going to come over here and pick up Hugs and drop him at his day care. It is kinda out of my way. But I could pick him up this afternoon," Fernando said hopefully.

"To tell you the truth, I don't care. He's your son, so why don't you drop him and pick him up? I have no plans to be anywhere near there today."

"Okay," Fernando said, trying to soothe the hostility in her voice. "You can drop him off tomorrow. I'll take my turn today. When you get off, why don't we go and have dinner as a family?"

"Look, cut the bullshit. I don't plan on picking him up tomorrow, or the next day, or the next. And as for that family dinner, fuck it. I don't eat with rapists or wife beaters. Now, if you'll excuse me, I have to get up and get ready for work."

Before he could find the words to reply, she had slammed the phone down in his ear.

Rolling out of Jamellah's guest bed, Fern went into the shower. After soaping herself from head to toe, she opened her hastily packed suitcase. Although most of the clothes she had taken were mismatched, she managed to pull together a snazzy work outfit. During her lunch break, she would either sneak back to her house to gather more clothes or go to Riverwalk and pick up a few new things. It depended on her mood.

Fernecia walked down to Jamellah's kitchen and made herself a cup of the gourmet coffee Jamellah had brewed before she left to go to work. As she expected, it smelled like heaven but tasted like shit. Pouring it down the sink, she rinsed out her cup and let herself out, using the extra key that Jamellah had given her to lock up.

Instead of heading toward work, Fern stealthily went toward the day-care center that Hugs attended. Upon arrival, she parked in the lot across the street, sat, and waited. After about half an hour, Fernando's Range Rover pulled up. Dressed neatly in a starched navy shirt and creased khaki trousers, he walked around to the passenger's side and lifted Hugs out. Sharing a laugh about something or other, father and son disappeared into the double doors of the center.

Seeing her precious son had actually given Fernecia courage to go to work and look on the bright side of things. She still had a wonderful job, a great best friend, and an adorable son. Turning onto the entrance ramp to the freeway, Fernecia headed toward work and her job, which often provided her with serenity.

"DOES THIS TASTE RIGHT?" Jamellah asked Fern while holding a long, threatening spoon out to her.

"Ummm . . . what is it supposed to taste like?" Fern asked suspiciously.

"Oyster bisque, but it probably tastes like axle grease." Jamellah laughed.

Taking the steaming spoon in her hands, Fern blew softly on it and took the creamy soup into her mouth.

"Girl, this is great!" Fern truthfully exclaimed.

"Ya think so?" Jamellah asked.

"Yepyep. Just grab that pepper mill and grind a little more black pepper into it and you're on the map!"

"I hope O'Kelley likes it. He seems to dig the domestic side of women . . ." Jamellah said while she stirred the bisque.

"Hmmm . . . oysters. Maybe I should leave after he eats this so you two can share the effects," Fern joked.

"Nawww! It's not even about that. In fact, I'll be much better off if you stay and keep us company," Jamellah said frankly. Her best friend had been at her house for over two weeks. Even though she loved her privacy, she enjoyed having Fern there with her.

"Now, you have this fine man coming over here to eat this fine food . . . all in all, it should be a fine evening. *Why* would you want me to stick around?"

"Okay, Fern. So you wanna forget all the times at A&M that I tagged along when you didn't want to give it up to Fernando?"

"All right, all right." Fern surrendered. "I'll stay and be the goonish third wheel. Lemme go upstairs and clean up."

"Don't get too clean now! Remember, I'm trying to hook him!" Jamellah laughingly warned.

Laughing and feeling young again, Fern tripped upstairs to take a shower.

"I'LL GET IT!" FERNECIA called as she bounded down the stairs. Opening up the door, a delicious-smelling O'Kelley waited with a decorated bottle of champagne and a bouquet of wild flowers.

"Well, hello," O'Kelley said in his silky baritone.

"Hey now," said Fern.

"Where's Fernando? I didn't know you guys were joining us."

"Oh, I'm not. I was just on my way out. And how have you been?"

"I've been great," O'Kelley replied. "Your friend is great company."

"Well, O, it gets even better. You'll get your socks knocked off when you see what the black Julia Child threw together tonight!"

Leading O'Kelley into the house, Fern yelled for Jamellah while she grabbed her purse. Jamellah flitted into the room looking like she had spent all afternoon getting pampered. She'd left work early and gone to the market, where she'd made a few purchases to throw together and reel O'Kelley in.

"Hey there," Jamellah said coyly while O'Kelley drew her into an embrace. While they hugged their hellos, Fern tried to make a quiet exit.

"Girl, where are you going?" Jamellah asked, spinning around.

"I have to go across town and pick up a few things. I'll be back later on."

"Now, Fern, that is so dirty! You said you'd eat with us!" Jamellah exclaimed.

"See you later, O'Kelley," Fern laughingly said while ignoring Jamellah. Even after slamming the door, her melodic laughter could still be heard. Shaking her head and grinning, Jamellah thought, That's my girl, before finally turning her attention back on to O'Kelley.

"Baby, I hope you like oysters!"

IT HAD TAKEN A couple of weeks, but Fernecia had finally managed to push the episode with Fernando to the back of her mind. To her, it would be much easier to avoid her house than it would be to try to work things out with him—everything was still too fresh. Now the heaviest thing on her mind was where to eat. She liked O'Kelley despite the fact that he was tight with Fernando. And in her mind, she knew that if given a chance, a relationship between him and Jamellah could work. All they needed was a push in the right direction and plenty of quality time.

Fern really couldn't decide what she felt like eating. Italian . . . nah . . . Chinese? Nah, she ate that too much. Hey, she thought. I'm always in the mood for BeeBee's. Turning the radio up, she sped toward her destination. Arriving at BeeBee's, Fern edged her Acura into a narrow parking space. Noticing that the lot was packed, she decided right then and there that tonight, she didn't care who she ran into. In fact, if she was still in a good mood after she ate, she'd go and visit Mom and the sisters.

Walking in, Fern spotted a booth in the back corner and made a beeline for it. A smiling waitress with a stiff weaved hairdo that resembled a double ice cream cone came to take her order. She ordered pork roast, smothered potatoes, gravy, and rice. Happy with herself, she settled back and waited for her scrumptious and greasy food to come.

Fern was lost in thought when she felt someone staring at her. Looking up, she almost keeled over when she saw Fernando's parents sitting at a table across the room from her. Oh no! she thought.

Not Mr. and Mrs. We're-It-and-Our-Shit-Doesn't-Stink. They'd never get caught dead in a place like BeeBee's, but she figured they never guessed they'd see anyone they knew. Waving at her in-laws, she smiled and then turned away. Fuck it, she thought as her food arrived. If they want to talk, they'll come over. The waitress arrived with her food and she turned her attention away from her in-laws.

The roast was tender and the potatoes were seasoned and chock full of onions, just the way she liked it. Just as Fern shoveled another forkful in her mouth and reached for her lemonade, she smelled the annoying scent of White Linen. Looking up, she pasted a smile on her face.

"Hey! How are y'all doing?" she asked her mother- and father-in-law. "I didn't know y'all liked BeeBee's."

"Hello, Fernecia," they replied in tight unison.

"We are doing fine," Francis Franklin, her father-in-law, continued for both of them. "But it is not us that you should be concerned about."

"Our son came to pick up our grandson the other week," his wife, Katherine, continued while gazing disgustedly at Fern. "It seems if he wouldn't have come to get him, his mother wouldn't have either. What we want to know is what kind of woman would abandon her son and leave her husband to fend for himself? Don't answer because we already know the answer."

Slamming down her fork, Fern stood up to face her in-laws and give them a piece of her mind. Before she could open her mouth to defend herself, her father-in-law pushed her over the edge.

"This is why we were dead set against Fernando marrying you in the first place. We knew you were the kind of trash who would eventually pull this kind of stunt. Well, you know what? We are there for our son and our grandson. They do not need you. We will give them all of the help they need. I hope he never takes you back!" he spat at her.

Stepping quickly out of the booth, Fern knocked her glass of lemonade over. Before she spoke, she could feel the hidden ghetto girl coming out. Raising her voice, she pointed to her father-in-law.

"Listen, I don't give a fuck what you two motherfuckers think. I loved your son until he took it upon himself to try to correct me." Ignoring the heads that were starting to turn in their direction, she continued with the tongue-lashing. "You raised him no better than common niggers. All his life, you led him to believe that he was better than everyone. But I am here to tell you that he is common nigger trash, just like you think I am. Now, he told you part of the story, but I guess his lying ass left out the part about beating and raping me, right?"

Looking into their shocked faces, Fernecia felt disgust rising. Opening her purse, she threw a twenty-dollar bill on the table in front of her barely touched food.

"Now, if you'll excuse me," Fern said in a mocking tone, "I must go. Instead of standing here and chastising me, I would strongly suggest you go over to your son's house and teach him who to fuck with because I am not the one."

Spotting the manager walking over, Fern slung her purse over her shoulder. Giving her in-laws a cold, assessing glance, she shook her head at the pitiful sight and walked out.

Starting her car engine, Fern sat in shaken silence and let her tears flow.

THE CHIMING OF THE doorbell caused Fernando to jump out of his light sleep. Reaching for his pajama bottom, he covered his naked body and headed for the door. Crossing his fingers, he silently prayed to God that it was Fern at the door and that she'd simply lost her key. Pausing at the door, he took a deep breath. Stepping back, he flung the door open. Instead of seeing the beautiful face of his sweet Fern, he was treated to the awful sight of his disgruntled parents. Before he could ask for an explanation or invite them in, they shoved past him and took seats on the couch.

"We don't know and don't care what happened between you and Fern, but that bitch has got to go," his mother began.

"Mom, what are you talking about?" Fernando questioned, once again feeling like a five-year-old who had been caught stealing cookies.

"We're talking about that black whore you married. Your father and I were out having dinner when she approached us and told us all kinds of lies about you."

Knowing that his mother was lying about Fern approaching them, he attempted to calm her down. The sooner they left, the sooner he could call Fern and find out the real story.

"We do not want our grandson growing up around that woman," his father said excitedly. "She needs to go back to the projects where she came from."

"Daddy, you're forgetting that 'that woman' is his mother. You and I both know that she is and will always be. Now, Fern and I have some problems but we'll work things out."

"Son, you don't know what kind of mistake you made by marrying her. Get out now while you have a chance. We'll help you. She abandoned her son. Can't you see what nigger stock she comes from now? You could be so much happier with someone else."

Just as Fernando was about to answer his father, the wailing sound of Hugs's crying floated into the room.

"Look, I understand that you two are concerned about my well-being but please, let me try to work this out for myself. Please. I promise, if everything fails, I'll let you help me," Fernando pleaded with his parents. "Now let me go see what's wrong with Hugs. Lock the door on your way out. I'll talk to you both tomorrow."

Bending down to hug his father and kiss his mother, Fernando fought to stop the tears from rolling down his cheeks. Turning away from his parents, he walked in the direction of Hugs's room.

"HELLO?" FERN SAID BREATHLESSLY, answering the phone so Jamellah wouldn't be disturbed. When she'd come in, Jamellah and O'Kelley were obviously busy in Melly's bedroom. She'd come upstairs to calm herself down and collect her thoughts.

"Hey," Fernando's voice said softly from the other end of the line.

"Hey," Fernecia answered, feeling helpless.

Relieved that she was not being hostile, Fernando contemplated his next move. Breathing deeply, he decided to lay his cards on the table.

"Fern, I'm sorry. I know that may never be enough, but I need you to know that. Fern, we need to talk. Can I come and get you?"

"Yes," was the only reply that Fern could muster.

"I'm on my way." Hanging up, Fernando grabbed his keys and gathered up Hugs, being careful not to wake him. He was determined to get his life back together.

Stopping in the kitchen, he again picked up the phone and called his parents.

"Dad, you said if I needed you, you would be there . . . do you think you could start out by watching Hugs until tomorrow? Thanks, Pop . . . be right over."

FERN SAT IN HER car in Jamellah's driveway. She'd thrown on a long Dr. Seuss T-shirt and some kneesocks. The radio played softly in the background, mellowing out Fern and calming her frayed nerves even further. She had just dozed off when she heard a soft tap on her window. Opening her eyes, she saw Fernando crouching down next to her car window, looking at her. Switching off the ignition, she put the keys in her shirt pocket and opened the door. Stepping out in her stocking feet, she stood next to Fernando silently, not knowing what to say.

"Wanna take a ride?" Fernando asked uncertainly.

Nodding, Fernecia followed him while he walked to his Range Rover and unlocked the door. Walking over to the passenger side, he opened the door and urged her in. Once she had settled, he pushed down the lock and shut the door. Getting in on the driver's side, he started the engine. Silently, they both listened as it purred to life.

After driving around silently and aimlessly for the better part of an hour, Fernando spoke up.

"I've missed you, Fern. Our son has missed you. It's hard not having you around."

He waited for her to respond. After hearing her sigh softly, he knew what he had to do.

"Fern, baby, I am sorry for what I did. There is not a minute or an hour that I don't think about it. I can only imagine what it did to you mentally, let alone physically."

Hearing her let out a rush of air, he turned to see her shoulders trembling. Crying was one thing Fern could never stop herself from doing. Her outpour of emotion soon caused warm, salty tears to slip down Fernando's face. Pulling over into the lot of a brightly lit Popeyes, he cut the engine off and had himself a good, cleansing cry.

WAKING UP AND LOOKING around, Fernecia was shocked as hell to see that she and Fernando had fallen asleep in the parking lot of a fast-food restaurant. Turning, she saw him quietly dozing with dried-up tears on his face. Reaching out slowly, she intended to wake him up. She found that she wasn't able to bring herself to touch him. Instead, she decided a verbal awakening would work better.

"Fernando? Fernando." She paused for a few seconds, surprised at the tenderness in her own voice. Making it a point to sound more gruff, she barked out his name. "Fernando!"

"Huh?" Jumping, Fernando woke up and looked at her wildly with bloodshot eyes. Without waiting for her to answer, he smiled sheepishly and started the engine.

"Fern, baby, let's go home."

Without even asking whose home they were going to, Fern nodded in silent agreement.

FERN SLOWLY WALKED AROUND her living room. It smelled the same. It looked the same. But for some reason, it just felt different. It was as though she had lived here not just a few weeks ago but years ago. Wandering down the hall, she heard the sound of running water. Coming to the door of her bedroom, she stopped dead in her tracks. Some invisible force was stopping her from entering it. Here, her very own bedroom, was the place where her marriage had started to crumble. She stood, just staring into space, until she felt droplets running down her cheeks.

"Come on, baby . . . time to take a bath and get some rest." Fernando stood in front of her, a little too close to her, in fact. In his hand was one of her favorite fluffy pink face towels.

"Just give it to me and I'll do it," Fern whispered slowly.

"But I'd like to help you. Come on, baby. I'll give you a bath and put you to bed. It'll be just like old times. Come on, boo," he coerced her gently.

"*No!*" Fern screamed, grabbing her hair and shaking her head like a woman gone mad. Crying, she screamed over and over and pounded on Fernando's face and chest. She beat on him until she was out of breath. Crumpling to the floor, she let the few tears she had left fall.

FERN WOKE ONCE AGAIN in a place she didn't expect to find herself. She felt the light, scratchy ruffles of the guest room's comforter. Sitting up, she assessed the area around her. Swinging her feet off the bed, she got up and wandered out of the guest room. She padded down the hallway until she reached the entranceway to her bedroom. The bed was in perfect order and the room was immaculately neat and clean.

Hearing strange bleeps and blitzes, Fern followed the sounds down to the five steps into the den. Sitting on the floor, Fernando was hunched over and staring up at the huge television screen. In his hands was the video game control pad. Game Day was the thing he always played to get his mind off whatever was bothering him. She stood at the bottom of the steps, watching him.

Jump, dodge, jump, swerve to the side. *Damn!!!* Throwing down the control pad, Fernando cracked his knuckles loudly. Arching his back, he stretched to the left and then to the right. His eyes burned, his feet were asleep. He had lost track of how long he had been playing. Feeling the weight of a stare, he turned around to see Fern staring at him.

"Hey, you . . . when did you wake up?" he said.

"A few minutes ago. I feel sleep-drunk. What time is it?"

Flipping his wrist and looking at his watch, Fernando let out a chuckle. "Twelve thirty."

"Golly geez. I feel like I've been asleep forever."

"Baby, you need some rest. Can I get you anything to eat?" Fernando asked gently.

"I'd like a peanut butter sandwich, but I can get it," Fernecia said, turning toward the door.

"No, baby. I am going to fix it. Toasted wheat, peanut butter on both slices and jelly in the middle, right?" Fernando asked as he started toward the kitchen.

"Yes . . . while you do that, I am going to take a quick bath."

"Sure, baby," Fernando called from the kitchen, already busy with Fern's sandwich.

SEARCHING THE LAUNDRY ROOM, Fern finally found an old gown that she hadn't worn in ages. She staunchly refused to go in the bedroom to get some sleepwear. She made a mental note to get her things from Jamellah's. Since she had to go through her bedroom to get to the bathroom, and the guest bathroom had only a shower, she decided to take a bath in Hugs's cute little bathroom.

Feeling her stomach turn, she turned to the toilet minutes before everything came flying up. She retched and retched until she felt her stomach ache from emptiness. After taking a spare toothbrush and brushing her teeth, she undressed and ran a warm bath.

Lowering herself into the blue tub, Fernecia smiled at the Winnie the Pooh murals on the walls and the matching shower curtains. All of her bath products were in her bedroom, so she lathered up with a bar of orange Tigger soap. After getting clean, she rubbed herself with some of Hugs's Baby Magic lotion and put on the gown. She felt funny actually wearing bedclothes, but she no longer felt comfortable being naked in front of Fernando.

Smelling Baby Magic, Fernando turned and saw Fernecia in a cute little granny gown. He wasn't used to seeing her in clothes at night, but he was okay with it. Besides, she looked charming. He hadn't seen her in weeks, so she could have worn a sack and he would have been happy. Plopping down at the table, she looked at him, busying himself with her food.

Fernando proudly set a perfect peanut butter and jelly sandwich down in front of Fern along with a glass of Tang. He loved the fact that his wife sometimes had strange tastes in food. He prided himself on knowing and remembering her favorite things.

"Aren't you going to have anything?" Fern asked as she tore into the sandwich.

"No, I have a bit of an upset stomach." Sitting across from her, his face in his hands, he watched her eat and thought about how much he'd missed her.

The sound of her pushing an empty plate away snapped him out of his reverie.

"Had enough to eat?" he asked, getting up and putting the plate in the sink.

"Yeah, thank you. Now I think I am going to go back to sleep. I feel exhausted all over again," Fernecia called over her shoulder as she walked toward the hall.

Watching her, Fernando hated the fact that he was instantly aroused by the sight of Fern in the gown without any undergarments. How he wished she would allow him to make love to her. It had been a while and he felt weak for her charms. He knew that he'd hurt her by forcing himself on her, but he wanted to make it all up. Clicking out the kitchen light, he followed her, wishing she would walk into their bedroom. Watching her rhythmic hip sway, his eyes followed her as she turned into the guest room. He decided to follow her, but before he could reach the door, he heard it shut and the lock click into place. Standing by the door, he felt like a criminal.

"Night, Fern," he said, low and inaudibly. Feeling defeated, he continued down the hall to his room to spend the night, once again, cold and alone.

THE FLASH OF LIGHTNING across the bedroom window woke Fernando out of his sleep. Hearing the loud boom of thunder, he rolled over to look at the neon face of the alarm clock. The face read 8:00 a.m., but outside, it looked black as midnight. He'd heard the news bulletins for the hurricane watch and assumed that the warnings had materialized. Oh, well. Louisiana was one of the states that made up Hurricane Alley, so he was used to it. Lying back to return to sleep, he heard sobbing coming from down the hall. Getting out of bed, he grabbed his robe and threw it over his nakedness. Walking toward the guest room, he was aware of the fact that Fernecia was very afraid of storms. Ever since she was a little girl, storms scared her stiff. As an adult, she could stay calm in regular rain but became frightened and childlike in storms. At work, if it began storming, Fern would often lock her door, crawl under her desk, and hug and rock herself until it blew over. If she happened to be driving, she'd pull off the road and pray until the storm let up.

Tapping on the door and then testing the knob, Fernando was surprised to find it unlocked. On the floor in a corner, Fern was curled up into the fetal position, hugging a pillow and partially covered with a blanket. She was shaking with sobs and didn't look up as Fernando stood towering over her. He was scared to touch her, but he kneeled and gently reached out to her. Surprised that she didn't jump at his touch, he pressed on further by lying down next to her and putting his arms around her. Rolling over to face him, Fern buried her face in his shoulder and sobbed softly, like a baby. Caressing her, he whispered soothing words into her ear and hummed softly.

"It's just a little hurricane, baby. It'll be over in no time. I'm right here . . . you'll be fine," he assured her in a cooing voice.

Smelling and feeling her warmth, he slowly let his hands wander lower and lower until he was holding her hips in a tender embrace. As he expected, she was nude under the blanket, and he was almost sure she'd shed the cute little gown as soon as she'd closed the door to him for the night. Feeling his manhood rising, he lifted her chin and brought her mouth to his. In all the years that he'd been acquainted with women, Fern was the only woman he knew with cherry-fresh breath first thing in the morning. But then again, Fern was phenomenal in every way. He kissed her tenderly and she was reluctant and tried to pull away at first. Soon, she kissed him back and wrapped her arms around his neck. Running his hands up and down her back, he realized once again that he missed her. With her hands, she shyly parted the robe that he'd hastily thrown on. Untying the waist, she reached down and grabbed what she missed so much. Removing her hands, he reached for her full and pendulous breasts and brought his head down to savor the taste of them. Crying out as he sucked harder and harder, Fern pressed his head against her breast as she felt a tempest rising in the center of her body. Finally pulling away from him, she rolled over onto her back and opened her legs to the man that she loved. Getting on his knees, he lowered his head and tasted the sweetness of his wife. Caught up in the ecstasy of pleasing her, he could hear her crying somewhere in the distance. Fernando did not stop because he knew that this time, she was crying for a much different reason. When he could hear her screams of passion, he rose up on his hands and knees and hovered over her. Kissing her, he shared the sweet taste of her body with her. She grabbed his manhood and slowly placed it near the tender place she wanted to receive it in. Gently, he pushed until he was inside of her. Moving in a slow, tortuous rhythm, he licked the salty tears on her face. Squeezing and kneading her breasts, he gave her pleasure that she knew she couldn't live without. He licked her nipples and hungrily sucked at them while he pumped away inside of her. Feeling his frenzied pumping grow faster, she wrapped her legs around his thick midsection and allowed him to hammer his passion into her. Breathing harder and harder until he began to shout, she could feel the warmth and the wetness of their joint climax flooding her.

Fernecia and Fernando lay there in silence, savoring the memory of their actions. Both lost track of time and eventually dozed off as Mother Nature raged outside the window.

THE NEON WALGREENS SIGN was a beacon in the heavy downpour. Dashing from her car, Jamellah ran inside and stopped inside the entrance to catch her breath. As she shook off, she watched a work crew frantically board up the glass front of the store. The store's cooling system was on full blast and the cold air hit her soaking-wet body. Smiling at the teenager behind the checkout counter, she grabbed a plastic handbasket. Walking up and down the aisles, she filled it with unnecessary items: hard candy, more cosmetics to add to her already large collection, magazines, Carpet Fresh. Approaching the feminine-care aisle, she got nervous. She passed the section twice before she found the nerve to stop and get what she came in for. The sky-high prices almost discouraged her, but she picked it up anyway.

Emptying the contents of the basket on the counter, she felt like a guilty teenager. She smiled again at the cashier, hoping she wouldn't comment on the item.

"You made it to the checkout just in time! We're closing in like ten minutes," she informed Jamellah.

"Well, I'll consider myself blessed, then," Jamellah said as she handed the girl her debit card. Squirming while the transaction was being handled, she couldn't wait to get home.

"Thank you and try to stay dry!" the cashier called as she handed Jamellah the card and her receipt.

"Thanks . . . It's a little late but I'll try." Jamellah giggled, picking up her bags and walking out of the store.

STEPPING INTO HER FOYER, Jamellah peeled away all her wet clothes. Bending to pick them up, she took them to the utility room and threw them in the hamper. Trudging up to her room, she threw her wet bags on the floor and went to the bathroom to shower and wash her hair. She really wasn't in the mood to deal with her hair, but nothing smelled worse than wet braids.

As she stood under the spray and rinsed out her hair, the contents of her bags were on her mind. Stepping out of the shower, she dried off and wrapped a towel around her hair. Prolonging the inevitable, she went downstairs to get a can of Fresca. She gulped it while standing, looking out the kitchen window into the still heavy rain. Tossing the can, she headed back upstairs.

Jamellah took the Early Pregnancy Test from one of her Walgreens bags and walked into the bathroom. She turned the instruction booklet over and over in her hands, blindly reading all but understanding nothing. Feeling the effects of the Fresca, she sat on the toilet and placed the tip of the wand in the stream of urine. Flushing the toilet, she placed the wand on the counter and wandered into her bedroom.

The time she spent with O'Kelley had been wonderful. He was a tender and thorough lover, a great listener, and had a heart of solid gold. She knew that like all men, he had a bad side that would come out sooner or later, but she was positive that when the time came, she could deal with it. The real question, though, was whether or not she would want to deal with it. Well, she thought, I'll cross that bridge when I come to it.

Pivoting toward the bathroom, she hesitated before taking any steps. The tip of the wand stuck out like a sore thumb. Picking up the instruction booklet once again, she read. Pink if you're pregnant, blue if you're not. Proven to be over 99 percent accurate in laboratory tests. Grabbing the filthy test wand, with its bright pink tip, she angrily broke it in half and tossed it in her garbage can. The last thing she saw before she was blinded by tears was the applicator sticking out among used Q-tips and facial tissue.

FERNANDO LOOKED INTO FERN's sleeping face and felt himself falling in love all over again. It was so hard not to love her. Even in slumber, her face held a smile. The pitter-patter of the rain on the window created a rhythm for her light breathing. Lifting his hand, he traced the outline of her eyes and slowly moved down to her lips.

Jumping at his touch, Fern woke up and smiled into Fernando's face. Without a word, she began caressing his bare shoulders. Moving onto his back, he watched as she rubbed and smoothed his skin with her velvety soft touch. In a soft, fluid motion, she rose and lowered herself onto his stiff manhood. Feeling it throbbing inside of her, she leaned down and kissed him. He placed his hands in her hair and held her to his lips while she rode the wave of his passion. Lifting his hips, he looked into her face and watched her deliciously distorted expressions.

"Oh, baby . . ." she gently muttered.

Instead of hearing Fernando's sweet reply, the guest room lights flew on and she heard a shrill voice.

"What the hell is going on in here?" a woman's voice screeched out.

Turning around, she saw Fernando's mother and father standing in the doorway. She reached out to grab the blanket and cover herself but lost her balance when Fernando pushed her off of him. Feeling the blanket being thrown over her, she saw him stand up naked to confront his parents.

"No. This is our house, remember? So I should be asking, What the hell are you two doing here?" he angrily barked.

"We've been trying to call and no one has been answering the phone. We left Hugs at home with Mama Maudie and came to see what was wrong. Now that we're here, we can see exactly what's wrong," his father said, eyeing Fern on the floor like she was a heap of garbage. "We're under a damned hurricane warning and all you can do is fuck? Do you not realize it's storming outside and your windows aren't even taped? What the hell is wrong with you?"

Although Fern was eager to get up and bitch her in-laws out, she was unable to move her mouth because she was so shocked. From Fernando she heard some of the harshest things that ever left his mouth. Not only was he standing up to his parents, he was putting them in their place. She couldn't believe it. When the tirade ended, Fernando took a deep breath and attempted to reason with his parents.

"How the hell did you get in here anyway?" he impatiently asked his father.

"You gave us a key, remember? And son, the least you could do is respect your mother and put on some damned clothes."

"If you cared anything at all about respect, you could have called or even knocked before you came barging in, so fuck respect," Fernando spat out. "I gave you the key for emergencies and for when you needed to get in the house in the event that we weren't here, but this is really some shit."

"Don't you talk to your father like that!" His mother stepped up. "We were here for you when that hooker left you and our grandson alone. Now we walk in here and she's fucking you like she's done nothing wrong. It is an emergency. This city is going to be hit by a category-three hurricane and we need to leave until it passes."

"Look, Fern is not a hooker. Fern is my *wife*. Accept it and get over it. You can evacuate if you like, but I happen to know that our house will be fine. Now, if you don't mind, we'd like some privacy. Leave."

"Son, if we leave, we're never coming back. Now, it's either her or us and we can't imagine losing our son to a tramp," his father said calmly. "Fernando, you don't know how serious I am, son."

"No, Dad, you don't know how serious I am. We'll be over to pick Hugs up in a while. Now leave."

"You will do no such thing. This bitch will come nowhere near our house. She fell off her rocker a long time ago and now we see that you've joined her. Our grandbaby will be around no such filth, you can forget it," his mother shot back.

"You can't tell me when I can get my own son. You must be out of your mind." Used to his parents' idle threats, he sighed and decided to calm down. "Look, if you want to amuse yourself with Hugs for a few days, fine. You guys are panicking over a simple tropical storm. Anyway, call me when you reach your destination and let me know how you all are. Other than that, good-bye."

Turning his back to his parents, Fernando bent down to comfort a sobbing Fern. He didn't turn around until he heard the front door slamming in the distance. Once again, his parents had gone overboard. But this time, Fernando thought, they'd gone too far. He knew that one day, he'd have to make a decision. And he'd used his head and chose his wife.

Reaching out to embrace her, he noticed Fern springing up and running for the bathroom. Following her, he reached the door right as she slammed it and locked it. Tapping on the door, he heard her retching loudly. Growing concerned, his taps became bangs. Taking deep cleansing breaths, he realized that she'd been very upset and was probably sick to her stomach. He heard the water tap being turned on and a minute later, Fern emerged, her eyes red and watery.

Giving him a sheepish smile, she offered no explanation as she brushed past him. Going down the hall, she turned into the bedroom. Shocked, he followed her and watched from the doorway as she flopped onto their bed. As badly as he wanted to join her, he didn't want her to change her mind about being in their bedroom.

Lying on her back, Fern felt lousy. She was oblivious to the raging storm going on outside, as she was concentrating on the riot going on inside her head. Silently she tried to remember the date of her last period. Dang, she thought. It's really been that long. The sluggishness she felt, all the crying, the temperamental moments reminded her of one other time in her life. When she found out that she was pregnant with Hugs.

Making her sign of the cross, Fern said a quick and pleading prayer to God . . . I'll be all right, she forced herself to think. Comforted by her prayer, she drifted off to sleep, with Fernando watching her from the doorway.

SWINGING THE HAMMER AND driving in the last nail, O'Kelley attached the last board outside Jamellah's picture window. She'd called him over, panicking because of the storm. He felt important. To him, things such as boarding up his woman's windows was his job, his automatic duty. Rain flew against his body as he moved from under the awning and ran up to the front door.

"Baby, it's done!" he called to Jamellah, who was in the kitchen banging pots and covers.

"Thank ya, baby," she called. "Dinner's almost done. By the time you take a bath and get changed, it should be on the table."

"Cool." Leaving his heavy, wet boots in the entranceway, he went upstairs in his socks.

He loved the decor of Jamellah's bathroom. The way she folded her towels, the scented candles that always seemed to be burning. In fact, there was very little that he didn't love about her. Peeling off his wet clothes, he put them into the hamper. Only a few weeks into the relationship, they already had sets of clothes at each other's houses, which was to him a totally good sign. Running bathwater, he noticed that there wasn't an open bar of soap. Opening the bathroom cupboard, he pulled out a fresh bar and tore the paper off. As he was about to toss the soap's wrapping into the wastebasket, he noticed the bright tip of a plastic pink wand. Reaching down to pick it up, he thought . . . My, my, my. What the hell is going on.

Sitting on the toilet tank with the wand in his hand, O'Kelley was dumbfounded. He knew what the wand's bright tip meant but he couldn't understand why Jamellah didn't tell him as soon as she saw it. Deciding to give her the benefit of the doubt, he placed the wand in his wallet, which was lying on the sink. He wasn't mad at Jamellah, he simply wanted to see how long it would take her to tell him.

COMING INTO THE KITCHEN, O'Kelley was assaulted by the delicious smell of spicy food. Jamellah had her back to him and was gazing out the window into the heavy rain. Hearing him pull out a chair, she turned around, startled.

"Hey there, baby," she said casually. Bouncing around, she filled up a plate and set it down in front of him.

Being a meat-and-potatoes man, O'Kelley adored Jamellah's cooking. Looking down at the meat loaf and garlic mashed potatoes, he felt his mouth water. The woman could turn simple comfort food into a masterpiece. The bright vegetables that adorned the outer rim of the plate looked crisp and picture-perfect. The meat loaf had a wonderful, glazed look. He couldn't wait to try it.

Waiting for Jamellah to sit down with her plate, he was surprised when she sat down with an empty saucer. Bowing her head and saying a quick grace, she reached out for a dinner roll. He watched as she broke off a small piece, sniffed it, and popped it in her mouth, chewing it slowly.

"Is that all you're going to have?" O'Kelley asked, digging into the meal.

"Yes, baby. I had a huge lunch," she answered.

He wanted to point out her lie, but he was enjoying the peaceful moment too much. Earlier, Jamellah called him over to board up her windows. He didn't arrive until much later because of the frantic traffic on the freeway. People in Louisiana did not take hurricanes lightly, no matter how many they'd been through. He'd pulled up shortly after five, and when he found her upstairs, she was in bed with her nightgown on. He clearly remembered her telling him that she hadn't been downstairs all day. The kitchen had been spotless and he remembered her saying she hadn't eaten anything. But instead of pointing that out, he ate and watched her as she continued to take tiny, birdlike pecks at the roll followed by sips of water. He was sure that she'd tell him; all he had to do was wait patiently.

As he expected, the food was wonderful. Before he could completely finish his first serving, Jamellah had stood and refilled his plate once again. When he reached for his glass of iced tea, he found it to be always full. Jamellah definitely knew how to please a man. In and out of the bedroom. She was just an all-around wonderful woman. But in the back of his mind, he wondered how long it would take her to tell him about the pregnancy test. Looking across the table, he saw her daintily sipping ice water and nibbling on the roll.

"You've outdone yourself again, Melly. Aren't you going to have some of this?" he asked.

"As I told you, I've already eaten," she lied again.

"Just a little, baby. I hate eating alone," O'Kelley pleaded.

Sighing, Jamellah stood and went to the counter next to the stove. He watched as she put small spoonfuls into a plate. She sat back in her chair and gave him a beautiful smile. Watching with great interest, he saw her take a bit of the potatoes on her fork, sniff it, and slowly place it in her mouth. She didn't chew or swallow, just gave him another big smile after she saw him looking at her.

"Good, huh?" he questioned as he watched her swallow like she had a mouth filled with motor oil.

"Yummy!" she brightly replied.

Just as she was about to say something, he decided he couldn't hold his question anymore. As he whipped his wallet out of his robe pocket, she saw the test wand with its bright pink tip sticking out.

"You want to tell me about this?" he asked, watching her carefully.

Clearly taken aback, Jamellah took a deep breath. She wasn't prepared to have this conversation. She felt that the pregnancy was something that she would take in stride and didn't want or need outside influences to affect her decisions. But knowing the kind of person O'Kelley was, she knew that her wishes were null and void.

"There's really nothing to tell. What do you want to know?" she asked quietly.

"I want to know everything. But you can start by telling me how long you've known about this."

"I took this today. I still don't know for sure because these tests can be wrong."

"I've never been a woman nor have I ever taken one of these, but from what I know, they are pretty accurate. So have you tried to schedule a doctor's appointment?"

"Not yet, but I'll get to it soon," Jamellah said as she moved the food around her plate.

"What do you call soon?" he said.

"See? This is why I didn't say anything. I knew you would nag me about it," she said in a teary voice. "This is a hard hit for me. Give it a chance to sink in, then I'll be able to handle business."

Looking at her, O'Kelley yearned to ignore her request but decided to grant her wish. He would give her a few days, and if she still hadn't gone to a doctor, he would take the matter into his own hands.

RIDING IN THE PASSENGER seat of Fernando's truck, Fern looked at the scattered mess that the hurricane dumped upon the city. Most of the minor roadways were closed due to flooding, but they managed to take major arteries to get to Fernando's parents' house. The fact that New Orleans was six feet below sea level worsened the effects of even the slightest downpour. Fernando's parents had panicked and evacuated, along with over half the city, but had returned the night before. She and Fernando missed their baby and had left at first daylight to drive and get him.

Pulling up to his parents' house in the Forest Wake gated community, Fernando killed the engine.

"I'll be right back," he said as he got out and went into the house.

Fiddling around with the radio stations, Fern hoped that his parents would have the good sense to stay inside instead of coming out to chastise her even more. She had been having unnecessary confrontations with them since day one and was really sick of it. In the beginning she simply let them get the best of her, but in later times she had done an excellent job of defending herself. Now she was tired of bickering with them over how she and Fernando lived their lives. Seeing Fernando come out of the house while balancing Hugs and his tiny little suitcase delighted her. They were so cute, the men in her life.

"Say hi to Mommy," Fernando told Hugs as he handed him to Fern. "Tell Mommy hi."

"Hey, my baby," Fern said, tickling his tummy as he tried to repeat Fernando's instructions. Giggling at his gibberish, she kissed him and inhaled his cool little scent. She'd enjoyed her break from motherhood, but she'd missed him so much.

"We missed him, didn't we?" Fernando chuckled as he watched Fern tickle Hugs and Hugs pretend that he didn't like it.

"We sure did," Fern affirmed. I wonder if he would like having a new little brother or sister, Fern thought. He was still so little and she had not planned on having children really close in age. As long as Hugs was her only child, she could lavish all her love and attention on him. It would be so hard to show two children equal attention while they were both still so little.

In the past few months, Fern's marriage really wasn't what she wanted it to be. Sometimes she just felt so trapped. It would kill her to lose Fernando, but she felt that she needed space. In the past, she always messed up in close-quarter relationships. She felt that if she didn't get the occasional break from Fernando, she would push him further and further away. Although most found her to be delightful, she saw herself as a bothersome, burdening person.

"Fernando," Fern began as they whizzed through the rain-drenched city. "How do you feel about having more kids?"

"Hmmm ... well, I never really thought about it. I'm pretty content with Hugs as well as the lifestyle we're living now. Too many kids could easily mess that up."

"What about one more?" Fernecia asked.

"You know what my father always told me? A woman's body is like a copy machine. Once it gets warmed up, it makes copy after copy after copy until someone pulls the plug out from the wall. One more will turn into two, which will turn into three, and so forth. Next thing you know, we'll have ten kids and be living in the Calliope projects. No deal," Fernando said with an air of finality.

Well, just kick me down, Fern thought. At this point, she knew what she had to do.

"Why are you asking me this? Is there something you want to tell me?"

"No. I was just wondering," she lied.

"Okay. If it ever comes to the point where you are seriously considering it, I might decide to give it more thought, but I doubt that I'll change my mind. Okay?"

"Okay," Fern answered.

*N*ovember breezed into New Orleans like an earth-toned palette. The rusts and ochers held court while the auburns and siennas vied for attention. Throughout the city, the curious smell of nutmeg hung in the air. Its origins were unknown, although no one really questioned it. The smell, coupled with the crisp, cool air, was a relief to many. To others it awakened a yearning. A restless hunger.

"MRS. FRANKLIN, YOU NEED to slip into this gown."

"Mrs. Franklin, you need to place your feet into these stirrups."

"Mrs. Franklin, you need to sign right here before we begin."

"Mrs. Franklin, have you considered all of the mental and physical repercussions of this?"

"Mrs. Franklin, is your husband aware that you are having this procedure?"

"Mrs. Franklin, this won't hurt a bit."

"Mrs. Franklin, wake up."

"Mrs. Franklin, wake up. Congratulations! You just killed an innocent baby."

"Mrs. Franklin, wake up, you selfish slut!"

"Mrs. Franklin, how could a grown woman be so careless!"

"Mrs. Franklin, how would you like to have a look at the dead fetus, you bitch!"

"Mrs. Franklin! Turn over and take a look at the life you just destroyed!"

• • •

SITTING UP RAMROD STRAIGHT in her bed, Fernecia could feel the sweat pouring down her temples. The voices always started so kind, gentle, and caring. Before long, though, they always turned malicious and patronizing, like a million collective demon voices from hell. They taunted her, coaxed her, berated her, and robbed her of sleep and sanity.

She began to hear them the moment the anesthetic wore off and she found herself on a cold clinic bed, a rough white sheet covering her midsection. This had been going on for the past month. Her lack of sleep was beginning to affect her work, her family, her everyday life. She didn't know what to do. The decision to abort the child she found herself stuck with was a hasty one. She hadn't even told Fernando. At the time, she could only think about herself and speculate on how it would ruin her marriage. She felt awful and wanted the secret to go to the grave with her. By the same token, she knew that she had to tell someone or it would kill her, sending her to an early grave.

"WASSUP, WITCH!" JAMELLAH CALLED out cheerfully as she bounced through the swinging doors in Fernecia's kitchen.

"Hey, pregnant witch," Fern replied as she leaned over the counter, chopping garlic as though she were killing an enemy. "Did you remember the basil?"

"Yep . . . sho 'nuff . . . I think the only place that has fresh basil this time of year is the French Market, and you know a sister wasn't down for driving across the city to the Vieux Carré. Instead, I got a bottle of the dried kind," Jamellah said as she walked toward the counter to set the plastic grocery bags down. Her earliest symptom of pregnancy was the fatigue that was constantly bringing her down. She couldn't even imagine how tired she would be now if she had driven to the French Market instead of the local grocery store.

"You did what?" Fernecia growled as she flung the knife on the floor. It landed inches from Jamellah's right foot. "I asked you something simple."

"Hey Fern, watch that, will you," Jamellah replied seriously as she slowly stepped back toward the door.

"I asked you one simple fucking favor and you couldn't even do that right," Fern screeched like a banshee as she flipped the cutting board of garlic onto the floor. "What is your fucking excuse? I asked for basil and you bring me some dried shit. After all I have done for you, was that too much to ask?" she screamed through her tears.

Jamellah was in such shock that she didn't even feel the groceries slip out of her hands and fall to the floor. Looking at Fern crumpled to the floor in tears, she felt helpless and scared. She had to go get Fernando. She didn't know what was going on. In all their years of friendship, she had never seen her act this way. Yep. She had to get Fernando.

"Fern, I didn't think that it was that serious. But look, I am going. I'm leaving now. I am gonna go find you some fresh basil even if it kills me."

"No! Don't fucking bother! You can't do anything right! Fuck this!" Fern yelled as she began bawling.

As Jamellah backed against the wall, the kitchen door swung open. Fernando rushed in, holding Hugs. Confused, he looked as Fern reached up for a terra-cotta soup tureen. Turning to Jamellah, he looked down and read the fear on her face.

"What the hell is going on? Melly? What did you do to her?" he said hurriedly.

"I bought dried basil," Jamellah replied in a zombie-like tone.

"You bought dried basil," Fernando repeated.

"Yes, and she went off on me like a loaded pistol," Jamellah told him in a pain-stricken voice as she reached out for Hugs.

"Fern, what is your problem?" he asked as he took a few steps forward. "Are you upset? Are you on your period?"

"You black motherfucker!" she yelled. "My fucking world is falling apart and all you can do is ask me if I am on the fucking rag? You shithead! I fucking hate you!"

Taking the soup tureen, she lifted it above her head.

"Fernecia. We bought that in Cozumel. It cost a fortune. You didn't even want to put anything in it and now you want to break it? Put it down, baby. Tell me what's wrong."

"You are such a motherfucking bitch! The only thing you fucking think about is how much shit costs. Fuck you!" Fern screamed as she threw the tureen at Fernando. He ducked just in the nick of time before it crashed against the wall.

"Hold up!" Fernando yelled, raising his voice several octaves. "I will not allow you to break shit and berate me in my house, no matter how mad you get!"

"*Your* house? Motherfucker, may I remind you that we are in Louisiana. A community-property state. This is *our* house and I will throw and break my share of shit if I choose to. Fuck you!" she said as she flung a blender against the steel refrigerator door.

A dark, angry, stormy cloud covered Fernando's face. He felt like hitting her. Hitting her hard. Instead, he leaned against the wall and drew a breath of courage. Turning, he addressed Jamellah, who stood frozen in place.

"Take Fernando Jr. into his bedroom."

"Fernando, I can't leave her like this."

"Jamellah, take my son into his room right now," he repeated, punctuating every word. "Please."

"But Fernando . . ." Jamellah hesitated. Tears began to roll down her cheeks. At times like this, she despised being pregnant. She couldn't stand the emotions.

"Please, Jamellah."

Jamellah stood there, still holding Hugs and crying loudly.

"Melly, standing there crying won't help her. Neither you nor Hugs needs to see this," he said in a coaxingly soft voice.

Hearing his tone, Jamellah spun around with Hugs on her hip and rushed toward the kitchen door.

"Thank you, Jamellah."

Turning back toward Fernecia, he looked at her just in time to see her pressing a fillet knife against her right wrist. The left wrist, as well as the floor beneath her, was already covered in blood.

"Mr. Franklin, did you see any signs of your wife being suicidal prior to this evening?" the caustic Asian social worker asked as Fernando nervously downed his fifth cup of bland, black coffee.

"Fern would never try to take her life," Jamellah shot from the other side of the waiting room.

"My question was directed to Mr. Franklin," the worker shot back.

"You listen here," Jamellah said as she took quick steps toward her. "The woman lying in there is my best friend. She is like the sister I never had. Fuck that! She is like the mother that I dreamed of having. So I don't care who the fuck you were directing the question to. I answered it!"

Looking at Jamellah through small, angry slits in her eyes, the social worker turned back toward Fernando.

"Has she had any type of depression?"

"She would cry often but she never let on that she would pull something like this," Fernando answered, fighting back tears. "The creature that we saw in action tonight was not my wife."

Fernando didn't know whether to be angry, hurt, or scared. His parents had rushed to the hospital after he called them from the ambulance. They were seemingly concerned about Fernecia, but he begged them to go home and to take Hugs with them. His family, the new family that grew out of his love for the woman he loved from so long ago, was falling apart. He had to stop it.

"Mr. Franklin, I would suggest getting help. Depression is common in black women, although little is often said about it. You need immediate help for your wife when she is discharged from the hospital. She could be a danger to herself and your child. She really needs help."

Standing to his full height of well over six feet four, Fernando crushed the Styrofoam coffee cup and slammed it in the trash can. Jamellah walked over to where he was standing.

"Mr. Franklin, your wife needs help," the parrotlike Asian repeated.

Both turning toward her, Fernando and Jamellah looked at her and said together with equal disgust, "No shit, Sherlock!"

Satisfied, they stalked off down the corridor to see what they could do to help Fern.

• • •

"Mr. Franklin, I was just coming to find you," Dr. Nicole Miller said as she closed Fern's door. "Who is this with you, if I may ask?"

"I am her sister," Jamellah said affirmatively.

"Very well," Dr. Miller replied. "Shall we sit?"

Walking down a few doors to the hospital chapel, they all sat as Dr. Miller looked over Fern's chart and her notes.

"I must say, this whole thing is a shock. The last time I saw Mrs. Franklin was when she came for an appointment and I confirmed her pregnancy."

"Now, Doc," Fernando said. "You saw her after that. In fact, you've seen her numerous times since my son was born."

"I even went with her to a routine appointment in July," Jamellah interjected.

"No, you don't understand," Nicole Miller answered in a confused yet compassionate tone. "Mrs. Franklin came to my office at the beginning of October. And from my memory and her medical records, I recollect that, at that time, she was several weeks pregnant. She has been my patient for three years and I know my patients' comings and goings as if they were my own."

Seeing the confused looks on their faces, Dr. Miller continued. "Keeping that in mind, once the hospital called me, I asked that they wait until I got here to medicate her fully because she was pregnant. They informed me that they had given her a test which was negative. Surely one of you knew that she miscarried? I, as her doctor, should have been informed of that."

"My wife never had a miscarriage," Fernando said quietly. "My wife was not pregnant. I would have known."

"Fern would've told me," Jamellah reassured the doctor.

"I am afraid that both of you are wrong. Mrs. Franklin did come to my office on October eighth and she did have a pregnancy test, which was positive. She is not pregnant now, which means that something happened to the fetus. Had Mrs. Franklin terminated her pregnancy, would she have told either of you about it? Surely one or both of you paid enough attention to her to know that she was pregnant?"

As they looked at each other with guilt in their eyes, neither Fernando nor Jamellah could decide which was louder: the silence that had fallen over the room or the roaring that had begun in their heads.

FERN'S MOUTH FELT AS if it had eaten all the cotton in the entire state of Georgia. Attempting to sit up, she decided to walk to the kitchen to get herself a drink. With a great shock, Fernecia realized that she was restrained to a bed. But not just any bed . . . a hospital bed. What was she doing in a hospital bed? Come to think of it, what was she doing in a hospital?

Taking a look around the room, she began to panic. The stiff white bandages wrapped around her wrists felt confining and forbidding. Seeing that the phone on the bedside table was clearly out of her reach, she found the call button on her bed. Squeezing down, she suppressed tears while she waited for someone to come and explain to her what she was doing here.

The dull wooden door opened and instead of seeing a familiar face, Fern saw a young white nurse peer timidly at her.

"Mrs. Franklin . . . how are you?" she asked shyly as she walked over to the bed and prepared to take Fern's blood pressure.

"I'm fine," Fern began. "But why am I here? And could I please have some water?"

"Why are you here?" the nurse echoed as she reached for the bedside pitcher and poured water into a cup. Handing the cup to Fern, she took a deep breath. "Well . . . your doctor is here, and after I get a reading, I'll call her in to talk to you."

"Dr. Miller? Here? Am I sick?" Fern asked while she gulped down the tepid water.

"I promise, Mrs. Franklin, she'll speak to you as soon as I finish."

"Can you take this off my wrists?"

"Dr. Miller will attend to that, Mrs. Franklin. Now I need you to relax," she said as she wrapped the cuff around Fern's upper arm.

Mere minutes seemed like hours as Fern gazed in silence at the fluctuating needles on the blood pressure gauge. Satisfied, the nurse recorded the reading and left the room, promising to send in Dr. Miller.

When the door swung open for a second time, Fern realized that she must have dozed off while waiting for Dr. Miller. She felt groggy and the dryness in her mouth had returned. Moving back into her semi-sitting position, she was elated when Fernando and Jamellah walked in along with Nicole Miller.

"What happened to me?" Fern begged of them.

Dr. Miller looked concerned and Jamellah wore a worried yet ashamed expression. A look of anger mixed with concern painted Fernando's face. All three looked at her and then glanced away.

"Is anyone going to answer me?" Fern asked as she began to cry helplessly.

"Fern, you tried to kill yourself yesterday afternoon," Fernando answered bluntly.

"No, I didn't. Hugs. Where is Hugs?" she asked Jamellah.

"He is with Mom," Fernando answered for her.

"How are you feeling, Fernecia?" Dr. Miller asked as she moved close to the bed and wrapped Fern in an embrace. The simple, tender gesture made Fern sob even more, and Jamellah started to cry too.

"I feel angry. I don't know what to say. You guys know that I wouldn't try to take my own life," Fern said softly through her tears.

"May I speak to Fernecia for a while?" Fernando asked, giving Dr. Miller and Jamellah a solemn gaze.

"Sure, we'll wait in the hallway," Dr. Miller answered as she steered a crying Jamellah out of the room and closed the door behind them.

"Fern," Fernando began. "Do I make life so miserable that you are just willing to throw it all away?"

Ashamed, Fern looked down and traced the patterns on the hospital gown she wore. In bits and pieces, yesterday evening was slowly coming back to her. She felt so bad. *What was I thinking? I messed up so bad.*

"Fern, look at me," he said as he lifted up her chin. "Quit talking to yourself inside your head. Talk to me."

"I don't know what to say," Fern admitted, pulling her chin out of his hand and facing the wall. "I want to say I'm sorry but I know that isn't good enough. I just don't know what to say."

"Fern, there are things that I need to ask you, but getting an answer may harm me more than it could ever help. Look at me," he said, turning her head back so that she was once again facing him.

"I am not crazy, Fernando. I know this says something totally different, but I am not crazy," she gushed out as she held up her bandaged wrists to him.

"The woman I married is not crazy. The woman that gave me my son is not crazy. The woman that I still love is not crazy. She is just disturbed by some things that need to be cleared away," Fernando affirmed.

"Fernando, please don't put me away. You know how I hate institutions. I know that I tried something stupid. But baby, those places are for crazy white people. Please don't do it," Fernecia begged.

"I am not going to 'put you away'; however, I do think that we need to get you some help," Fernando said frankly.

A knock on the door indicated that it was time for Fern's medication. Within minutes of taking the dose, she began to doze off. Somewhere, in the fog of sleep, she heard Fernando say that he was going to check on Hugs and would be back at the hospital in no time.

FERNECIA WOKE UP AND instantly felt the bush that her hair had become. Geez, I must look like who dun it, why he did it, and he bet' not do it no mo'! She'd always taken so much pride in her hair and she wasn't about to stop now. Swinging her legs over the side of the bed, she got up in pursuit of a comb or brush and a mirror.

The next thing she noticed was the white woman in the next bed, fully dressed, sitting up, and peering at her curiously. She then noticed that she was not in the same hospital room she was in the last time she was awake. This place was as clean but much less sterile-looking. It reminded her of a hotel room.

"Where am I?" she asked the woman.

Letting out a loud snort, the woman began to laugh loudly. She sounded like one of the stinking hyenas from Hugs's *Lion King* video.

"Listen, if you don't want to tell me, then fine. I'm going to find out myself."

"They got you too, I see! My parents had me towed here while I was too sauced to even remember. Sugar, welcome to Meadowlark."

"What the hell!" Fernecia's head began to spin. Her firm had handled the sale of the property on which Meadowlark was built. It was known throughout New Orleans as the detox/mental health rehab hospital for the rich and overprivileged. She needed to call Fernando to get her out of this fucking nuthouse.

"I need to use the phone. Where is the nearest one?"

"There is a pay phone in the corridor," the woman answered as she lit a stinking Virginia Slim. "I came here to drop my coke habit and now I'm hopelessly addicted to nicotine. Ain't that some shit?"

Ignoring her, Fern felt around for change to use the pay phone.

"Listen, can I borrow a quarter? I don't have any money on me right now but I am good for it. I gotta call my husband to get me out of this place."

"Sure. But I doubt that he'll get you out when he's the one who threw you in here," the woman said as she eyed her skeptically.

"Please. Just give me some change. I'll repay you. I have money," Fern pleaded, her patience wearing thinner by the minute.

"Oh, I know you have money. If you didn't, you'd be at the state joint," she said as she handed Fern a small handful of change. "Here you go. Knock yourself out."

THE FIRST PLACE FERN called was Fernando's parents' house. She had to check on Hugs. No answer. She then called her own house.

"Hello?" A female voice that she recognized as Fernando's mother's answered.

"Where is my baby? And what am I doing here? As a matter of fact, why the fuck are you answering my phone?"

A dead dial tone was the only response that Fern got. Inserting more coins, she tried her house again. The phone was picked up and then dropped loudly on its base. Taking a few breaths to steel herself, she dropped more coins into the slot and called again.

"Hello?"

"Fernando. God, am I glad to hear your voice. Your mother is tripping. Come and get me. I'll be ready by the time you get here. You can explain everything then. Okay?" Fernecia gushed.

"Fern, baby . . . I can't come and get you. We've decided that you need to stay there awhile. They're good people. They'll help you get things together. I am here for you every step of the way. I've done this for us," Fernando said rationally and a little too calmly.

"What do you fucking mean, you did this for us?" Fern said loudly, drawing the attention of the staff huddled at the nurses' station.

"I want our marriage to work. I want to see you become a good wife and mother. I believe in you and me, Fern," he said.

"Save that bullshit for Whitney Houston. I am getting out of this fucking joint," Fern said evenly. This time, it was her turn to slam the phone down.

"You have a collect call from—" Jamellah heard just before Fern yelled out, "Melly, come get me!"

Quickly following the automated operator's instructions, she pressed 1.

"Fern, where are you? I went to the hospital and you were gone. Fernando isn't answering any of my calls. I am worried as hell," Jamellah said, her voice thick with tears.

"Melly, I'm in Meadowlark. Please come get me. I hated to call you collect, but I wasted all my money trying to get Fernando to come and get me. Please, Melly, I don't wanna be here," Fern pleaded with Jamellah.

"Baby, hang up and I am going to call the administration to see what I need to do to come and get you. I promise, you'll get out," Jamellah said while reaching for a phone book. "Talk to you in a little while."

Jamellah, if anyone, knew that Fern was not crazy. Surrounded by craziness, yes. But crazy? No. Fernecia was the closest thing to a true family that Jamellah had. It had been months since she'd spoken to her own mother and siblings. They were concerned about her well-being only when it was beneficial to them. She sometimes purposely went for months without calling her mother just to see if anyone would pick up the phone to call her, simply to see if she was still alive. They knew nothing about present-day Jamellah. They couldn't tell you what her favorite food was or even what she did for a living. They didn't even know that she was pregnant. But one thing they did know was this. If you called her with a sob story and begged long enough, she would probably send you a check. Fern's family was the exact same way. Jamellah and Fernecia had had each other's backs forever. And it wasn't about to stop now.

"Hey now," O'Kelley sang out as he entered the kitchen. "What's wrong now?" he asked impatiently after spying fresh tear tracks on Jamellah's cheeks.

After telling him about Fern being committed, she drew a breath for strength. She went on to tell him that since Fernando had gone to the courts and filed an order of protective custody because Fern was a threat to herself and others, it would be seven days before Fern or anyone could sign herself out of the facility. She felt helpless. Jamellah could think back to a time when her mother had used up all the food stamps and welfare money feeding and entertaining her weekly card-party guests. Fernecia was the one who'd smuggled boxes of macaroni and cheese, cans of potted meat, tubes of Ritz crackers, packs of Kool-Aid, and sugar in Ziploc bags so that Jamellah would have something to eat. In their first years of college, it was Fern who would filch items from the deli where she worked so Jamellah, who often missed cafeteria meals because of classes, could eat. Fernecia had always operated on the "If you're broke and I got a dime, then we both have a nickel" theory. Fern had always been the flame. But now that Fern was at the lowest point in her life, there was virtually nothing Jamellah could do to help her.

"Are you even hearing me, Jamellah?" O'Kelley asked as he shook her shoulder a little too roughly.

"Yes, I am hearing you, but I am not listening . . . what are you saying? What did I miss?"

"What I was saying is this," O'Kelley began. "You have me now. I understand that she's your friend, but you need to move on. Learn to please your man. You can't save the world."

"You black son of a bitch," Jamellah said coolly. "I was drawing breath for twenty-four before you came in the picture. I love you, but it's quite possible that you're only a temporary fixture. You may or may not be here tomorrow. But Fernecia? Fernecia is *here!*" Jamellah exclaimed to him as she pounded a fist over her heart. "And no nigger is going to move her."

"You are one crazy black bitch." O'Kelley chuckled. "The woman wanted to beat the shit out of you because you didn't get fresh parsley."

"Basil, motherfucker. Basil. Get it right. She may have had a moment, but she's still here. Don't ever let a foul word about Fern slip out of your vile black mouth," Jamellah said, growing even angrier. "You are a man. A dick. Baby's father or not, you can be replaced. My best friend can never be. And I only know one black bitch. *So,* if you want to talk to a black bitch, pick up the phone and call that mama of yours."

"Oh?" O'Kelley questioned, raising a brow. "She's a bitch, is she? I'll show you who the bitch is."

Seeing him make his way to her as swift as a panther, Jamellah rose and threw the chair in his path. Her heart raced. She had spent the last few months getting to know and growing to love this man, and now he was chasing her as if he were going to harm her. This had to be a bad dream. She was carrying his child, for Christsakes. Running through the living room, Jamellah stumbled over an end table and fell.

The first lick didn't hurt. The second stung vaguely. But the third, fourth, and fifth caused Jamellah to curl herself up into a ball and tuck her neck in to protect her and her growing fetus. If this nigger ever stopped swinging on her, she was going to kill him. Without a doubt.

O'Kelley swung, kicked, punched, cursed, and yanked while Jamellah rocked on the floor. She muffled her cries of pain, hoping that if she showed no emotion, he would stop.

"I tried to make somebody out of you. I love you. I will not have you disrespect me. You hear? You hear me?" O'Kelley said breathlessly as he pulled hunks of Jamellah's braids upward, causing her face to lift to him.

"Yes, baby," Jamellah agreed. She would have done or said anything in order for him to let go of her hair. "I promise, whatever you want, I promise."

As abruptly as the licks started, they stopped. Getting up from his crouching position on top of her curled body, O'Kelley extended a hand to help her up. Ignoring his hand, Jamellah ran her hands over her swollen belly and felt her crotch for the wetness of blood. Her only concern was her baby, not the man who'd just beaten her and now had the nerve to try to help her up.

"You don't want any help? Then fine. Come to bed when you're ready," he said as he retreated toward the stairs.

Thunderstruck, Jamellah remained in her fetal position. Her mind raced. Never did she have any indication that O'Kelley would flip on her. He was the most stable person she had ever met. This was crazy. The world was spinning out of control. Was Armageddon here? Fernecia was in a rehab center, but Fernando was the one who'd really lost his mind. She was lying on the floor, pregnant and panting, having just received the worst beating of her life. Spitting out a mouthful of blood, she realized that the craziest part of the whole thing was the fact that the man who had just beaten her and threatened the life of her child was still alive. In fact, he was upstairs, singing to himself and taking a shower. Oh, hell no. Sooner or later, you have to go to bed. Sleep with one eye open, motherfucker.

"FERNECIA, THINK BACK. I want to help you release all this anger. I want you to tell me when it all started."

Rolling her eyes at the handsome black man whose name tag read SEAN SIMM, MD, Fern took a long drag on the Kool that she borrowed from one of the other patients in the dayroom. Her so-called doctor had just arrived and was interrogating her in a casual setting, pretending that he was her friend.

"Fernecia, you don't have to be ashamed. You have some people who are very concerned about you, including me. Whatever it is. Don't be ashamed. I am sure that I have heard worse," he coaxed.

"Okay, Doc . . . you wanna talk? Let's talk," Fern said as she mashed out the cigarette.

"Great, I knew you could do—"

"Then shut up and listen," Fern said, cutting him off. "Suppose you grew up with a family who only gave a fuck about themselves."

"I understand, Fernecia. Many families aren't sup—"

"I said shut up. You said you wanted to listen, so listen," Fernecia said. "Imagine waking up when you were no more than a child with a different nigger trying to hump you every night. Imagine your mother being in the next room, acting like she was asleep. Not wanting to wake up and have proof that her newest boyfriend was a piece of shit.

"Imagine having to look out for a sister the same age as you as well as younger siblings because your mother was too busy living from orgasm to orgasm to pay attention to any of you. Imagine that. Imagine growing up around temptation. Niggers pawing you on street corners while you walked to school. People saying you wouldn't grow up to be anything but a fat slut. Imagine beating the odds. Growing up, going to college. Learning to live instead of simply surviving. Then, imagine being handed the life that you've always dreamed about. On a silver platter. But then, out of the sweet pot come crawling slimy memories of filth. Not being able to suppress the bad memories even though your life has become pure sugar. Then, imagine hitting rock bottom. Then you start to elevate. You realize that you are tired of being the victim. Imagine that you knew you had to make a change and knew how you needed to go about doing so. But you were locked up in a fucking *nuthouse* so you couldn't do anything. Now, once you take all of that into consideration, then you can approach me with this pyschobabble," Fernecia said, standing. "Now you have a *nice* day, Doctor."

"JAMELLAH, ARE YOU COMING to bed?" O'Kelley said from the bathroom. Spitting out the last mouthful of antiseptic and realizing that there were no more traces of blood, Jamellah rinsed her mouth once more and turned off the tap.

"And put on something sexy," he called out.

This nigger just beat his woman and his unborn child and now he wants to fuck? Jamellah thought incredulously. Flipping off the lights, she walked out into the bedroom. Lying down next to him in a daze, she stared at the ceiling as he climbed on top and penetrated her. While he slobbered and smothered her face with kisses, she was quiet. Shock could be a silencing thing. When he rolled off, she sensed that he was finished. Turning on her side, she knew that she had to take a shower.

"You don't need to clean up right now, come here, baby," O'Kelley said sleepily.

"I'm hungry," Jamellah said as an invisible lightbulb appeared over her head. "I didn't get anything to eat."

"You sure are right. I could go for some eggs and pan sausage right about now," O'Kelley mumbled dreamily.

"I'm going to go and make you a meal that you'll never forget," Jamellah promised as she started out the bathroom door.

After adding salt, Jamellah waited for the water to come to a rolling boil. Reaching for a phone book, she found Meadowlark and dialed the number. Giving the operator the patient number that Fernecia had given her earlier, she waited for Fern to come on the line.

"Hello," Fern said eagerly.

"Fern, it's me. Don't talk. Just listen. Some crazy shit is going on. But I am going to get you out of there. I don't care if it's the last thing I do. I'm gonna find a way to get you out. Sit tight."

"Okay," Fernecia mumbled with tears in her eyes and choking

her throat. It seemed far-fetched, but she couldn't remember a time when they'd let each other down. And she doubted that it was going to start now.

"O'KELLEY . . . food's ready," Jamellah said as she pressed the Ziploc bag full of ice onto her bruised and swollen eye. Letting the cool sensation penetrate the wound, she held it there for a while and then put it down when she heard him bounding down the stairs.

"Are those cheese grits I smell?" he asked as he took a seat at the table, the very table that she'd nearly jumped over a few hours ago in her attempt to escape him.

"They sure are," Jamellah said as she stirred the pot on the stove.

"Great. I haven't had those in months," he said hungrily.

"Then you'll be happy to know that I made the whole pot just for you," Jamellah said as she flung the boiling grits onto O'Kelley. The screams and smell of scorching flesh were drowned out by her deep sense of immediate satisfaction. Flinging the empty pot onto the floor, Jamellah stood with her hands on her belly and watched as he writhed in pain, not unlike she had done as he beat her. Satisfied, she turned and began to walk away. Stopping short, she turned back and looked at the suffering, screaming man on the kitchen floor.

"Oh, if you need an ambulance, the phone is right there," she said, pointing to the counter as if he were coherent enough to see. "Next time you decide to hit a woman, make sure you pick one that won't strike back."

THE MINUTE THE FIRST police car arrived and she opened the door to a sea full of uniforms and neighbors, Jamellah was worried. She was not worried about the moaning man who was carted out on a stretcher and into an ambulance. She was not worried about her unborn child that she knew was now safe. She was worried about Fernecia. She had to go and get Fern. As a million flashcubes popped in her face and a plastic-looking black reporter stuck a mike in her face, she was worried about Fern. As the police officers cuffed her and shoved her body into the backseat of the cruiser, she was worried about Fern. How would she go and get Fern?

FERN SAT ON THE bed, brushing her hair. Her roommate, whose name she learned was Sandy, sat on her bed, flipping channels and yapping about her drug habit. Sandy, it seemed, had the habit of going between New Orleans' three news channels. Fernecia was a news junkie and was addicted to CNN, MSNBC, and BET's nightly news, but she hated the local stations. They bypassed important things like politics and major crimes in order to report petty crimes and events in the inner city. She decided that lying back and counting ceiling tiles would be more interesting than watching the plastic-faced blonde yap away about liquor-store robberies and welfare mothers.

Fern stopped short when she happened to glance up at the television to see a very pregnant Jamellah being placed into a police car.

"What the fuck!" she yelled as she grabbed the remote from Sandy and turned up the volume. She listened as the stone-faced reporter said that Jamellah was being booked on charges of aggravated assault and possibly murder.

"Sandy, gimme some change," Fernecia yelled. This time, Sandy took one look at the determined expression on her face and complied.

AFTER DIALING THE NUMBER for Pop-a-Lock, she whispered into the phone that she needed the ignition changed and new keys issued on a 1998 Acura Legend. She assured the locksmith that she'd meet him at her house in about thirty minutes. Then, as calmly as she had made the transaction over the phone, she exited out the corridor door at the end of the unit, setting off a myriad wailing security alarms. If they wanted her, let them catch her.

TAKING OFF HER THREE-CARAT wedding set, Fernecia put it in the waiting palm of the cabdriver.

She'd run like never before until she finally got to the main road and hailed a cab.

"Lady, I can't take this," the dreadlocked cabbie said.

"It's worth a thousand times more than I owe you for this ride," Fernecia cried out. "You know it's real."

"No, that's not what I mean, sister. These rings could feed my family for months. But I can't take them. It's not any of my business, but obviously you needed a ride. I believe in God. I believe that the second coming of Jesus Christ is walking the earth right now in the form of a person who needs help. You may be that person. Have a nice evening," he said as he handed her back her rings.

"What's your name? I could send you the money in the morning," Fernecia said as she watched the Pop-a-Lock truck pull into her driveway.

"I have no name." The cabbie smiled and rolled up his window as she closed the door. He gave her a final wave and a warm smile as he pulled away.

"I know you have no name," Fernecia said to herself as the cab retreated down the street. "Most of God's angels will always remain anonymous."

PUFFING ON YET ANOTHER cigarette, Fern happily recalled how the real estate agent who first showed them their house bragged that the neighborhood was so good, car doors didn't even have to be locked. Luckily, the last time she'd parked her car, she'd exercised that right.

"Okay, ma'am. That'll be a hundred and ninety even," the smiling white man said.

"I don't have any money," Fernecia explained.

"No money?" he said as he took in Fern's house and yard. Looking at the car, he turned back to her with a doubtful look.

"Can I pay you tommorow?" Fern begged.

"Ma'am, you have no idea how many times in a week I hear that," he said apologetically.

"I just got out of the hospital. I don't have any money. I don't have any keys to get into my house. I don't even have a pair of clean underwear. But I do have my word. And my word is bond. I don't care what I have to do. You'll get every penny that I owe you in the morning," Fernecia said as she said a silent prayer.

"I'm sorry, ma'am. Taking promises to pay are against our company policy."

"Shit!" Fern yelled as she felt herself losing control again. "Isn't there something that I can do?"

"I tell you what, what kind of car insurance do you have?" asked the Pop-a-Lock man thoughtfully.

"State Farm . . . comp and collision at least."

"Let me see a copy of your policy. Depending on the type of coverage you have, having a new set of keys made may be covered under emergency roadside service," he said, smiling.

As Fern climbed into the passenger seat and opened the glove box, she realized for the second time that night that there really was a God.

Flying down I-10 in the direction of the precinct where Jamellah had been booked, Fernecia picked up the cell phone mounted to the console of her car. Fernando hadn't been at home to thwart her efforts, but she knew where to find him. Punching in his parents' number, she navigated the freeway.

"Hello?" his mother, Katherine, answered angrily.

"Put Fernando on the phone," Fernecia barked.

"I refuse to do that, you fugitive! You mental hospital escapee. Meadowlark called and said how you escaped. I'm calling them right now to tell them—"

"No disrespect, but listen here, bitch," Fern said, cutting her off. "Put Fernando on this fucking phone *now*."

Within seconds Fernando came on the line.

"Fern, listen . . ."

"No, *you* listen. I am on the way to rescue a friend. A real friend. Here is what you are going to do. You are going to get in your vehicle, drive to Meadowlark, and sign a fucking release. Not tomorrow. *Now*. Next, you are going to have my baby bathed, dressed,

Checkout Receipt

Library name: MU

Current time: 08/06/2014,
11:44
Title: The sex chronicles :
shattering the myth
Call number: ZANE
Item ID: 33206008091765
Date due: 8/20/2014,23:59

Current time: 08/06/2014,
11:44
Title: Love is never painless
: three novellas
Call number: ZANE
Item ID: 33206060605018
Date due: 8/20/2014,23:59

Current time: 08/06/2014,
11:44
Title: Mockingjay
Call number: COLLINS
Item ID: 33206007287430
Date due: 8/20/2014,23:59

Total checkouts for session:
3
Total checkouts:3

Renew by phone at:
577-3977
or online at:
www.sanleandrolibrary.org

and ready first thing in the morning. Have *all* of his shit packed for when I get there to pick him up. Mama is coming home," Fernecia said boldly and confidently before she pressed the end button. Satisfied, she parked in front of a bail bondsman's office building adjacent to the jail. She had never been good at standing up for herself. Once again she realized how tired she was of playing the bad guy. The victim. Now it was time to get this show on the road.

"MY NAME IS FERNECIA Franklin. My very best friend is sitting in that jail across the street. I am not about to let her stay there a minute longer. I have money, I own half of a house and two rental properties. I have a savings, a checking, and a money-market account. I can't access any money tonight because my husband has my purse, along with most of my other possessions. However, if you have Internet access in this office, I can access my accounts online to prove that the funds are available for withdrawal. As soon as the banks open, I can have them pull my signature card and pay you," Fernecia said. Looking at him squarely in the eye, she gave him her most serious look. "I don't care if it takes every penny that I own. I don't care if you have to call every judge in this stinking city. I don't care if I have to give you the deed to my house. I don't care what measures you have to take. Get her out."

Sitting back in her seat and lighting the last of the borrowed Kool cigarettes, Fernecia waited for him to make it happen.

"TURN AROUND. LIFT UP your hair," the deputy said. Jamellah had been booked three hours ago, and after being moved from a holding cell to the second floor, she'd been forced to undress and stand under a freezing-cold shower. Choking on tears, she meekly lifted up her hair while the female deputy sprayed an awful-smelling liquid onto her body.

"Why?" Jamellah managed to choke out. Being arrested had to be the most dehumanizing thing in the world. She understood that she'd nearly killed a man, but didn't the fact that he beat her black-and-blue count for anything?

"We need to make sure that you don't expose any of the inmates to any new strains of head or pubic lice. We have enough problems controlling the strains that we have up there," the deputy said kindly. This woman didn't look like she belonged in jail, the deputy thought. But then again, neither did half of the male and female inmates. Handing Jamellah a pair of shower slippers and an orange jumpsuit large enough to accommodate her pregnant body, she waited while Jamellah dressed slowly and blindly through her tears.

Vaguely, Jamellah heard the two-way radio on the deputy's hip crackle. Watching as the woman walked away while talking into the radio, she took a few minutes to try to compose herself. She felt like trash. Being treated like a common criminal. All for what she saw as defending herself.

The female deputy returned and handed Jamellah the clothes that she had been booked in.

"Get dressed . . . you've bonded out."

As Jamellah put on her clothes at the speed of light, she wondered who on earth had the money or the time to come and get her.

WALKING OUT OF THE central processing unit, the large metal door slammed behind Jamellah. She was free again.

Standing at the counter, signing forms saying she would be responsible for Jamellah until her court date, was none other than Fern. Turning around, she took the six steps toward Jamellah and embraced her in the warmest hug either of them had ever experienced.

"I knew dawn would not come without us bringing it in together," Fernecia said as she held on to her friend. Her only friend.

Crying onto Fern's shoulder, Jamellah could only sob in agreement.

DRIVING UP TO FERNANDO'S parents' house, Fernecia noticed that Fernando's truck was absent from the driveway. Picking up the cell phone, she punched in his cell number.

"Where the hell are you?" she spat.

"I'm at Meadowlark, doing what you asked . . . no, what you told me to do. Hugs is inside the house with my parents," Fernando said in a defeated voice.

"Good boy," said Fernecia in a patronizing tone before hitting end and once again hanging up on him.

Smiling at Jamellah, she pulled up the emergency brake.

"You wait here . . . I'll be right back."

Getting out of the car, Fernecia walked up to the palatial house and banged on the front door. When her fist began to hurt from banging, she leaned on the doorbell until she was sure she would burn it out. After about three minutes, Fernando's mother appeared holding Hugs, who was dressed and smelling clean. Balanced on her other arm were two overstuffed baby bags that contained all his things.

Grabbing her baby and embracing him, she stared at him and then at Fernando's father, who had walked up behind his mother. Snuggling to Hugs's warm little body, she said with finality, "Mama's home."

Daring them to say anything to knock her last words out of the air, she grabbed the bags off her mother-in-law's shoulder. Looking squarely at them, she shook her head in a sad way that indicated it was they who deserved pity.

"I've spent the past few years being someone else, thinking it would please your son and praying that it would please you. In fact, I've tried so hard to be what I am really not that I forgot who I really am. Did any of you appreciate it? No. Do you know who I am? Have you ever even given thought to getting to know the real Fernecia? I doubt it." Shaking her head slowly and looking at her mother-in-law's open mouth, Fern continued.

"Trying to be someone else hurts yourself, but it also hurts the few people who actually know the real you. I've finally figured out that you and Mr. Franklin have pretended to be someone else for years and you've done it because the thought of who you really are disgusts you. Do yourself a favor—come down from the ivory tower and get to know what real life and real people are about. You'd be surprised whom and what you've missed out on."

This time, walking away was the easiest thing that she had ever done in her life.

STRAPPING HUGS INTO HIS seat, she felt her heart melt as he beamed up at her.

He giggled in his adorable baby voice: "Mama home."

"That's right, my baby. Mama's home."

Shutting the door, she jumped into the driver's seat and looked at Jamellah. Reaching over to rub Melly's tummy, she let out a laugh.

"How would Buddha like some BeeBee's?" she said.

"Sho 'nuff, gurl!"

Reaching over to give her friend a hug, Jamellah decided that tomorrow didn't look so bad.

ACKNOWLEDGMENTS

I would like to acknowledge my family: Gloria, Freddie, Ellen, Murray, Marvin, and Mitchell. You have seen my best and my worst but have always believed that there was better to come.

Eileen M. Johnson

Love Is
2 Blame

V. ANTHONY RIVERS

CHAPTER ONE

Too Hard
to Shake

*M*alcolm sat at his desk in his home office, writing furiously. He tried desperately to compose a letter to the woman who broke his heart. Why am I doing this? he thought to himself. He slammed his pen down on the desk, eased back into his chair, and placed his hand on his chin. Malcolm sat deep in thought. He couldn't shake Shaylisa's face; without warning she had recently ended their two-year relationship. She'd probably planned it well in advance and just waited until she knew she could fuck with his mind. Malcolm had been getting very little sleep at night as a result.

Lately, anything that resembled thinking had become an exhausting experience. Constantly Malcolm searched his mind, trying to determine where and how things went wrong. How could a man be so giving 24/7, 365 days a year, only to be rewarded with that slap in the face known as I don't want to see you anymore.

"I don't want to see you anymore, Malcolm. It's over between us."

Those words echoed constantly in Malcolm's mind as he continued to sit at his desk. He looked down at the crumpled pieces of paper on the floor. There were five pieces balled up, representing as many attempts to write a letter that deep down he knew he had no business writing. Malcolm picked up his pen once again and began to write.

"Fuck you, Shaylisa," he scribbled, just before being startled by the sound of his phone ringing.

"Hello?" Malcolm answered.

"Hey, Malcolm, what you up to, man?"

"Not a whole lot, Jamal."

Jamal Richardson was Malcolm's best friend, running buddy, and part-time psychiatrist. Malcolm never hesitated to unleash all his issues and complaints on Jamal's shoulders. Jamal always teased Malcolm about paying him for the time they spent laboring over why a woman just ain't right!

"I hope you not sitting over there still sulking over Shaylisa!" Jamal said.

"Nah, I'm just flipping through the TV channels," Malcolm lied.

"Yeah, right . . . Listen, if you not doing anything that's gonna get you out of that darkness you call home, then hang out with a brotha and at least see if you can't look at you some booty."

"Where you headed to?" Malcolm asked somberly.

"I'm about to go to Venice Beach, buy me some cheap sunglasses, munch on some hot dogs, and, as I said, look at some booty. The only difference between me and you being, I plan on talking to whoever possesses that booty . . ."

"You know those things will make you go cross-eyed, don't you?" Malcom said.

"What will?"

"Those cheap-ass sunglasses!"

"Oh, thought you was serving up some jokes about booty watching."

"Oh, nah!" Malcolm laughed for the first time today.

"That's a welcome sound, my brotha."

"Yeah, I needed that. Thanks, Jamal."

"No prob. So, we on or what?"

"Yeah, what the hell."

After hanging up the phone, Malcolm returned to his letter. *Am I really bold enough to send something like this?* He pondered that question over and over while writing and rewriting. Once again, he slammed the pen down on the desk and took a few deep breaths, trying to relax his mind.

He closed his eyes and rubbed his forehead, hoping to ease the pain of his thoughts. He wasn't very successful, but an image of Jamal speeding through yellow lights on his way to pick him up caused Malcolm to suddenly open his eyes and stand up from his black leather chair. He had to get ready. His disposition didn't allow him to show much enthusiasm as he looked inside his bedroom closet to decide what he might wear on a Saturday afternoon in the spring in L.A.

Malcolm pulled out from his closet a white T-shirt, blue carpenter jeans, and a black Rocawear jersey with the letters RW emblazoned on the front. Now all he needed to do was put on his Timberland boots and he was good to go. Killing some time while waiting on Jamal, he pushed play on his CD player, returned to his office, and sat back down in his leather chair. The letter still sat on top of his desk. Ignoring it, he picked up a magazine lying on the floor beside his chair. It was the latest edition of *Essence*, with Sanaa Lathan on the cover. Malcolm smiled but felt strange as he gazed upon this very beautiful actress. He was admiring her because she reminded him of Shaylisa. Actually, pretty much everything and everyone reminded him of his ex-girlfriend.

Losing himself in the latest issues of magazines with chocolate honeys on the covers, Malcolm at first didn't hear Jamal pounding on his front door. Startled, Malcolm finally realized that there was some noise coming from somewhere. *Damn, is that my door?* he asked himself.

Jamal continued to pound and wasn't giving up until his depressed good friend opened the damn thing up.

"I'll be right there!" Malcolm shouted as he tossed the magazines on his way to the front door.

"Man, what took you so long?" Jamal said as Malcolm opened the door.

"I was reading something and didn't hear you knocking."

"Aw, man, no wonder, shit, you over here blasting some Marvin Gaye! You trying to just drown in your pain and self-pity, huh?"

"Not really. You know I like to listen to that old stuff sometimes. A man can't be listening to Ice Cube, Jay-Z, Dr. Dre, and all the others twenty-four hours a day!"

"I hear you, Malcolm, but I still think you trying to get you a first-class membership to the Sad Brothas of America Club. You ready to go yet? Venice gonna be off the chain. I can feel it!"

Malcolm walked to his bedroom, picked up his keys, put his silver Kenneth Cole watch on, and turned off the CD player. He took one last look around his bedroom as well as all the other rooms that he happened to walk past on his way to the front door. He wanted to make sure that everything was turned off so he could leave the house knowing that nothing was causing his electric bill to go up.

"You got everything, man?" Jamal asked.

"Yeah, just making sure," Malcolm responded.

His mind wasn't completely focused yet but he knew that Jamal was about to show him a great time no matter what. Jamal's enjoy-life-to-the-fullest attitude always made him the life of the party, especially where he and Malcolm were concerned. Malcolm was always the more serious of the two, but Jamal wanted to take full advantage of the fact that his best friend was now a single man and, in his opinion, in desperate need of a new woman in his life.

"Brotha, it's gonna be on and poppin' once we get to Venice Beach!" Jamal proclaimed.

JAMAL SLOWLY DROVE THROUGH the neighborhood streets searching for a parking space close to Venice Beach. It had been about four months since the last time he'd been to this area and already the cost of parking had doubled and in some cases tripled.

"Shit, look at the price of parking for that lot!" Jamal shouted. "They must think this is the damn airport or something!"

"Yeah, parking is pretty ridiculous."

"These fools need to be thrown in jail, charging fifteen dollars just 'cause their lot is the closest one to the beach. Mofos ain't right, shit!"

"Is this how you gonna cheer me up today, Jamal?"

"Nah, I'm through, I'm through. It's all good . . ." Jamal switched his attention to looking for a street to turn down so he could find a place to park for free.

Soon after that, he found a parking place near a small elementary school located a few blocks away from the beach.

"You hungry?" Jamal asked while holding his stomach and looking like he was in some sort of pain.

"I'm not really starving, but I don't mind getting a little something to eat."

"Well, I'm stopping at the first place I see that got hot dogs on a stick. I've been craving that shit all week! Weekends ain't made for watching your diet. I can do that from Monday to Friday, 'nah mean?"

"If you say so . . . I don't know how you come up with your philosophies, but as long as you feel good about what you're saying then I feel good too."

"That's a good thing, since I haven't heard you mention Shaylisa's name yet. Don't you think that's a positive sign, bro?"

"I don't know. It could be, I guess."

"But you ain't sure. Well, Malcolm, we gonna have to work on that and this could be the first step. You know, I'm surprised you didn't come prepared with your camera!"

"My camera for what?"

"Damn, man!" Jamal chuckled. "You know this place be littered with honeys walking around, making you wish you had a Kodak moment so you can remember in full detail just how good that booty looked."

"Yeah, it's usually some pretty ladies here, I'll have to admit."

"Pretty ladies? Boy, you need to stretch your imagination and tell me what you really see out there!"

Malcolm was past ready to get out of the car and find out what this day had in store for him. The way he was feeling, he just wanted time to go by and the weekend to be over so he could return to work. At least there, he didn't have to think about things to do to amuse him 'cause keeping company with himself had definitely been a challenge lately. It didn't take much time for his sadness about Shaylisa to evolve into moments of anger, when he'd get really pissed off.

"I see you didn't forget *your* camera," Malcolm said as he noticed Jamal readying his Sony digital video camera.

"Nah, I ain't missin' no opportunities, my brotha."

JAMAL AND MALCOLM STEPPED onto the infamous Venice Beach Boardwalk. They were instantly met by the noise of skateboarders, street performers, and constant foot traffic. It was already a warm day outside, but on the boardwalk the temperature was even warmer due to all the body heat going around. It didn't take Jamal very long to notice his first image of self-proclaimed heaven.

"Aw, damn, look-a here!" Jamal gestured with his chin, pointing in the direction of a lady strolling along, looking at some artwork.

"Yeah, she looks pretty good," Malcolm replied.

"Who you telling? Looks like Chante Moore got a twin, forget about having a muh-fuckin' man!"

"Funny . . ."

"Maybe I should say hello to this young lady and pretend like I'm an artist or something."

"Yeah, you could probably pass for one, although you don't look like you're starving."

"All the better, my brotha, 'cause you know sistas in L.A. ain't too crazy about a moneyless mofo trying to vie for they time."

Malcolm watched as Jamal led the way, in the direction of the Chante Moore look-alike. Jamal himself had the kind of looks that ladies rarely passed on, plus he possessed a quick wit along with his streetwise charm.

Malcolm drifted off slightly to the right of Jamal so that his buddy could have room to work that infamous charm. Jamal turned off his video camera. He had already filmed the woman for a few minutes while she was appreciating the oil paintings and hand-sculpted mini-statues of men and women embracing.

Jamal cleared his throat. "Nice, isn't it?" he asked.

The woman looked at Jamal, who was standing to the left of her with his eyes on an oil painting, though he only pretended to really be interested in it. She didn't respond to his comment, but clearly she was pleasantly surprised by who she'd seen standing next to her. The woman smiled and then returned to examining a piece of sculpture that was on display.

"My name is Jamal, and I hope you don't mind a brotha going out on a limb by approaching you."

"No, you seem genuine," she replied.

"I like the sound of that. I especially like the sound of your voice, umm . . ."

"Cindy," she said as she picked up on Jamal's attempt to ask for her name.

"Cindy, that's cool. So, Cindy, you think that my efforts might lead to a phone call or even dinner?"

"Possibly . . . you never know until you try."

"Okay, that almost sounds like a yes."

Cindy smiled bashfully, but she scrutinized as much of Jamal as she could without getting caught. Jamal was a tall brotha, six feet two, dark brown complexion, dreadlocks, a goatee but no mustache. He oozed with masculinity and sexuality.

"You still thinking about it?" Jamal asked.

Cindy continued to examine the sculpture. Jamal had a feeling that Ms. Cindy was doing some heavy-duty fantasizing but didn't want to admit to it. She could probably envision herself and Jamal, intertwined in a position similar to the sculpture she was touching. Her fingers glided across the statue in a motion that was borderline sensual.

"What the heck," she said. "I'll give you my cell phone number."

"Oh, okay. I can handle that." Jamal had to humble himself and accept something tht he deemed of lesser value.

"Well, you could be anyone, so I can't just give you my home number without getting to know you better."

"No prob. I'm looking forward to talking with you real soon. Is tonight okay to call you?"

"Tonight is fine."

"Beautiful."

Cindy turned and noticed Malcolm standing by as though he were waiting and listening to the conversation between her and Jamal.

"Yo, let me, um, introduce you to my buddy Malcolm," Jamal said as he noticed a perplexed expression on Cindy's face. She didn't mind Jamal giving her so much attention, but seeing another man watching her made her feel really uncomfortable.

"Hi, Malcolm," Cindy said.

"Hey, how you doing, Cindy?"

Cindy turned her attention back to Jamal. "So, I guess I'll be talking to you soon then, huh?"

"Yes, you will. Very soon, in fact. You wanna hang out with two handsome fellas? We about to grab something to eat. I think my boy wants Chinese but I'm about to splurge on some corn dogs."

"No, I'm just taking a break from some studying I had to do, but now it's time to get back to the books."

Cindy stood with her hands in her back pockets, bashfully appreciating the attention of two black men standing so close to her. She definitely favored Chante Moore a great deal and appeared to be in the same kind of incredible shape too. Her thighs, that ass, her voice! Though she was merely talking and not singing, she looked and sounded incredible. Malcolm couldn't help but examine Cindy's body with his own eyes and imagination, but she was clearly taken by Jamal and his not-so-subtle way of saying we should get together soon and do the do.

JAMAL DROWNED HIS TWO corn dogs in mustard. He sprinkled a few onions on top and attempted to bite into his food without making a mess. His attempt proved to be unsuccessful, and he searched for a napkin to wipe the dripping mustard off his chin and from the side of his mouth. Meanwhile, Malcolm was ordering some Chinese food from a nearby food stand.

"I'll have some sweet-and-sour pork, and a couple of egg rolls," Malcolm said, his eyes still fixed on the menu.

"Anything else?" the Asian lady asked.

Malcolm continued to look. He was hungrier than he'd thought, but he had a hard time deciding on what he wanted.

"I guess that's good enough," he told the lady.

Before Malcolm could take a sniff of his food, Jamal had walked up behind him with his culinary mess of corn dogs.

"What you get, bro?"

Jamal was never one to pay attention to that old saying "Don't talk with food in your mouth." Why waste the energy when you can do two thangs at once! He'd tell you.

Jamal listened as Malcolm spoke about his craving for Chinese food and how he couldn't really decide what he wanted. Malcolm spotted a place where they could sit, talk, and indulge in some serious people watching.

Days like this were perfect for watching folks walk up and down the Venice Beach Boardwalk, especially the regulars—like the brotha on the skates, playing guitar, and even that dude with the big hat who tries to improvise a little rap song using the names of the people he's trying to get donations from.

"Yo, did you ever check out Michael Colyar when he used to tell jokes down here?" Jamal asked while chewing the last of his food.

"Yeah, I saw him back in the day, he was pretty funny."

"It's been a while since I been down here, bro."

"I thought you were here last month!" Malcolm said.

"Oh yeah, but that's one of those moments I'm trying to forget, 'nah mean?"

"You forgetting a moment, Jamal, is like me getting back with Shaylisa . . ."

"It'll never happen!" they both exclaimed.

"You were with Annette the last time you came out here, huh?" Malcolm questioned.

"Yeah, and I thought the girl was all that too! I'm talking banging body, had some auburn locks in her hair, café au lait complexion, what else?"

"Umm, a cool walk too, I believe you said."

"Yeah, the girl had fools breaking they necks trying to watch how her ass jiggled from side to side. I mean, even though she had a skirt on, a brotha could still see imprints on how fine that ass was," Jamal explained.

"But didn't you just have one date and nothing happened?" Malcom said, questioning his seriousness.

"Anyway!" Jamal attempted to change the subject. "Did you get a fortune cookie with that stuff?"

"Yeah, why?"

"I wanna check out your fortune. Usually them messages be right on point and that always trips me the hell out!"

Malcolm handed Jamal his fortune cookie. Jamal opened the plastic and broke open the cookie. He read the message. He smiled, read the message again, and returned to watching the people walk by.

"What?" Malcolm wondered aloud, noticing a little smirk on Jamal's face.

Jamal cleared his throat. "Check this out," he warned. "From a past misfortune, good luck will come to you."

The two men looked at each other.

"So?" Malcolm was clueless and needed Jamal to make his point clear.

"You and Shaylisa . . ." Jamal assumed that the mere mention of Shaylisa would be enough for Malcolm to get the point.

Malcolm remained clueless. "What about us?"

"Well, my brotha, you and Shaylisa gonna end up getting back together, you watch."

"I thought we already agreed there was no possible way for that to happen."

"Yeah, that's true, but now that I've seen this fortune cookie, things have changed!"

Malcolm paused. His motivation for having fun had left his body completely. He wanted to go home, turn on some music, and finish writing that damn letter.

CHAPTER TWO

Always Wanna
Know Why

*S*haylisa Jones loved to eat pecans and drink sparkling cider late at night. She would end her day that way, along with reading a good book or calling up the girlfriend she'd met two months ago. Their meeting struck an instant chord of sisterhood and friendship for both of them. Recently, most of their conversations involved complaining about men. They wondered why most if not all of the ones they knew seemed to have the same first name, Ex.

Shaylisa had dealt with several by that first name, but only one made her wonder if she'd said good-bye a little too soon. Two years was a long time to just throw something away on a whim. How could she possibly wake up one morning, thinking and wondering about somebody else being the ideal man in her life? When did the man she was seeing become less exciting to her? When did things change? Doesn't it matter that he gave her so much? Did she ever really care about him in the first place? Doesn't she remember all the dreams she talked about sharing with him? She even looked him in the eye one day, assuring him that she hadn't changed her mind about him being "the one." She was probably motivated to lie because she and Malcolm were enjoying an all-expenses-paid vacation at a resort in Palm Springs. All expenses were paid by him, as was typically the case.

"Girl, I'm sick of trying to explain myself! Why can't he just move on?" Shaylisa asked her girlfriend on the phone.

"Does he call you a lot?"

"No, he doesn't call me. I got caller ID, so I know he's never called me since we broke up."

"You mean, since you broke things off."

"You know what I mean, girl."

"Uh-huh, so, why are you frustrated with him?"

"'Cause I got this letter from him. It just screwed up my whole day too! Almost made me want to call him up and curse his ass out."

"Why, was it that bad?"

"Not really bad, just one of those guilt-trip letters. Plus, I guess he doesn't want any memories of me because he put all the pictures he had of us, of me, in the same envelope as the letter and sent them."

"Damn, that man is wounded, girl. I hope he doesn't pass that pain on to someone else."

"Should I feel guilty about that?" Shaylisa replied defensively.

"I'm not saying that, it's just—"

"Listen, it's not like I just disappeared one day. I didn't leave some funky message on his voice mail. I told him in person how I felt and what I no longer felt about him."

"Then why are you feeling so guilty now?"

"Because of the letter . . . He's not a bad person. I don't know. Can we just change the subject?"

Shaylisa couldn't take what she was feeling. Instead of drinking sparkling cider, she put her girlfriend on hold so she could go into the kitchen and pour herself a glass of Merlot. Shaylisa brought the whole bottle with her and turned off the television before picking up the phone again.

"You still there, Cindy?"

"I'm here, what did you just do?"

"Poured a glass of Merlot, 'cause I need something to calm my nerves down right now."

"You sound like an old woman! What were you watching anyway?"

"*The Sopranos* . . . although to be honest, I'm not really in the mood to watch anything tonight."

"Yeah, I turned my TV off a long time ago, girl."

"Hope I'm not keeping you up too late, Cindy."

"No, before I called you, I was talking to this guy I met this past Saturday. He's fine, girlfriend. He seems to love talking and I don't mind listening to him either. I think we might be going out next weekend."

"Seems like you're not sure about him."

"I only hesitate because he seems like a player. I mean, I met him at Venice Beach, and for all I know he probably collected a lot of phone numbers besides mine. I'd rather be alone than to be with some man I got to share."

"I hear you. I guess I never had that problem with my ex because all he wanted to do was spend time with me. I couldn't bribe him to spend time with somebody else."

"Well, this guy seems like any lady in his life would come second to his own ego."

"He's that bad?"

"Hard to say, but it seems like it."

"That's funny, Cindy. Girl, maybe you should just leave his ass before you even start down that road."

"Don't think I haven't thought about it, Shaylisa. That's why I turned down his offer to have Sunday brunch. But he's got this sexy voice that had me rocking my leg back and forth when we talked tonight. He was saying some stuff to me that, oh my God . . ."

"Cindy?"

Cindy laughed as she anticipated Shaylisa's next question.

"Did you just have phone sex with that man?"

"No, I didn't!"

"Cindy Griffith, did you?" Shaylisa repeated her question, waiting for an affirmative answer.

"Girl, I almost did but I held my ground. He definitely stirred a little something inside of me, but I had to end that conversation and tell him that I'd call him later in the week."

"What did he say to that?"

"He just brushed it off and said cool. You know how men with huge egos try to play like nothing disappoints them."

"Yeah, I guess so. I mean, that's the thing about my ex, if I told him that I needed to go somewhere, he'd say it was okay and then he'd tell me that he'd miss me until the next time," Shaylisa said while imitating a sweet-sounding man.

"What's wrong with that?"

"Nothing, I guess, I mean . . ."

"Shaylisa, I know we haven't known each other that long, so I can't really say much about your ex, but you have me constantly wondering who's the real villain in your breakup. But don't get mad and think that I'm putting you down . . ."

"No, it's okay, Cindy. You have a right to question it, but all I can say is that for whatever reason, I woke up one morning not feeling like I wanted to see him anymore. I wanted to see someone different, if I was to see anyone at all." Shaylisa attempted to explain, but her words only revealed the uncertainty of not really knowing what she wanted in a man or for herself.

Shaylisa and Cindy continued to talk into the wee hours of the night. Shaylisa's CD player had gone from one CD to the next. In the course of their two-hour conversation, Cindy could hear a wide range of music through the earpiece of her cordless telephone.

"Girl, I need to come over to your place and copy some of that music," Cindy commented.

"Anytime!" Shaylisa laughed.

Cindy was impressed by the selection of music, which included the Isley Brothers, Nina Simone, Will Downing, and Bob Marley.

"I didn't think anybody young listened to Nina," Cindy said, complimenting Shaylisa on her musical taste.

"I wish I could take credit for that one, but actually, my ex turned me on to her. He always teased me about listening to Phyllis Hyman all the time, so he figured I needed a change."

"He must've been deep then, huh?"

"I guess you can say that. He's definitely sensitive, ultrasensitive!"

Cindy began feeling as though all the traits that Shaylisa found unappealing in her ex were things that she had always desired in a man. She couldn't understand why Shaylisa gave up on him, but she didn't want to jump to conclusions before knowing the full story. Cindy carefully brought up the subject of the letter again. "Do you think you'll ever respond to his letter?" she asked.

"I'm not sure. I really don't know what to say except to tell him what I've already said. He and I can never get back together, and because he is so sensitive, I can't see us being friends either. How can he want the best for me if he's still feeling wounded about me breaking up with him?"

"That's true."

"What do you think I should do, Cindy?"

"I don't know."

Shaylisa sighed and looked toward the bedside dresser drawer in which she'd placed the letter. She twisted her body so that she could reach over, pull open the drawer, and take the letter out. "You want me to read some of it to you?" she asked, quietly hoping that Cindy would say no.

"Yeah, I'm curious . . ."

"Okay. Let me warn you, though—"

"What, he curses a lot in the letter?" Cindy interrupted.

"No, nothing like that. He just tends to be very poetic and creative when he expresses himself. You should see all the cards, letters, you name it! I have so much stuff that he's written to me from day one!"

"Oh, that's sweet. Sounds like a romantic . . . Oops, sorry, girl." Cindy apologized for letting her appreciative words get the best of her.

• • •

" 'DEAR SHAYLISA,' " Shaylisa started.

" 'Words normally flow through me like the wind blowing through your gorgeous curly hair. Forgive me for that description, but I can't imagine that I'll ever forget all the images that I captured of you through the lens of my camera. I wrote something in my journal the other day. A quote that's kind of sad but nevertheless hits home with my thoughts that exist now. I wrote, "Physical pain is almost a luxury compared to its emotional counterpart." I don't know if you'd agree with my quote or not. This breakup is something you wanted, not I. You should see how many times I've written this letter only to throw it in the trash can because I couldn't formulate my words and thoughts without expressing anger toward you. I imagine my letter to you doesn't exactly warm your heart, and seeing those pictures probably makes you wonder what my problem is. Well, to answer that question, *love* is my problem.

" 'I recall a time when we drove up to that exclusive neighborhood that had model homes, opened for public viewing. We walked inside those homes with our mouths dropped to the floor. We wondered out loud if it could be possible for us to own such a home, together. Well, Shaylisa, when I dream, it ain't just a motion that I'm going through. All that I said I wanted to do? I wanted to do. Everything that I wished to give you, I wanted to give to you exclusively. I'm a man that keeps his word to the nth degree. I'd rather give up on life than give up on a promise. So, just when I thought I'd found my own everything, she decided that I wasn't what she had been looking for, two years later. Funny, but I didn't realize that in the midst of sharing dreams, talking about the future, making love, laughing, and enjoying each other's company . . . I didn't realize you were still looking.

" 'The breakup has been tough for me to swallow, but I'm trying to find a way to ease the pain. I'm trying to find something "real" to drink down so that this lump in my throat will go away. Maybe God is just putting me through something so that, if I'm lucky, I'll walk away with a deeper understanding of my life, as it should truly be.

" 'I don't mean to rain on your parade with this letter, but I figure if you're confident in your decision, then you can merely classify what I've written to you as one man's opinion on love. What was that quote you used when you said our breakup was inevitable? I believe you said, "Love is never painless"? I second that statement, 'cause right now, it hurts like hell.

" 'Peace and blessings, Malcolm Savoy Tyler.' "

CINDY SAT SPEECHLESS ON the other end of the phone. Her eyes had filled up with tears as Shaylisa read the words of a wounded man pouring his heart out as though it were his epitaph.

"There, that's what he wrote me. I was pissed when I first read it but now it's no big deal. I'm thinking that once I get some batteries for my paper shredder, I'm gonna make confetti out of his letter." Shaylisa spoke with very little emotion and received no response from Cindy. "Cindy, you still there?" Shaylisa asked.

"Uh-huh, I'm here. I just took a sip of some water," Cindy lied.

"Oh. So, what do you think about his letter?"

"Honestly? I don't know what to think. I'm speechless because I've never heard a man express his true feelings like that before. I'm telling you, Shaylisa, hearing or even reading that type of stuff coming from a man is rare, girl!"

"If you say so . . . I felt like he was putting me down, but he just did it creatively. Plus, I don't need all these pictures back! I know what the hell I look like!" Shaylisa laughed.

"Yeah," Cindy replied with false humor. She didn't agree with Shaylisa's feelings on the subject of the letter, but she didn't want to offend her new best friend.

"Well, as I said, Malcolm is a good man, but just not the man for me. Maybe I'm used to a different kind of man and for that reason I needed to be free of Mr. Sensitive."

"You said his name is Malcolm?" Cindy asked, as the name began to dawn on her with a reflection of familiarity. Even though Shaylisa had read his name at the end of the letter, it did not register the first time.

"Yeah, that's his name, why?"

"Nothing . . . just making sure I heard what you said." Cindy's heart pounded because she suspected that Shaylisa's ex was the same Malcolm she'd met at Venice Beach. Nah, I'm sure there's more than one Malcolm in this city, she thought to herself.

"Anyway, are we through talking about Malcolm. We should both probably get some sleep. I didn't expect for us to be talking all night."

"What time is it anyway?" Cindy asked while glancing at the digital clock on the front of her VCR. "Wow, it's almost five a.m., damn! Let me go to sleep, I have to get up in about three hours!"

"You work at UCLA, right?"

"Yeah, been there for about four years now."

"That's not too far from where you live."

"Everything is far, now that there's so much traffic in L.A. these days," Cindy said, sounding slightly disgusted.

"Well, that's true, Cindy. Listen, I don't want to keep you up too much longer."

"You act like you don't have to get up early, Shaylisa."

"Nope, I'm off tomorrow, or should. I say today . . ."

"Lucky you."

Shaylisa laughed. "Good night, Cindy."

"Good night."

CHAPTER THREE

Heart Made of Cellophane

What can I say, that girl found a perspective that feels comfortable to her. And with that said she's able to move the fuck on," Malcolm attempted to explain to Jamal on his cell phone.

"That's deep, my brotha," Jamal replied. "What's all that noise in the background? Where you at?"

"I'm sitting on a bench at Balboa Park right now. You probably hear the construction going on in the distance. I needed a change of scenery so I could do some writing."

"I forget you got it like that, Malcolm. You can just leave your job with no problems and go hang out somewhere. Must be nice to be you, my animating, don't-punch-a-clock brotha."

Malcolm laughed. "You jealous, Jamal?"

"Nah, I'm proud and trying to put my influence on you so you can take advantage of moments like these."

"Oh, I'm gonna guess this refers to women somehow?"

"That's right, bro. You should be checking out some honeys right now. I mean, you could've picked out two so that I could join y'all when I get off work. I work a real job out here at the airport, so I don't get them same kind of opportunities as you, ya heard me!"

"I hear you talking a lot of noise!"

"Oh, my brotha is trying to be funny now, huh?"

"Yep, and you noticed that I stopped flying as soon as I learned that you fix airplanes," Malcolm joked.

"Uh-oh, you gonna pay for that!"

"I'm just kidding. But, hey!"

"Yeah, what's up, Malcolm?"

"What happened with that girl you met last weekend?"

"Cindy? I don't know. One minute she's serious and the next minute she can't decide. She sound like one of them last-minute chicks, and if she wasn't so cute, I'd probably forget I ever saw her. Next time she call a brotha, I'm thinking about giving her my ghetto response."

"What ghetto response?" Malcolm asked, a look of confusion on his face.

"Who you is, girl? Who you is?" Jamal responded with a ghettoized southern accent.

Malcolm laughed. "Funny. You're crazy as always."

"Last time I talked to Cindy, she asked about you."

"Oh, really? Why?"

"I don't know. I think homegirl might want to do the double-date thing. Maybe she got a friend she thinks would be good for you."

"Oh, I don't know if I want to do that."

"Bro, you gotta take a chance on a lady."

"Yeah, eventually."

They said good-bye and Malcolm opened his journal. His plans for the day were to take advantage of the beautiful weather and do as much writing as possible. His animation work was all caught up, leaving him with the rest of the afternoon and evening to concentrate on himself. He figured this was the dawn of a new era in his life. He felt a sense of relief after sending that letter to Shaylisa. It was hard enough that he had to endure six months of reliving over and over in his mind the last conversation he'd had with Shaylisa.

On that day she'd done most of the talking, and the worst thing about it for him was that she'd had the last word.

His anger and disappointment kept him from responding to the things she'd said. The letter was just the beginning of what he wanted to get off his chest. Malcolm's plans were to open his journal and pour out his soul on every page, hoping that one day he'd awake on the other side of this experience, a wiser and hopefully happier man.

Malcolm focused his attention deeper until becoming oblivious to the noise around him. He zoned out all the construction activity. He could no longer hear the sounds of children playing, basketballs being dribbled on the pavement, or car horns honking in the distance. Malcolm opened to the first page of his journal. He titled this page, "A letter to myself before I stopped believing in LOVE." Malcolm began to write.

I wanna be in a situation where we can talk about life and feel understood. That beautiful kind of vibe where smiles coincide with fond memories of what used to be or could become ... No blank stares following that overused, familiar exclamation point of "You know what I'm saying?" We can talk until the wee hours of the night, only stopping every once in a while for passionate lovemaking. We'd understand the true importance of getting to know each other. I wanna be able to say things that go beyond love. It's a beautiful feeling to say I love you, but after the passion has subsided, I want to continue feeling proud of the person that I've come to truly know. And within that pride, I imagine there would always be some sort of motivation to keep the passion simmering and the effort would always be mutual. That last word should be underlined in everyone's consciousness. Mutual ...

Malcolm sighed and looked over what he'd just written. His heart was pouring out on the pages of his journal as he recalled how he used to think before his experience with Shaylisa. It seemed so foreign to him now to actually believe that love was possible or that trust could be fact, rather than fiction. A woman actually giving and not just taking from the relationship? Malcolm shook his head in disbelief as he returned to writing in his journal. His thoughts seemed to take on a more doubtful perspective. He continued . . .

Sometimes I wonder if I've taken the wrong route toward my recent discovery. For whatever reason, God took a while to turn the lightbulb on and present to me the reality of how coldhearted love can actually be. I've been in situations that had no strings attached or so we tried to convince ourselves. Personally, I believe there's always a string attached. That string is about life and discovery. Sometimes on one end you'll find an optimistic heart while on the other end you'll find a selfish soul with a talent for manipulation. Sort of like some chick who will come up with a scheme to get what she wants by giving you a choice on what you should buy for her rather than her trying to do the shit for herself. I used to be so optimistic before, but rather than become manipulative too, I choose to be alone.

A tear fell from Malcolm's eye. His anger felt justified, but it didn't feel like an emotion he could hold up with pride. He wondered how much time would go by before he could trust love again.

As Malcolm raised his head and glanced at the children playing, he began sketching an image of himself as a young child. Even back then he believed in love. He could remember the nervousness and sweaty palms as he held the hand of a little girl. An onslaught of laughter would ensue and he and the little girl would return to running around the sandbox or playing on the swings. Malcolm immediately shook off that memory. Love is no longer innocent like that, he thought to himself. He glared, as all memories that included the opposite sex seemed to slip toward the negative. He stopped sketching for a moment to look at the image that seemed to come to life on the open page of his journal. The young boy he had drawn had a smile and looked upward, his face covered with innocence.

Malcolm slowly closed his journal, stood up, and walked over to his black Lexus ES300. Fumbling with his keys, he noticed a woman across the street with an ample serving of hips, chocolate brown complexion, and the desire to smile once she saw Malcolm approaching his car. The woman blushed as she slowed her steps, perhaps hoping that Malcolm would change his direction and approach her instead.

Malcolm made eye contact but didn't smile. He wanted to, but he couldn't. The woman looked away for a moment, feeling somewhat uncomfortable as she noticed Malcolm's glare.

Malcolm opened his car door and sat inside, waiting a moment before turning the ignition. He slammed the door shut and rolled down the power windows. An instrumental jam was playing on the radio. He had the dial turned to a college radio station that often played really cool jazz. Malcolm felt a sense of relaxation as the sound filled the inside of his car. Music and Malcolm got along perfectly. Any mood changes or demands could always be controlled by his own will, depending on what he felt like listening to. That sort of control never existed whenever there was a woman in his life, because being selfish had no place in his thoughts.

Before Malcolm could pull away from the curbside where he was parked, the woman had slowly driven her silver Audi A6 right next to his car. She rolled down her passenger-side window and spoke.

"What, you not gonna say hello to me?" she asked while adjusting the volume of her sound system. She was yet another sista who probably liked to recite lines from a Jill Scott CD. She was no doubt sniffing and trying to see what Malcolm was all about.

"You don't want to talk to me either? Do I look that bad?" The beautiful chocolate sista kept trying.

Malcolm laughed.

"That's a start, I was beginning to wonder!" She smiled, flashing her pearly whites and exposing the beautiful dimples in her cheeks.

"Sorry about that," Malcolm said. "How you doing?"

"Well, I'm doing okay but I'm a little worried about such a handsome man looking so mean. Are you a hitman or something?"

"That's funny. No, I'm an animator, actually."

"Oh, that's so cool!"

"Hey, no disrespect, but I think you should probably move your car from the middle of the street," Malcolm said, causing the woman to stop smiling,

"Are you gonna drive off and not talk to me?"

"No, I'll wait here for you," Malcolm reassured her.

"Okay, let me park my car."

The woman backed her car down the street and found a parking space not too far away. Malcolm kept his promise by not driving off and leaving the woman wondering what his problem was. He had a mental picture of her doing that and it wasn't too pretty.

"Glad you found a parking space back there," Malcolm said as the woman walked toward him with a slightly nervous smile, trembling between curious and unsure.

"Wow, I didn't think you were that tall!" she said excitedly.

"Yeah, a little bit."

Malcolm spoke in a soft, nonchalant tone. To say he was calm, cool, and collected would be an understatement. He showed very little emotion even though he recognized the woman as being very lovely.

"I like a tall man."

"Thanks."

"I guess I should introduce myself so you can at least call me by name," the woman said. "My name is Zahara Hubert, and yours is?"

"Malcolm Savoy Tyler."

"That's quite a name! And you say it so well."

Malcolm laughed. "Thank you, Zahara. I guess I'm fond of saying my full name 'cause I think my middle name is cool. I hope that doesn't show signs of being self-centered in any way."

"Hmm, I couldn't say just yet. Have you ever considered just using your first initial and then going by your middle name?"

"No, I like the name Malcolm a lot too."

"Alrighty, then! Nice to see a man in love with his name!"

Malcolm smiled, wondering if Zahara was being serious.

"Hmm, is there a woman that shares your name with you?" she carefully asked.

"You mean, am I married?"

"Yes, are you?"

"Nope, you?"

"Actually, divorced, one kid."

"Oh."

"Geez, don't sound so enthusiastic!" Zahara chuckled.

"No, I don't mean anything by it."

"You have any kids?"

"Nope."

"That's almost hard to believe. A good-looking man like you, career oriented, nice car . . ."

"Yeah, but stuff like that don't guarantee love. And at the same time, I'm not trying to be a magnet to women who want more than they wish to give."

"I come in peace, Malcolm." Zahara held up her right hand, palm facing him, an innocent smile on her face. "I'm not the enemy, sweetheart," she said.

"I know, and I apologize if I came off too serious."

"That's okay. I like intelligent, serious men, although I hope there's a fun side to you as well."

"Comes and goes."

"Okay. Do you like sports? Do you go to museums? Concerts?"

"So many questions, Zahara. Maybe we should sit down."

"How about inside your car?"

Malcolm hesitated for a moment. "Okay," he said before opening the passenger door for Zahara. He couldn't help but glance at the just-right thickness going on inside her jeans. After he closed her door, he quickly rounded the car, opened the driver's-side door, and sat down beside her.

"It smells so fresh in here," she complimented. "So, now you can answer my questions."

"You asked quite a few."

"Well, you can tell me if I'm getting too personal, Malcolm. Although I don't think those questions were so bad."

Malcolm nodded. "No, they weren't."

"You do enjoy sports, right?"

"Yeah, football, basketball . . ."

"Lakers fan?"

"Yeah, I guess."

"You have a cute smile, Malcolm. You should definitely use it more often."

"Yours is nice too, Zahara."

"A compliment? How long did it take before I got one?" Zahara laughed.

Malcolm smiled but slipped inside his shell. There was a moment of silence.

"I hope I'm not keeping you from going somewhere or perhaps from someone?" she asked.

"No, as I said, I'm not married."

"Girlfriend?"

"Nope."

"Do you have plans?"

"For what, to get married?"

"No, silly . . . Do you have plans for tonight or even right now?"

"No, none that I can think of. I was just gonna go home, probably watch a little TV, and then do some preliminary sketching for tomorrow. I have some ideas in the back of my mind that I'd like to bring forth."

"An artistic man is such a turn-on to me!"

Malcolm smiled.

"You're a cutie, Malcolm. You shouldn't be so serious all the time."

"I don't always get inspired to smile that often."

"And I inspire you?" Zahara asked with her hands spread out against her chest.

"Yeah, I guess you do."

"Hmm, that sounded like another compliment!"

Zahara watched Malcolm blush slightly. He seemed to be somewhat uncomfortable with showing signs of happiness.

"Do you consider yourself spontaneous, Malcolm?" Zahara asked while glancing out the window. Before Malcolm answered, she turned her head back to make eye contact with him.

"In what way?" he asked.

"You either are or you aren't."

"I guess I always need to know why there's a need for me to possibly be spontaneous. I don't see myself doing something just 'cause it's there, but if you let me know what's up, then I might go along."

"Loosen up, Malcolm!" Zahara teased. "I'm just playing. But anyway, I said that because I think it would be nice to do something together right now. We could go see a movie or just hang out at Starbucks or something. If you're into museums or galleries, which I love, we can go there too. Let's do something!"

"I'm driving?" Malcolm asked sarcastically.

"Umm, yeah!"

MALCOLM DECIDED AGAINST THE movie. There just wasn't anything out there that he was interested in seeing. The only new films out that week were family films and cartoon features. Working as an animator, sometimes for eighteen hours a day, you don't really get that excited about watching a two-hour animation flick.

"Maybe we can see a movie another time?" he offered.

"That's fine. Hmm, you said another time, so that means you kind of like me a little bit, huh?"

"Yeah, I guess."

"Alrighty, then!" Zahara chuckled.

Malcolm drove through the canyon, which separates the San Fernando Valley from the L.A. area. He was headed toward L.A. and felt pretty good about having met Zahara. His feelings weren't obvious by any means, but he enjoyed her company.

"It is such a beautiful day!" Zahara commented. "Where are we headed?"

"I was thinking we'd go over to La Cienega Boulevard first. They have some really nice galleries along that street."

"That sounds nice. And here I thought this day was gonna be boring for me."

"Where's your kid? You have a what?"

"I have a five-year-old daughter. She's with her father for this week until I pick her up on Sunday."

"Oh."

Zahara studied Malcolm's expressions closely. She noticed something whenever she mentioned she had a kid. Malcolm's reactions would become less enthusiastic.

"Can I ask you something, Malcolm?" she asked, warning him of the seriousness of her next question.

"Yes," he replied while keeping his eye on the road.

"Is there a problem with me having a kid? Is it gonna be a roadblock as far as us liking each other?"

Malcolm struggled for a moment to answer. He looked away, pretending to be too focused on making a left-hand turn before he could answer her question.

"No, it's no problem," he answered without making eye contact.

"Are you sure?"

He paused before answering. "Yes. I guess I hesitate because of past experiences with women who had kids. I'd have some serious reservations when they would always say that they spent the day with their baby's father. One time my suspicion proved to be true."

"What happened?"

"Several visits with the baby's father led to her getting pregnant again."

"Oh, well, there's no baby-daddy drama with me. There used to be, but we seem to have grown up in the last two years. We've reached an understanding now that seems to be working. There were times when my ex would show up at my door unannounced and that was not too cool. A few of those times happened when I had company over."

"Oh. You date much?"

"A little bit. How about you?"

"Nope, not really."

"Why not?"

"Just don't want to. Dating is difficult for me to do, I suppose."

"I think you need someone to help you bring that wall down. Is there any chance that you and I could date?"

"Haven't we begun that already?"

"Hmm, it's a start, Malcolm. This should be interesting."

"Hey, I'm gonna pull over. This is a great spot right here." Malcolm pointed to a cliff side that allowed for a breathtaking view of the valley below. The sky was a beautiful powder blue with very few clouds and no smog.

"Ooh, it is nice up here. I've only driven this way a few times at night but never during the day," Zahara said, gazing out the window and looking in the direction Malcolm pointed in.

"Oh, it's especially beautiful at night. Maybe we'll pass through here later on after the sun goes down."

"Hmm, sounds romantic. What do you have in mind?" Zahara smiled.

"Umm, well, you never know."

Malcolm parked on the side of the road, facing the view of the canyon. Zahara was feeling the breeze a little too strongly as she got out of the car. Her silky straight black hair was blowing in the wind and her fashionable top couldn't protect her from freezing to death.

"Hey, you look cold. Let me give you my jacket!" Malcolm said as he walked around to the trunk of his car.

"Such a gentleman!" Zahara replied.

Malcolm pulled out a black leather Avirex jacket and handed it to Zahara.

"Aww, I thought you were gonna put it around me. Show me how much of a true gentleman you really are."

Malcolm hesitated for a moment and then walked toward Zahara as she turned around, facing the beautiful view of the valley. Malcolm stood close behind her, opening the jacket and then placing it around her shoulders and arms. As he closed the jacket, he could feel the natural softness of Zahara's breasts. Zahara leaned her head back as Malcolm leaned in toward her, embracing her from behind.

"Mmm, now this feels good," Zahara whispered softly.

"Yes, you do."

Malcolm tried to control what he was feeling at that moment, but it was getting very hard. Zahara may have noticed just how hard. She smiled as she gazed upon the view below. "I bet this is really beautiful at night," she said softly.

"Yes, I think you'd like it."

"Hmm, I think so too, Malcolm."

Thoughts of passionate kissing and warm hugs filled Malcolm's head. He wondered if Zahara shared the same feelings but he was too cautious to ask. One thing he noticed, though, was that she really enjoyed being in his arms. She smiled and sometimes she closed her eyes so that the breeze could flow across her face as she continued to lean back in his arms. Her expression made her look as though she were in heaven and completely lost inside her fantasies. Maybe she was.

"What are you thinking about, Zahara?" Malcolm asked, interrupting her feeling of bliss.

"Hmm, so many things, but mostly I'm just feeling everything, you know."

"I think so."

"This feels so nice, right now. And I almost feel you losing some of that tension inside your body too. I think I may have to give you a massage someday so I can get the rest of it out of you."

"Maybe so, but it's probably gonna take a lot more than a massage to relieve me," Malcolm replied, half serious.

"I could take that in two ways, but somehow I think you're remembering the past. When I invite you over for dinner, I hope you'll leave some of that baggage at the door."

"I don't know, Zahara. We shall see . . ."

"Well, I don't know what else you have planned for us today, but I am really enjoying this right now, Malcolm."

"Me too . . ."

Zahara leaned her head back once again before breathing in deeply and sighing. She opened her eyes, smiled, and pressed her dimpled right cheek against the left side of Malcolm's face.

"Hey, do you ever listen to Jill Scott?" Zahara asked.

Oh, here we go! She's about to quote from the new sound track to the black woman's empowerment movement. He was actually a huge fan of Jill Scott too, but lately he'd noticed the common bond that so many women had with respect to loving that extra-fine lady of poetic soul.

"Yes, I like her a lot, she's cool," Malcolm replied. "Why do you ask?"

"Well, earlier I was listening to that song called 'Gettin' in the Way' . . ."

"Yeah, I'm familiar with it."

"Well, Malcolm, as I lean back in your arms and feel so content, so warm inside, I just hope I'm not getting in the way of what you may be feeling."

"I'm not sure I understand."

"Hmm, well, warn me if I'm treading on tough terrain or exclusive areas with warning signs that your door might slam shut . . ."

Malcolm chuckled. "You sound just as deep as Ms. Scott, speaking like that."

"I have my moments, I guess."

Malcolm adjusted himself and held Zahara even tighter. "I guess you do," he replied.

"You're making me forget what I was gonna say." Zahara laughed.

"I guess you can tell that I have some issues lying underneath."

"Yes, Malcolm, it is apparent that something unkind is going on inside your heart, sweetie."

Malcolm kissed Zahara on the side of the cheek. "I like the way that sounds," he whispered in her ear.

Zahara turned around so that she could look deeply into his eyes.

"You like the way what sounds?" she asked.

"When you say 'sweetie.'"

"Feel free to get used to it, Malcolm."

Zahara wrapped her arms around Malcolm's neck, pulling him toward her for a gentle first kiss. They both smiled as they rested their foreheads against each other. Malcolm couldn't resist kissing Zahara again. This time it was much deeper. Malcolm could feel Zahara's soft hands caressing the back of his neck. They kissed even deeper still. Zahara felt heat flashes and Malcolm felt dizzy. He wasn't supposed to be enjoying this so much. This beautiful woman had just stepped into his life. Earlier he was sitting on a park bench writing a hate letter to the emotion known as Love. Now here he stood embracing a woman and kissing her as though there were no tomorrow. God doesn't always play fair, but He definitely knows how to make a point, Malcolm thought to himself. Malcolm, no longer convinced of anything, held Zahara close and kissed her once again . . . deeper.

MALCOLM COULDN'T MAKE HEADS or tails of the artwork he and Zahara looked at, but he was extremely happy to be with her.

Now they were at a café. Zahara found a table and two chairs near the window as Malcolm ordered two drinks and a pastry for himself.

Malcolm grabbed the drinks and headed toward Zahara. She watched his every step and was guilty of having all sorts of sexually charged thoughts. She didn't dare ask him what size he was, though she thought about it. Malcolm's height alone was very appealing to her, so she could only imagine what else he could be packing.

"What size shoe do you wear?" Zahara asked before laughing at her own question.

Malcolm placed the drinks on the table and sat down next to Zahara.

"What size shoe?" Malcolm repeated.

"Never mind . . ." Zahara smiled.

"It's okay . . . I wear a size-thirteen shoe, why?"

"Just wondering."

Malcolm looked at Zahara's drink. "I never had one of those, how does it taste?"

"Very sweet, it's good! Try some."

Malcolm took a sip. "Hmm, I like that. You don't mind me drinking from the same cup, huh?"

"No, I love to share."

Malcolm smiled and eased back into his chair. He looked at Zahara. Her deep, dark brown eyes opened wider as she wondered why Malcolm was staring at her. She wondered what was going through his mind. He sat there appreciating her whole energy and feeling as though he'd met a woman who had really special qualities about her.

An hour went by filled with light conversation and people watching. To her amazement, Zahara enjoyed witnessing his animation talents as he drew several characters on a napkin, including one that resembled her.

"Why did you draw my lips so big, Malcolm?" Zahara laughed.

"This is just a caricature, not a portrait," Malcolm replied.

"Yeah, right . . . You didn't mind my big lips up on that hill, did you?"

"No, I love your lips."

"Are we being silly?" Zahara asked.

"Yep, a little bit."

Zahara leaned in and Malcolm met her halfway with a very soft kiss, followed by another kiss. She smiled. He smiled. Malcolm returned to sketching something on the napkin. Zahara wondered if today had been a fluke or if it was always going to feel like this. I'm already falling for this guy, but I'm not sure he could handle that revelation. He might become dysfunctional if I get too close to his heart, Zahara thought to herself. She also wondered if perhaps it was too soon to ask her next series of questions, but there was no sense in holding back.

"Malcolm, do you think today is happening too fast?"

"What do you mean?"

"Umm, you know, how we met, the holding each other, kissing.

I feel like, before you know it we're gonna be talking about what sort of wedding we've always dreamed of."

"I don't know. I don't feel like things are being rushed. This day has definitely been an unexpected surprise, Zahara. I mean, with what I was feeling before I saw you across the street, being with a woman was the last thing on my mind."

"Is that why you were looking so mean?"

Malcolm smiled while still looking down at the napkin that he'd sketched on.

"Yeah . . . I had just finished writing some thoughts in my journal that weren't too kind, I guess you could say."

"Oh. Were they about someone? I guess I shouldn't ask that question."

"I think you can sense the answer."

Zahara touched Malcolm's arm and brushed it with her fingertips. She tried to show that she meant no harm with her questions. It was obvious that the answers were attached to painful memories. He didn't seem to be too keen on offering information about his past or to pick up on the hints she'd given him, in the hope that he'd embellish his answers with more details about his experiences.

"You think they'd give me some water here?" she asked.

"Yeah, I'll get you some."

Zahara watched as Malcolm left the table to get her a cup of water. She laughed at herself because she didn't have the guts to ask Malcolm about his ex or what he was writing in his journal. Secretly, she wished she could read all of it.

Malcolm returned to the table holding her cup of water. "You miss me?" he asked.

"You know I did," she replied.

Silence surrounded the table as Zahara began sipping her water and occasionally glancing at Malcolm. His attention was on the various people walking outside. A white couple holding hands had passed by, followed by a homeless person pushing a cart and stopping at each newspaper dispenser, hoping that he could find loose change. Then a young African-American man strutted by, giving

Malcolm a what's-up type of nod while recognizing that he was sitting next to a very lovely lady. It felt like the whole world was walking by as Malcolm observed from the corner of his eye that he too
was being watched.

"What's the matter?" he asked Zahara.

"Nothing. I'm fascinated by what goes through your mind, especially when you get so quiet."

"Oh."

"You're not gonna tell me, huh?"

"Well, mostly I was watching the people outside, more so than
actually thinking anything. Nice to know that I fascinate you."

"Listen, I'd like for you to meet my daughter sometime when
she comes back from spending time with her father."

"Okay, sounds good."

"You don't mind?"

"No, it's cool. I'm looking forward to it."

"Well, you don't sound overly enthused."

"Zahara? What's your daughter's name anyway?"

"Imara. It means strong."

"It's a pretty name, actually."

"Thanks. I think she's gonna be a strong lady when she grows
up, and not to mention beautiful like her mother. You were supposed to make that comment, by the way!"

Malcolm chuckled. "You are beautiful, Zahara."

Malcolm and Zahara mutually decided to forgo making a return trip to that beautiful view in the canyon. Instead, Zahara felt
comfortable enough to invite Malcolm over for a Blockbuster night
that she'd promised herself. Malcolm was pleased with her decision
and relished the moment when he found himself walking a half step
behind Zahara, on their way upstairs to her apartment. Malcolm's
attention was so focused on Zahara's backside that he wasn't prepared for her to stop so suddenly. He bumped into her and lost his
footing.

"Are you okay?" She laughed. "What happened?"

"Nothing, just didn't see that last step."

"Well, this is my apartment. Don't be trying to make fun of it either. I wasn't expecting to bring someone home with me today."

Malcolm worried for a moment. This lady might be a slob when she's at home!

"Why are you hesitating to come in?" Zahara asked.

"I'm not hesitating."

"Looks like it to me, sweetie."

Malcolm wasn't prepared for what he walked into. Zahara's warning had him thinking the worst, but in actuality, her place was almost immaculate. As soon as Malcolm stepped inside, he noticed a beautiful cream-colored sofa with silk brown throw pillows, a very clean beige carpet, a really cool entertainment system, and plenty of pictures on the walls and on the round coffee table.

"I'm speechless," Malcolm said.

"I had you fooled then, huh?"

"Yes, you did."

"I wonder what I'll find over at your place when I come over. You live in a house, condo, or apartment?"

"I live in a town house, actually. More questions, huh?"

"Well, it's not like you're offering me much information, Malcolm."

"You're right. So, can I sit down?"

"Please. I'm gonna change into something more comfortable."

"Why do women always say that?"

"I don't know, but my feet are hurting and we spent an unexpected long day together, Malcolm. Not that I'm complaining, but a woman like myself wants to feel comfortable when she's at home."

"You get no complaints from me."

"What videos did you rent?" Malcolm asked when Zahara returned and put a tape in the VCR. She stood with her behind facing him, legs slightly parted, leaning over to see if she was operating the VCR correctly. In his opinion, she knew exactly what she was doing. I mean, how long does it take to stick a tape in the machine? he thought. Zahara was showing off that lovely five-feet-seven, thick-in-all-the-right-places frame of hers. And she was causing him to struggle with his attempts at remaining a gentleman.

"What?" Zahara asked.

Malcolm paused. "Please," he said, gesturing that she sit down next to him.

"You got anything to munch on?" Malcolm asked.

"Hmm, let me go check." Zahara stood up, but Malcolm stopped her from walking to the kitchen.

"Let me look. Maybe I can throw something together, depending on what you have in there."

"Oh, so you cook too? Aren't I the lucky one to stumble upon a man that can cook?"

"Yep. One day you should let me cook for you."

"That would be nice," Zahara said as she sat back down on the sofa.

Malcolm walked into the kitchen. "Check this out!" he said.

"You found something?"

"No, I mean your kitchen is really nice!"

"Oh, thanks. They remodeled this building a few years ago, so we have a lot of modern amenities in here."

Malcolm peeped into the living room. "I wish you could say that about your food selection, Zahara."

"What do you mean?"

"All I'm seeing in here is Ritz crackers, refried beans in the can, pancake mix, umm, Campbell's tomato soup . . ."

"Well, I haven't been to the store yet, and since Imara is with her father, there's been no reason for me to have a bunch of food in the house."

"Oh, so you've been starving yourself?"

"You want to go to the store, Malcolm? Is that what you're trying to say?"

"No, I'll just have some of these brown sugar Pop-Tarts and some water." He laughed.

"I didn't invite you over to eat anyway," Zahara said with a hint of seduction in her voice.

"Huh, what did you say?" Malcolm stuttered.

"I think you heard me, sweetie."

"No, I was getting my, umm, Pop-Tarts."

"Come on and sit down so we can talk and watch the movie!"

Zahara smiled as she patted the sofa, gesturing for Malcolm to sit next to her.

Malcolm walked over and sat down. Zahara snuggled really close, smiling and excited to have him over. Malcolm showed signs of excitement too; embarrassed, he kept his hidden for the moment. Zahara had secretly been looking forward to this moment ever since the two of them stood embracing on top of the hill. She now had her chance, a real chance to get inside the head of this man who had grown from an instant attraction to a deep curiosity. Malcolm looked so good to her and it wasn't just physical.

"Malcolm?" Zahara asked, her voice sounding as though she had a question that was either personal or flirtatious.

"Yes?" he replied cautiously.

"Am I someone that you would like to get to know better?"

"What kind of question is that?"

"I want to know how you feel about me."

"Why can't we just see how things go?"

"I don't know, I guess I've always liked knowing my boundaries. I don't want you to think that I'm not gonna be patient with you or that I don't respect the fact that you've been hurt. I merely wonder are you truly open to getting past that hurt and accepting me as someone potentially very special in your life."

"Zahara, how can I really answer that? I could simply say yes, but would that really satisfy your need for a clear-cut answer?"

"I don't know . . ." she replied, feeling somewhat discouraged.

"I think a lot of people have too much discussion time when all they should be doing is enjoying each other's company."

"Would you like me to stop asking you questions, Malcolm?"

"No, I'm not saying that at all. It seems like in this day and age, love is about taking the ultimate chance. Up until today, I haven't taken any chances, Zahara."

"None?"

"Not since my heart was crushed."

"Can I ask you about that?"

"Can we talk about it another time?"

"Yes, we can." Zahara let Malcolm off the hook this time. His avoidance of her questions only added to her desire to hear the answers one day. For now, she chose to refrain from pushing the limits of his sensitive boundaries.

Her curiosity continued to grow as she slipped into a moment of silence. She adjusted her head on Malcolm's chest and noticed rapid changes in his heartbeat. The silence and avoidance of Zahara's questions seemed to put Malcolm on edge. He appeared to be a little tense and uncomfortable. He sighed. He cleared his throat. He laughed nervously as the men in the movie sat around a table, playing cards and talking about women.

"You okay?" Zahara asked.

"Yeah, I'm okay," Malcolm answered softly, but he wasn't being completely honest. Deep inside he'd wrestle with the realization that talking about his past with Zahara might be good for his soul. Perhaps it could be therapeutic in a way. He'd had many conversations with Jamal, but his perspective would usually turn toward a find-some-new-legs-to-get-between mentality. Not that Jamal wouldn't be understanding or wise with respect to relationships, but he could only stay serious for so long. Jamal is a fool, but he's my buddy, Malcolm thought.

Malcolm tilted his head slightly and kissed Zahara on the top of her head. She smiled and made a gentle sound, showing how content she was inside his arms. Her contentment only added fuel to the reasons why he wanted to be more open in discussing matters of the heart.

Malcolm sighed. "Zahara, what do you want to know?"

Zahara turned her attention to him.

"I want to know about you, sweetie. I want to know the inner layer of Malcolm and why you're not able to really let go."

"Let go?"

"Yeah. I bet it's been a while since you laughed so hard until you had tears, huh? I've seen your cute smile and heard you laugh softly, but I can also see the pain so deep in your eyes. You're like a little boy behind an iron gate, wondering what it's like on the other side."

"You really see that in me?"

Zahara sat up on the sofa so she could face Malcolm. She held his hands in her lap and looked into his eyes. Malcolm looked deeply into hers as well. Zahara leaned forward to kiss him, softly, but only to reassure him that everything was okay.

"That's enough," she warned. "I want you to know that I'm here for you."

Malcolm smiled. "So, you said you wanted to know about me, the inner layer, as you put it?"

"Maybe I should simply ask you to tell me about her?"

"Shaylisa?"

"She's the one whose name is attached to the pain that you feel, right?"

"Yeah, if you could see the wall around my heart, you'd probably see her name spray-painted across the front, graffiti-style." Malcolm sighed.

"I can kind of tell. How did you meet her?"

"Met her outside of a comic-book store on Melrose Avenue. I go there often to buy the old collectible stuff and also to see some new animation. You know, do some research, sort of . . ."

"Yes, go on . . ."

"Well, when I was coming out of the store one Friday afternoon, there she was with a sleeveless summer dress on, looking incredible. I let her know with my reaction that I was instantly attracted to her. I mean, I'm not the type to approach women, but she had me smiling and saying hello as though I wanted to grab her and never let her go."

"Sounds like you still wish that to be true, by the way you tell the story."

"That was then, Zahara. When I look back on that moment, I can place myself there as though it were happening now. If someone were to ask me about how you and I met, I guarantee you they would see the same kind of excitement as the day it actually happened."

"I believe you and I don't mean to put you on the defensive, Malcolm. I envy the fact that Shaylisa found you at a time when you weren't in the midst of trying to heal your heart."

"I guess that's true," Malcolm said as he studied Zahara's expression. He feared that revealing his thoughts about Shaylisa might make Zahara decide against continuing to see him.

"Are you sure that it's okay for me to speak about Shaylisa?" Malcolm asked cautiously.

"Yes, I feel it's good for the both of us. We've all been in love before, and I want to understand who you are right now in your life."

"Okay."

Malcolm released Zahara's hands for a moment. "Where are you going?" she asked.

"I wanna get some more water. You want some?"

"No, go ahead. Thank you."

Malcolm smiled and then walked into the kitchen. He could feel Zahara's eyes on him as he walked away and he worried. He had images in his mind of stepping into deep, dark holes and not knowing how to get out. As he shared each memory of his early days with Shaylisa, he wondered if Zahara would in turn begin her process of pulling away. That's a process that he was all too familiar with. If you'd try to play a word-association game with Malcolm and said the word "relationship," Malcolm would answer back immediately with "struggle." He could feel that emotion right now as he stood in front of the refrigerator, pouring a glass of water. Zahara, on the other hand, sat patiently on the sofa, waiting for him to return.

Malcolm sat back down on the sofa, took a sip of water, and returned to holding hands with Zahara. He looked into her eyes with concern.

"You know, Zahara, I wonder if this kind of discussion is putting a damper on such a beautiful day. Do you really want me to continue talking about Shaylisa?"

"I don't know, I guess I did get slightly jealous a moment ago, hearing about how you were so taken by Shaylisa the first time you saw her."

"Jealous?"

"Yeah, we do get that way sometimes!"

"Okay . . ."

"But as I said, we've all been in love before and we've all come across people that have instantly excited us. I could tell you about the day I met my ex in college and how we spent so many days and nights making love, talking, teaching each other, studying together—and perhaps have you feeling slightly jealous too. So, with that said, I want you to know that I'm cool with whatever you share about Shaylisa."

"You sure?"

"Yep, I'm sure."

THEY TOOK A BREAK from the serious talk, and Malcolm was moved to tears by the marriage proposal at the end of the movie. Zahara stared at him. She was touched by his show of emotion and sensed that she was sitting next to a man with a very tender heart. Why else would his eyes fill up with tears when he had seen the movie several times before? She smiled at the potential of his love, yet feared the thought that he might not allow himself to grow from his experience with his ex.

"Malcolm, do you mind me asking you what was the reason for your breakup with Shaylisa? You don't have to answer if you don't want to."

Zahara watched as Malcolm adjusted himself. It was as though he wanted to think through what he would say before he said it.

"Seems like it was a combination of things. Sometimes I'm not exactly sure what the reason was." He sighed.

"You're not?"

"No, but I feel like it had to do with her basically becoming bored with me. At least that's how she made me feel when she explained her reasons."

"What did she say?"

"Something about realizing after two years that she needed something else."

"Like what?"

"I'm not sure. I think she met someone, probably a thugged-out brotha who blew her mind, but I don't think it lasted. Then she also mentioned about me not showing enough passion for life away from her."

"Do you consider her to be a cold and callous person?"

"I don't know, I can't really say."

"She seems that way. I can't see someone ending things so suddenly, although I know it happens . . ."

"Yes, it happens all the time!"

"Maybe so."

"Well, I feel as though there was a certain cruelty about her actions, but because of my feelings for her, I guess I can never write her off as being a cold person. I just can't."

"Let me tell you this, Malcolm, and then maybe we can put the subject to rest until another time, if necessary . . ."

"Okay."

"Your quiet sensitivity, your tenderness and thoughtfulness have affected me already, very much. It would be so cruel of me to listen to what you've said and then to walk away because you happen to have loved someone before I came into your life. I'm very patient, especially with someone that opens up to me and is always honest with what they're feeling. Lying is what causes me to walk away."

He smiled at her. "Thanks, Zahara."

CHAPTER FOUR

Confessions
Between Friends

*S*haylisa had a busy week screening calls for a boss who wasn't always accessible to his clients. She worked demanding hours as an executive assistant to a VP at Warner Brothers. In the smallest corner of her mind, she missed the days when Malcolm would stop by her job to bring her flowers or see if she was busy for lunch. He always came through when she needed to escape.

Shaylisa was not suffering being single. She'd had two dates in the past week and had been on several since her breakup with Malcolm. Sitting on her desk was a beautiful arrangement of flowers given to her by "him." That's all she cared to call that particular person. The man turned out to be a desperately-seeking-a-female-ear-to-listen-to-him-bitch-about-his-ex kind of man. Shaylisa had enjoyed the food and managed to throw in a few "Oh really, she was wrong for doing that" comments.

That was one experience that she didn't want to repeat anytime soon. However, she wasn't about to throw the flowers that he'd given her away, especially considering his growing status in the company. Thinking about that experience, Shaylisa wondered what was in store for her next. She'd been through several disappointments similar to that one, her biggest one being a guy she thought was the answer to all her dreams and fantasies.

Victor Allan was a six-feet-nine, dark-complexioned, bald-headed cross between Kevin Garnett and Michael Jordan. He had youthful energy and a what-the-fuck-you-looking-at attitude. He also possessed a certain style, clothing-wise, just like Mike. The man drove a Benz with tinted windows and the shiniest chrome wheels. The first thing Shaylisa thought when she laid eyes on the man was, Damn! Then, when he approached her, she uttered, "Mmm-mm!"

Shaylisa was in heaven at that moment, the kind of heaven that women experience when they find themselves on the dance floor with a man worth over a million dollars. Victor was an entertainment attorney for a major agency in town and also invested in real estate.

Shaylisa was coming out of Bloomingdale's one evening when she heard a "Psst!" followed by a "Hey, young lady." The voice she heard was just as dark as the man who uttered the words to her.

"Hello," she replied, amazed by his height. "You are so tall!"

"Yeah, that's what they say. You have a name to go along with that banging body and lovely smile?"

Shaylisa laughed. She usually came off as very bashful at first, but Victor took her by complete surprise and she wasn't sure how to respond.

"I'm Shaylisa," she said, reaching forward to shake his hand.

"I see you did some major shopping, huh? You buy something for your man?"

"No, I'm single. This is all for me."

"I heard that." He smiled. "I saw something in there that would look really lovely on you. If I show you, would you try it on for me?"

"You're kidding, right?"

"No, lady, I'm serious."

"But we just met!"

"Yeah, and?"

Victor didn't have to do much convincing. Shaylisa blushed

all the way up the escalator as she took advantage of his offer. She couldn't resist his confident charm and she loved the way he took charge of the moment. The excitement sent charges through her body. She was smiling uncontrollably when they reached the third floor of the department store.

"Hmm, you have me wondering why you would be up here in the first place, Victor. I can't see any reason why a man would come up to this level unless he was buying something for his woman. Or, maybe you might be a cross-dresser?"

Victor chuckled slightly but brushed off Shaylisa's attempts to be funny. "Nah, lady, the restroom is on this floor."

"And what made you look at this outfit you're gonna show me?"

"Damn, you always try to ruin the moment when a man wants to surprise you? I'm gonna show you how I can sense what your style is like. If I guess right, then you're gonna have dinner with me, tonight."

"I give you points for creativity . . ."

"Yeah, well, check this out." Victor walked over to a golden halter top and a double-layered silk skirt displayed on a mannequin.

"Wow, you have great taste!"

"Sounds like I have a dinner date."

"Hmm, I guess that was the bet, huh?"

Victor winked. "Yes, ma'am."

He stood there, glancing at Shaylisa from head to toe. She assumed that he'd only wanted to guess her taste in clothes, not buy her anything, so she began walking back toward the escalator.

"So, what's up?" Victor asked, stopping her from taking another step.

"Huh, I thought we were leaving. I'm gonna hold up my end of the bet."

"That's cool, lady, but don't you want this?" Victor asked, pointing at the outfit.

Shaylisa couldn't believe what he was asking her. She had a look of astonishment on her face that could be read from clear across the room. "You are not serious!" she shouted.

"Let's find your size."

"You do this with all the ladies, huh? You just got all kinds of money you can throw away, huh?"

"You're ruining the moment again, girl. Think of this as a mutually beneficial investment."

"How so?" Shaylisa said.

"You get a really nice outfit and I get to see you in it."

Victor had Shaylisa swooning. Twice she began fanning herself because she was getting some serious hot flashes. Victor stood so tall, so confident, so in touch with the fact that he was sweeping Shaylisa off her feet.

Victor stood waiting for Shaylisa to come out of the dressing room. She agreed, without much hesitation, to allow him to buy the outfit for her, and when she stepped from the hallway leading to the little rooms, he was very pleased with what he saw. The outfit complemented her and seemed to inspire even more sexiness in her walk.

"Damn, lady. I think that outfit is loving you!" Victor exclaimed.

"I love it, Victor."

"Cool. Plus, I got to say that seeing you walking barefoot does something to me."

"You into feet or simply old-fashioned?"

"That's funny. Nah, I'll just say that you do have some lovely feet."

"Thank you. I still find it hard to believe that you're doing this!"

"Please, believe it. You ready for dinner?"

Shaylisa nodded her head yes and returned to the dressing room. Victor watched her until she was no longer in sight. He'd pay for the clothes and then wait for her to return.

REIGN WAS THE PLACE that Victor chose for dinner. The decor and food was upscale, contemporary southern soul. Victor spent a lot of time there networking as well as impressing dates with the black Hollywood types and athletes who frequented the Beverly Hills restaurant.

"I've always wanted to come here," Shaylisa said as she looked around the room. Her mouth began to water when she saw a waiter carrying a plate of smothered pork chops. The smell alone had her daydreaming about the extra ten pounds she'd put on as a result of all the good food.

"I think you'll enjoy yourself here very much. The food is all that and then some! You got to try the fried green tomatoes."

"You're making me hungry, Victor!"

"Good, don't hold back, lady, I want you to enjoy yourself."

"I can't believe how you've spoiled me today."

Shaylisa sat across from Victor, mesmerized by his mere presence. She hadn't even begun to focus on the beautiful Michael Jordanesque gray suit that Victor was wearing or the bling-bling on his wrist and finger. All of that stuff only highlighted the fact that this man sitting before her was just as fine as can be!

"I need to bring my girlfriend here!" Shaylisa said.

"Yeah, I recommend you come here for any occasion. This is definitely the place to have power lunches and do business while the gravy drips down your chin."

Shaylisa laughed.

"Hey, lady, you mind if I make a phone call?" Victor asked.

"No. Do you have to go outside to the pay phone?"

"Nah, I'm gonna use my cell."

Victor pulled out his phone and began dialing. "Thanks, this won't take long, okay?"

"Okay," Shaylisa replied as her heart tightened. She witnessed the warning sign. Watching Victor talk business and show Shaylisa very little attention was not going over very well with her. Was she there just for show? Maybe that's why he wanted to pick something out for me to wear so badly, she thought to herself. Victor sat there grinning from ear to ear, talking with whoever was on the other end and being a Mr. Hollywood showoff. Shaylisa didn't like what was going on one bit.

She smiled, excused herself to the ladies' room, and went to check if there were taxicabs outside that could take her back to the mall where her car was still parked. When Shaylisa peeked back inside to see if Victor was off the phone, she could see him still talking, probably not even noticing that she was gone. The waiter passed by with the food that she and Victor ordered.

"Excuse me, but can I get that to go instead?" she asked the waiter.

"You're not staying?"

"No, something came up, but my friend will still be here."

"Okay, let me put this in a box for you."

Shaylisa kept her eyes glued to Victor, seeing if perhaps he'd begin to wonder what happened to his date. No such luck at all . . .

On that day, when she'd met that fine-ass-chocolate dream stick, her only consolation was that she was able to take home with her a banana-cream pie and some smothered-in-gravy pork chops. She ate good that day and felt only slightly guilty that she'd gotten a free dress out of it all too, but she wasn't gonna stress over her unexpected moment of romance. Not at all and no way . . .

FRIDAY EVENING AFTER WORK and it was now happy-hour time for two ladies who needed to release some stress by talking major shit! Shaylisa had planned to meet up with Cindy at a local spot for drinks and gossip. It was a ritual they'd enjoyed doing the last two weeks. This time, however, Shaylisa didn't have much gossip to add to the conversation. With all her sighing and attitude around the workplace, she was starting to feel the effects of jumping ship too soon and leaving a good man behind.

Shaylisa wasn't going to keep stressing over leaving Malcolm. The way she stood in the restroom, adjusting her outfit and fixing her hair, it was obvious her vanity was on the rise. Get it together, 'cause this is your world! she thought to herself as she blew a kiss at the mirror. On her way out the door, she could read the minds of several ladies giving her that no-she-didn't look and smacking their lips at the same time. It was as though Shaylisa were being followed by paparazzi, because she could hear a bunch of clicking sounds, the kind that sound like lips a-smacking. They can kiss my ass!

Shaylisa didn't think twice about those girls at the office. She was more interested in getting her drink on with Cindy at the Café

Del Rey in the marina. She grew tired of her feelings of guilt and for thinking about how her post-Malcolm days hadn't been so successful in terms of the men she'd dated. For one thing, it wasn't like she was looking to start a relationship, so any determination or measuring stick for success at this moment could only be based on what fucking felt good! When Shaylisa pulled into the parking lot of Café Del Rey, parked her car, and adjusted her off-white, three-button long jacket, she proclaimed, "I'm a woman and I ain't did shit wrong to nobody!"

Shaylisa walked up the stairs and into the restaurant.

"Good evening. Table for one?" the hostess said as Shaylisa approached.

No, she didn't just look me up and down and ask that question!

"Umm, no, I'm meeting someone at the bar and she's probably here already, thank you."

"Okay, please, walk right in. The bar is to your right."

Bitch!

Shaylisa smiled. "Thank you."

She did a quick scan of the restaurant and bar, looking for Cindy and also hoping that she might catch the attention of some fine man sitting alone or with other fine men. The lighting inside the restaurant was very dim, so Shaylisa had to pay close attention to her feet, because it would be mad embarrassing if she fell and slid across the slippery wooden floors.

In the dark distance, Shaylisa could see a hand waving. She squinted a few times and came to the realization that it was a white man waving, not her friend Cindy.

"Hey, girl!" a familiar voice shouted from the opposite direction.

"Cindy, hey!" Shaylisa shouted back.

The two of them embraced and gave each other the once-over, looking at each other's outfits and dishing out high-fives.

"Cindy, look at you!" Shaylisa noticed the gold leather pants and sequined top that Cindy wore. She probably wasn't the only one in the room amazed by Cindy's outfit.

"Look at me what?" Cindy responded innocently.

"You just sparkling and trying to show off your little booty in those leather pants, girl. I thought I had it going on."

"Oh, this little outfit?" Cindy tried to play it off. "I picked this up last month and only wore it maybe twice."

"Uh-huh. Let's get us a drink and then you can tell me what's going on in your life, 'cause mine has been boring as hell lately."

"I have a table already," Cindy said, pulling Shaylisa to where they would be sitting.

The two ladies sat down and the waiter came over immediately.

"What can I get for you two?" he asked.

Shaylisa responded first because she was anxious to get her drink. "I'll have a glass of Merlot, please."

"Yes, and I'll have a glass of Chardonnay," Cindy ordered.

"Very good, I'll bring your drinks right over. The special tonight is black-bean soup and grilled salmon."

Neither of them paid attention to the waiter, but they both gave him a smile, hinting perhaps that his presence wasn't needed.

"Thank you," he said, before picking up on the hint.

"So, Cindy, what have you been up to? You got a new man in your life?" Shaylisa asked.

"Not really new but yes, someone is in my life."

"Yes? Wait a minute, girl. It's not like we haven't been talking on the phone this week, so why haven't you told me anything before?"

Cindy beamed. "Oh, I wanted to keep it a surprise and tell you in person. Plus, I wasn't sure about him 'cause he's not the quiet type that I usually go for. He keeps me laughing, though . . ."

"That's a good thing."

"What about you?" Cindy asked.

"What about me what?"

"Here you are, ladies," the waiter interrupted as he placed the drinks on the table. "Need more time with the menus?" he asked.

"No, I'm gonna have that soup and salmon," Cindy said.

The waiter's attention turned to Shaylisa. "And you, miss?"

"Let's see, I'll have the Thai shellfish sausage."

"It's one of our most popular dishes."

"Fine, I'll take that."

As the waiter walked away, Shaylisa took a sip of her Merlot and focused her attention back on Cindy. "Now, tell me more about this man."

"You ain't shy, Shaylisa. What you want to know?" Cindy chuckled.

"No, I'm not shy but you are, a little bit."

"Yeah, compared to you I am."

Shaylisa raised her hand. "Puh-lease!"

"Well, as I said, he definitely makes me laugh a lot, but he's pretty romantic too. He ain't no rich brotha like the ones you meet, but he's got a good job at the airport."

"What you mean, like I meet?"

"You know who I'm talking about . . . what was his name?"

"Victor."

"That's it. Are you sorry you left him in that restaurant?"

"I can't miss what I never had, girl."

"Which means what?"

"Yeah, I wish I had stayed."

Cindy laughed.

"But you know me; I can't sit around and watch some man talk on his cell phone, knowing full well that he should be giving me all of his damn attention."

"You are something else, Shaylisa."

"Well, whatever. We're supposed to be talking about your semi-new man anyway!"

"Yeah, well, as I was saying, he works for the airport, fixing planes, so you know he has some strong hands."

"Big hands?"

Cindy giggled. "Yes, very big, and thick too!"

"What, his hands?"

Cindy laughed.

"Girl!" Shaylisa said before taking another sip of her Merlot.

Cindy held her glass up to her forehead in an effort to tease

Shaylisa. She used her napkin to fan herself as though she were hot and bothered by the memories of her man.

"You're trying to make me jealous, aren't you?" Shaylisa asked.

"Who, me?" Cindy replied innocently.

Both women sat at the table, shaking their heads and looking at each other with smiles on their faces.

"Okay, so have you found anything wrong with the brotha or is he truly Mr. Right for Cindy?"

"Hmm, no, there's nothing really wrong with him. At least I haven't noticed anything yet. It's still very early, but all indications point to him becoming very special in my life. I know that before me he was a big-time flirt and he might be still. But anybody can change, and I can't put him down for being a ladies' man before he met me, so long as he's stopped now."

"Listen at you!" Shaylisa said, noticing the confidence in Cindy. "So, describe this handsome brotha who's got you open, figuratively and literally."

"What literally?" Cindy replied, shocked by the connotation.

"The way you talking and giggling over there, I can tell you had sex with him."

"Maybe."

"Uh-huh, maybe my ass!"

"Yes, we've been intimate a couple times."

"Don't try to hide that you been getting your freak on, girl! That's why we here, to talk about some good dirt. If my sex life were happening right now, then I'd tell you everything. But for now, I have to live through you, Cindy."

"It won't be long for you, Shaylisa. Already you got men looking at you in this restaurant and I know how open you are about approaching men."

Shaylisa looked around. "Where? Who's looking at me?"

"The guy over here on our left has been checking you out so hard that I think he's reading your lips," Cindy whispered.

"He's also sitting with a woman, so I ain't about to be messing with somebody's man, okay!" Shaylisa replied.

"Maybe he wants you to join them for a threesome?"

"Puh-lease!"

"You might like it, Shaylisa. Don't knock it till you tried it!" Cindy laughed.

"That's what I'm afraid of, liking it. Lord knows I don't need no man-woman, woman-man drama in my life. The brotha would probably get mad 'cause he thinking I'm focusing too much on the coochie, and Miss Thang would get mad 'cause I'm climbing the walls and riding that brotha too much. Nope, I don't think so!"

"Shaylisa, you are crazy! The things you say sometimes."

"Yeah, whatever, girl. You still haven't described your man."

"Well, to be honest, Shaylisa, I think you know him."

"What you mean, I know him? This ain't someone that I used to date, is it?"

"No, but he is the friend of someone you were seeing."

"What friend, friend of who?"

"Malcolm's best friend, Jamal."

Shaylisa paused. "Oh, that friend . . ."

Silence surrounded the table for a moment, until the waiter finally brought the food over. The aroma of the black-bean soup had both ladies breathing in.

"Wow, that looks delicious!" Cindy said, looking over at Shaylisa's plate.

"Yours looks good too, girl. Maybe I should've ordered that soup."

"Hey, Shaylisa, I hope it's not gonna be a problem between us that I'm seeing Jamal."

"No, Cindy, it's not really. I guess the immediate shock needed a second or two to wear off, you know."

"Yeah, that's why I hesitated."

"And probably why you haven't mentioned it all week to me, huh?"

Cindy looked away. "Yeah, I confess, I've been holding back on you."

"It's okay. I'm glad I know and yes, Jamal is a good-looking man, although I've never noticed the thickness of his hands."

"I have, Shaylisa, and oh my!"

"Girl!"

Cindy laughed nervously at Shaylisa's response. Deep down she worried that there might be a conflict if she continued to spend time with Jamal.

"So, how's Jamal doing anyway?" Shaylisa asked before taking a bite of her sausage.

"Oh, he's always good. I don't think I've ever seen him down about anything. He's constantly giving pep talks to anybody that'll listen, and he and Malcolm seem to have a really genuine friendship."

"Yes, that's why I know Jamal so well. Sometimes I think those two are joined at the hip, because they love to hang out together. I imagine you'll be competing against Malcolm when it comes to spending time with Jamal."

"So far, I haven't. I've only seen Malcolm once, but Jamal talks about him all the time. You know, my boy this and my brotha that . . ."

"Maybe he's keeping to himself these days," Shaylisa said, hoping to get the scoop on Malcolm.

"Yeah, maybe so," Cindy quietly replied as though she were keeping a secret.

Shaylisa suspected that Cindy was still holding back. Cindy couldn't bear to look Shaylisa in the eyes, and she seemed to be having a hard time eating because of nervousness. Her glass of Chardonnay was just about gone because she'd been gulping it down ever since she'd confessed she was dating Jamal.

"Maybe you should order another drink, Cindy. You over there trying to get a buzz, huh?"

Shaylisa made the suggestion in the hope that Cindy would relax a little bit. She figured that eventually Cindy would get around to saying whatever it was that was making her feel so uneasy. It would have to take some creative prying on Shaylisa's part in order to get Cindy talking.

"You okay, girl?" Shaylisa asked, noticing Cindy so quiet.

"Yeah, I'm fine. So, what have you been doing all week besides working, Shaylisa?"

"Let's see, besides working? Absolutely nothing . . . I go home, fix myself something to eat, watch some news, flip through the channels, get fed up with television, read a book . . ."

"Girl, come on! I know for a fact that men try to hit on you all the time. Isn't there someone who has interested you?"

"I'm not trying to do the office-romance thing, especially after *him*; and besides, when I'm at work, I'm all about being professional."

"I hear you, but now that work is over . . ."

"Yeah, I intended to get my flirt on, but first I wanted to catch up with you and all the juicy gossip. I didn't expect to hear about the Jamal situation, though."

"See, now you have me feeling guilty that I said anything."

"Why are you feeling guilty?"

"Because I may have ruined our get-together by telling you about him. I know that anything I say about Jamal probably makes you think of Malcolm."

"A little bit, maybe. But no, you shouldn't hold back, Cindy, and besides, I'm the one that broke up with Malcolm, remember?"

"Yeah, but—"

"Don't even trip, girl."

Cindy and Shaylisa were silent again and focused on the food sitting before them. Shaylisa kept glancing over at Cindy, thinking and wondering what the big deal was and what she was holding back. All the speculation going through Shaylisa's mind was driving her crazy.

"Cindy, are you holding something back about Malcolm?"

"Kind of, yes . . . Malcolm is seeing someone."

"Oh, is that all?" Shaylisa laughed as if the news were no big deal or surprise to her.

"You're okay with it?"

"Yeah, girl . . . How many times do I have to remind you that I broke up with him? He's the one that's been writing me letters and acting like his damn life was over! Shit, it's about time he moved on and started dating."

"Jamal is trying to have us double-date with them, but I've felt weird about it because I wasn't sure how you'd feel."

"You can go, I don't care."

"Okay. Malcolm seems to be very happy with this girl. He spends a lot of time with her and I think she has a daughter . . ."

"Cindy, did I ask for all that information?"

"Oops, sorry about that, I didn't mean it. Just thought you might want to hear about her."

"Spare me the details, okay?"

Cindy smiled and nodded her head.

"What's the girl's name anyway?" Shaylisa asked.

"Thought you didn't want to hear about it."

"I don't!"

"Her name is Zahara."

"Za-what?"

"Zahara, like Sahara but with a Z."

"Oh, okay. So, that heffa can't spell, huh?"

Cindy laughed. "Are you gonna start talking bad about her?"

"Whatever, girl. I hope she got plenty of patience, 'cause she's gonna need to wait awhile before Malcolm gets over me."

"You're funny, Shaylisa."

"Uh-huh, well, you watch what happens."

"Why, you gonna call him or something?"

"No, he'll probably call me eventually. I'm not trying to mess up his happy home with Safari."

"Za-har-a!"

"What-ev-er! You'll see, Cindy."

"See what?"

"Malcolm will be calling me, very soon."

"If you say so."

Shaylisa returned to eating the last bit of her food. She had a devilish grin on her face, which made Cindy wonder if perhaps she hadn't been the only one holding back tonight.

For the rest of the evening, Shaylisa refused to talk about Malcolm. She refused to believe that Malcolm could open his heart to a new woman without major difficulties. She figured that once things got deep, he'd start tripping like most men do. He'd run away and hide within the walls of his own self-pity. He'd start writing more letters to himself, to her, and to Zahara. Shaylisa knew Malcolm better than anyone else did, and all her predictions would be right on point.

Shaylisa and Cindy both proved to be very hungry women. Their plates were completely empty, though their glasses were half full—they'd had enough of the wine. Shaylisa suggested some coffee and Cindy immediately agreed. The atmosphere of the restaurant changed and Cindy noticed more single men hanging out at the bar. One man in particular looked like he was going to approach their table.

"Don't look now, but I think this man is gonna try to talk to us." Cindy pointed by raising her chin in the direction of the man walking toward them. He was clean-shaven, with a light brown complexion and hair cut close to his head, and wore a tan-colored sport coat over some light brown pants. The man was conservative in dress, but in Shaylisa's opinion, the man was putting his ego in his own hands.

"If he says the wrong thing, I'm gonna embarrass his ass!" Shaylisa warned.

"Be nice, girl."

"That's about as nice as I can get, especially with his polyester-wearing self trying to walk over here and get his mack on."

"Give him a chance, he hasn't even said hello yet!"

The man adjusted the lapels on his coat as he approached. The smile on his face seemed to say, Which one of these ladies is gonna give me some play tonight?

"How you ladies doing tonight?" Mr. Tan Sport Coat asked.

"She's fine and I'm good," Shaylisa snapped.

"Wow, excuse me!" he said, obviously unprepared. "Maybe I caught the two of you at a bad time?"

"Honey, I don't think you could find a good time if you tried."

The smile left his face. "Why you got so much attitude?"

Cindy interrupted the potential drama with an apology. "I'm sorry for my friend. Maybe you should just walk away."

"Okay, but if either of you change your mind, here's my business card. That's me there, Curtis Spencer."

"Puh-lease!" Shaylisa held up her hand to fend off what she recognized as game mixed with bullshit.

"Thanks, Curtis, you have a good night," Cindy replied, hoping that Curtis would leave before Shaylisa started in on him.

He did just that and returned to his seat at the bar, scoping out other potential victims of his charm and lucky recipients of his card. Shaylisa couldn't contain her laughter after Curtis walked away. Cindy just sat back and gazed upon her best friend's display of wickedness.

"You are so evil, Shaylisa!"

"That man deserved it, girl, I'm sorry."

"Do you see any man around here that would interest you? I mean Shaylisa, why are you acting bitter about men when you seem to be the one in control of your relationships?"

"I am not bitter! Let me look around this room and see who's up in here."

Shaylisa looked to her right and noticed a man eyeing her as the lady sitting at his table focused on her plate of spinach. Behind him sat a man with his attention focused outside the restaurant, looking at the boats in the marina. Hmm, he appeared to be somewhat attractive, Shaylisa thought, but perhaps he was a loner with issues stacked on issues—and Shaylisa wasn't thinking of magazines. She lingered for a moment, staring at the man before putting an end to thoughts of his potential. Nah, he could be another Malcolm. On her left, she noticed a bunch of men standing at the bar, hoping for female attention and making fools of themselves, possibly after having had a hard day at work. She saw no potential in any of the men in the room, or perhaps it was her attitude, which blocked everything. Shaylisa felt the need to excuse herself from the table and go to the ladies' room.

"I'll be back, girl," Shaylisa said in a somber tone.

"What's wrong with you?" Cindy asked, concerned about the suddenly sad expression on her friend's face.

Shaylisa tried to play it off with an instant happy face and a laugh. "Nothing's wrong, I'm just a happy camper!" she said before retreating to the restroom.

Once inside, Shaylisa took a deep breath and closed her eyes for a moment. She sighed before opening them, looking in the mirror and seeing a reflection that she wasn't too proud of. Yeah, she was physically attractive enough to interest the best-looking men or women in town. What they wouldn't see was the sadness behind Shaylisa's eyes as she stared in the mirror. Maybe a little makeup would do the trick. Shaylisa had been blessed with great eyelashes and beautiful brown eyes. She could make a man appear dumbstruck during the most lighthearted conversations because he would be so focused on her eyes.

"Get it together, girl," Shaylisa demanded as she checked her pearly-white teeth and noticed that she needed to add a little something to her lips. For all she knew, once she walked back into the dining area, she'd find new talent awaiting her careful inspection. It was wishful thinking, but she needed all the motivation she could find to remove what she felt deep inside.

Maybe she needed some professional help. A psychiatrist might be able to shed light on her confusion. Or maybe visiting one of those psychics could reveal something to her about her past and future lives. Cindy had mentioned several times a psychic she'd used before. She claimed the guy was very insightful and mentioned that she would have an exciting sex life once she'd met the right man. Shaylisa teased Cindy for a long time about that revelation, and it still made her laugh to think of trying that route for self-discovery.

"I am tripping and don't know where to turn," she spoke into the mirror.

"Excuse me, did you say something?" a woman asked as she entered the restroom.

"No, just talking to myself, that's all," Shaylisa replied as she put her lipstick back inside her purse. She fumbled with her eyeliner, trying to decide if she still needed to touch up her eyes.

"I love that coat you're wearing," the woman said as she made eye contact with Shaylisa in the mirror.

"Thank you. Aren't you cold wearing what you have on?" Shaylisa noticed the woman wearing a plum-colored jersey slip dress with spaghetti straps. The front was draped slightly, revealing a little cleavage. The woman was very lovely, sort of Halle Berry–ish but with auburn-colored, curly hair that came to the tops of her shoulders.

"I have a jacket at my table," the woman answered, smiling and waiting for Shaylisa to pick up on the offer.

This woman was trying to flirt and perhaps see if Shaylisa would be interested in joining her for a drink at her table.

"Did you want to use this particular mirror or something?" Shaylisa asked sarcastically.

"I didn't mean to stare, I'm sorry. I just find you very attractive and thought . . ."

"O-kay, umm, I can hear my cue . . ."

"I apologize again. But hey, if you ever need a friend to talk to who's willing to listen, perhaps rub your shoulders, relax you in a way that I'm sure you've never experienced before, then feel free to call me. My name is Gina."

Shaylisa was so amazed and shocked by this woman coming on to her that she didn't realize she'd handed the woman a pen to write her phone number down on a piece of paper towel.

"Here you are, call me anytime. What's your name?" Gina asked, handing the pen and paper towel to a somewhat stunned Shaylisa.

She cleared her throat before answering nervously, "Shaylisa."

The woman smiled. "Nice meeting you, Shaylisa. I hope to hear from you really soon."

Shaylisa shook her head as if to snap herself back to reality. "Yeah, right! Girl, I've got enough problems already!" she uttered before leaving the restroom with that familiar get-out-of-my-way-before-you-get-hurt attitude in tow. And it didn't help that nothing had changed inside the dining room; no good-looking men or even a halfway-decent brotha attached to a platinum card, wearing size-eighteen shoes. I want a man with something big on his plate!

Shaylisa thought to herself before laughing at the very notion of what she'd imagined. Not to mention her momentary brush with Ms. Auburn Halle Berry in the restroom. What was Shaylisa thinking? Why was she still holding the piece of paper towel with the phone number on it as she returned to the table?

"What's that in your hand?" Cindy asked.

"Huh, what is what?" Shaylisa appeared more dumbfounded than innocent.

"In your hand, girl!"

"Oh!" Shaylisa laughed. "You'd never believe it, but some girl tried to hit on me in the restroom!"

"She must've been successful, 'cause you got her number in your hand. That is her phone number, right?"

"Yeah, girl, puh-lease! I just haven't had time to throw it away yet."

"Why, the trash cans are full in there?"

"Cindy, stop!"

"Ooh, Shaylisa. What deep, dark secret are you hiding?"

"No, no, no, watch this," Shaylisa said before crumpling the paper towel and dropping it inside her wineglass.

"Okay, but I'm still gonna wonder about you. Nothing's wrong with it . . ."

"I've said this time and time again to you, Cindy, *puh-lease*!"

Both ladies erupted in laughter.

"Okay," Cindy replied.

"Good, it's getting late, and even though you're my girl, I'm ready to go home!" Shaylisa announced.

"Yeah, I need to get home myself."

"You expecting a call from your sweetie pie, Jamal?"

"Yep, he calls me every night."

"I don't miss that kind of shit at all!"

"You're just evil, Shaylisa."

"Whatever, let's get out of here!"

Cindy chuckled as she shook her head in disbelief.

Shaylisa took a last look at her wineglass. "I am seriously out of control now!" Shaylisa said as she strutted out the door.

Cindy walked right behind her girlfriend, teasing her the whole way until they got in their separate cars and drove away.

AFTER LEAVING CINDY, SHAYLISA had no place to go but home: that lovely condo with plenty to do inside and that beautiful pink comforter lying on top of her bed, awaiting her warm, sexy body to come and spend time with it. It was the only thing that Shaylisa imagined would be caressing her body anytime soon. None of the male prospects seemed promising, and besides, she had so much attitude right now that no other soul could possibly break through her wall of disenchantment. No other soul indeed.

"Yo, lady!" a man shouted in her direction at the stoplight.

Shaylisa's windows were up, so the sound of his voice was muffled. She decided to take a look in his direction and see what sort of response he required from her. He was in a white four-door Corolla with purple-tinted windows and a clothes hanger for an antenna. Shaylisa pressed the button to roll down the passenger-side window.

"Will you please shut up!" she screamed in his direction.

She drove off before he could wish her well or mistake her name for something beginning with a *b*. She shook her head in amazement at the day she'd experienced and wondered what would happen next. Even the radio stations weren't giving her much play. She had to listen to nothing but the same ole shit, and it didn't help that she was sick of her own music tapes that she'd sat up all night recording last weekend. Shaylisa was about to take drastic measures to end her evening on a positive note. She'd thought about calling Malcolm to see how life had been treating him, but she passed. She even considered going to a club, anonymously, as a woman in heat and in desperate need of some nooky. She passed on that as well. She gave Ms. Auburn Halle Berry a millisecond of thought but remembered that the infamous telephone number was left behind, drowning inside her wineglass back at the restaurant. Drastic measures were still needed.

Shaylisa decided to do something she'd been craving to do for a while now. She took a right turn and pulled into a parking lot on La Cienega near San Vicente Boulevard. She went inside a small green shack where the aroma could be described as heavenly, and she could hear the sounds of burgers on the grill and fries getting mad crispy in the deep fryer. One of those oh-my-God-I-don't-need-this expressions was written all over her face, right behind the hurry-up-and-give-me-my-damn-hamburger stare. The Latino brother behind the grill was taking way too long, and Shaylisa sent him subliminal messages that told him she was about to go ballistic if he didn't hurry up with her food.

"Okay, that's one King Fat chili burger and one order of chili-cheese fries to go?" The young Latino smiled as Shaylisa dug inside her purse for the money. Underneath that I-wanna-eat exterior was still a fine-ass woman, no matter how bad she treated folks who looked at her wrong. Shaylisa walked out of the eatery determined not to taste her fries before she got home.

"Stay strong, girl!" she told herself.

She placed her food in the backseat of her BMW 540i and prayed for strength as she turned the ignition. She couldn't ask for a better theme song to drive home to. The radio station she was listening to was playing a blast from the past. It was that old jam by Roy Ayers called "Everybody Loves the Sunshine." Shaylisa turned up the radio and rolled the windows halfway down. The wind blew her hair as she drove farther up La Cienega and then turned right onto Beverly Boulevard. Her whole attitude had done an about-face; she found herself feeling great, hearing an old song that always sounded good whether it was the original or somebody sampling it. The night air was like an aphrodisiac, making it easier for Shaylisa to enjoy even those annoying moments when she'd hit a pothole or someone would cut her off. Life felt beautiful.

Is that my phone ringing? Shaylisa asked herself. She could hear familiar chimes under the loud music.

"Hello," she answered while turning the music down.

"Hey, girl, you still ain't made it home yet?"

"Cindy?"

"Yeah, who else you expecting, that lady from the restaurant?"

"Puh-lease! What you want?"

"Nothing, just to talk."

"I thought you would be getting you some extra good loving from Jamal by now!"

"No, he told me that he and Malcolm made plans to see the Lakers play tonight, and then after that they were gonna hang out at the Staples Center sports bar. Where are you at anyway?"

"I'm on Beverly and La Brea, about to turn left."

"Oh, so you're almost home, then."

"Yeah, uh-huh. So, what did you want to talk about, Cindy? Something must be up, since you couldn't wait for me to get home."

"No, just wanted to talk."

"Don't play me, what's wrong?"

"I don't know, it's kind of silly, actually."

"What is?"

"Something that I want to try with Jamal."

"You either want to do a threesome or have anal sex!"

Cindy laughed. "No, that ain't it, girl."

"Then what is it?"

"Well, Jamal and I have had sex a couple of times and we used a condom."

"Yeah, go on."

"Before him it had been a long time since I'd been intimate with anyone, so I stopped taking the pill. Well, I've been having all kinds of thoughts about him entering me without a condom on. I mean, I am craving to feel him inside of me, bare. I get this tingling sensation inside of me from my hair follicles to my toenails, thinking about this."

"Girl, you need to quit!" Shaylisa exclaimed. "Anyway, Cindy, you go ahead and both get tested for AIDS then get your freak on, girl. Just make sure I get to be your baby's godmother."

"You had to go there, huh?"

"I'm teasing, but anyway, let me hang up 'cause I'm about to pull into my driveway, okay?"

"Okay, thanks for your advice, Miss Thang."

"Girl, puh-lease . . ."

BEING AT HOME WAS the best feeling in the world to Shaylisa. She turned on a couple of lights, the television, and the stereo and laid her keys and purse down on a small table near the front door. As she kicked off her shoes and took off her jacket, the aroma of her burger and fries beckoned. She ripped open the paper bag and unwrapped the burger. Mmm, it's been so long! she thought. She chewed slowly, as though she were making love to her food. It felt like centuries had gone by since she'd eaten this type of glorious junk food. The burger tasted so good that she could've sworn it was talking to her.

Don't worry 'bout the weight, 'cause you've been wanting me for a long time! a voice said to her.

I'm tripping. Let me see what's on television.

Shaylisa plopped down on the couch with her burger in one hand and the remote in the other. With her thumb on the button, she scanned through the channels. Conan O'Brien, infomercial, Shopping Channel . . . How can this heffa seriously sell some earrings for $19.95? Shaylisa continued to scan while munching on her burger. The chili dripped down her chin, making her look like the sexiest slob in the world. She turned the television off. There was complete silence before she got up from the couch and tuned to the radio station that was playing Roy Ayers earlier. Once she found the station, she immediately recognized the syncopation of that old familiar Stevie Wonder jam "Boogie On Reggae Woman." Shaylisa twirled her body around and around, dancing and smiling. She'd forgotten all about her chili fries sitting on the table, but those things are never any good once they get cold anyway. She'd lost her appetite by the time Stevie got to playing his harmonica at the end of the song. It didn't matter, because Shaylisa was actually enjoying herself. She'd been stressing about men ever since she'd left work, but in the comfort of her condo, all those negative feelings had been lifted, and she continued to dance in the middle of her living room.

•   •   •

WHAT IS IT ABOUT candles that relax the soul? Shaylisa thought to herself. The late night–early morning hours cast the mood for her feelings. She couldn't sleep. She surrendered her thoughts to memories of Malcolm. Those times when he'd call to say good night or when she was too sick to get out of bed and desperately needed some sympathy as well as some vitamin C, Malcolm would rush to her aid. And yes, sometimes she'd call him over 'cause she needed a certain itch to be scratched. Shaylisa beamed as she lay in bed, surrounded by candlelight and the vivid reflection of her memories. I need to quit, she thought to herself, her fingertips lightly touching her nipples through the soft fabric of her silk nightgown. Shaylisa sighed as she found herself becoming aroused by thoughts she would otherwise feel she had no business indulging in.

"Stop it, girl!" she cried as though her hand had a mind of its own.

Shaylisa sat on the edge of her bed trying to rid her mind, body, and soul of what she was feeling.

"Damn him!" Shaylisa uttered.

She reached for a notepad and pen on the nightstand next to her bed. So many thoughts of Malcolm had her wondering if it was a sign that she needed to write his ass. She didn't wish to get back with him, but for some strange reason, she wanted to know that he still had feelings for her no matter who he was currently dating.

"Hmm, dearest Malcolm . . ." Shaylisa whispered out loud.

She'd begin a letter that she hoped would have Malcolm drop everything, including his lady friend, Zahara.

CHAPTER FIVE

Special
Pleasures

*Z*ahara and Malcolm were like wine and roses. Impossibly, the two lovebirds couldn't get enough of each other. Malcolm had found a way to leave his baggage at the door and Zahara rewarded his efforts constantly.

A weekend spent at his town house would always lead to something very special. Intimacy didn't always mean sex. Zahara appreciated Malcolm's willingness to talk and share his feelings so openly. He'd talk about his childhood, his work, his sexual fantasies, and his plans for the future. The two of them loved to sit up all night conversing. Malcolm was extremely patient when Zahara attempted to probe his mind. He'd answer everything: Where do you see yourself in five, ten years from now? Do you ever wish to get married? Do you believe in God? Do you get along with your mother? Would you like to have kids one day? Are you still in love with your ex? Ouch. With that question Malcolm would always pause. He'd change the subject to any topic other than her, his ex, Shaylisa. Zahara would follow that up with a forgiving "Never mind," letting Malcolm know that she too possessed a great deal of patience.

• • •

SITTING IN FRONT OF Malcolm's town house was a silver Audi A6, a familiar sign that Malcolm had a very special visitor. This time, however, he had two special visitors.

"Malcolm, honey, can Imara see some of your drawings?" Zahara asked as she and her daughter sat in the living room while Malcolm prepared an exceptional dinner for three.

"Yeah, take a look in my office. There's a folder on my desk that I keep some of my drawings in."

Zahara retrieved the folder from Malcolm's office as Imara sat quietly in the living room. She was not sure what to make of the new environment. Occasionally glancing at Malcolm, she'd wonder who he was and why her mother was so friendly with him.

"Look, sweetheart, isn't this nice?" Zahara asked, showing off Malcolm's drawings to Imara.

She responded with a slight nod of her head. Gradually Imara's interest grew as Zahara continued to turn the pages of Malcolm's book. His drawings were amazingly lifelike.

"Honey, you really should consider doing portraits too!" Zahara suggested to Malcolm.

"I've done a few before, but right now animation is what's paying the bills."

"I hear you. How about drawing Imara one day?"

"Sounds good. Hey, dinner is almost ready. I made some sweet-potato fries too. You can grab some now if you want."

Zahara walked into the kitchen and Malcolm instantly smiled. He relished the fact that Zahara felt so at home whenever she came over. An indication of her comfort was the fact that she'd always remove her shoes and walk around barefoot. What is it about a woman being barefoot that's so appealing to a man? Whatever the answer to that question, Malcolm didn't waste time pondering. He showed his appreciation for Zahara's presence by wrapping his arms around her waistline before she could exit the kitchen and return to the living room.

"Hmm, what are you up to, Mr. Tyler?" she inquired.

Malcolm smiled and kissed her softly on the lips.

"Thank you. Let's not get anything started, 'cause I may not be able to stop," Zahara cautioned.

"Is that so bad?" he asked, smiling wickedly.

"With my daughter sitting in the other room? Umm, let's stop because I'm getting hot and bothered and I can't do what I want to do . . ." She giggled. Then the oven timer rang.

"Well, you've been saved by the bell 'cause that sound means dinner is about to be served," Malcolm joked, and led Zahara to the kitchen.

Malcolm prepared a dinner that even Emeril Lagasse would be honored to eat. "I prepared a grilled portobello mushroom salad and roasted lamb chops."

"Where did you learn to cook like that, from your mother?"

"Nah, she can't cook. I learned on my own. My creativity has no boundaries. I'm gonna prove that to you later tonight!"

Zahara blushed. "Imara, Mommy hasn't forgotten about you!" Zahara yelled into the living room. "Are you okay?"

"Yes, Mommy," Imara replied.

Malcolm smiled with pride as he removed the food from the oven. He couldn't wait for his creation to be sampled.

Zahara searched Malcolm's cabinets for plates and silverware to use. She took the initiative, since he'd done all that hard work putting together such a delicious-looking meal. She wasn't making much headway, but she did make a lot of noise, opening and closing the cabinet doors.

"Umm, the plates are there on your left and the silverware is right here, Zahara." Malcolm smiled with delight as he watched Zahara trying to be helpful. It kind of threw him off for a second. He wanted to tell Zahara to stop trying but instantly realized that it might offend her. She had her heart set on doing something, so Malcolm remained patient.

DINNER WAS AN ABSOLUTE delight. Imara appeared to break away from her shyness and made an effort to speak with Malcolm. He wondered if she'd ever look at him, let alone say something. Malcolm feared that Zahara's daughter could be a major obstacle to the relationship, and with Imara having just spent her spring vacation with her father, he was still fresh in her mind. How could she be expected to adjust to a strange man touching her mother? he wondered.

Malcolm acted fidgety until Imara laughed at him for dropping his fork and knocking over his glass of grape soda in an attempt to whisper to Zahara. What is it about kids finding humor in physical mishaps? Malcolm smiled at that moment because he felt a breakthrough had occurred. Zahara laughed. Malcolm wasn't surprised by that reaction, because women definitely laugh when a brotha stumbles like that.

Dinner was cool and satisfying. Malcolm was pleased with the outcome, and his greatest reward came afterward. He'd sat down on the couch at Zahara's request, watching two gorgeous ladies remove dishes and clear the dinner table. Once again Zahara made it apparent that she wasn't a woman who would sit back and allow a man to do for her without her giving in return. She was so true to every honest man's desire: a woman, feminine yet strong, gorgeous, and a smooth complexion that matched the quality of her voice, which reflected the essence of her soul at any given time. Now Zahara seemed to be in a good place, happy, thankful, and energetic. She'd smile so sincerely after sharing her thoughts with Malcolm.

"You look so fine sitting over there on that couch, baby. Did you get enough to eat?" Zahara said flirtatiously.

"Not yet." Malcolm winked.

"Umm, you nasty man!"

"Shush, there's young ears in the room . . ."

Zahara smiled and continued clearing the table. Certain parts of her body wiggled and jiggled, causing Malcolm to sit up and take notice. He cleared his throat and grabbed a magazine from his coffee table. Imara continued to help while occasionally stopping to wait for instructions from her mother. Zahara noticed Imara yawning and looking tired. Imara wiped her eyes and smiled, yawning again. She walked over to the couch and sat down next to Malcolm.

"Hey, you tired?" Malcolm asked.

Imara nodded her head yes.

"Did you like the food?"

Again she nodded.

"I'm glad. I hope we can hang out sometime, Imara. Maybe go to the park or something."

Imara smiled and rested her head against Malcolm's arm. It wasn't long before she drifted off to sleep. Malcolm wasn't sure what to do because he didn't want to disturb the little angel from resting so comfortably.

"She had a long day, huh?" Malcolm asked Zahara.

"Yeah, we did a little running around. I wanted her to look good for you, so I bought that outfit that she's wearing."

"Oh, wow, really? That's cool . . ."

"I told you, Malcolm, you're very special to me and I always want you to know how much. I knew my baby would eventually warm up to you."

"Well, I'm not gonna lie, Zahara, I was nervous about your daughter."

"Nervous?"

"Yeah. I didn't think she would like me."

"She does."

"I can see that now, but before?"

"She's a tough young lady. I'm to blame for that, 'cause I don't want her to instantly like all strangers. I want her to be nice and ladylike, of course, but not be so naive."

"I feel you. She's beautiful, just like you."

"Yeah, well, despite her shyness today, she will speak her mind and talk your ears off, so be prepared for that."

"I will . . ." Malcolm smiled.

Zahara sat down beside Malcolm and Imara. She'd finished with the dinner table and wanted to relax with her two sweethearts. Imara was still fast asleep on the couch and Malcolm tried desperately to keep his focus on an article he was reading in *Black Enterprise* magazine about tax-free investing.

"I need to figure something out so Uncle Sam won't be taking so much money out of my checks!" Malcolm uttered.

Zahara chuckled. "Why you reading that anyway?"

Malcolm shrugged his shoulders, trying to act nonchalant but knowing full well that he had a very sensual chocolate delight sitting nearby with freaky thoughts on her mind. He tried to act as if he didn't notice, but if he'd been asked to stand up, it'd be clear that Malcolm was quite aware of Zahara's presence. The hairs on his arms were even standing at full attention.

"You're bad, Zahara," Malcolm said while still flipping through the pages of the magazine.

"Honey, I'm horny and I'm not ashamed to admit it!"

Malcolm laughed. "What about Imara?"

"She's too young and she better wait until she's thirty before she starts thinking about sex!"

"Oh, well, I didn't think we could do anything with your daughter around."

"You mind if I put her in your other bedroom?" Zahara asked.

Zahara kissed Malcolm before attempting to pick up Imara without waking her up. Imara mumbled and resisted at first, then opened her eyes and allowed her mother to remove her from the couch. Zahara gave Malcolm a flirtatious sidelong glance before walking away with Imara in her arms.

"Don't go anywhere," she told him seductively.

"I'll be here . . ."

Malcolm thought he had a better chance of hitting the Lotto than of Zahara making love to him on his couch with her daughter so close by. He'd gotten the feeling that she talked a good game but probably couldn't deliver on some hot-sweaty-passionate-freaky-can't-get-enough sex. He couldn't see it, couldn't believe it, and couldn't imagine it.

In the distance he could hear Zahara quietly closing the door of his guest bedroom. After that, she opened the door to his bathroom.

"Give me a second, okay, Malcolm?" Zahara said before going inside.

Malcolm picked up another magazine. He thumbed through the pages, stopping on an article about Tiger Woods before being interrupted by a smooth yet delicate sound.

"Malcolm . . ."

Zahara couldn't have said his name better than the way she'd said it just then. He smiled before turning his attention to her. At first glance, he was captured. His bottom lip hung down as if he'd seen a ghost, albeit the most beautiful ghost to ever scare a man into submission. Zahara stood in a sexy pose with one hand on the wall and the other on her hip.

"What are you doing?" Malcolm asked, confused and caught totally off guard.

Zahara stood near the arm of the couch wearing her Victoria's Secret Body Bare bra and matching string bikini.

"Can't handle what you see?" Zahara teased.

"Nice color."

"It's called Nude Croco."

"Oh, okay."

"I've been wearing it all day, but now I think it's time to remove it. Would you like to help me take it off?"

Malcolm nodded his head.

"Can't you talk, honey?"

Malcolm sighed. "Not too well right now."

Zahara snickered. She was acting seductively, gesturing for Malcolm to come to her. He stood up and walked over to her almost immediately. His nervous right hand touched the top of her left thigh. He played with the string on her bikini.

"If you want to rip it off, I won't be mad . . ."

"I'll buy you a new pair," Malcolm promised.

"Maybe I won't need to wear any when I'm around you."

Malcolm smiled and proceeded to tug at the string. Zahara placed her arms on the top of Malcolm's shoulders. She quietly chuckled at Malcolm's attempts to remove her string bikini. She could see the gentleman in him come out, because he really didn't want to ruin what she was wearing.

"Look at me," she said softly.

As Zahara looked deeply into Malcolm's eyes, she reached down with her left hand and was somehow able to undo the strap without struggle. She smiled, bringing attention to what she'd done. Malcolm glanced downward to find Zahara's bottom half completely exposed. She leaned forward to kiss him. His excitement more than compensated for his nervousness, and he returned her kiss with a passionate embrace and some uncontrollable moaning.

Zahara slipped her hand between their bodies and began pulling at Malcolm's belt buckle. She then toiled with his pants, causing them to fall to the floor. The kissing got hotter and the breathing faster as Zahara lifted herself and wrapped her legs around Malcolm's waist. Zahara's own excitement revealed itself, as Malcolm was able to feel the wetness between her legs pressed against his skin. He held her close and entered her. The force of her pushing against him caused Malcolm to sit on the arm of the couch, but the sexing never stopped or missed a beat, like a slow jam that you grind to, wondering if it could get any better. It did.

Zahara continued to thrust her hips forward and ride Malcolm furiously as he made attempts at removing her bra. His concentration wasn't too good, so he gave up on the bra and held on to Zahara as if he were holding on for dear life. Malcolm's legs were hanging off the couch and Zahara was moving steadfastly on top of him.

"Mommy?" Imara uttered.

There was a sudden stop in the action. Zahara grabbed a pillow, since it was the nearest thing she could find to cover up. Malcolm tried to hide by remaining seated and not moving an inch. He gave Zahara his shirt so she could look a little less suspicious than she already did, holding a pillow against her half-naked body.

"Baby, go back in the room for Mommy, okay?" Zahara cried out, totally embarrassed.

"I had a feeling something like this would happen," Malcolm said.

Zahara blushed. "What am I gonna tell her?"

"Make something up."

"You are not helping."

"I tried to warn you, though."

"Whatever, Malcolm."

Zahara fixed her face and buttoned the shirt that Malcolm covered her with. She walked carefully toward the guest room, occasionally looking back at Malcolm, who was smiling and giving her a supportive nod.

"It'll be okay, she'll understand," he said. Malcolm watched as Zahara opened the door and entered the guest room.

"Imara?" That was the last thing Malcolm heard before Zahara closed the door behind her. He walked to his own bedroom to find something else to wear. He didn't think it would be too cool to remain sitting around without his shirt on and his pants down around his ankles.

THIRTY MINUTES HAD GONE by before Malcolm heard the doorknob of his guest bedroom turn. Zahara stepped out into the hallway still wearing Malcolm's shirt and trying to be extra quiet as she closed the door. She listened for a moment before turning her attention to Malcolm, who was standing at the end of the hallway leading to the living room.

"Everything okay?" he asked.

"Yeah, she's fine. She didn't really say much, but I think everything is okay."

"We shall see."

"What do you mean?"

"Well, you never know what she might say when she's with her father the next time. Would it bother you if she told him about us?"

"It might bother me a little if she tells him what she saw, but eventually my ex is gonna know about us, so . . ."

"Well, I guess we shouldn't worry about it until it happens."

"No, I was just wondering if it would be okay for us to spend the night."

"Oh, okay."

"You don't mind, do you?" Zahara asked with an innocent look on her face.

"No, not at all. But, I think we should be cool as far as the sex goes."

"I'll be good, Malcolm." Zahara snickered.

CHAPTER SIX

Love Took
the Change
Out of Me

 *M*alcolm and Zahara awoke to a beautiful Saturday morning in the suburbs of L.A. The skies were a powder blue and there wasn't a cloud in sight, as the wind had been blowing so fiercely all night. Malcolm hadn't felt so good lying next to a woman since Shaylisa. That memory didn't make him proud, but he did feel really good lying next to Zahara. She made it very hard for him to get up. She slept so close to him all night. They spooned each other continuously. One moment it was Malcolm behind Zahara and the next moment the position was reversed. Either way, Malcolm never felt an ounce of cold anywhere on his body.

In the distance he could hear the sound of the television playing in his guest bedroom. Saturday-morning cartoons were a welcome sound as he watched Zahara continue to move around so seductively, though it was purely unintentional. Malcolm kissed her on the forehead and removed his half of the covers so he could get out of bed. He figured that Imara might enjoy some breakfast with her cartoons. Maybe she'd like some pancakes or his special homemade waffles with some old-fashioned ribbon cane syrup that he'd bought one day while traveling through a small town in the South.

"Where you going?" Zahara said as she rolled over.

"Gonna fix some breakfast. You want anything special?"

"No, but Imara loves pancakes and scrambled eggs," she replied, still half asleep.

"Hmm, okay, cool. Well, feel free to join us if you happen to be awakened by the smell."

"Okay, honey, I will," Zahara said, though not convincingly.

Malcolm put on his robe and slippers, walked into the hallway, and turned right into the kitchen. The sound of water running, pots and pans banging, and the cutting board being put to good use attracted the attention of some very young but pretty eyes.

"What are you doing?" a cute little voice asked.

"Hey, good morning, Imara, would you like pancakes and eggs?" Imara smiled.

"How many you want?" Malcolm asked.

Imara shrugged.

"What you watching on television?"

"Nickelodeon," she replied. "Are you gonna give me some milk too? I like a lot of syrup on my pancakes!" Imara exclaimed.

"Yes, ma'am. Anything else you desire?"

Imara laughed. "I eat pancakes only on the weekends. Mommy doesn't have time to make it before school. Sometimes we're late."

"Oh, really? Well, I hope you like my pancakes, Imara. That's a pretty name. Do you have a middle name too?"

"Michelle."

"That's nice. Imara Michelle."

"My daddy's name is Michael, that's why."

"Oh."

"He makes me pancakes even if I want them for dinner. Sometimes we go to the restaurant too."

"That's really nice," Malcolm responded, feeling somewhat uncomfortable talking to Imara about her father.

"Can I watch your TV in that room?" Imara asked while pointing in the direction of the living room. Malcolm had a big-screen television in there.

"Sure, just press the on button of the remote, okay?"

Imara went to the living room and Malcolm continued preparing breakfast. Imara talking about her father gave Malcolm a strange feeling. He didn't like the idea of competing for Imara's attention or trying so hard to get her to like him. Perhaps he was just experiencing feelings that he needed to get used to. He'd never really seriously dated a woman with a child. He'd never had someone's child spend the night. He never had to wake up the next morning and make attempts to entertain that child. It was strange to be feeling this way, considering he was basically an animator for kids. That's how he made his living, but trying to entertain a child, face-to-face, was a whole new ball game. Life could be that way sometimes and Malcolm could do nothing at the moment but shake his head, sigh, and make sure he didn't overcook the eggs. He'd hate to see little Miss Thang giving him those looks as if to say, *Tsk, tsk, yo ass can't cook!*

Imara was still enjoying herself in front of the television when Malcolm heard Zahara in the bathroom. He smiled knowing that Zahara had finally gotten up and that he'd be greeted with a good-morning kiss. Those kinds of thoughts got the brotha instantly warm. Memories of last night danced across his mind, and waking up with Zahara's butt cheeks pushed up against his ooh-what-is-this chunk of manhood made Malcolm forget he was standing in front of a hot stove. He didn't burn himself, but he came pretty close to pouring pancake mix on top of the eggs he was cooking. Startled by the realization that he'd been daydreaming, he jumped back slightly.

"Good morning, cuteness!" Zahara said, sounding like she was on some early-morning talk show, not walking into a kitchen barefoot and wearing another one of Malcolm's shirts. "I hope you don't mind?" she said, drawing attention to what she had on.

Malcolm was speechless, but his raised eyebrow and half-smile indicated that he didn't mind one bit. Zahara had put on one of the sweatshirts he'd bought a few years ago at a Bob Marley festival. It fit Zahara very nicely. She tried to act like it needed adjusting, but Malcolm could tell she was only trying to seduce him and get his little big man to rise to the occasion—again.

Malcolm smiled and shook his head. "You don't stop, huh?"

Zahara smiled. "Well, it's nice to know that I keep you from concentrating on other things."

"Yes, you do accomplish that quite often, Zahara."

Malcolm turned his attention toward the food. He placed all the pancakes he cooked on a big round plate and the eggs on a separate dish. Zahara took both plates from Malcolm's hands. "Let me help you with that," she said.

Zahara turned and walked to the dining room area, leaving Malcolm behind with a combination what-am-I-getting-into and I'm-a-lucky-man kind of glare—that part of him that needed space to figure out what was going on. Zahara was looking like everything he wished to find in a woman and then some. And as a mother, she had Malcolm smiling as he witnessed the closeness she shared with her daughter. Zahara sat next to Imara, cutting her pancakes into little slices so that she could eat them without making a mess. Malcolm stood quietly, watching, thinking, and wondering before reality hit him in the face and he had to stop daydreaming. The phone was ringing . . .

"Hello," he answered.

"What up, bro?"

"Jamal, hey, what you been up to?"

"Ah, man, working my ass off, doing my thang, and romancing my little honey, Cindy. Shit, routine got a brotha feeling good right now!"

"Routine?"

"Yeah, working and romancing."

"Oh. So that means you've been spending a lot of time with Cindy, huh?"

"Yeah, homegirl is cool. She don't bring no stress with her and I like that."

"Sounds good."

"Yeah, it's been better than good. It's nice for a change to have a lady who likes to laugh and be all about enjoying the simple things. And get this, Cindy be bringing me flowers! Is that some shit or what?"

Malcolm laughed. "Yeah, but the question is, what do you do with them?"

"Ah, man, don't front! I went to IKEA the other day and bought me a couple of really cool-looking vases . . ."

Malcolm snickered at Jamal's purchase.

"Oh, so you got jokes about a brotha's discovery of his romantic side, huh?"

"No, I'm teasing."

"Uh-huh, so what you doing anyway?"

"Oh, I just finished making breakfast for Zahara's daughter. They both spent the night."

"Cool. You two couldn't get loud, though, huh?"

"Uh, nope."

"You ain't did nothing, stop trying to lie. Is it cool, you being on the phone right now?"

"Yeah, it's cool, wait, hold on . . ."

"Yo ass better ask permission!" Jamal laughed.

Malcolm whispered to Zahara, "This is Jamal, you mind if I talk with him?"

Zahara shook her head. "No, go ahead, we're fine."

"Okay, I'm back." Malcolm could hear Jamal laughing.

"You a good man, bro," Jamal teased. "When we gonna hang out and talk the shit?"

"We can do it anytime."

Jamal didn't believe him. "Now, you know that ain't true. Even I've been realizing that I gotta put Cindy first. Ain't no woman in recent memory had me acting like this. I'm on some old exclusive tip right now and it's got me trippin', dude!"

"You sound like you're enjoying yourself to me, Jamal."

"Shit yeah, I'm having fun and I'm even thinking about surprising Cindy with a cruise to Ensenada."

"Oh yeah? Mexico?"

"Yeah. That way we'll be on the high seas and she'll be enjoying a brotha while surrounded by some muh-fuckin' fresh ocean air, I mean . . ."

Malcolm chuckled. "Jamal, you don't talk like that with Cindy, do you?"

"Hell yeah, shit!"

Malcolm laughed so loud that both Zahara and Imara looked over at him. He held his hand up to apologize for the sudden outburst.

"I can't believe you talk to her like you talk to me, Jamal."

"Nah, but on the real, she's cool with me talking shit to her 'cause she said that's me and at the same time it makes her laugh. I mean, that's what's been so cool about the whole situation, Malcolm. Cindy is so down to earth and real. She ain't trying to change a brotha and I ain't even mentioned how she got it going on behind closed doors. She was all shy when I stepped to her at the beach that time but once we got to talkin'? A brotha struck gold!"

"What do you mean, gold?"

"Freak city. She got fantasies up the kazoo, bro. Homegirl don't seem to be running out of ideas! Yo, I let her put a blindfold on me and tie my wrists to the bed."

"No you didn't."

"Yep. I mean, she ain't done nothing kinky to me, though. Nah, she just ran a big-ass feather up and down my body. You know, tried to tease a brotha . . . How's things with you anyway? I know how you are when you really into a lady."

"It's cool. Things been going really nicely."

"Have you heard from Shaylisa recently?"

"No, why, have you?"

"Nope."

"Why you ask, then?"

Zahara turned to look at Malcolm, noticing the obvious change in the tone of his voice. He tried to brush it off. He could feel Zahara's concerned and attentive eyes all over him. He placed the phone in his left hand instead of his right, hoping that he could block any view of his saddened eyes and quivering lips.

"So, what's up, bro? I think we definitely need to talk if you over there having thoughts about Shaylisa when you know you should be focused only on that lady you got with you now."

"Yeah, I guess so." Malcolm stood up, exited the living room, and went inside the kitchen. He couldn't talk freely with Zahara watching him so closely. Jamal had opened a floodgate of feelings and emotions with the mere mention of Shaylisa's name. Malcolm couldn't shake it off, and sitting in front of Zahara only made matters worse. He could already envision her asking if everything was all right, and the worst part of it was that he'd have to lie and say yes.

"Man, I can't believe after all this time you still carry feelings for that girl," Jamal said.

"I don't know. It's like this morning I was having these uneasy feelings when I was talking with her daughter. She started bringing up things about what her father does for her and that had an alarm going off inside my head. The first thing that came to mind was wishing I was back with Shaylisa."

"Damn, bro, you can't let that get to you. Of course the little girl is gonna be missing her father and making you feel like an outsider, but at the same time, you can't start bringing back those Shaylisa memories and screwing things up with Zahara. She probably can already sense that something is up. Ladies got radar when it comes to shit like that. Watch what happens when you get off this phone. She gonna look at you like there's already another woman in your bed, you feel me?"

"Yeah," Malcolm replied somberly.

"Yo, but check this out. Cindy knows your girl."

"Who, Zahara?"

"No, Shaylisa."

Malcolm hesitated for a moment and then leaned against the kitchen counter.

"What do you mean, she knows her?" he asked.

Jamal told him about Cindy's friendship with Shaylisa.

"She talks about me?"

"Yeah, but I ain't up on details about they conversations, a'ight?"

Malcolm listened closely to Jamal, unaware that Zahara had walked into the kitchen. With her eyes glued to Malcolm leaning against the counter, Zahara was puzzled by the sudden change in his behavior. She wondered if this had to do with someone else or if maybe she'd said or done something wrong. Either way, Zahara didn't like the vibe she was feeling and hoped that she and Malcolm could talk about it.

She continued to stand there looking at Malcolm. Zahara was astounded by the fact that Malcolm hadn't noticed her enter the kitchen. He just kept listening to Jamal, and the expression on his face was one of worry and confusion. Zahara thought for a moment and realized that she'd come into the kitchen for a specific reason. Moments ago she'd heard a noise at the door and wanted to let Malcolm know. She cleared her throat to alert Malcolm that she was in the room. But he was so deep into the conversation that he didn't hear Zahara at all.

"Excuse me, Malcolm?" Zahara finally got his attention.

"Hold on, Jamal. Yeah, what's up, Zahara?"

"I heard a sound at your front door. Maybe someone's out there?"

"No, that's probably the um, the mailman. They usually deliver around this time of the day."

"Oh, okay. I was just wondering 'cause it startled Imara and me."

"No, that's probably what that was, just the mail."

"Hey!" Malcolm uttered before Zahara could turn and exit the kitchen. "Would you mind getting the mail for me? I'm expecting my American Express bill, which I know I'm gonna end up paying late this month." Malcolm attempted to smile.

"Sure, okay."

"Thanks."

Zahara flashed a fake smile before leaving Malcolm in the kitchen so he could return to his conversation with Jamal.

"Yo, Malcolm!" Jamal alerted. "You still kind of native, my brotha. How you be drawing all those details with your characters and still can't pick up on the obvious in your real life?"

"Huh?"

Jamal laughed. "Nothing. I'm just trying to show you the warning signs that you might be headed for some more drama. Look at you now, all concerned about Shaylisa instead of trying to hurry me off the phone 'cause you got company. I mean, homegirl in there seems cool, plus she got that bangin-ass body, which you should be putting your hands on right about now."

"Yeah, you right. I don't know. I just still wonder about Shaylisa. And now that you tell me Cindy is friends with her—"

"Yeah, I know," Jamal interrupted. "That's some more shit that I probably shouldn't have mentioned to you."

"Yeah, but we don't keep things from each other, right?"

"No, we don't, bro. I'm always gonna be real with you and tell you what I know."

"I appreciate that, Jamal, really."

"Well, I'm being real with you now, Malcolm, when I say you need to get rid of that baggage and do it before you lose out on a sista who's really gonna make you happy."

"Yeah, you're probably right," Malcolm replied, though not convincingly.

Malcolm's entire body language had changed at this point. He stood there, no longer the man who'd been enjoying a special weekend with a gorgeous lady and her daughter. Instead, he looked like one big question mark, filled with self-doubt. His behavior bordered on selfishness and stupidity. He'd begun his descent into the abyss of heartache and the illusion of believing that he'd be better off if Shaylisa was still the center of his life.

"What you doing, bro?" Jamal asked, noticing the silence had lingered longer than usual.

"Nothing, just thinking . . . Hold on, here comes Zahara."

Zahara walked toward Malcolm, waving the mail in her hand and giving it to Malcolm. Although she delivered the mail in an exuberant manner, Malcolm noticed her somber expression as soon as he placed the envelopes on the counter beside him.

"Thanks," Malcolm said as he leaned forward to kiss Zahara.

At the last second she closed her eyes and turned her face. She could feel his lips press against her cheek, but something was missing. She could sense that something was truly wrong with the man that she'd been falling in love with. She had something on her mind that needed addressing and that something could no longer wait.

"Malcolm, I think you have a letter from your ex," Zahara said calmly, pointing to the mail lying on the counter. Malcolm made a casual attempt to look at what she was referring to and could sense that trouble was brewing. Zahara's eyes were penetrating and filled with intense displeasure. Malcolm felt as though he were two seconds away from hearing that familiar cry, Don't fuck with me! He decided it would be best to end the phone conversation with Jamal.

"Let me call you back," he said.

"A'ight, I'll be here if you need me," Jamal replied.

Malcolm hung up the phone. "Now, what's wrong, Zahara?"

"Are you and your ex still talking?" Zahara asked.

"No, why?"

"I think you have a letter from her. Isn't her name Shaylisa Jones?"

"Yeah, but I haven't been in touch with her for a while now."

"I wish I could believe you, Malcolm."

"Why would I lie?"

"You tell me."

"Nothing to tell except that I haven't seen or spoken to her, as I said, since we broke up."

Malcolm chuckled nervously as Zahara stood with her arms folded and her attitude on the rise. She saw no reason for any attempt at laughter and found nothing humorous about the discussion they were having.

"Well, Malcolm, if that's the case, then is it all right for me to read the letter that she wrote to you?"

"Why do you keep talking about a letter, what letter?" Malcolm replied angrily. He still hadn't looked through the mail to see what Zahara was referring to.

"You're acting strange, Malcolm. It's like you're keeping something from me. I don't want to be in a relationship that's not open and honest. If you still have deep feelings for your ex, then maybe we shouldn't see each other."

"So what, you're just gonna walk out because I got a letter in the mail? That doesn't seem like you're being very understanding, Zahara."

"And you're not being very honest with me, Malcolm."

"I haven't lied to you!" Malcolm raised his voice slightly.

"Then you won't mind if I read the letter . . ."

Zahara reached for the letter but Malcolm intercepted her attempt. He thumbed through the mail and found the letter addressed to Malcolm Savoy Tyler. The handwriting was instantly recognizable.

Malcolm held up the letter. "Why would you think that I had anything to do with her writing to me?"

"Why else would she if she broke up with you?"

Malcolm shrugged. "I have no clue."

"Then let me read it . . ." Zahara voiced her command for the third time and that was it. Malcolm had struck out.

"I can't let you do that, sorry."

"I think I need to go, Malcolm."

"Go, why?"

"You really need me to tell you why?"

Zahara held her emotional ground despite the fact that her heart was hurting so much. Malcolm had quietly dissed her and disappointed her in such a profound way with his continued loyalty to someone who had supposedly broken his heart. Zahara came to the quick resolution that in a crisis, Malcolm would surely run to his ex first instead of the new woman in his life, who not only attempted to help him heal but also tried to show him that love could once again feel like something special. Love could become his center, his inspiration, and his motivation for wanting more out of life than just a cool place to live and a nice car.

As Malcolm continued to prevent Zahara from reading the letter, his gesture opened one of Zahara's deepest wounds. She'd hoped to never find herself in a situation where she would give her heart to someone who continued to love another.

"Imara?" Zahara cried out while maintaining eye contact with Malcolm in the kitchen. "Get your things, sweetheart, we're leaving!"

"You don't have to leave, Zahara," Malcolm uttered quietly.

"I don't like what I'm feeling, Malcolm, so it's best that I do leave."

Malcolm couldn't figure out what to say next. He stood there holding the letter he'd received from Shaylisa as he watched Zahara turn and walk away. It wasn't long before he heard the front door slam and an aftermath of silence engulfed his town house. There was no television noise coming from the living room, no sounds of running water coming from the bathroom, and no beautiful voice calling his name. He was alone with a letter from someone who continued to permeate his thoughts, long after that person told him it was over. Did she want to come back? Did she miss him? Did she struggle to move on with her life, just as he did with his? Did she ever reach out for him, only to open her eyes and feel a part of her was missing?

After sitting in silence for a while, Malcolm debated whether to read the letter from Shaylisa. His first reaction was to put it down because he feared what she may have written. He followed that up with thoughts of trying to forget the letter even existed. Maybe he could throw it away, therefore proving that he was completely over Shaylisa and wasn't interested in anything she had to say. Malcolm sighed heavily. There's absolutely no way I could find the strength to do that! he thought.

• • •

THE MORE THINGS CHANGE, the more they stay the same, Malcolm thought to himself. He couldn't believe that one letter from Shaylisa would stir up the kind of emotions that would leave him confused and yearning to finally be over this woman who apparently impacted his life significantly. She'd become a constant memory that presented itself in the form of an emotional roadblock. A very addictive memory, to say the least. He'd even toyed with the idea of seeing a psychiatrist, or maybe somewhere out there was a self-help group for victims of can't-get-over-my-ex-and-don't-know-what-to-do-about-it syndrome. Malcolm had listened to a radio program the other night that spoke of self-determination and how people control their futures. At this very moment, Malcolm felt no sense of control and fought constantly against the determination to move on. Inside his soul was a serious war going on between thoughts of Zahara, feelings for Shaylisa, and that selfish demon lurking about that made him want to shut off the world and tell everybody to fuck off.

Why so committed? His heart wouldn't change the direction it was headed since the first day he met Shaylisa. Why? That's the question he pondered intensely. He had been carrying himself unaware of the fact that he wouldn't let go.

Then there was Zahara. She was exactly what he needed. A woman who in the past couple of weeks had shown him what it was like to be loved, nurtured, appreciated, and adored. All of these were ingredients he'd never truly seen with Shaylisa but believed existed somewhere underneath the surface.

Malcolm sat on the sofa in his living room, still wrestling with his thoughts about opening the letter. This is so crazy and so stupid, the way I'm acting! Malcolm thought. Still, that realization couldn't motivate him to rip open the envelope and read what was inside. He placed the envelope on the coffee table, sat back, and glared at the address written on the front by Shaylisa. Her handwriting stirred up so many memories. Those times when he relished the fact that she'd written him a thank-you note for something he'd done for her, or when he came home to find a flirtatious message on the refrigerator telling him to be available for some lovin'. Malcolm smiled. His thoughts, though surrounded by silence, spoke volumes to what he continued to feel. He leaned forward to pick up the envelope again but was interrupted by the telephone ringing. Malcolm was startled, causing him to sound out of breath when he answered.

"Malcolm? This is Zahara."

"Yeah, I know."

"Oh, you know, huh?" Zahara replied with a hint of anger in her voice.

"I don't mean it that way . . ."

"I really hate that I walked out on you, but I didn't know what to think or how to feel. I mean first it was the phone call and then the letter . . ."

"The phone call? What do you mean?"

"You seemed to have changed all of a sudden. Your tone of voice, emotionally, everything!"

Malcolm paused for a moment. "I'm not sure what to say, Zahara. Jamal told me something that kind of brought back feelings, you know?"

"No, I don't know, Malcolm. Last night felt really good between us—"

"It was good, it was great!" Malcolm interrupted.

"Was?"

"You know what I mean."

"No, I'm not really sure what you mean, Malcolm, or even how you feel at this point. I thought you and I were headed somewhere very special. I've never been with a man who was so willing to share his feelings, or so I thought! Now it feels like you're not even the same person."

Zahara's emotions simmered rather than boiled. She didn't allow herself to lose her cool, though she wanted to. She wanted to scream and cry. She felt as if her heart had been wounded and wasn't sure if Malcolm even cared. Pain was oozing from her pores. She even imagined hurting Malcolm with the intention of showing him how she felt right now. There was one problem; he already knew.

"Malcolm, am I merely someone you're seeing on the rebound? I feel set up. I feel angry, Malcolm. I feel like I wasted valuable time with you. It's as if you've been stringing me along until you saw the first sign that you could return to your ex."

"This wasn't a rebound situation, Zahara. I care for you. I enjoy being with you, a lot. I had so much fun last night and cooking for your daughter was really cool too."

Zahara took note that Malcolm only said he cared for her and didn't mention love. "All that sounds great, Malcolm, but it still seems to me like you carry deep feelings for your ex. Is she still your ex?"

"What do you mean?"

"Maybe in that letter she's asking you to get back with her."

Malcolm looked at the envelope, forgetting for a moment that he was on the phone with Zahara.

"Hello. Well?" Zahara asked, sounding like she was losing her patience.

"I don't know. I haven't opened the letter yet."

"You expect me to believe that, Malcolm?"

"Why would I lie? I really haven't opened the letter."

"Whatever . . . Listen, Malcolm, I think you really need to figure out how you feel about me, about her . . . maybe then we can sit down and talk things through. I don't believe we can go any further unless you know where your heart is."

"So, when am I gonna see you again, Zahara?"

"I'm here, Malcolm, that's really up to you."

Malcolm paused. "Okay. I'll call you later."

Zahara hung up without saying anything.

Malcolm decided it was time to open the letter. He leaned forward, picked it up, and began slowly tearing it open. The sound of it tearing was magnified by the silence that engulfed his living room. The letter was now open and Malcolm gazed at the first words written on the page. "Dearest Malcolm," Shaylisa had written.

Seeing those words immediately caused Malcolm's heart to beat rapidly. Dearest Malcolm! Could it be that she's about to apologize for breaking up with me and wants to get back together? He could hear Shaylisa's voice so vividly, as if she were sitting right next to him. He closed his eyes and imagined just that. His vision comforted his anxiety. He opened his eyes slowly and began reading the letter.

Dearest Malcolm,

Yes, it's me, and I can already picture the surprise and shock on your face when you find this letter in your mailbox.

I hope this letter finds you in good spirits, though I wouldn't be surprised if it took you a while before you opened it. I'm probably not the most welcomed person in your life right now. The sight of me, the thought of me probably doesn't give you a good feeling. I heard that you're seeing someone now. I want to say that's great, but selfishly speaking, I didn't expect you to get over me so soon. That's mean of me to say, huh? Smile. Well, I don't want you to think that I'm making attempts to pry or mess up what you have right now. I know all too well how loving and sweet you are. I know that once someone enters your life and you see there's hope of something special, you focus all your attention on that person. I'm not gonna lie, I miss that kind of attention. I miss being spoiled by such a giving man.

Well, let me cut to the chase. I was motivated to write you because I looked at my calendar yesterday. In a few days it will be April 30th. You remember that day? I probably shouldn't ask you that because you were the one that always reminded me. I laugh when I think about how you surprised me by remembering the first day that we'd met. Before you, I'd never had a man in my life who would remember important days in a relationship. That's usually something that women do, and I sort of resolved not to pay attention 'cause I'd been so fed up with being the only one to remember. You made me feel guilty many times about not remembering things. Well, Malcolm, here I am, remembering and asking if maybe we could talk or perhaps do lunch, just to celebrate the day we met. Maybe I shouldn't say "celebrate" because of recent events between us, but I think it would be nice to recognize somehow that very special day.

I have a lot to say in this letter, huh? Smile. Well, call me and let me know if you want to get together. You can even come over here if you'd like. I'll cook that meat loaf you always go crazy over. That makes me smile because you know it's my mother's recipe and yes, it is the bomb! Smile. Anyway, let me know, okay? And Malcolm, I'm not trying to make you uncomfortable. There's no pressure. Let's have a good time and see what happens.

Love,
Shaylisa

"See what happens?" "Love, Shaylisa?" Malcolm's heart was on fire. His hands were shaking as he tried unsuccessfully to fold the letter into its original state. He wasn't sure what to do. Not even sure how to respond or to feel. This was what he'd wanted?

Malcolm nervously opened the letter again. He gazed at the section that spoke of how he is, or was, when a woman entered his life. It was true that he'd shower that woman with attention and show her what it's like to be loved in the most sincere way by a man unafraid to do so.

His thoughts made him sit back in silence. He reflected. He thought about Zahara and then he thought about Shaylisa. Her letter was a beacon of light. The brightness was so profound as he leaned forward to pick up the telephone.

He needed to make this call because he'd discovered what he truly wanted. He found that place in his heart that was real and felt right. A dreamy place with no sadness or stress to speak of. In this place he could reflect on one person who inspired him and contributed to his feeling like the man that he knew he could be, especially if given the opportunity. A confident man and a man unafraid to discover the kind of love that lasts beyond forever. He dialed the phone number with a gentle smile on his face. He listened; after two rings, there was a voice on the other end.

"Hello," she answered.

"Shaylisa, hello, this is Malcolm."

"It's really nice to hear from you. I guess you got my letter, huh?"

"Yeah, I did." Malcolm smiled. "I'm blessed to hear from you and surprised that you remembered. I guess you could say that it made my day and I was touched."

"That's sweet."

"Yeah, just reading your words really took me back, Shaylisa. I mean memories started flowing like crazy. My feelings just seem to have picked up where they left off. I don't know, but it felt . . . good, interesting . . ."

"It's nice to hear you say that, Malcolm. I thought for sure that you would've thrown the letter away as soon as you saw it was from me. You didn't think about doing that?" Shaylisa chuckled. "I figure you'd say a few curse words too!"

"No, I was nervous about reading it but never had any disrespectful thoughts."

"What am I gonna do with you, Malcolm? You're still a sweetheart, still the same even when someone has done you wrong."

"I guess I'm stuck with being like this."

"Well, you should never change . . ."

"Hmm . . . change." Malcolm paused. He thought for a moment and smiled. "I can't really speak about change but I can do my best to grow . . ." he told her.

"I like the way you grow too, Malcolm," Shaylisa said flirtatiously, attempting to take the conversation in a more sexual direction.

"Thanks, but I'm sure you know what I mean, really. I'm growing, Shaylisa, and I want to thank you for that."

"I aim to please, sweetheart."

"Yes, I remember, but this time you've done more than that. You shined the light on what I've wanted for a long time. You took me back to how I felt when you and I first met, and yet, that memory or perhaps discovery has now opened my eyes to the importance of what I have now."

"You mean, when we get together for our anniversary?" Shaylisa asked.

"No, I'm talking about love, true, sincere, passionate, totally-into-and-don't-want-to-part kind of love . . ."

"Malcolm, I told you there was no pressure between us. Let's get together, have fun, talk . . . and whatever happens just happens!"

"It already happened, Shaylisa."

Malcolm felt relaxed. He smiled and relished the fact that Shaylisa had no clue what he was speaking of, nor did she know the beauty of what he'd been feeling.

"Malcolm, I'm not understanding you. Did you want to come over here for our anniversary or you want to go out somewhere? I know this really cool club in Santa Monica that has poetry-reading rooms and in other rooms you can shake your ass and all that good stuff." Shaylisa chuckled.

"Shaylisa, thank you for showing me what love is truly about. Thank you for reminding me of how I approach and pursue love. Thank you for reminding me of who I deserve in my life. A wise person once told me that one day when I least expected it, someone special would find me and she'd be the one. Today you showed me that I've indeed been found!"

"You're so sweet, Malcolm. So, what time are we gonna get together? Shoot, the way you're talking, you can come over now!"

Malcolm paused. "No, as I said, you allowed me to really rediscover who I am and how I love, so I've got to say thank you, and I've got to say good-bye."

"What?"

"Yeah, I have to call my lady Zahara, apologize, and pray that she accepts my growth, my discovery, and my wish of being her man, if she'll have me."

"Listen, I wrote you a letter—"

"Yes," Malcolm interrupted, "and I am so thankful to you because it came when I needed it the most . . ."

"You gonna have me wasting time like that and turn me down?"

"Stay sweet, Shaylisa. I don't want this moment to turn ugly. Thanks so much again . . . truly, you pointed me in the right direction."

Malcolm hung up before he could hear Shaylisa's last words. They didn't sound too kind and he didn't really want his last memory of her to be her idea of where he should go. He was feeling like the weight of the world was off his shoulders, and he couldn't wait to begin his new journey. He felt whole, and he needed or perhaps wanted to be in the presence of a woman who was also whole.

"Hello?" a beautiful, silky voice answered.

"Zahara, this is Malcolm!" he said with pride, smiling.

It felt incredible to hear the voice of someone who he'd shared such an instant connection with. A beautiful, intelligent, spiritual, sensual being that knew without a doubt the sincerity behind a man's voice and eyes, and the depth of his soul. Zahara felt like home. Zahara felt like a prayer. Zahara felt like the wind whispering love in his ear. Malcolm listened and shed a tear. His heart was ready to take on its biggest challenge to date and he was ready to be a whole man.

"Hey you, I'm glad you called," Zahara replied.

"Me too . . . more than you'll ever know, but I intend to change that. I was wondering if I could, share my feelings with you, beginning now."

ACKNOWLEDGMENTS

Much love and endless thanks to Zane and Sister Charmaine for everything and more. Opportunities are endless and blessings come often when inspired by your examples . . . Also, special thanks to Malaika Adero and Krishan Trotman.

Special shout-outs to the women that broke my heart. Thanks for the inspiration that runs real deep . . .

Warm Blessings,
V. Anthony Rivers
Dreamstyle@aol.com

$\mathscr{S}$taring Evil in the Face

ZANE

*This novella is dedicated to all the people in the world
who have ever tried to make a failing relationship work.
Remember that everything happens for a reason
and if you never face pain, you will never recognize pleasure.*

ROBIER

Tiphanie slid in the house like a snake, trying to prevent me from hearing her. The time was five past noon on a Saturday. She had been missing since Wednesday evening. Once again, she had failed to pick up the kids from school that day. Embarrassment was the least of my emotions. How could a mother forget about her own kids? Over and over? The answer was simple. My wife, Tiphanie, was a drug addict and drug addicts only care about one thing: getting high.

"Tiphanie, are you all right?" I asked her, entering the foyer from the kitchen, where the kids were eating the chicken fingers, fries, and applesauce I had prepared them for lunch.

She was stunned by my appearance. She thought she would make it upstairs and hide under the covers for at least a few hours before we caught wind of her being home. Not a chance. We had been around that block too many times.

"I said, are you all right?"

"I'm fine, Robier."

She leaned against the banister, letting her right foot rest on the bottom step. She was bone-thin and frail. If someone blew on her too hard, she would probably tip over.

"You don't look fine. You look like a skeleton."

"Shit! Do we have to go through this bullshit every damn day? I'm sick and tired of you treating me like a fucking baby!"

There it was. The anger. The lashing out at me as if I were the one who had neglected our home and family for three days.

I lowered my voice to a whisper, hoping she would not yell out again with the kids in the other room. "Tiphanie, we don't discuss this every day. You're not here half the time. Hell, you just got back from another disappearing act."

She sighed, glared at me, and put her hand on her hip. "I need to get some sleep."

I caught up to her by the time she made it to the fourth step and grabbed her elbow.

"No way. My mother's on her way over here to watch the kids. I was going out to search for you but now I'm taking you to the emergency room."

She tried to yank her arm away but was too weak to do so.

"The only place I'm going is up here to bed. I need to take some medicine and lie down."

"Medicine?" I asked, feeling myself getting heated. I had promised myself that I would be compassionate with her, if and when she did turn up. "You mean pain pills?"

"What-the-fuck-ever!"

"Mommy!" I heard Lennox call from the next room.

Our four-year-old son was extremely attached to his mother. He would soon be crawling down from his chair to come see her. I didn't want him to see his mother like this, so I let Tiphanie's arm loose. She ran up the stairs. She did not want him to see her in that state either. She never did.

"Tiphanie, I love you. I'm here for you, baby," I called after her. "Let me help you help yourself."

She glanced down over the railing at me. "I don't need help with shit!"

"The truly sad part is that you probably honestly believe that nonsense."

"It's not nonsense." She paused at the master bedroom door. For a second, I saw the real Tiphanie flicker in her eyes. "Seriously, Robier. I'm exhausted. Let me grab some sleep. We'll talk later."

No sooner had she closed the door than Lennox came rushing into the foyer. "Was that Mommy?"

"Yeah, little man," I said, coming back down the few steps. "Mommy's home but she's resting right now."

He frowned. "She's always resting."

I lifted him up in my arms. He had the same curly brown hair and sparkling brown eyes as his mother.

"Lennox, sometimes she needs a little more sleep than the rest of us."

"Is Mommy sick? Where has she been? Why didn't she pick us up from school the other day?"

I bit my bottom lip, not knowing how to respond. I did what was normal for me: I tickled him. This worked sometimes, but I realized that it wouldn't always work as a method to distract him from concerns about his mother. Sooner or later he would figure out Tiphanie was not a normal mother. His eleven-year-old sister, Carson, already had; her disappointment and sadness were growing daily. What a terrible thing it is that today's children grow up so much faster and know more about adult issues than we did. Carson had surely heard Tiphanie come in but made no move to come check on her.

I flung Lennox over my shoulder and carried him back into the kitchen so he could finish his lunch.

Fifteen minutes later, Momma was at the door. I had called her on her cell to alert her that Tiphanie was back. Like everyone else, she had been worried sick. I did not want to wait for her to arrive to put her somewhat at ease. To some degree, my pain was her pain, but her main concern was her grandchildren and the stability of their home. My parents had witnessed it all over the years. My father remained calm but my mother was fed up. Her attitude toward my wife had turned to straight-up resentment.

"So where is the crazy bitch?" Momma asked the second I opened the door.

"Momma, don't talk about my wife like that. Please. I've asked you many times before."

I glanced toward the family room in the rear of the house, where Carson and Lennox were watching music videos. The last thing I needed was for them to hear Momma and me going at it too.

"Son, the time has come for you to face reality. Tiphanie is beyond help." She came all the way in and closed the front door. "The woman you married and had children with died years ago."

I was floored. "How can you say that?"

She held her palm up in the air, her religious stance. Both of my parents were devout Christians. "Because it's the gospel."

I found myself rolling my eyes, something I rarely did to anyone, much less the woman who birthed me.

"Are you still willing to babysit the kids?" I asked.

She flung her heavy purse from one shoulder to the other. "As far as I'm concerned, I can't babysit my own grands. They're as much my babies as they are yours."

"I'll take that as a yes."

She went to the coat closet, opened it, and started getting coats off hangers for Carson and Lennox.

"I'm not staying here with them. We'll be at my house." She eyed the master bedroom door, probably hoping she could bore a hole through Tiphanie with her X-ray vision. "They're only going to be young once and neither one of them needs to be subjected to this nightmare."

I decided the best thing to do would be to rush them out of there. Momma was on the verge of losing her religion and going on a rampage.

"Thanks for coming to get them, Momma."

"It's not an issue, Robier. But if you don't do something about that cra— woman soon, it's going to become an issue. Your daddy and I are reaching the point where we're ready to petition the courts for custody."

My knees weakened and I had to find the wall to hold me up. "Oh, God! Momma, no!"

She stared me down. "Someone has to protect those children." She pointed to the family room, where we could hear music and the kids laughing. "I realize you didn't set out to marry a drug addict and Tiphanie certainly didn't intentionally become one. Still, facts are facts and the situation is what it is. You need to make a choice."

"A choice?"

"Yes, Tiphanie or your children." She waved her index finger in my face. "There can never be one happy family in this house. You've practically run yourself into the ground, trying to help her and chase her down from drug house to drug house. How are my grands going to benefit with a father in the ground and a mother in a crack house?"

I was angry then. Not because she was wrong. Because she was right. I had been suffering from anxiety attacks and chest pains lately. The stress was taking an obvious toll on me, both emotionally and physically.

"That's enough, Momma!"

I was ready for her to slap me for disrespecting her. Even grown children are supposed to respect their parents. Instead, she grabbed my chin and kissed me on the cheek.

"No, Robier, it's not nearly enough." She sighed and headed for the family room to gather the kids. "But it will have to be enough for today."

Momma decided she would keep them overnight and take them to church on Sunday. Lennox was delighted because a visit to his grandparents' house meant ice cream sundaes and baking home-made cookies. Carson had made plans with a neighbor girl to go to the movies. This forced her to change those plans, but she managed to keep a straight face as she went upstairs to her room to pack an overnight bag. She realized it would be better for her to go to her grandparents'. There would likely be serious drama at our house when Tiphanie woke up, and she did not want to be a witness to it.

Once they were gone, I went into the kitchen and fixed some chicken-noodle soup for Tiphanie and me. She would be starving when she finally resurfaced. I sat at the kitchen counter and lost myself in thought. How had it all happened? We once lived a fairy tale. Now we were both staring evil in the face.

SPRING 1990

The first day of spring lived up to its word, bringing green grass, a bright sun, and a clear blue sky that almost seemed mystical. I was feeling great about life and it showed as I used my perfected pimp walk to make my way across campus. I was on the way back to my dorm from a marketing class. I had already nailed straight A's on an eighteen-credit course load, but the second semester of my freshman year at Blake University was destined to be more special than the first.

Among the things that made my experience unique were the honies on top of honies at the school, nestled at the base of the Virginia mountains. The campus was small but big enough to enjoy a pleasant social life, including enough sex to tide a brother over. The student population was multiracial. Since I'd grown up in Washington, D.C., that was a new situation for me. Prior to then, all of my classmates—with the exception of ten or fewer—had been African-American like me. But I adapted quickly, realizing that people are simply people and that was cool.

I had dated more than my share of cutie pies during that first semester, acting like a starved homeless man who had suddenly come across a feast meant for a king. I had sampled Afro-Cuban, Asian, Indian, and Puerto Rican cuisines. The African-American sisters in my classes did not seem to be feeling me. I was ready for them, though. The majority of them were sensual enough to grace my bed any night.

My roommate was a guy called Muffin—a shitty-ass name for a man. But he liked it. Muffin's real name was Derrick Connors. It was obvious his nickname derived from the fact that he was on the chubby side. Derrick claimed an ex-girlfriend had tagged him with the name because he had a huge, fat dick. I had no aspirations to gain knowledge of another man's dick size but couldn't help but notice, by the flatness of the front of his jeans, that he was exaggerating big-time. Either way, he loved the name enough to let it follow him to college from Los Angeles. After all, no one would have possibly figured out his nickname was Muffin if he had not revealed it.

Both of us were majoring in marketing, which was why they roomed us together. But that's where our similarities ended. Otherwise, Muffin and I were like night and day. I loved to party; he loved to study. I wanted to get laid; Muffin wanted to get married. I wanted to be rich; Muffin wanted to make a difference. I wanted to drink beer until I passed out and blast R&B music; Muffin wanted to drink herbal tea and listen to gospel music.

Muffin had pictures of his family all over his side of our room. It seemed like someone's grandmother's house instead of a bachelor pad. I was embarrassed to bring women in there. My side of the room had posters of sexy women adhered to the wall with various color thumbtacks. His side of the room had professionally framed photographs of his immediate family. He was the oldest of three kids. He had two younger sisters, Tiphanie and Angelica. He kept his side as neat as a pin, while I enjoyed my sudden newfound freedom from my parents and threw a piece of clothing here or there for good measure. Momma couldn't get on my back daily for not picking them up and I found that awesome.

I tried to stay out of the room as much as possible, choosing to hang out in the room of my buddies Craig and Neal, two white boys from West Virginia who acted "blacker" than me. They taught me more about rap music than BET. People may think inner-city youths are the biggest buyers of rap CDs, but the ones in the country really keep them in business. The hip-hop lifestyle is exciting to them because they don't witness the downside of pimping and drug slinging. Still, I was digging Craig and Neal and I had to pass the time in some way. I did have one other pastime, though: pussy.

I was getting a lot of pussy in college. I swear it helped me with my grades. The adrenaline from a "great fuck" worked wonders for my brain activity. Without a doubt, I was the typical "pitbull" and proud of it. I was not looking to settle down in a relationship. I had been in two serious ones already and I was only eighteen. First there was this girl Kendall Trueman who had kept me on lockdown all throughout middle school. Then Lisa Edwards occupied my high school years. I believed that I was in love with Lisa. But, as it turned out, she was in love with practically everyone else but me. My high school sweetheart was riding every dick she could hop on. Since she was the finest sister in school, getting play was easy for her. I only wish she had clued me in earlier. To think about all the bomb-ass pussy I missed out on because of her was sickening. Now I was making up for lost time and had zero intention of settling down.

Yet, as crazy as it seems, I was growing obsessed with one girl, someone I had never actually met. Because I did at least sleep in my room, I would often wake up and find myself staring at a photo of Muffin's sister Tiphanie. The rising sun seemed to spotlight it in its silver frame with a vine border. She was a senior in high school and the most beautiful woman I had ever seen. She had this smile that lit up the entire room, even through a picture. She had curly brown hair and sparkling eyes. She looked innocent but I imagined making love to her on a sandy beach in the middle of nowhere, having her stare up at me with desire in those eyes and whisper my name.

She often called the room looking for Muffin. We talked but our conversations were always brief. "Hello, is Muffin there?" "No, he's not here right now. Can I take a message?" "Yes, could you tell him that his sister Tiphanie called?" "Sure, no problem." "Thanks. Bye." "Bye."

Her voice was soft, pleasant, and sweet, adding to my fantasies of her. It got to the point where I found myself daydreaming about her in class and even pretended like I was boning her a time or two when I was drilling my dick into other women from behind. Quite honestly, it was getting kind of scary. Being infatuated with a stranger was wild, a stranger who was undoubtedly as religious and subdued as her brother.

Muffin did at least engage in sex, although half the time he seemed like he might be afraid of an actual pussy sighting. He was dating Selma, this sophomore from Atlanta. Selma was as nerdy as they come, but he was digging her and it was his business. They did things like play lacrosse and ride horses. How fucking lame could they get? I wondered if Tiphanie was sexually active or celibate, or possibly even still hanging on to her virginity. As if I would ever get to find out!

Then it happened. Muffin came in the room one day, that first day of spring, and rocked my world.

"Robier, heads-up. My parents and sisters are coming to visit for a couple of days."

"Really!" I jumped up off my bed before I could control myself. Muffin chuckled. "Wow, I didn't expect that reaction."

"What reaction?" I asked, clearing my throat and sitting down at my desk. "I only hopped up because I forgot there's a paper due in tomorrow and I haven't started it yet."

"Oh," he replied. "You mean the one on product placement?"

"Yeah, that one." I had done the paper already but pretended to be busy anyway, flipping through the textbook for that particular class.

"Okay. Well, anyway, they'll be here Friday and they're staying the weekend."

I glanced up at him. "In here?"

He chuckled again. "Of course not. The two of us can barely fit in here. Why would my parents and sisters stay here?"

I shrugged. "I don't know. Just asking, since you said you were giving me a heads-up."

"They will be coming by. Of course, they want to see where I stay. Los Angeles isn't exactly a hop, skip, and a jump from here."

"True that."

"Since you're my roommate, they'll want to meet you. See who my new friends . . . acquaintances are."

I turned my chair around to face him. "Muffin, we are friends. We don't have a lot of the same habits, but that's what makes life interesting."

He grinned at me, a rarity. "Great! I was beginning to think I was getting on your nerves. We do have many obvious differences. I don't want to seem imposing."

"It's all gravy with me."

There I was, lying. He did get on my nerves with a lot of his bullshit, but hey, it was time to butter him up. I needed to do more than "meet" his family. I wanted to get to spend some bonding time with Tiphanie.

•   •   •

I walked in the room that Friday evening to find the entire gang. Mr. and Mrs. Connors were pleasant and looked exactly like their photos, which was strange. Most people appear slightly different in pictures. Angelica was a thirteen-year-old cutie who seemed fascinated with being on a college campus. Tiphanie was sitting on my bed, right the hell where she belonged. She was ten times finer than her pictures, something I did not think was humanly possible until the vision was before me. She smiled at me after I had shaken hands and introduced myself to the rest of her family. I smiled right back at her and took her tender, soft, delectable, tasty-looking right hand into my left.

"I'm Robier Martin," I said.

"Tiphanie Connors."

"Nice to meet you."

"Nice to meet you."

"Robier, we were about to go have dinner in town," Mr. Connors said. "Would you like to join us?"

"I'd love to. I'm starving," I said, not missing a beat. I had eaten in the student union thirty minutes earlier but did not hesitate to accept his invitation.

We went to this overcrowded steakhouse. In small towns with little else going on, the few restaurants they do have stay packed on weekends. That is one of the few out-of-the-home activities most of the residents have to enjoy. Feeding their faces and spending all their extra cash in the local Wal-Mart. The wait for the table was more than an hour. I purposely snuggled up next to Tiphanie on one of the benches out front while we listened to them yell out party name after party name. They were not modernized enough to have those hand buzzers many restaurants use today, so every few minutes a country-ass voice yelled out someone's surname.

My goal was simple: Convince Tiphanie to attend Blake when she graduated. She had zero interest in that at the beginning of our conversation, having settled on staying close to home and attending UCLA in Westwood. That was not an option for me. She had to attend Blake or bust.

"You know, there are a lot of advantages to attending a small school. At larger universities, you're nothing but a number. You'll get lost in the mix."

She had me hypnotized with her eyes. "But Blake is in the middle of nowhere. What do you guys do for fun?" She surveyed the restaurant. "Surely this can't be all there is."

"Oh, no," I said. "We have tons of fun. Take Muffin, for example. He and his girl play lacrosse and ride horses all the time."

Tiphanie threw her head back in laughter. I thought it was because of the activities I listed. I was incorrect.

"Muffin has a girl?" she asked incredulously. "This must be some school, if Muffin has a girl."

Muffin eyed us suspiciously from across the walkway, where he was waiting on the opposite side on a bench with Angelica and his parents. It was a mixture of expressions, one stating that I better not be spreading his business and the other stating that I better not try to lay a hand on his sister.

It suddenly dawned on me that Selma was noticeably absent from the list of dinner invitees. He was trying to hide the fact that he was boning a chick from them. I chuckled under my breath.

"Tiphanie, can I ask you a serious question?"

"Sure."

"You promise you won't be offended?"

She shrugged. "We just met. How could you offend me?"

"Your brother is kind of different. Not in a bad way, but different. I guess what I'm asking is, are you like him or are you normal?"

She snickered and punched me gently on the arm. "You're funny!"

"I'm trying to keep it real. I'll keep it even more real." I took her hand, a bold move considering her entire family was staring us down. "Ever since I first saw your picture, I've been interested in getting to know you better. I realize this sounds absolutely crazy, but I think you're the right woman for me, as much as there can be a right woman."

"Robier, how old are you?" she asked me.

"Eighteen, and you?"

"Seventeen."

I grabbed her hand tighter. "Your point?"

"Aren't we kind of young for you to make that determination?"

"Maybe. Maybe not."

"Hmmph."

I did not like that "hmmph" at all. "What does that mean?" I asked.

"It means that I'm pondering what you said."

"But I'm only getting started. I have a lot more to say."

She glanced down at her watch on her free wrist. "Well, we probably have at least another forty minutes before they call us to a table, so . . ."

"So?"

"Go for it. Tell me what's on your mind. You're handsome, you seem nice, you seem safe enough, so holler at a sister."

We both laughed. No, Tiphanie was definitely not like Muffin. She was straight-up cool and I was about to do exactly what she suggested and "go for it."

DINNER WENT OFF WITHOUT a hitch. Everyone filled their bellies with oversize steaks, stuffed baked potatoes, and gigantic salads. It never ceases to amaze me how large the portions of food are in American restaurants. I traveled most of the world with my parents as a child and noticed the difference even then. American restaurants feed us to death and then everyone wonders why so many of us are overweight.

Tiphanie and I had spent the additional waiting time, which turned out to be exactly fifty-seven minutes, to get to know each other and to make plans. We were rushing the others through dinner because of those plans they knew nothing about. When they decided to order dessert, I almost screamed. I could not wait to get her alone.

AT EXACTLY MIDNIGHT, TIPHANIE snuck out of the motel room she was sharing with Angelica—adjacent to her parents'—and got into my black 1980 Chevy Caprice. I sped off from the gravel parking lot, kicking up pebbles like we were Bonnie and Clyde. Muffin had caught hell from Selma when we returned from dinner. Someone in the small school had decided to stir up trouble and had spilled the beans about his family being in town. Selma demanded to know why he had not "shown her off" to them at dinner and Muffin looked like Boo Boo the Fool. It gave me the excuse I needed to clear out of the room, so I was content. I told them to handle theirs and pretended like I was going to go chill with some of the fellas.

Tiphanie and I drove up to a secluded and romantic spot by the lake at the bottom of a mountain. I had discovered it one day when I was out canvassing the area for wildlife. The one thing I did enjoy about the outdoors was hunting. My father had been taking me since I was eight and I loved it. I wanted to get the lay of the land so I could invite him up to join me. My parents had been to see me a few times, but I went home to D.C. two weekends a month.

"How long do you think you can hang out?" I asked her, placing my arm around her shoulder.

She did not even flinch. "My parents sleep like logs and even if Angelica wakes up, she's not about to tattle. I have way too much dirt on her for that."

"Angelica?" I was stunned. "What kind of dirt could you possibly have on that sweet, innocent child?"

Tiphanie giggled. "Angelica has had at least three pregnancy scares already."

"You can't be serious?"

"I kid you not." She moved over closer to me on the seat. "But we're not here to talk about her, are we?"

"No, we're here to talk about us."

"Talk about us?" Tiphanie eased herself up so my face was mere inches from hers and drew my bottom lip into her mouth, suckled on it, and then let it go. "Or be about us?"

My dick instantly perked up. "Be about us?"

"Robier, I'm only here for a couple of days and rest assured that most of the time, my folks and Muffin will be watching me with eagle eyes. So that means we have tonight and tomorrow night to figure out if what you feel for me—all that you so adamantly spoke of earlier—is something to explore or discard."

"Wow, you sure you're only seventeen?" I asked jokingly. She seemed so sincere in her statement and it sounded like something that would come out of the mouth of a fifty-year-old woman.

"I'm seventeen but I know something good when I see it."

I took her hand in mine and slowly kissed each of her fingertips. "So do I. I've been thinking about you ever since I saw your picture on Muffin's wall." I leaned over and kissed her neck. "I've fantasized about you, over and over."

"What have you fantasized about, exactly?"

"Making love to you." Now I had gone and stunned myself. Even with Kendall and Lisa, the *L* word had never escaped my lips, and I had dated each of them for years.

I had cocked the gun; Tiphanie pulled the trigger. "Then make love to me, Robier. Right here, right now."

She began to unbutton her blouse, and I took it all in as she finished and it cascaded off her shoulders, revealing a white satin bra. "Do you like them?"

"I like the bra, but what's underneath?"

She grinned, reached behind her back, unsnapped her bra, and took it off. I drew in a breath. I had seen a lot of tits in my day, and had definitely sucked my share, but hers were special. Her nipples reminded me of small grapes, sweet and juicy. As she took off the rest of her clothes, all I could think about was her loveliness. She was everything I had ever imagined and more.

She reached for me and I went to her, climbing on top of her in my front seat and showering her with a rainstorm of kisses. She reciprocated and before I knew it, I was naked too. To this very day, I do not recall whether I or she took my clothes off. Tiphanie Connors had me sprung.

Once I entered her, I wanted to live inside of her forever. Her pussy was so wet and tight, I shuddered while she contracted her inner muscles, enveloping my dick like she was milking me of everything I was as a man. I stared into her sparkling eyes and promised her, "No matter what, this night will live forever in my heart."

She pulled my head onto her shoulder and whispered in my ear, "As it will in mine."

That night I fell in love with Tiphanie Connors. She fell in love with me. She did attend Blake and we dated throughout our college years. I changed to a double major, marketing and business administration, so I could stay in an extra year to be with her. We graduated together. Made love together. Grew into adulthood together. Then we got married, had a beautiful baby girl named Carson, and believed the future held nothing but success and happiness. We were so damn wrong.

SUMMER 1996

"Mr. Martin, I'm sorry to interrupt."

I was irritated at the sound of my secretary's voice blaring through the intercom. I had arranged a meeting with one of the top auto dealerships in the area to pitch a marketing campaign to them and had left express instructions not to be disturbed.

I grinned uneasily at the three men sitting at the conference room table with me as I picked up the phone, hitting her extension.

"Excuse me for one second, gentlemen." She picked up. "Yes, Harriet?"

"You have an emergency phone call."

"From whom?"

"Howard University Hospital. It's your wife."

If someone had ripped out my heart at that very second, I probably would not have noticed.

"Mr. Martin? Mr. Martin? Are you there?" Harriet yelled into the phone, waking me back up from the dazed stupor I had fallen into.

"I'm here. I'll be right out." I got up from the table. "Gentlemen, I apologize. I'm going to have to reschedule."

"Is everything okay?" the general manager of their company inquired.

"Something has happened with my wife. I have to go."

I dashed out the room before anyone could respond and headed for Harriet's desk. I grabbed the phone from her before she could blink twice at me.

"This is Mr. Martin."

"Mr. Martin, this is Dr. Boulder from Howard University Hospital."

"What's happened to my wife?" I demanded to know.

"Mrs. Martin was involved in a multivehicle accident on Florida Avenue. She's been admitted."

"Is it serious?"

There was a pause. "Mr. Martin, do you have someone who can drive you here? You should get here right away, but don't drive yourself. Maybe the young woman who answered the phone can—"

I hung up and ran for the elevator, banging on the down button with one hand and loosening my tie with the other.

I was in my 1995 Ford Explorer within two minutes and flying out the parking garage of my office building at Connecticut Avenue and K Street downtown.

"I hate this fucking traffic!" I slammed my fist repeatedly on the dashboard, wishing I could turn the SUV into a hovercraft.

When I arrived at the emergency room, there were people rushing around everywhere. I finally located a nurse who informed me Dr. Boulder was in surgery.

"Who is he operating on?" I whispered, already knowing the answer. "I'm Robier Martin. Is he in there cutting on my wife?"

The nurse seemed apprehensive. "Sir, why don't you have a seat in the waiting room. I'm going to have another staff doctor come out to speak with you."

Realizing no further information was forthcoming from her, I did as she suggested and sat in the crowded waiting room. I fought back tears. She was not dead. They would have told me when I first came in, even if they didn't want to tell me over the phone. She was the one in the operating room. She had to be. She could not be dead. If Tiphanie was dead, that meant I was dead too.

• • •

THE FIVE OR TEN minutes it took for a female doctor to appear and head toward me seemed like an eternity.

"Mr. Martin, I'm Dr. Stanton."

I stood up to face the music. "Tell me what's going on with my wife, please."

"Your wife was in a car accident and—"

"That much I know already!" I caught myself. "I'm sorry. I didn't mean to lash out at you. Please continue."

"She had some spinal-cord damage. Dr. Boulder is trying to repair it now. She's going to make it; we're confident of that, but . . ."

"But?"

"We can't make a determination on the extent of the spinal damage or what effect it will have on her quality of life."

"Quality of life?" That was a term I had hoped to never hear, not about anyone I held dear to my heart, especially not my wife.

"Mr. Martin, I won't attempt to cut corners with you. At this point, we can't be sure whether or not your wife will be able to walk again. She could end up as a paraplegic or quadriplegic. We simply can't tell."

I grabbed her shoulders. "Tiphanie can't live like that. It'll destroy her."

"Sir, please let me go."

I felt like such an ass. I released her and apologized. "I'm so sorry. I'm having a hard time with this. This morning, my wife and I made love, she left with our daughter for day care, and now this." I panicked. "I need to call my mother so she can pick up Carson."

Dr. Stanton touched me on the arm. "Mr. Martin, don't think the worst, but at the same time, you need to be prepared. Pray on this, and I'll pray with you. God does work miracles."

I got my father on the phone. He stayed calm—like that type of thing happened every day—but he did so for my sake. He said he would go get Carson himself so Momma could come to the hospital. He knew she would want to be there. He promised that he would take good care of his granddaughter and arrange for their neighbor to watch her when she got in from work. That way, he could come to the hospital to be by my side as well.

I went to the hospital chapel and prayed like I never had before. I prayed to the Lord to spare Tiphanie and to take her pain away, to give the pain to me instead. I prayed for Him to take me instead, if He needed another soul to leave the world that day. I needed Tiphanie. Carson needed Tiphanie. We needed to hold our family together.

TIPHANIE SURVIVED WITHOUT PARALYSIS, but she did experience excruciating pain. I could see it in her face. We all could. For the first month, they had to keep her on drugs constantly so she would be able to bear it. They slowly eased her off medication so she could be more alert and somewhat function.

Tiphanie was an interior designer, a far stretch from her college major of finance. She was content and that was all that mattered to me. Designing the furnishings that made others comfortable in their environments excited her. Now that she had to stay laid up in bed all the time, the joy had slowly dissipated from her life. She hated the fact that she could not play with Carson, an eighteen-month-old at the time. She hated the fact that she could not perform her regular household duties like cooking and cleaning. Taking care of her family was important to her. She had been raised to believe that a wife and mother does certain things.

I tried my best to convince her that everything would be fine. Marriage was for better or for worse and I was prepared to live up to my vows. I cared for her like she was an infant, caressed her all night long, and told her how much she meant to me.

Tiphanie seemed to make a full recovery about a year later. She was up and about and playing with Carson, cooking gourmet meals, and making love to me on a nightly basis like we were teenagers back at Blake. The new Tiphanie was amazing and I had never been more in love with her.

One day I came home from work early, wanting to surprise Tiphanie with roses and an offer to take her to her favorite Italian restaurant. Momma and Daddy were keeping Carson overnight and we needed the time alone. Her car was in the garage when I arrived, but I did not see her anywhere on the ground floor. I went upstairs and found her sprawled over our king-size mattress. The bed was stripped bare and the vision right away struck me as odd. Tiphanie never believed in lying on an uncovered mattress. She was meticulous in that way. Yet, there she was, facedown on our bed, still as a rock. I rushed to her and listened to her breathing. It was shallow. I shook her but she did not wake up. I flipped her over and shook her some more. Her eyelids fluttered but did not open all the way. Then I spotted it. A bottle of white pills that I recognized immediately. They were Percocets and, to my knowledge, she had not been prescribed pain pills in months. There was no label on the bottle—it had been scraped off—but I knew what it contained just the same.

I called 911 and told the dispatcher that I thought my wife had overdosed on pain pills. The few minutes it took the ambulance to arrive seemed like a thousand, but I was relieved when they pulled up and started working on her. They said her heart was not functioning properly and that she had to have her stomach flushed immediately. They gave Tiphanie something to help her throw up in the ambulance on the way to the hospital. Normally I would have been appalled, but not this time. Her vomit was like a Christmas present to me.

TIPHANIE

FALL 1997

Robier could be so overdramatic. After I was released from the hospital, it felt like I was on house arrest. I could perfectly understand Robier's concern, but I had only fucked up one time by taking too many pain pills. Even the strictest of states usually give first offenders a second chance. He had a zero-tolerance policy, so it seemed. He was giving me no chance. I loved Robier more than I loved breathing; always had. But he did not understand the excruciating pain I had endured since the accident. He was overreacting.

It's crazy how one moment in time—sometimes merely a second—can change the direction of your entire life. I had reenacted that horrible day in my head a thousand times. What if I had left the office ten minutes earlier or ten minutes later? Five minutes earlier or five minutes later? Two minutes? What if I had stopped at the previous light when it turned yellow instead of rushing through it before it turned red? What if I had stopped by the ice cream parlor on the way to pick up Carson instead of deciding to take her with me so the ice cream wouldn't melt? What if? What if? What if?

For whatever reason, the accident was meant to be. My deeply rooted spirituality dictates that He who watches over us never makes mistakes. The accident, the hospitalization, and the possibility of never walking again had given me a new outlook on life.

Even though I had to walk through a valley—the valley of pain and affliction—I was still blessed enough to be alive. Alive to cuddle up with Carson on my favorite down comforter and pinch her chubby cheeks. Alive to hear Robier tell me why I complete him and how he will love me forever and a day. Alive to be able to call my parents and sister in California and reminisce over the past and make plans for the future. The loss of another child would have been too much for them to bear. Their burden was already heavy—too heavy—because of what had happened to Muffin.

I don't believe Daddy will ever recover from losing his only son. Momma fakes her acceptance of it, but those closest to her knew she suffered in silence. The year after Muffin graduated summa cum laude from Blake University with a marketing degree, he made a silly mistake. The one moment in time that drastically altered the course of his life was when he decided to go to the Wet Pussy, a redneck titty bar in West Virginia. Muffin had accepted a job as the token African-American for a small corporation in Bull Run, West Virginia. They had offered him a starting salary of sixty thousand, ten to fifteen thousand more than the average marketing graduate. Hosts of corporations set up locations in small towns to save on real estate, affording them the opportunity to offer bigger salaries than their counterparts. Muffin had accepted the job—appeared to like it, even—but there wasn't much for an African-American man to do there socially. Heaven knows I am not a racist. Without a doubt Robier was playing the "international lover" role before he hooked up with me. I had no issue with that. Yet and still, Muffin had developed a predilection for white girls during his senior year. His desire for them—and only them—did not sit quite well with me. Interracial dating is okay, but brothers who resort to bad-mouthing and demeaning sisters to justify why they do it irritate me. Muffin had pissed me off, reminding me of a famous movie star who had had the nerve to proclaim the reasons why he wasn't feeling women of his own race in a magazine whose subscribers were 90 percent African-American. When his next few movies flopped, he got the message.

Muffin had his nose wide-open over this girl named Mindy, who was uneducated and out of his league. She frequented the Wet Pussy, so he was eager to get there to try to get into her pants later that night. Unfortunately, a few rednecks from out of town were traveling through with a biker club. They rode loud-ass bikes, bathed when they felt like it, and spit out tobacco indoors or out. I don't know all the details, but sometime during that fateful evening, my brother got into a verbal altercation with one of them and, like the pack of rats they were, they attacked him and beat him to death while Mindy watched alongside everyone else. They say she even left the bar that night with one of the bikers who later on ended up charged with Muffin's murder. Three of them had been convicted of manslaughter and were serving various terms ranging from ten to twenty-five years. While justice—if you can even call it that—had been served, Muffin's life was still lost for absolutely no reason and my parents had to deal with that loss. We all did.

Robier missed him as well, since they had roomed together for four years in college and Muffin was due to be his best man at the large wedding we originally planned. He died three months before, so we decided to have a small, intimate wedding instead. Muffin would have wanted us to go through with the extravaganza, but out of respect for him, we kept it simple.

Angelica and Momma had both offered to come to D.C. to help with Carson, but I didn't want them to feel obligated. Daddy needed Momma out in California with him and Angelica had just started law school in Arizona. She was young, beautiful, intelligent, and didn't need to be bogged down with my issues.

Thus, I did what I had to do in order to survive; I took pills. At first the pain was unbearable but as time went by, I learned to numb it with various medications, some prescribed and some not. Doctors are something else. They give you medicine to mask the pain—almost like a bandage—instead of actually fixing the problem. Granted, the damage to my back was not their fault, but making people dependent on pain medication and then ripping it away without warning is. They determine when they think a person shouldn't need it anymore. That is what happened to me. Dr. Boulder didn't cut me off completely—at first—but my allocated dosages decreased and then became practically nonexistent.

I was one of the lucky ones. I didn't have to comb the streets searching for a "street pharmacist" to hook me up. Because of the physical therapy I endured at the hospital on a regular basis, it was easy to befriend those who could hook me up with what I needed. Even they had an agenda. At first, they gave me freebies—everything from Percocets for pain to Flexerils, nicknamed "home plates" on the street, for muscle relaxation. They got them from doctors who either got tons of samples from pharmaceutical reps or prescribed them under the table. I thought they were simply being cool by giving me what I needed. Then their real game began. They started charging me—after it was apparent I couldn't function without them.

Percocets could go for twenty a pill and Flexerils or other muscle relaxants for ten. That all began to add up, especially when I became immune to small dosages and had to start taking several at a time. My interior-design business had tapered off but I started picking up clients whenever I could to make more money. Half the time I wouldn't tell Robier about new jobs. He would have questioned my revenue stream, or lack thereof.

I didn't view what I was doing as a problem. It was a way to make it through the day without being bent over in pain or feeling like I wanted to cry. For a while, right after the accident, I wished I was dead. The pain was that much out of control. Prayer got me through. I realized that life still had some goodness in store for me, no matter what trials I had to endure to get to my rightful place.

After the so-called overdose episode, Robier began clocking me on an hourly basis, always checking up on me like I was his child, not Carson. In the evenings, I would drink some wine or make piña coladas in the blender—added on top of the drugs in my system—and seduce Robier to make him more trusting. Sometimes it worked. Sometimes it didn't. Our love was stronger than ever, but I began to feel smothered.

We were lying in bed one night when the angry words finally came out.

"Tiphanie, something's not right."

I had my head resting on Robier's chest. I glanced up at him and then swept my tongue across his right nipple and started caressing his dick underneath the black satin sheet.

"What do you mean?" I asked. "I thought the sex was awesome."

He pushed my hand away. "It's not that. You know I adore our lovemaking."

I grinned and sat up on my elbow. "Tonight was especially good. I like sixty-nining. We need to experiment like that more often. I was reading about these wild sex positions in *Cosmopolitan* and—"

"Tiphanie, I said it's not about the sex. It's about the drugs you've been shoving down your throat."

I feigned ignorance. "What drugs? I told you I stopped taking those pills after that incident."

"Baby, I know you're being untruthful and so do you. Half the time you can't even wake up in the morning."

"That's because I've been having a little wine or a frozen drink before bed. It helps me to relax."

"You don't think I know that's a cover-up, a way to try to explain away your behavior?"

"Robier, we've been having a wonderful night. Please, don't go and ruin it."

"You want me to pretend to be as delusional as you, and that shit's not happening."

I pushed away from him, shoved a pillow between us, and flipped over so my back was to him. "I'm going to sleep. I have no intention of arguing with you tonight over complete nonsense."

"Tiphanie, Jocelyn told me what she saw."

I sighed. "Nosy bitch!"

"No, not a nosy bitch but a concerned friend."

Jocelyn was this bimbo who worked with Robier. She thought she was God's gift to men and carried herself accordingly. Everything about the woman was fake, from her unbeweavable hair to her colored green contacts. She had the hots for my husband and was willing to do anything to get in his good graces. I had run into her the week before at a happy hour. I was there to make a "connection" and she was lurking around the bar, pretending to be enthralled in a conversation with a trollish dude with bug eyes. When my upper-middle-class dealer and I exchanged white envelopes under the table, I glanced up and saw her staring. That should have been my cue to bounce, but the pain in my lower back had me ready to scream. I slipped into the ladies' room, ripped open my package, took two Vioxx out, and was about to dry-swallow them when she burst in like SWAT.

"So what are those?" Jocelyn asked, grinning.

"My business," I replied nastily.

"Didn't I hear something about you taking too many pain pills about a year ago and almost dying?"

"Didn't I hear something about your name being in the paper for being stabbed by a crazy woman who can't stand your ass?"

She seemed confused. "My name's never been in the paper for any such thing."

"Oh, my bad. I was thinking about tomorrow's edition." I reached into my bag and pulled out the switchblade I kept in the side zippered pocket. One could never tell when something might set off in the city, especially in the circles I was beginning to travel in.

Jocelyn's eyes almost popped clear out of her head when I clicked the blade open and swiped it across my throat a few inches from my skin.

"You're sick," she said, before yanking the door open and rushing out.

I thought that was the end of it, figuring she would be too embarrassed to mention it to anyone. I was wrong.

"Tiphanie . . ." Robier snapped me back into reality. "What were you taking in the ladies' room? The pills Jocelyn saw you purchase and then take?"

Hmmph, well, at least she apparently had not mentioned the

knife. "Jocelyn doesn't know what the hell she's talking about. I was taking some pills: Tylenol. Unless it's a crime to take acetaminophen these days, I was doing absolutely nothing wrong. She's a drama queen and she's trying to fuck you. She thinks she has half a chance if she can get me out of the picture or cause turmoil in our relationship. I can't believe you're bringing that bitch's name into our bedroom." I was furious and not even trying to hide it. I got up from the bed and covered my nude body with a satin bathrobe. "I'm going to check on Carson. In fact, I'm going to sleep in her bed tonight. The air in here is too thick."

"Don't you walk out of here!" Robier demanded from the bed. "We're not finished talking!"

"You might not be finished but I am. I'm sick of you trying to treat me like a child. I can't even go out for a drink without being questioned. For your information, I was there to meet a client and he was paying me for my services."

"She said you handed him something under the table also."

"Yes, a receipt for the material I ordered for his custom draperies. Would you like me to call you when they come in so you can go over to his house and watch the installers hang them?" I asked sarcastically.

Robier's eyes dropped. "I'm sorry, baby. I should never have doubted you. You promised me you wouldn't take any more of those pills and I believe you."

He got up from the bed, dick swinging left and right as he came to me in the doorway. "Please forgive me. I love you. I need you." He kissed me on the lips. "I can't survive without you. I worry about you sometimes, that's all."

"Now you make me a promise," I said.

"Anything."

"Don't ever bring that tramp's name up to me again. She's nothing but trouble."

He grinned. "I promise." He unfastened my robe and let it drop off my shoulders to the floor. "Now, can we get back to cuddling?"

"You're going to have to do more than a little cuddling to make this up to me."

"I know just the thing. How about one of our special showers?"

I giggled. "You ain't said nothing but a word."

Robier and I had this thing about doing it in the shower. Having a steam shower made the experiences highly erotic. We would get into our stall, which was really big enough for four people and had a bench, and scrub each other clean. Robier would rub my pussy with a body sponge and then take care of my ass, slipping a finger in seemingly by accident and then watching me as I moaned.

That night, we stayed in the shower for more than an hour, fucking first when standing and then lying on the bench. It never ceased to amaze me how Robier could come and then be ready for another round within minutes. I never imagined that I would grow to love sucking dick, but that's exactly what had happened over the years. It got to the point where I would damn near beg him to "dick feed" me. I even swallowed, and that was something I felt was disgusting when I saw other women doing it in pornos. But with Robier, there were no limitations for me.

He seemed sated when we crawled back into bed in the morning. More important, I had regained his trust and that was essential. Everything within me wanted to confess that I was still taking pain pills and muscle relaxants, but he wouldn't be able to understand. I hated keeping secrets from him but it was a necessary evil.

"I love you, Tiphanie," he whispered in my ear as we fell asleep. "Forever and a day."

"Forever and a day," I replied.

$\mathcal{R}$OBIER

JANUARY 2002

Tiphanie claimed to have had postpartum depression after the birth of our son, Lennox. I wasn't buying that. For years, I had ignored the obvious. In retrospect, that was the worst thing to do because I had become her enabler, or at least one of them. For a second, I tried to put the blame on her parents, but they—along with Angelica—were clear across the country and had no way of knowing how common Tiphanie's undesirable behavior had become.

Lennox was barely six months old when everything really hit the fan. You never know what or whom the devil will come disguised as. In our case, it was in the form of Eva Holt, one of Tiphanie's best friends from college. Eva had attended Blake for two years before she was expelled for poor grades. She was originally from Columbia, South Carolina, and from what I knew, she had returned there after her expulsion. I had no idea that she and Tiphanie had even kept in contact over the years. I never liked her. She was trouble from day one. She was an easy woman with whorish ways and I feared her "looseness" would rub off on Tiphanie. I worked overtime to make sure Tiphanie did not have a chance to hang out with Eva and various dudes who had nothing but fucking on their minds. Still, Tiphanie found something in Eva she liked, and so they would go shopping and work out together in the campus gym.

Tiphanie was heartbroken when Eva left, and I had to keep myself from break dancing.

I came home from work one Friday afternoon and there was a black BMW parked on the street in front of our house. It had Virginia tags and I had no clue whom it belonged to. When I opened the door and found Eva sitting on my sofa—in an expensive pantsuit and tons of jewelry—I almost lost it.

She jumped up. "Robier! Give me a hug!" Eva raced over to me and grabbed me like we were long-lost lovers. "You look great!"

"So do you, Eva," I replied, telling the truth. She did look awesome, the bitch! "Where's Tiphanie?"

"Oh, she went upstairs to check on the baby. He's asleep. That Lennox is the most adorable thing I've ever seen. How did you and Tiphanie make such a beautiful baby?"

I chuckled. "Well, she did most of the work. I was simply the sperm donor."

"Good sperm, then." Eva walked over to the mantel and picked up a picture of Carson. "She's absolutely lovely too. I can't wait to meet her."

An uneasiness settled in my stomach. "So, Eva, what brings you to D.C.? Is that your car out front?"

"Yes, it is. I live right in northern Virginia. I ran into Tiphanie at B. Smith's in Union Station a few weeks ago. She didn't tell you?"

I shook my head and crossed my arms. "No, she never mentioned it. I'm sure it was merely an oversight. So, what are you up to these days?"

Eva sat back down. "I'll be honest."

Oh, brother, I thought to myself. This is going to be a doozy.

"I run an escort service in Alexandria," she casually blurted out.

"An escort service?" I practically yelled. "You mean hookers?"

Eva gave me this sarcastic look and then smirked. "It's not even like that. My clients pay to have a fox on their arm, not a mink in their bed."

"Mink?"

"Yes, you've never heard the term: fuck like minks?"

"No, but I obviously don't travel in the same circles as you, Eva."

I sighed and glanced up the staircase, wondering what was taking Tiphanie so long. I wondered if she knew about the so-called escort service. Of course she knew, I told myself. If Eva blurted it out so quickly to me, Tiphanie had to know all about it and then some. That certainly explained why Tiphanie had not mentioned running into her.

"Anyway, it is a legal business and it pays extremely well," she added, playing with her diamond-crusted watch. "Besides, a girl's got to earn a living, and you know how those bastards at Blake tried to play me."

"Eva, didn't you flunk out?"

She glared at me then. "So they say, but there were some underlying reasons behind my expulsion."

Now I was simply being nosy. "Like what?"

"Like I was doing a certain professor, his wife found out, and they needed to get me out of the picture to save face."

That made absolutely no sense to me. "That's weird, because it would seem like they would kiss your ass royally instead to keep you silent. By kicking you out, they risked a serious lawsuit, if you had pursued it."

"They knew I wasn't going to pursue shit. I was a kid. One who needed love and affection, and I'll admit that back then I was searching for dick in all the wrong places."

I let that sink in for a moment. "But by running an escort service, you are searching in the right places now?"

"Hey, I have a man. We're going on three years. My business is just that and I don't even go out on calls. I have more than two dozen sexy vixens on my roster."

"I see," was all I could manage to say. I was too stunned to say anything else.

"Listen, Robier. Tiphanie needs to get out of the house for a while and clear her head. Do you mind watching the kids so she and I can hang out?" Eva asked.

Tiphanie had been cooped up in the house, except for work, since Lennox's birth. I was surprised that she was in B. Smith's long enough to even run into Eva. However, I was not crazy about the idea of her "clearing her head" with the likes of Eva.

"Where are you two planning to go?" I inquired. "I suppose that I could get Carson from school and watch both kids, but how long will you be gone and where are you headed?"

Eva sucked in some air. I could tell that she was not used to having to report anything to anybody, even though she said that she was going on three years with some man. "We're going to hang out in Georgetown and have a nice dinner and some drinks. She said she's never been to Clyde's, so we'll see if there's a long wait there. We won't be out half the night or anything. I have an early morning."

Tiphanie came running down the steps, and it was then I realized what had taken her so long. She was dressed in a pantsuit similar to Eva's, her hair was curled, and she had applied fresh makeup. It was an ambush all along.

"Hey, baby." Tiphanie caressed my cheek and kissed me on the lips. "Aren't you surprised to see Eva?" she asked, like it was a pleasant thing.

"Yes, I'm definitely surprised. You didn't tell me that you'd run into her."

"I knew she'd be coming by soon and decided to spring it on you so you'd be shocked. It's been so many years. I feel like a kid again."

Tiphanie was so blissful that I could not deny her, even if it meant succumbing to Eva.

"You look great, Tiphanie. Eva asked if I'd watch the kids and I'm more than happy to. You go out and have a wonderful time."

Tiphanie sighed, then grinned. "You sure?"

"Positive. I'll keep the home fires burning. You two ladies go do your thing."

AT FOUR IN THE morning, the panic set in. Where the hell were they? I got up from the bed, where Lennox was sleeping peacefully, and started pacing the floor, staring out the window every few minutes to make sure they were not in the driveway. I had started calling Tiphanie's cell phone shortly after one. As I dialed it again, I realized it would go straight to voice mail like the dozen or so times before. How I failed to get Eva's cell number was pure stupidity.

At eight thirty-five exactly Tiphanie came strolling in without a care in the world. "Good morning, Robier," she said, beaming like a ray of sun.

"Um, maybe I'm crazy, but when did dinner and drinks start taking all night?"

She giggled. "Oh, I'm sorry, baby. Eva and I got to playing catch-up and it just went on and on and on."

I stood there, tapping my bedroom shoe on the tile in the foyer. "I called your cell phone time and time again."

"Oops," she said, removing it from her jacket pocket. "I had it on vibrate and didn't hear it ring."

Now, who was she trying to fool? "On vibrate, you would have felt it in your jacket. What gives, Tiphanie?"

"Robier, stop trippin'." She started for the steps. "I'm exhausted. We'll talk after I get some sleep."

I grabbed her wrist. "No, we will stop right this second. It is almost nine o'clock in the morning. This type of behavior is not acceptable. You are a mother and a wife."

Tiphanie laughed. "Do you honestly think that I'm not aware of that? Come on, baby, don't give me a hard time about this. Eva and I hung out like old times. She ended up taking me to see her place, and we'd had a few drinks, so I dozed off. No big deal."

Her explanation seemed plausible enough, and that would give credence to her not feeling her cell phone vibrating. "Okay, fine, but please call me if you don't think you'll make it home again. I was worried sick and ready to call the state police and hospitals. After that last accident, my mind is on overdrive with what could happen."

She kissed me gently on the lips. I could smell alcohol on her breath. "Oh, sweetie, I didn't even think about it like that. I'm sorry. Please forgive me."

"I could never stay mad at you, Tiphanie."

• • •

TIPHANIE AND EVA CONTINUED to spend a lot of time together. I was not happy about it, but she seemed so peaceful when she came home that I could not voice my objections. She did not stay out all night again and our family life was great until . . .

. . . I found something wrapped in a towel in our master bathroom cabinet that I hoped was not what I thought it was: a crack pipe. I had never actually held one or seen one in person, but I had seen them on television shows like *COPS*. I tried to tell myself that it had landed there by itself; it could not possibly be Tiphanie's.

The kids were asleep, and I was waiting on the living room couch in the dark when Tiphanie showed up at about three in the morning, the latest she had since the night she had been gone all night. She tried to come in quietly, but the alarm bell chimed when she opened the door. I watched her silhouette as she kicked off her pumps and removed her jacket in the foyer, debating what words to say. She was walking toward the kitchen when I spoke up.

"It's almost three. Where have you been, Tiphanie?"

She practically jumped out of her skin, and then turned to the sound of my voice. "Robier, is that you?"

I reached over and turned on the light on the end table. "No, it's the boogeyman. I'll ask you one last time. Where have you been?"

"There you go, treating me like an infant again," she stated angrily. "I will not tolerate you . . ."

I held the crack pipe up so she could see it. "What is this, Tiphanie?"

She bit her bottom lip. "I haven't a clue. What is it?"

"I'm not an expert, but from the shape of it and the burnt glass, I would call it a crack pipe."

"A crack pipe?" She seemed dumbfounded. "What the hell are you doing with a crack pipe, baby?"

"I found it wrapped in a towel in our bathroom. I guess this explains why you stay locked in the bathroom for long periods of time lately. You've been in there doing drugs."

"Don't be silly." She sat down in the armchair on the other side of the coffee table from me. "You know me better than that; I would never do crack."

"The old you wouldn't have. You've graduated from the pain pills, huh? Or are you doing a combination of both?"

"I'm not doing a damn thing. Look, I don't know where that came from. Maybe the plumber who came a few weeks back to fix the toilet left it. You never know about these service people." She laughed uneasily. "Bonded or not, we need to be careful who we let into our home."

I sighed in dismay. "Tiphanie, the plumber did not leave a crack pipe in our bathroom. It was not there two days ago when I got a roll of toilet tissue from the same cabinet. This is your crack pipe and you need help, sweetheart. Please, let me help you."

"I don't need your fucking help!" She stood and paced the floor. "Okay, the damn pipe is mine. Now what? I deserve to relax every now and then. You have no idea how much pain I'm still in from the accident. The pills and yes, even the crack, help me to relax. It's only recreational use. I swear."

"So if it's only recreational, then that means you can quit in a heartbeat, right?"

Tiphanie went silent.

"Right, Tiphanie? Recreational use is just that; you can take it or leave it."

"I'm going to get some juice and then I'm going to sleep."

Tiphanie walked away as I buried my head in my hands and wept.

THE NEXT DAY I went to the public library and did some research on cocaine addiction. I felt ten times worse after I left and prayed that Tiphanie was in the early stages and not totally hooked. According to what I read, only about 8 percent of those who went through drug rehabilitation were able to refrain from drug usage permanently. Most went right back to using. I could not help but shelter part of the blame for it. I should have banned her from seeing Eva, who I suspected was behind Tiphanie's introduction to cocaine, if not her actual dealer.

I wished Muffin was still alive, because he would have been the first person I'd contact to discuss his sister's problem. He had been a dear friend and a realist. He would have helped me rationalize everything that was going on. I considered phoning California and dropping the dismal news on her parents but could not bear causing them emotional pain. I was sure my parents would understand, but after all was said and done, I could not openly discuss it with anyone I cared about. I was sitting there on a bench outside the library when the anger set in. Then I went to find Eva.

Eva's upscale escort/hooker agency was called Stimuli, an obvious name for selling pussy by the hour. She had an office on King Street in Alexandria. When I entered the reception area, there was a scantily clad woman seated at a contemporary glass-top desk who greeted me with a smile.

"Welcome to Stimuli, where it is our pleasure to be your pleasure. How can I help you today, Mr. . . . ?"

"Martin. Robier Martin. I need to see Eva."

"Is she expecting you?"

"No, she is definitely not expecting me, but I'm sure she'll see me. We attended college together and she's dear friends with my wife."

"Oh, you're Tiphanie's hubby." She seemed delighted to figure out that fact. She picked up the phone and pressed the intercom button. "Tiphanie's husband is here to see you. Yes. Okay, I'll send him right in."

When I entered Eva's office, she was sitting at an expensive desk, flipping through a stack of headshots and full-body photos of gorgeous women. "Hey, Robier," she said without giving me even a courtesy glance. "Have a seat. I'm almost done."

"Looking for some new women to victimize, huh?"

Eva giggled and then finally glared at me. "Robier, I don't victimize anyone. I simply meet a supply and demand."

"Does that pertain only to sex or drugs also?"

"Whatever do you mean?" she asked nervously.

"So, you're running both a prostitution ring and a drug ring out of this high-class joint. I should turn you over to the feds right this second."

"You must be on drugs, because you're obviously hallucinating."

"I wasn't hallucinating last night when I confronted Tiphanie about the crack pipe I found in our bathroom."

Eva frowned and worry lines set in deeply along her brow. "Tiphanie's on crack?" she asked innocently.

"Give it up. I know you got her started on the shit, and more than likely you're selling it to her."

"If I did use drugs, and I am by no means saying that I do, I would not use crack; I would use cocaine. There is a major difference in quality." She hesitated and then added, "So I hear."

I'll be damned if what she said did not make sense. Eva did not strike me as the type who would use the cheaper version of drugs. I remained convinced that she knew something, though.

"Eva, please, you care about Tiphanie; at least you act like you do. Help me to help her, before she gets too deep into this. I went to the library and—"

"The library? You can't learn shit in the library." Eva sat up slightly in her executive chair. "Listen, Robier, I do care about her, so I am going to tell you what I know and then I'm going to have to insist that you leave my office and never come back here. Deal?"

"Deal. Now, what's going on with my wife?"

Eva sighed. "It's that damn back of hers. When she and I first started hanging out again, she was already hooked on those pills, but you knew that already."

"I thought she had stopped."

"She never stopped; she simply graduated. That first night we went out she met this dude at a club and—"

"What dude? What club?" I asked anxiously.

"Do you want to hear what I have to say or not?"

"Please, go ahead," I prodded.

"He tried to pick her up and she told him she was married and all that. That is one thing you can rest assured about; Tiphanie does love you. Anyway, I overheard her asking him if he had any home plates—muscle relaxants—and he said he didn't but he had something much better. Next thing I know they had disappeared outside for about ten minutes. She came back in and was spaced the fuck out. She sat on a sofa and stared at the wall for at least an hour. When I tried to talk to her, her tongue was tied and I knew she had done cocaine. I've been around the block a time or two and I recognize the symptoms. I ended up dragging her from the club, bringing her home with me, and letting her get it together before I dropped her off at home. That's why it was way over in the morning. Contrary to what you believe and what I may or may not be, I do care about my girl and I would never do anything to hurt her."

"So why have you been keeping her out so late all the time? Last night, she didn't get home until three."

Eva seemed to be debating what to say. "Tiphanie was not with me last night. I rarely see her anymore, but she told me that she uses me as an excuse for being out, just in case you should ever ask."

"Then where the hell has she been?"

Eva shrugged. "Ask dude."

"Does dude have a name?"

"I believe they call him Deliverance. He hangs out at Club Urbana."

"Deliverance?" I asked in disbelief.

"Yeah, sounds like a drug-dealer name if I've ever heard one," Eva replied as I stormed out of her office.

TIPHANIE

I had to be more careful; it was as simple as that. How stupid could I be? Leaving that pipe under the cabinet. I was stoned out of my mind and forgot it was there. Robier was upset, but I was determined to sweep it under the rug and make him forget about the incident. I was not an addict; that was for damn sure. Like I told him, it was for recreational use only, and I needed something to ease my constant pain.

Deliverance met me at our usual spot in Capital Plaza to make an exchange. He was looking as suave as ever in black leather pants and a gray cashmere sweater. If I weren't married, I probably would have let him hit on me that night in the club. He often tried to sleep with me but I remained committed to Robier. There were a few times—when I was totally out of it—that I discovered my clothes slightly disheveled when I came down off my high. I had not been fucked, though; that feeling is unmistakable. A woman knows when someone has invaded her pussy, drugged up or not.

I decided to tease Deliverance to break the ice that day by asking, "Hey, did you feel me up the other day when we were over your friend's place?"

He would sometimes take me to his friend Lee's house to use when I did not want to use at home. He would never tell me his real address. Drug dealers—at least smart drug dealers—never took people to their actual houses or apartments, just in case someone decided to turn on them.

Deliverance chuckled. "Naw, baby. The day I feel you up, you will definitely realize it. You'll be begging for this dick one day. Trust on that."

"I've never begged for dick and I'm too old to start now," I replied jokingly. "You have my stuff?"

He eyed me quizzically. "You have my stuff?"

I was behind on what I owed Deliverance, but I needed to get high. "I have most of it. I still need you to front me this time."

"Tiphanie, you're fine and all, but since you're not giving up some ass, I can't keep hooking you up for free. This is a business."

"I'm aware of that." I reached into my purse and pulled out the money from the pawnshop where I had taken the portable DVD player Robier had given me for Christmas and one of our digital cameras. I had been pawning a lot of little electronic items lately; luckily, Robier hardly used any of them. "This is all I have," I said, handing it to him.

Deliverance did not count it. He never counted money out in the open. "You need someplace to get set up?"

"Yeah, that would be cool." I thought about what had happened the night before. "I don't want to go home and use."

I woke up several hours later, coming down off my high. I felt something wet and sticky between my thighs and looked down to see Lee eating my pussy. I tried to scream but nothing escaped my throat. I could barely even sit up. My jeans were wrapped down around one of my ankles and Lee had my knees resting on his shoulders while he went to town on me. "Deliverance," I managed to whisper, hoping he would save me. "Where is Deliverance?"

Lee glanced up at me. "Deliverance went to handle his business and I'm handling mine. You think you can keep using my crib and not give me a damn thing in return? You are so wrong, bitch. Luckily for you, my dick can't get hard when I'm high, but I love eating me some pussy, especially when it's fresh like yours. Most crack hoes don't even wash their asses. You haven't gotten to that point yet, but you will."

I lay there, zeroed in on a dead fly on the ceiling, and tried to allow my mind to carry me elsewhere while he finished doing what he was doing. Then I got up, struggled to get my pants back on, and drove home to my husband and kids.

ROBIER

Everyone at Club Urbana played dumb when it came to Deliverance. They had either never seen or heard of him, or they hadn't seen him in a long time and he didn't hang out there any longer. It was apparent that they were all lying; I could see it in their eyes. After I'd read up on the symptoms of drug use at the library, it was like a rude awakening. A lot of them had rubbery-looking skin, their faces were extremely oily, they had nervous tics, and they seemed either sedated or volatile, depending on whether they were in the process of going up or coming down. Pipe dreams; they all had one. Deliverance was probably their savior, the one who kept them in their various states of euphoria. There was no way they were going to tell me shit. I even pretended to be trying to buy, but they probably thought I was an undercover narc or something. I definitely did not fit the bill, if there was such a thing.

I decided to give it up for the night and go home to see if Tiphanie was there. The kids had gone out of town with my parents to Colonial Williamsburg. At least they were having fun at Busch Gardens and the old-time villages, seeing how people survived back in the early years when drugs—at least the powerful ones—were not around. They healed themselves with natural herbs and tree bark, not man-made poison.

As soon as I turned the key to unlock my car, I heard a noise behind me. I turned and saw no one, but the sound had been distinct. There was someone there.

"Who's there?" I asked, feeling a sense of danger.

Normally, fear was not a part of my personality, but leaving a club full of addicts who needed money to get their toxin had me on high alert. I rushed to get in the car but I was not fast enough. Something hit me across the back of my head first. I fell to the ground and then the kicks began. To my ribs. To my chest. To my head. I could not make out anything but big boots coming at me as I tried to shield myself with my hands.

The beating stopped as suddenly as it began. Then I heard a voice.

"Why the hell are you looking for me?"

I spat blood and replied, "You must be Deliverance."

My vision was still blurry but I could make out a man of about twenty-five who looked like the typical playa, dressed in brand-name clothes and sporting a lot of fancy jewelry.

I tried to pull myself up by my car door but collapsed right back down. "I'm Tiphanie's husband. You know a Tiphanie?"

He smirked. "I know a lot of bitches, fool."

"This one spells her name with a *p-h*. You know her now?"

He grew silent. "What if I do? What the hell does that have to do with you looking for me?"

"Stop selling her drugs. I came here to ask you to please stop selling my wife drugs," I pleaded. "She has kids at home who love her. We need her."

Deliverance knelt down beside me and grabbed me by the collar. "Listen, I'm going to do you a favor, but this is a one-shot deal. Normally you would be found dead out here in the alley tomorrow morning with a bullet in your head or be swimming with the fish in the Potomac. But I like Tiphanie and, on good principle, that means you're all right with me too."

He stood and pulled me up by the hand. "Get in your whip and go home, man. Tiphanie comes to see me because she wants to." He spread his arms open and swayed from side to side, like a man claiming his kingdom. "They all come see me because they want to. I'll admit that I gave her the first hit, but I didn't force it on her and

I never have. Your wife is hooked, man. Big-time. She's one of my best customers."

"You did this to her," I managed to whisper.

Deliverance shook his head. "Naw, my man, she did it to herself. If you're smart, you'll cut her loose. Things are not going to get better. I tried to tell my mother that same shit when my older sister got strung out when I was in middle school. She didn't listen either. She tried to save her and I was happy as hell when Sis overdosed and put us all out of that misery."

I spat some blood on the ground. "If that's true, then why would you be a contributor to this? Why would you help destroy families?"

Deliverance chuckled. "Shit, do you have any idea how much money there is in slanging dope? I'm paid and I'm not about to go flip burgers or pick up trash. Fuck that!" He pointed to the side of the club building. "When I step up in this piece, everybody wants to suck my dick, you know what I'm saying? Everybody. They are willing to do anything, to sell anything, to get what I have. That's power. I don't give a fuck how they got here, as long as I walk out with two pockets full of cheddar."

I suddenly came to my senses. "You're right. This is not your fault. It's not your fault or Eva's."

"Who the fuck is Eva? Another dealer? That bitch better not be cutting into my flow."

I held my palms up. "No, I thought she was, but she had nothing to do with it, other than bringing my wife out to this club."

Deliverance licked his lips. "Aw, you mean that fine bitch Tiphanie was with that first night. She's a keeper. I tried to get her to step outside with us but I think she sensed what was up. Tell her I said to come see a brother if she ever gets lonely."

I winced, partly from pain and partly from disgust. He was serious. Then something else invaded my mind, a visual that I could not stand. "Are you fucking my wife?" I blurted out.

"Naw, not yet," Deliverance replied. "But bro, the way she's headed, it's only a matter of time before she gives up her goodies for my goodies. She's already pawning shit. You probably haven't even noticed."

"Tiphanie went to a pawnshop?" I asked in shock.

Deliverance shook his head. "You're still in make-believe land, so allow me to enlighten you. Drug addicts have to get drugs. That means you need to lock everything down worth value in your home, you need to keep her the fuck away from any joint bank accounts before you lose everything right along with her. If you're smart, you'll kick her the fuck out and keep it moving."

"You're crazy!" I lashed out. "I can't do that to my wife!"

"You better do her in before she does your ass in. I'm her dealer and I'm telling you that shit. You seem like a cool brother, trying to take care of his family. You better protect those kids of yours, my man. Momma's got a brand-new bag."

With those words, Deliverance walked off and left me there. When he was nothing but a distant blur, I struggled to get into my car. On the drive home, something told me to stop by the ATM at the local branch of our bank and check the balance on our high-performance money-market account. There should have been nearly ten thousand dollars in there. It was overdrawn. I got back into my car, turned on some slow jams, and tried to reason with insanity.

An hour later I found Tiphanie washing dishes in the kitchen sink. She started screaming when she saw my face and asked if I had been mugged. I confronted her right there, sitting in our breakfast nook. I told her about my talk with Eva and the beat-down Deliverance had given me, along with a description of how bad her drug problem was. She cried. I cried. We cried in unison. Then she admitted that some man had eaten her pussy earlier that day when she was laid up in his apartment getting high. I could not believe my ears. Another man had touched my wife, and she had voluntarily been in his place to use drugs, so there was nothing we could do about it. What could we say to the police? Tiphanie was taken advantage of by a man who sucked on her clit, but she was in his place to use crack and had been over there dozens of times?

"I want to get help, Robier," Tiphanie whispered in my ear as I held her close. "Please, I want to beat this. I can do it."

"I'll help you, baby." I clutched her in my embrace. "We'll get through this. I promise."

I went on the Internet, made a few phone calls, and the next morning I drove Tiphanie to an inpatient drug rehabilitation center in Annapolis. She stayed for ten days, and stupid me, I thought that would be enough to cure her. I attended the family session and film presentation and was convinced their therapy would work wonders.

Tiphanie came home, excited about a new beginning. She had put on about ten pounds during her stay and looked healthy for the first time in ages. She left the very next evening to attend her first outpatient session. We did not see her again for four days.

THE SECOND REHABILITATION CENTER Tiphanie entered was in Wilmington, North Carolina. It was recommended to me by a friend whose father had gone there for his alcoholism. He had managed to fully recover, and I held out hope that they would be able to work wonders for Tiphanie as well. It was a two-week program, but Tiphanie called and insisted that she wanted to leave the program early to attend a friend's wedding. I was a groomsman and she did not want me to be embarrassed by attending the festivities alone. The counselor at the center told me that she thought Tiphanie was playing a game, making up an excuse to leave early. The counselor stated that Tiphanie was not serious about being rehabilitated and was simply "doing her time."

I wanted so much to believe that my wife was better, and I realized that she would be upset to miss the wedding of our close friends. I agreed to let her leave early and picked her up at the airport on Friday morning, the day of the rehearsal and rehearsal dinner. When we got home, she stated that she wanted to go to the hairdresser right quick to get her hair fixed, since it had not been done in weeks. As it was less than ten minutes away, I thought it would be okay. I told her to be back in time to go check into the hotel over in Arlington, Virginia, so that I could be at the rehearsal on time. She never came back.

For three days, I was devastated. Everyone was at the wedding, including my parents, and Tiphanie was missing in action. Of course, they all wanted to know where she was, and my friend—even though it was his wedding day—was more concerned about my feelings than anything else. It was a nightmare.

I still did not give up, although my parents tried to convince me that I was fighting a losing battle. Our kids needed their mother. Her behavior became worse, more volatile and unpredictable. After much prodding, I convinced her to go to a center in Atlanta. Again, she relapsed. Then she went to a center in California. I figured being near her parents, where they could visit her on family days, would be good for her. It did not work. All four times she went to rehab, Tiphanie went back to using within forty-eight hours. The ups and downs were taking a toll on me, both emotionally and financially. It got to the point where I could not eat without getting an upset stomach, and my chest often hurt from the stress. Still, I could not give up. After all, Tiphanie was my wife and I had loved her seemingly since the beginning of time. The old Tiphanie would resurface. I was convinced of that. I did not know the day or the hour, but I had my faith and I allowed that to sustain me.

ROBIER

PRESENT DAY

Momma's words rang out in my ears. Was she for real about fighting me for custody of Carson and Lennox? My parents had always been so supportive of me. Now it had come down to this.

I decided to wake Tiphanie up after she had slept for about six hours. She and I needed to have a long talk. She was in that anger stage, in the process of coming down from her binge.

"Tiphanie, sweetheart, I made you something to eat. You hungry?"

"Leave me the fuck alone, Robier!"

I yanked the covers entirely off her and the bed. "No, I will not leave you the fuck alone! Tiph, I love you and I've tried to help you. Are you ever going to want to help yourself?"

She sat up and leered at me. "I've been to four rehabs. What more do you want from me?"

"A fifth one. I've been doing some research and—"

"You and your fucking research! Rehabs do not work!"

"The ones you've been going to are too short. You need to go to a long-term facility."

Tiphanie rolled her eyes and lay back down, turning her back to me. "We can't afford something like that. Our insurance company said they aren't paying for any more treatment."

"Then I'll pay for it."

"Robier, those places can be up to two grand a day. We don't have that kind of money."

"We don't have any money and we never will as long as you're using crack. I'll take out a personal loan to pay for the rehab, whatever it takes."

I could hear Tiphanie sobbing and realized what would be next. It was always the same routine.

"Well, why don't I just do everyone a favor and kill myself," she said right on cue.

I had learned not to take her suicide threats seriously. They were a way to get pity and to make me think I was badgering her too much. I had been to enough Narcotics Anonymous meetings to recognize that power move. Tiphanie had no intention of killing herself. The selfishness that resided within her was more important than our marriage, our kids, and everything else. She had stopped working altogether, not that she really had a choice. She had started stealing items from her clients' homes and offices. Twice, someone had threatened to press criminal charges, but I managed to smooth it over by replacing the items or retrieving them from local pawnshops.

Tiphanie's own wedding ring was long gone. She had pawned it nearly a dozen times before I refused to get it back again. It was a sick routine. She would pawn it to buy drugs. I would ask her where it was, as if I did not know. She would lie and say that she had put it away for safekeeping. Then a special occasion would come around and she would ask me to get it out of the pawnshop so she would not be embarrassed by not wearing it. I would drive her to go get it, but by the next week or so, it would be pawned again.

I had to play hardball, so I formulated a response to her mention of suicide. "Fine, Tiphanie. Make sure you pick out the outfit you want to be buried in before you kill yourself. I've never been good at selecting your clothes and I want you to feel comfortable in your grave."

Tiphanie leapt from the bed. "You bastard!" Before I could grab ahold of her, she yanked her purse off the foot of the bed and dashed into the bathroom, locking the door behind her. "Why don't you pick out what the fuck you want me to be buried in? Fucking bastard!"

I banged on the door. "Tiphanie, open this door right now!"

I had searched the bathroom while she was gone and tossed out all of the drug paraphernalia I could find. She had become an expert at hiding them, everywhere from inside the toilet bowl to behind it, from a hidden compartment she had cut into the cabinet to the showerhead. The master bathroom was her drug haven, when she was not occupying crack houses. She would stay in there for hours upon hours, claiming to be constipated. Sometimes she would run the shower for a long time; our water bill had shot up tremendously over the years. It was a costly, sick game and I was struggling to keep things afloat. I could barely afford to pay the kids' tuition or purchase their uniforms. It should not have been like that.

"Either you open this door or I'm calling the police to come get you out!" I shouted, trying to ram into the door with my shoulder to knock it down. I realized it would not work; I had tried before countless times and I could have smacked myself for not making the lock on that door inoperable, as I had planned.

"Call the police! I'll tell them you're abusing me!" she yelled from her sanctuary.

She had often made that threat and there was not a doubt in my mind that she would carry it out. Truth be known, she was the one who was abusive. Tiphanie would often hit me and issue threats. She even once threatened to burn the house down with me and the kids in it. I did confess that to her father during a recent call, but he did not want to come to terms with the fact that Tiphanie was so far gone. Her parents had stopped coming to visit altogether and felt it was better not to face the truth. They were safely out of it in California while I was living a nightmare in D.C.

I attempted to discuss it with her sister, Angelica, as well. She really laid the guilt trip on me. "Would you leave or discard my sister if she had cancer?" she asked me sarcastically. "You took vows to love her for better or for worse, did you not?"

In desperation I even reached out to Eva, who had ceased coming around. Eva said, "I've had a lot of experience with drug addicts, Robier, and they have no grasp on reality. My only advice is not to let her take you down with her. Look at how many celebrities had it all—fame, money, and power—and lost it all because of addiction. You're going to fuck around and be homeless, wondering what the hell happened."

"Tiphanie, open this fucking door!" I yelled again, banging as hard as I could.

"Little pig, little pig, let me come in," she said giddily. The drugs had kicked in and she was acting childish. "Not by the hair on my chinny chin chin."

"Tiph, baby, please come out." I was on the brink of tears. "I need you to come out here and talk to me. We can get you some help."

I recalled a story one woman had related to us at a family NA meeting. She said that she had gotten so desperate once that she actually smoked her boyfriend out of the bathroom. Bathrooms across the world were havens for crackheads, when they weren't laid up with other crackheads in communal drug houses. I was desperate and willing to try anything, even if it made absolutely no sense. On top of everything else, I was also angry.

I left the bedroom, went to the kids' bathroom down the hall, and got the bottle of rubbing alcohol Carson used to clean the posts of her pierced earrings. A pair of silver ball earrings were soaking in the cap, so I grabbed the open bottle and headed back. I grabbed the long-handled lighter Tiphanie used to light bedroom candles out of the nightstand drawer and poured the alcohol underneath the bathroom door.

"Tiphanie, I'm telling you one last time to come out of there. Open the door."

"You're the big bad wolf. Huff and puff and blow the door down!"

I lit the alcohol and waited. Less than ten seconds later, "What the fuck!" came through the door and I could hear Tiphanie panicking as she tried to stomp out the fire with her bare feet. She yanked the door open. "Are you out of your fucking mind? You tried to kill me!"

I pushed past her, grabbed a bath towel, wet it quickly in the sink, and then snuffed out the fire with it. In retrospect, I should have gotten the fire extinguisher from the kitchen before I lit the alcohol.

"I told you to come out," I said nonchalantly, recognizing that my behavior was becoming as irrational as hers. The damage to the floor was minimal, but with all the flammable material and products in the bathroom, I could have literally burned our house down trying to teach her a lesson. The irony of me carrying out the threat she had issued to me herself was nothing short of pure madness.

"I'm getting the fuck out of here," she said as she threw on a pair of sweatpants and some unlaced tennis shoes. "You're sick!"

"We're both sick, sweetheart." I took her into my arms from behind and she started crying. "I'm sick because you're sick. My heart can't take any more of this and yours is going to give out if you keep doing damage to your body. The kids need you. I need you. Let's both get better."

"I've tried, Robier. Nothing works."

"Then try one last time. One last time." I turned her to face me, forcing her to gaze into my eyes. "Baby, I lie awake at night, all night, wondering whether you're alive or dead. Even when you are here, I stay up watching you, afraid that you'll stop breathing in your sleep and never wake up again."

"I'm sorry, Robier. I'm so sorry." For a moment, I saw the old Tiphanie, the one who loved me once. "Please forgive me, baby."

She kissed me and I could not deny her. I needed her as much as she needed me. It was a bad dependency that we often played out in each other's arms, as we did again that evening.

We undressed and made this crazy, passionate love. I couldn't suck her breasts enough. I couldn't eat her pussy enough. I couldn't fuck her enough to satisfy my craving for her. She reciprocated by doing everything I needed, everything I yearned for. When it was over, Tiphanie had once again convinced me that she had a better chance of healing at home than in a rehabilitation center.

As we dozed off together, I issued one last idle threat. "Tiph, you mess up one more time and it's all over. I will protect the children from you if I have to."

$\mathcal{I}$ promised Robier that I would stay away from drugs, a promise I had made a hundred times if I had made it once. Every time the words left my lips, I sincerely meant them, but crack had a power over me that I could not fight. At first, I told myself that I could cut back, like I was talking about drinking two caffeinated sodas a day instead of four. Crack did not work that way. The more you used, the more you became immune to it and the more you needed to try to achieve that pipe dream, that feeling you felt the first time you got high. I had learned during rehabilitation that the initial feeling could never be re-created and that is why people stay hooked; they never get what they need from it.

Robier, his parents, my parents were all enablers. I am not sure they realized it but I did. They let me slide, time and time again, without doing anything significant to stop me. I did not care, as long as I had my crack. I loved my kids and wished that I could be the mother they needed and deserved. Even though Robier thought that I was kidding about suicide, I really was not. There had been many times when I thought about driving my car off the road into a tree, but I was afraid that it might not do the trick and I would end up a vegetable or something. I could not stand the sight of blood; otherwise I would have slashed my wrists. I had seen that fail a lot of times as well. A few times I did take a ton of pain pills, but my body had become so immune to them that I'd fall into a deep sleep—but I would always wake up. I decided that it must not be my time and that there was some purpose for me to be around. In the end, crack was more important than anything else. I did not want to die because I did not want to stop doing drugs. There were no other real considerations. Robier and the kids would have been better off without me. Time heals all wounds. I knew that I should leave and go someplace alone, so that others would not be subjected to my disease. Yet I had no money and could no longer work. Hell, I could barely function as a human being. My self-esteem was completely gone, evaporated. That was how I ended up with Deliverance.

"BEG ME," DELIVERANCE SAID as he stood before me with his manhood dangling in my face. "Beg me for this dick."

Tears were streaming down my face as I spoke the words. "Please, give me your dick. Let me suck that big, juicy dick of yours. Please, Deliverance, let me suck it."

That was what it had come down to. All the money had run out. There was nothing else to pawn because Robier had locked all the electronics in a room and my wedding ring was history. I had thought about fucking someone else to get some money to pay Deliverance, but that made me even sicker to my stomach than fucking him. At least he was attractive, and no one else would have to know but the two of us.

I was weak and almost gagged as he rammed his dick into my mouth. It was salty and nasty and I closed my eyes, trying to pretend he was Robier. It did not work. I sucked his dick like my life depended on it; in many ways it did. I needed the crack and had to do what I had to do in order to get it. Once he came down my throat and made me continue to suck him until he was hard again, I begged him for the drugs. "Come on, baby, I took care of you. Now take care of me."

He picked his pants up off the floor and gave me enough to get started. I yanked it from him, put some on a spoon, melted it with a lighter, and handled my business. The drugs kicked in as Deliverance took off all my clothes and went to town on my pussy.

"Yes, bitch," he whispered in my ear. "I told that husband of yours that one day this pussy would be mine. You're hooked and I'm gonna take care of you. Don't worry. As long as you give it up, it's all good."

It was saddening but I was happy all the same. If all I had to do to get high was spread my legs for Deliverance, then I had it made. He was not hurting me, just fucking me. I felt guilty about my wedding vows, but Robier could not possibly understand what I was going through. I shut my eyes again as Deliverance pushed and grunted, pushed and grunted until he had gotten all the pussy he needed for the day.

AFTER TWO WEEKS OF fucking Deliverance, he decided to pass me around to his buddies. There was nothing to do at that point but comply. I was giving it up out both sides of my drawers, anything to get my drugs. Most of them were decent-looking but a few looked like trolls. I lost count of how many men would take their turn with me, passing my ass around like it was a joint. I was no longer embarrassed to sit naked in a room full of men and other women who were there for the same thing. If they did not have the cash, they had to give up some ass. Some were mothers and some were grandmothers. The men did not care. Pussy was pussy to them. One dealer made his own wife suck off three men because he was mad at her about something. She did it like it was nothing. Then her husband fucked her right there on the dining room table of the crack house in front of everyone who cared to watch. It was a sick existence, but it was the only reality I knew.

ROBIER

Everyone had tried to persuade me to let Tiphanie fall by the wayside, but I could not convince myself to do it. It took the words of a child to change everything. My eleven-year-old daughter, Carson, came to me one night when her mother was missing, and her words cut me like a knife.

"Daddy," she began, as I sat on my bed watching the evening news. "Where's Mommy?"

It had been ages since she asked that question. In the beginning she would wonder if her mother was home and then it came down to "Did Mommy come home last night?" No child should have to think that way.

"She's away on a business trip." I lied, not wanting to say "Mommy's in a crack house someplace."

"Can we call her? The hotel has a phone, right? Does she have her cell phone with her? I tried to call her cell about ten times and it went straight to voice mail."

"I'm not sure about the name of the hotel, honey." I moved nervously on the bed. I hated lying to my flesh and blood. "She'll call in the morning to check on things."

"What city did she go to?"

"I'm not sure."

Carson sat down beside me. "Are you sure about anything?"

"Look, baby, Daddy's a little exhausted right now. We had

to launch a new marketing campaign today and it was more work than we expected. I can't think that clearly at the moment."

That much was true. My career had also been affected by Tiphanie's behavior. Marketing was really a creative process—like that of a writer or musician. Your mind had to remain clear in order to be inspired, and not knowing whether my wife was alive or dead half the time had taken its toll.

Then Carson said the words that truly made my hurt flutter. "Is Mommy a crackhead? Michael, this boy in the fifth grade, said my momma is a crackhead."

"Michael needs to shut his filthy mouth!" I yelled out in anger. "How does he know anything about your mother?"

Carson shrugged. "He said that his daddy saw Mommy coming out of a crack house."

"In order for his daddy to see that, he must have been there himself."

I felt foolish. There I was, trying to justify Tiphanie's behavior by casting a negative light on someone else's. I was always telling my kids that two wrongs don't make a right, but I was going against that.

"He also said that Mommy gives head for drugs. What does that mean?"

I started shaking and I could not control my anger. "Carson, go to bed now."

"But Daddy, what does it mean?"

"Take your little ass to bed now!"

She started crying and ran out of the room.

I picked up a pillow and buried my screams into it. Carson would only be a child once. It was only a matter of time before Lennox was asking the same questions, and his innocence would be lost as well.

Tiphanie had even stolen some money from Carson's room once and then helped her search for it, making her feel irresponsible for losing it. Tiphanie had neglected to pick them up from school time and time again. It was too much. It was over. Tiphanie was gone and unless I did something, the rest of us would be gone too. I had also read on the Internet that spouses of drug addicts tended to die sooner than spouses of nonaddicts because of the stress. I did not want to end up as a statistic.

TIPHANIE

I returned home after four days of straight fucking and getting high. Robier had had enough; the locks were changed and my clothes were in plastic bags out in the garage. I banged on the door but he would not answer. I am not even sure he was there. I went to his office but security would not allow me to go past the lobby. I called him but he would never take my calls. I went to his parents' house and his mother laid into me like there was no tomorrow. She could finally call me every name in the book without fear of repercussions from Robier. I was every version of bitch, whore, and tramp she could conjure up.

I went to a shelter but they kicked me out when they realized I had a problem. They said they could not allow that kind of behavior there—for fear that I would start stealing from other women—and suggested that I try to get into a rehabilitation center. I tried, but only short-term facilities had free beds. Short term was not going to do shit for me. I was trapped, and like a trapped animal, I went into survival mode. Less than a week later, I was at Deliverance's mercy to do as he wished, with whomever he wished.

Robier finally did take a call from me, but he was brief and hurtful. He said, "I love you, Tiphanie, but this relationship is unhealthy. It's unhealthy for you, for me, and for our kids. It's getting to the point where I don't hate you, but I hate myself for what I am becoming because of you."

I hung up. I could not take any more because he was right. There were two of me: the Tiphanie who loved him, Carson, and Lennox and the Tiphanie who did not give a fuck about even herself. I thought about throwing myself off the Woodrow Wilson Bridge that night. I even pulled over and got out of the car. Then I started having a pipe dream and went to find Deliverance, so that he could deliver me back into evil.

ROBIER

Tiphanie tried to fight me on the divorce, demanding half my earnings, half the equity in the house, and full custody of the kids. Momma was worried sick, to the point where she almost ended up on bed rest from the stress. I tried to reassure her that judges were judges for a reason and that they heard more crack stories than anyone. Like Judge Judy would always say on her television show, "If it doesn't make sense, it's not true." I knew that the master in charge of our case would feel the same way, and Tiphanie's lies were so obvious they were pathetic.

Half of her brain cells were destroyed to the point where she could barely recall anything on the stand during her testimony. She claimed to be the primary caregiver of the children, but my contention was how could she be the primary caregiver when she was missing half of every week? When confronted about her failure to pick the kids up from school on numerous occasions, she feigned ignorance and said it never happened. She committed enough perjury on the stand to be thrown up underneath the jailhouse.

The judge refused to even grant her temporary maintenance because he knew all of it would go straight up her nose. I had to support our children, not her drug habit. Her parents showed back up in the picture, along with Angelica, enveloping her in a cocoon and making me out to be the devil. Amazing how they were nowhere to be seen or heard from when I had reached out to them time and time again for help. Now they were at every single court date, like a group of vultures waiting to pick the skin off my bones.

Battle lines were drawn. My parents and me on one side, Tiphanie and her family on the other. The close-knit family relationship was destroyed because of crack cocaine. We had a story that was becoming all too familiar in today's society. After days of useless testimony by witnesses—part of Tiphanie's attorney's attempt to help her get whatever she could, even though she had clearly pillaged anything she would have been entitled to sans the drug addiction— the judge made a final divorce decree. I had proof of most of the damage: the pawned items, the damaged vehicles that had been willingly handed over to drug dealers as collateral, the money that had been shelled out on rehabilitation center after rehabilitation center.

Tiphanie was granted no money and limited visitation with the kids: two hours every other Saturday in a supervised church environment. She would have to remain drug free for six months before any further visitation would be considered, and her prognosis for recovery was not good, according to the court-appointed psychiatrist. He had suggested to me that I read a book about malingering personalities and deceptive behavior. Tiphanie fit that build. She had become "a narcissist with a sense of entitlement that was beyond belief," to quote his words exactly.

I wished the best for Tiphanie. It was hard to let go of someone that had played such a significant part in my life for so many years. The Tiphanie that I had fallen in love with was a memory, replaced by a person with no morals and no goals. I hoped that her family would someday see the light and stop contributing to the problem. They would all need counseling before they could realize it, but they refused to go to family therapy.

Tiphanie would try to call me from time to time, attempting to ease herself back into my good graces. After a while, I refused to speak with her at all and would make her leave messages on my voice mail, giving me the required seventy-two hours' notice that she would make visitation. There were no more words to be said between us. She was content to be on her path of self-destruction; I was on a journey of self-discovery.

I decided to take a cruise to get my mind off things, a quick three-day jaunt to the Bahamas. Besides, the trip was free, a bonus I had won from my job. I barely left my suite, except for meals. Then I would go back and catch up on some recreational reading.

There was a young lady that I had seen in passing. She had caught my eye, not only because she was extremely attractive but because she had this pleasant glow about her, like she was at total peace with herself. Something I craved to be.

The last night of the cruise I decided to go down to the gallery where they displayed the photos taken when we boarded the ship. Others had taken photos throughout the cruise, like during formal night the evening before. When I was searching for my photo, realizing it was the only time I had likely smiled and deciding to get it as a souvenir for the kids to prove I had a great time, I spotted her photo from formal night. She was wearing wire-rimmed glasses, but even through the clear lenses, I could see that she had the kindest eyes I had ever seen. I found myself staring at her for several minutes, like she was right there before me.

One of the females who had tried to step to me on day one came by and touched my hand. "Hey, sexy, how's it going?"

"Everything's good," I replied. "So have you enjoyed the cruise?"

"I have but I'm depressed."

"Why is that?"

"The cruise is almost over and I was hoping to have some real excitement before we docked back in Florida." She winked at me and her seduction play was obvious. "You have any thoughts?"

The woman before me was sexy in her own right, but much too aggressive and not my type, as if I had one. It had been so long since I had been with anyone other than Tiphanie—since my college days of being the pussy bandit—and the thrill for me was really gone. I was too grounded for such things. Sex for me had to mean something, that much I was sure of.

"I'm not feeling well," I stated casually, even though I felt fine. "I get horrible motion sickness. I'm going to purchase my picture for my kids and then go chill in my cabin for the rest of the cruise."

She started rubbing her fingers up and down my arm. "I can keep you company, nurse you back to health with these," she said, dropping her eyes down to her voluptuous breasts.

"Look, you seem like a really nice young lady. I forgot your name, but—"

"Florida, my name is Florida, like the state."

"Florida, that's pretty."

"Thanks. Do you think I'm pretty too?"

"You're gorgeous, but I'm just getting over this nasty divorce and I don't want to mislead anyone."

"You wouldn't be misleading me. I would recognize it for what it is: a vacation fuck. I came on this cruise for several reasons and one of them was to get some sex action. I'm beginning to think there's something wrong with me."

Even though she was beautiful, it was obvious that she had a self-esteem problem. Some man had probably recently hurt her and she was trying to teach him a lesson, at the same time trying to prove to herself that men still desired her.

"There's nothing wrong with you. You're one of the sexiest women on this ship. Maybe it's simply not in the cards for you this trip. You never know, someone might be protecting you from being hurt."

"Hmmph, I've been hurt. Nothing can hurt me anymore," she stated vehemently, proving my previous thoughts to be correct.

"My former man decided he wanted my so-called best friend more than me."

"Well, then, they're both fools. He's a fool for thinking the grass is greener on the other side and she's a fool for jeopardizing a close friendship for something that could never last."

"You're preaching to the choir, my brother."

I had actually made her laugh.

"Did you find your picture?" she asked.

"No, I didn't. I'm sure it's around here somewhere, but it's not in the numbered area where it's supposed to be. I'll come back in the morning before we dock, when most of the pictures are cleared out, and see if I can find it."

"Want me to help you look for it?"

"Thanks, Florida, but I'm cool." I glanced one last time at the picture of the woman with the kind eyes. "On second thought, I might not head straight back to my room. Care to join me for a drink?"

"Sure," she replied giddily. "Maybe I can change your mind about that other thing as well. You know, nursing you back to health with my tatas."

"Let's just start with the drink," I said, knowing full well that I would never sleep with her, but I wanted to do a good deed for the day and help heal her wounds in some way.

After three Miami Vice drinks—a mixture of piña colada and strawberry daiquiri—Florida ended up dumping me at the bar in the casino for a man who was definitely ready to bed her down. In less than five minutes they were all over each other and headed to one of their cabins. She did not even bother bidding me farewell. I chuckled and shook my head, thinking you can't knock the hustle. Florida was going to get some dick and hopefully feel better about herself in the morning.

I was walking back to my cabin when I heard this horrendous singing coming from the karaoke bar. I was in need of some light-hearted entertainment so I went inside. Much to my surprise—or dismay—the woman singing was the one I had been hoping to run into one last time before we docked. There she was, in the middle of the stage, wearing a red shorts set, belting out "We Belong Together" by Mariah Carey. Miss M did not have a damn thing to worry about because girlfriend sounded like a hyena. She was sexy as all get-out, though, with her body movements. I quickly grabbed a chair and watched her finish her act, wondering if she actually thought she sounded good or was simply making a mockery of herself on purpose.

The audience applauded when she was done. I ogled her as she made her way up the tiered seating area and sat down at a table with two other African-American females. They were flipping through the book of song titles. I had turned in my playa's card ages ago, but I wanted to meet her and devised a plan in order to accomplish that goal. I walked over to their table and stood over her.

"Hey, you did a good job up there. Want to do a duet with me?" I asked, trying to maintain a serious expression on my face.

One of her friends spoke up first. "Are you deaf? Ayricka can't sing a lick."

"I thought Erica sounded fantastic."

She said something to me for the first time. "My name is Ayricka, A-Y-R-I-C-K-A, not Erica."

"How do you pronounce it correctly?" I asked, yelling over the family of four who had taken the stage to sing a country-western song.

"*Air*-reek-a."

"Oh, okay, well, I thought you were great, Ayricka. My name is Robier. Where are you from?"

"New Jersey. You?"

"D.C."

"We're from New Jersey too, in case you give a damn," her sarcastic friend added.

I grinned. "What part of New Jersey do you young ladies grace with your loveliness?"

The other friend spoke up. "I like him, Ayricka. If you don't jump on him, I damn sure will."

Ayricka rolled her eyes at her friend and then glanced at me with those eyes. "We're from Trenton."

My heart suddenly grew heavy. I realized what it was about Ayricka that attracted me so much. Even though she was a totally different complexion than Tiphanie and had none of the same facial features or hair, her eyes were almost identical. I had fallen for Tiphanie because of the pictures that used to hang on Muffin's wall. Now I had seemingly fallen for this woman because of her picture on the wall of the cruise-ship gallery. Was I officially on the rebound and trying to replace her?

"You ladies have a good evening," I said in dismay as I began to walk away from their table.

I was about twenty feet away when I heard Ayricka yell, "Hey, what about that duet?"

I turned and grinned. "Maybe some other time."

I decided to take a walk out on the deck, something I had not done since I boarded the ship. The cool breeze rising up from the waves was soothing to my soul. I went to the helm of the cruise ship and looked over, and I was reminded of that scene from *Titanic* when Leonardo DiCaprio and Kate Winslet are standing there enjoying the view during the daylight. Then I recalled the scene where they're at the same helm, about to sink after the cruise has taken a tragic turn. I began to feel sick to my stomach, although I had no reason to sense danger.

I was going to go back to my room and finish the book I was reading about forgiveness and finding the strength to move on after being betrayed.

"Enjoying the scenery?" I heard Ayricka say as she came up behind me.

"It's breathtaking."

"Yes, I love cruises. Being out here in the middle of nowhere reminds me of what life is truly about."

She had my attention. "Share your philosophy with me. What is life truly about?"

"Deciding that no matter what the devil throws in our paths, we will live each day with a new vision and try to do something productive."

"That's deep. Sounds like you've experienced a lot in your tender years."

She giggled. "I bet you and I are relatively the same age."

"How old are you?"

"You first." We both laughed. "Age is only a number, but you're right, I have been through a lot. In fact, this is my 'waiting to exhale' cruise. I'm recently divorced and trying to start anew."

"That's something we have in common. I just got divorced as well."

"I'm surprised you're not here with someone. Then again, I shouldn't make presumptions. You might have someone lying in your cabin right this second."

"No, no such thing. I came alone. I won this trip on my job. It was for two people, but bringing someone along would have only complicated matters. I've met a few women but I'm not dating."

"And you didn't think a cruise was the appropriate way to begin dating? Some would call it romantic."

"Only if no drama ensued. Would you spend three days with a complete stranger in a cabin, without knowing whether you were compatible with them or not?" I asked, trying to feel her out.

"You've got me on that one. These cabins are kind of miniature."

"I have a suite and I'm still falling on top of myself."

She came closer to me. "So, Robier, why did you ask me to sing with you and then take off?"

"I didn't want to pressure you."

"But I wanted to sing with you. I had even picked out a song and everything."

"Really. Do tell. Which song did you think the two of us should have graced the microphone with?"

Ayricka laughed again. "I had narrowed it down to 'Fire and Desire' by Rick James and Teena Marie or 'U Got the Look' by Prince and Sheena Easton."

It was my turn to laugh. "Wow, that would have been something. I must confess, I can't sing a lick."

"Like I can?" she asked in mock disgust.

"I thought you were serious up there, like those contestants on *American Idol* who sound like they crawled up out of caves."

"Yeah, the best part is the original auditions, when people mess up. My girls and I fall out laughing."

"You seem really close to your friends in there. I can see the three of you sitting around a television set, eating popcorn and making fun of people."

"I am close to them but I meant my daughters, Ardith and Ariel."

"Aw, you have two little ones. Something else we have in common. I have a son and a daughter, Lennox and Carson."

AYRICKA AND I SPOKE until well over in the morning, after most of the people on the ship were fast asleep. Her ex-husband had been bipolar and it seemed like she had endured a nightmare of a marriage as well. We traded war stories, but at the same time found that we were really feeling each other. At about three, I convinced her to go back to my cabin. I had no intention of coming on to her physically, but in all honesty, nothing had ever felt so natural as when I took her into my arms and kissed her. We did not make love that night for two reasons: I did not want her to think that I was a user like that, and we only had a few hours before we docked. I wanted to take my time with her. Yet I also wanted to give her something to remember me by. We lay naked in each other's arms and talked as I kissed and sucked every inch of her, even her toes.

If I am being honest, I have to admit that Tiphanie's spirit was there in that room with us that night as well. All the things I was doing were things I had often done to her over the years, trying to make her feel special and in order to prove my love for her.

Ayricka allowed me to drive her back to the airport in my rental car while her friends went in theirs. I kissed her good-bye, not knowing whether it was the beginning of something real or the end of a brief fantasy. She called me that night, after she was back in New Jersey and I was back in D.C. We talked for hours a day until I invited her to meet me in the Poconos three weeks later. There, we made love for the first of many times.

Going through that nightmare of a marriage with Tiphanie had taught me one valuable lesson: how to recognize and appreciate a special woman like Ayricka. She did not drink, she did not do drugs, she did not even drink coffee. She believed in parenting above all else and our children ended up getting along like they had always been siblings. A year later Ayricka and I were married on the beach in the Bahamas. We honeymooned at the famous Atlantis hotel. There, she got pregnant with our son, Samuel.

After a while of visitation, Tiphanie stopped trying to prove a point and gave up. The drugs took over completely and her parents and sister had to face facts. I had always held out hope that she would someday recover. On Christmas Day, 2006, I received the phone call that I knew would someday come. Tiphanie had been found dead, outside of a crack house. I paid for the burial and made sure that she looked as beautiful as possible, despite the fact that she was skin and bones. Momma had been right. The woman I had married and had children with had died many, many years earlier. I could only hope that she found the peace in death that she could not find in life.

ACKNOWLEDGMENTS

This book has been a long time coming, mostly because I was personally dealing with painful relationship issues myself. No one is immune, but I have bounced back fine and have moved on to a better life and a better love. I would like to thank my faithful readers for your patience and understanding as I took a yearlong hiatus that probably seemed more like ten years. The good thing is that I feel stronger—both as a writer and as a person.

Thanks to my parents for their continuous love and support as I make both good and bad decisions in life. Thanks to my children for being my main inspiration in life. The best days are the ones I spend with the three of you, no matter where we are or what we are doing. Thanks to my sisters for being there and always remaining faithful to the cause. You are such a tremendous backbone system.

Thanks to Pamela Crockett Fish, Esq., my attorney and dearest friend. We really had to buckle down and fight the "trash" this past year, but we were ever confident because we knew that we were right. Let's put all of that behind us and do the damn thing. "Hollywood on the Potomac" is about to be more than a fantasy. Bank on that.

Thanks to Destiny Wood for being my ear late at night or early in the morning and for being so protective of me, both emotionally and physically.

Thanks to Sara Camilli. As always, you have been a wonderful agent and friend.

Thanks to my Simon & Schuster/Atria family: Judith Curr,

Malaika Adero, Kathleen Schmidt, Melissa Stoeckel, Kitt Reckford, Krishan Trotman, Dennis Eulau, and Carolyn Reidy. Without your belief in my ability, this would have been a much harder road to travel.

Thanks to the Strebor family: Charmaine, Carlita, Dante, Destiny, Pamela, and all of the authors. Please visit www.simonsays .com/streborbooks and check out the vast selection of titles we now publish. This is only the beginning of a much larger legacy.

Thanks to Suzanne de Passe for taking me under your wing and mentoring me through the filmmaking process. I am a fast learner and hold up my end of the bargain when it comes to de Passe–Zane Entertainment.

A WORD FROM ZANE

*I*f you have ever watched someone self-destruct, you know it can be one of the most traumatic experiences life has to offer. Even worse is when a person on a path of self-destruction attempts to drag you down into the pits of hell with them. Your first inclination will probably be to hate them. Then you will certainly wonder what you have done in your past to deserve it. Day after day, instead of concentrating on your career, you have to sit by the door or phone, wondering whether or not the person is in the midst of another disappearing act. Instead of being able to plan family activities, cook dinner, and relax by the fireplace, you have to go into protect mode in case the person comes home lashing out at you and the children in anger. The person will often make themselves out to be the victim when they are victimizing not only the people in the household but anyone they come in contact with.

You probably think I am talking about some crazed person, but in actuality, I could be talking about your mother or father, your son or daughter, your neighbor or coworker, your doctor or even your minister. So many things happen behind closed doors, horrible things most people can barely imagine. I find myself staring at people in passing, wondering who has gone through the same drama that I have, who has endured the pain. The basis for it all comes down to one five-letter word: drugs. A tiny word, but its impact is worldwide.

I have lived with an alcoholic and drug addict who had absolutely no grasp on reality. One who felt it was okay to pillage my belongings—which I busted my behind to acquire—to support his habit. One who had no goals or aspirations in life other than to achieve his next high and help his so-called friends do the same. One who thought vanishing for three to five days at a time was acceptable behavior. One who, to the very end, tried to destroy everything I had—even my health—to get what he wanted. One who seemingly put drugs in front of me, his children, and definitely himself. One who thought I was responsible for supporting not only him—a grown-ass man—but his entire family as well. They were all gold diggers, all of them bottom feeders, all of them enablers who were out to see what they could get while my life was being destroyed.

When it came time to write my story for *Love Is Never Painless*, choosing a story line was a no-brainer. I was living it already. For many years I had endured exactly what the main character, Robier, endures: I had been "staring evil in the face."

If you have a loved one addicted to drugs or alcohol, realize one thing. Unless they truly want help, you cannot save them from their demons. They have to save themselves, and the fact of the matter is that some of them are so far gone that they do not want to come back. It is impossible to reason with someone who is delusional and irrational.

Overcoming the chemical addiction is often the easy part. Dealing with the underlying psychological issues is a much deeper battle to fight. If they do end up in the small percentage of those who kick the habit, then they have to face the music and deal with all the damage they have done: physical, emotional, and financial. They have to attempt to make amends with all the good people who had to suffer. They have to look in the mirror and, for the first time, stare their own evil in the face.

Do not take what I am saying out of context. Most addicts are full of potential and many were successful, law-abiding citizens at one point in their lives. Many, like the character Tiphanie in my story, became chemically dependent on prescription drugs for pain, and when their doctors abruptly cut them off, they were forced to turn to other means to deal with their needs. I remember reading a magazine article a few years back which stated that several million women in the United States were addicted to pain killers. Since then, it has become a major news story and there is no end in sight, with Ecstasy and crystal meth taking over inner cities and suburbia nationwide.

I hope that my story—"Staring Evil in the Face"—will help others, because it was certainly a cleansing experience for me, a way to express the hell I have lived through without being totally autobiographical.

Peace and Many Blessings,
Zane